BLOOD LILY

a novel

by Spencer Stephens

BOOKS FOR ALL
SAINT PETE PRESS

For Catherine, who knows me completely,
and loves me anyway.

ONE

Father would have me dress in men's clothes so I could drive without being arrested. Some places, if I'd been caught, a mob would have stoned me and dumped me in the desert. For so long, our men were the only ones to drive. Women were mostly at home without permission to leave. A woman wanting to change that would make the men feel threatened and if a Saudi man feels threatened by someone less important, the law says it's fine if he wants to be a murderer or a rapist. So, most women are on permanent alert. Does that man think I shamed him? Does that one have a mind to force himself between my legs? The vigilance—it's always.

Before I drove, when I was thirteen, Father put me in male robes and led us places where women were forbidden by Sharia—restaurants and soccer stadiums where it was only men. When I was out as a male and we went to visit people, Father acted like everything was excellent. He grinned at me when talking to men he was planning to kill. He was showing me what it looked like to have no fear.

I wore men's robes with a corded keffiyeh that covered the sides of my face. I used deodorant for men so I smelled right and I kept my nails manicured, masculine, the way that's popular with rich Saudi men. When I was fifteen, Father handed me keys to the Range Rover. He sat in front, gave directions and there I was, driving through cities, driving on highways. All these cars driven by men and in one there was me, just a girl, learning how to act like a boy. My hands were sweaty because of the fright.

I'm twenty-eight now. Sometimes I'm driving and my hands get sweaty for no reason.

Eventually, I felt like a male. I was always in the mind of a male, making my shoulders square, trying to be dominant. I'd invested so much in avoiding femininity—and life was easier that way. I could look men in the eye without being accused of anything and didn't have to worry about rape.

Lots of Father's business was in homes, nice homes where you might be looking over the Red Sea and they had mosaics on floors, the pretty curtains blowing. With Muslims—you know, right?—no alcohol. So, men share boiling tea with honey and plates of chocolates. We would have something melty and sweet, talking with men who needed things from Father. He was at the top of the Saudi Security Directorate, which meant he had our King's permission to do almost anything. He could have someone's business taken away and have their hands cut off.

Father's friends, some owned big companies and some were government ministers. Some made yachts for Russians that cost a hundred and seventy million dollars. One man, his business processed and distributed a third of the world's sugar supply and for part of every week, he became the Saudi minister of commerce. He had ceremonial visits and gave speeches and decided if your business deserved special treatment. His ocean tankers and his trucks were always moving around the planet and, somehow, he never had trouble with customs or pirates.

Father told people part of the truth—that I was a member of the Saud family. But he lied and said my mother ran away and that my father died while serving our King's family. He gave men a reason to be sympathetic and trusting.

He told me to learn from the richest men. How did they rise above and how did they stay there? One day, he promised, I'd live in America. I'd work for Father and I'd rise above. I was so sure of what that meant, I never asked. I was a teenager. I was stupid and didn't know it. Father knew and he took advantage.

He was practiced in the art of deception. He had wealth in the billions and collected ancient books that he never read. He told stories about history like he'd been there. People were fascinated, and some never saw that with Father, it was always a competition, even after they'd lost to him.

Dominance was essential for Saudi manhood. Men couldn't stand to be diminished. They'd get violent. I got so afraid that once I asked Father what would happen if people found out I was a girl dressed as a boy? Would he protect me? He said everyone is a fool in love with an idea about what could never happen. They'd never suspect that the head of the Security Directorate was passing his daughter off as a male, just like the King wouldn't give away his money.

I persisted. What if? Would he protect me?

Father looked proud, like I'd made a discovery. He told me people fall into two groups. Most people are stupid. They always avoid the things that make them afraid.

The smart ones do nearly everything they want. They act like they have power and control. People fear them, the same way they fear God.

Father never did answer me. Instead, he made me confident things would be fine. He stopped me from asking questions about threats to my life. In that way, absolutely, he was brilliant.

* * *

The President of Russia was on his elbows, leaning over a conference table and scrutinizing a satellite photo dotted with Cyrillic words. The brutalist symbols made it look like every place on the map had reason to be hostile and he'd always spoken as if that were true. He rapped a knuckle on downtown Washington, DC. That's where I want to invest, said the President of Russia. That might be the world's best real estate.

Six feet away, a Russian lawyer on the business side of a computer screen was preparing to begin a video call. She had a finger ready to press a button and sniffed with impatience at the interruption. How can you be so sure? she asked him.

That's an idiot question, said the President of Russia. I know because I know. He motioned big with one hand and demanded the lawyer get busy with the conference call.

The lawyer scolded the President of Russia. Don't be an ass, she said. Her finger got back into action. It tapped a button on her laptop. She reminded the President of Russia that for the duration of the video call, he needed to keep his mouth shut. Don't imagine you can control the conversation, not if you want to stay anonymous, she said.

The President of Russia remained silent, hidden from the computer's camera.

From Washington, DC, six thousand miles removed from Moscow, the faces of two American realtors became visible on the computer. They were eager to learn more about the lawyer's plans to purchase office properties in their city. The market was primed for a move and the lawyer's timing could hardly be better, said one of the realtors.

It's not me, it's my clients doing the buying, said the lawyer in beautiful English. They see Washington as a top-shelf city. First-class.

Remember to say springtime, probably March, whispered the President of Russia.

You saw in my e-mails, we won't sign purchase agreements until next spring, definitely not until March, said the lawyer. She'd given the realtors her clients' budget, their timeline, examples of buildings that appealed to the clients. Right now, we're identifying targets, she said. Send us pro forma financials on each building you're recommending.

The realtors agreed, confirmed they had correct contact info, offered flattery in case it was required, and ended the call. The lawyer closed her laptop.

You were loud enough I know they heard you, she told the President of Russia. They know who they're dealing with now, I'll bet. And they already know we're planning for March. You made me write the e-mails so that was obvious.

He shook his head as if to offer regret without apology.

If we see a bargain, shouldn't we put it under contract right away? asked the lawyer.

Something is going to happen in Washington, DC, said the Russian President. Soon. Come spring, it will be a buyer's market for Washington real estate, he said. He went back to his map. As his eyes followed Connecticut Avenue into downtown—a corridor of luxury office properties—he mindlessly fingered the inside of one nostril. He had a good scratch and pretended not to see the moistened fleck that fell onto the satellite photo. Wordlessly, he kept studying the image.

The young lawyer was repulsed. Dad—really? she said. That's disgusting.

TWO

The Canadian female had pure white skin. She was slender and fast—faster than the brown Saudi policemen who chased. Her black abaya trailed, flags flying on Arabian winds. Her feet and legs pumped. Fear and loathing forced her shocking green eyes wide open. She sprinted along on Mecca's sidewalks, a fossilized grid that ran between mirrored high-rises, each one hiding any hint of a soul. Past street vendors selling dirty shoes, past beggars with weeping sores. The sun blistered all. She ran in a straight line through a gaggle of men in white robes waiting at a Starbucks window for iced coffee.

The midday Saudi heat was outrageous; the Canadian's sweat came in rivers.

Mustafa, the more aggressive of the two uniforms that pursued, screamed at her. In Arabic, he threatened her and ordered her to stop. A pistol and a truncheon flailed on his belt as he chased.

The young Canadian bolted across a street without slowing, slid against a dirty Toyota taxi that stopped short and she fell flat. She jumped up, her black costume concealing everything but her white hands and those emerald eyes. The soles of her running shoes beat a frantic rhythm on concrete.

Heads turned all along the sidewalk, men, women and children alarmed by the reminder that in Saudi Arabia, the police are never denied.

The Canadian screeched like an ambulance and some people escaped her path. She hurdled a child, almost lost balance, pushed off a parked truck and left a sweaty handprint.

Mustafa got close, leapt, grabbed an ankle and tackled. The young woman flopped, her face and body bounced and slid, tearing away the top half of her robes. The side of her face oozed. White heat lit up her nipples. An earlobe dripped crimson. Flat on her back on the sidewalk, she swore at Mustafa in French, clambered and kicked at Mustafa's hands, which held fast on one ankle. Mustafa reached out, and his fingernails tore at her legs. He tore off the rest of her robes and tossed them. Kneeling at her feet, looking up the length of her, he'd rendered her nearly naked. She was his prize.

She kicked more and she tried to punch, her face red and slippery with her fluids and pocked with sandy grit. She briefly broke Mustafa's grasp, bashed a heel into his teeth and made him scream.

Wearing only Reeboks and powder-blue panties that had ripped, she rolled and rose, looking to dash away on runner's legs. Mustafa rose as she did and took the rod from his belt. He swung side-armed and struck her jawline, breaking teeth and spraying blood. She screamed, fell again and kept kicking with her long legs even after there was no point in trying. A gazelle had been taken down by a practiced predator.

Mustafa lay on the slim girl, pelvis to pelvis, and trapped her on the pavement. He pinned her wild hands, zip-tied her wrists, brought her to her feet. The remains of her robes lay twenty feet away, blown into a pile by hot winds. Grown men and boys considered her underpants, her quivering rump. She bent at the waist, hands behind her, urgently trying to conceal herself, fighting for slack in Mustafa's hold.

Mustafa straightened her, spit in her face. He held her so she faced the crowd of witnesses. Blood discolored his chin and his khaki uniform. He shook her captured wrists and threatened to yank her arms out of their sockets. Infidel bitch, he told her, you're dead by next week.

Ibrahim, the second policeman, arrived at a gallop. He kneeled low and could scarcely talk for the need to breathe. She's ordinary, he wheezed. He paused to breathe more. The owner of her home says she is Canadian, he said. A student. A caretaker. For his children. She is in Mecca for only two weeks more. A Canadian sorcerer? Does that make any sense?

You saw her room, said Mustafa. Talismans and idols. Ibrahim, she prays to idols. She ran from the law. She knows she's guilty.

She's Christian, said Ibrahim. A crucifix and a Bible. A Catholic necklace. Mustafa, please. Ibrahim laced his fingers across the top of his head, as if it would make breathing easier. She's not a sorcerer, he said. She'll throw out her things if you ask. A girl. Is she twenty? Her employer says if she's not with his children, she's in her room. Ibrahim's gaze lingered on her breasts. He caught himself, his head shook and he looked away.

An old man with a cane smacked Ibrahim across the tender side of his neck and was ready to hit again when Mustafa's free hand stole the cane. You're sinners and you're decrepit, said the old man. She's naked. You should be whipped.

Mustafa threatened to hit the man. You interfere with Mustafa? he demanded. With the Mutaween? If you are a blasphemous asshole, I can have you burned alive. You and your family too.

I'm not afraid of you, said the old man. I know Nassir Saud. He was my student. Should I tell him what I've seen? Nassir would hate you if he knew. The old man moved on Mustafa, seized the handle of his cane. He yanked and ordered Mustafa to let go.

Mustafa released and the old man fell on his ass. Mustafa sneered. I could kill you and Nassir would never care, he said.

Cover the girl's body, ordered the old man's wife, from under a niqab. Shame on you, on you both. Her vagina. It's obvious. And here, where it is holy?

A crowd assembled, emboldened by the woman's tone, and began to harass.

Mustafa yelled back, defended himself. We are agents of God! he yelled. We do God's work. The uniforms, khaki under black berets, announced to the crowd that Ibrahim and Mustafa were Mutaween, weaponized enforcers of Wahhabi morality. They had the power to police the campus of a transnational conglomerate, heavily invested in petroleum and owned by the same few families for centuries. The campus took up nine hundred thousand square miles. The enterprise supported thirty-five million people and lifted a lucky few hundred into extravagant wealth. The Mutaween were famous for being above sin, morally fit to sit in judgment of those who insult God. They whipped people who ignored sexual norms and confined convicted blasphemers scheduled for execution. They arrested shop owners who refused to close for prayers and sometimes held them long enough that the shops failed and became somebody else's.

The question among members of the Mutaween was always about how they'd been chosen to serve, who must have recommended them. Someone influential had seen them and thought they'd been righteous in defense of Islam. Once appointed, they had power to arrest anyone for all things illicit, obscene or offensive. If they accused a person of blasphemy, execution was given. Certain Saudis, devoted to certain sacred words reportedly uttered by one sacred man centuries ago, demanded order. People told stories about the sacred man after he died. Years later, scholars put his words on paper and those words became Wahhabi gospel. They were literally and strictly enforced.

The crowd issued damnation for these two Mutaween who'd desecrated the holy. To make an arrest, they'd publicly exposed the sexual organs of a female—they'd made her naked—in sacred Mecca and claimed to have done it in the name of God.

The crowd surged with anger and people screamed their condemnation. The anger was more uncomfortable than the heat; people yelled at the uniforms that they had disgusted God, that they were loathsome.

Mustafa's sweat bled through beneath his armpits and his reaction to the ugliness was to remove the pistol from his belt and wave it. At the image and sound of a crazed man, bleeding from the mouth, a naked hostage in one hand and a firearm in the other, people ducked and scattered. *Go away!* he screamed.

The old man and his cane did not retreat.

Ibrahim, holding his bruised neck, pleaded with the man to leave. Then, to Mustafa: Must we? Do we have to arrest her?

She is a sorcerer and she is caught, he told Ibrahim. Mustafa sheathed his gun, pulled out his mobile and called for a police car. Together, they marched with the nearly naked Christian Canadian nanny over a distance of two city blocks, along busy sidewalks, before a bigger audience, to meet a police vehicle.

People stared, moaned, appeared repulsed. Ibrahim looked no less certain of himself. What will anyone gain from this? he asked Mustafa.

Mustafa whined through clenched teeth. Do you see what she did to my face? And Mecca is pure and holy, only for Muslims. Did you forget? You are new to this uniform, said Mustafa. These stars on your collar mean your job is to protect the sacred. You should be more concerned for public safety than for hers.

Will we have to answer for this? pleaded Ibrahim. It's not wrong to wonder, is it? She is naked in public. In Mecca. What happens if the palace finds out?

Mustafa took a handful of Ibrahim's uniform, pulled him close. He cast off a sulfuric breath. Do you worship idols? Is that why you want to save her?

From thirty feet away, people with iPhones had filmed Mustafa's tackle, the capture, the crowd's jeers, the cane slapping Ibrahim's neck, Mustafa waving his pistol—everything but the voices of the officers. Two weeks later, the Internet buzzed worldwide about two Mutaween who'd exposed holy Mecca to the venereal. On Reddit, the video of the woman got downvoted one hundred and forty thousand times and upvoted two hundred thousand more.

Two of the Saudis' holiest, esteemed by fundamentalist Wahhabis, were guilty of blasphemous sin. They'd sullied the purity and innocence of Islam. And worse? Everywhere on earth, people saw.

* * *

Victor Ivanov opened the armrest in his Lexus sedan, pulled out his mobile, checked an account balance and it came up zero. The cold of Moscow was heavy enough to be dispiriting. Despite it, Victor's face smoldered. He told Siri to call Taras Kulikoff and when Taras answered, Victor was demanding. I don't have what I'm supposed to, he said. Fix it. Victor was an amphibious reptile with demon jaws; he would have his mouthful of flesh.

There was whining. Please, I'm sorry, said Taras. The money will be there next week. I'm not lying.

Even on the phone, Victor could impose the kind of silence that made people squirm.

Please, I'm sorry, said Taras again. Next week I can pay. Thursday— we get money from sales in Kuwait. Don't hurt me.

Victor came at him. You are an idiot, he said. A man who wants to buy favors from his president and doesn't pay on time is a man with problems. Men like you get poison in your tea. If you don't pay by Wednesday, this goes to Gazprom, he said. Either way, you'll owe me, and when I tell you what you owe, you don't dare say no.

Taras Kulikoff didn't say a word.

When he got home from work that evening, Victor Ivanov told his wife and his nineteen-year-old daughter they'd have to wait on his promise of a new Lexus for each. His cut of the oil equipment money hadn't come in and they'd have to wait a little longer. His wife, a woman confident of her rank, raised a hand to him. He flinched and offered hasty apologies, begged forgiveness. Don't hurt me, he pleaded. It couldn't be helped, he said. The man promised next week and I believe him.

When she got the news, Victor's daughter shrieked. You promise and you promise, she said, tearing up. And it never, ever happens. Why should I ever believe you?

Polina, the daughter, and Nadia, the wife—they shamed him. Nadia was the daughter of Russia's Prosecutor General. I deserve a better husband, she shouted. She told him he had a penis like a queer man.

He went to bed furious and couldn't sleep.

Wednesday, when Victor checked his phone, the money was there. A few days later, Taras Kulikoff got an e-mail from the purchasing office for Russian Land Forces Command that said it looked forward to working with Taras's organization, the Irkutsk Oil Company, to develop and fabricate cluster slider rigs, portable drilling platforms used for oil exploration through permafrost.

Victor called the Lexus dealer who promised to send a driver for Polina and Nadia the next morning. They'd have their pick of his inventory. Victor Ivanov got a kiss on the cheek from his daughter. Daddy, I love you again, she said.

His wife wouldn't touch him. You don't deserve me, she said.

One morning, Victor and his Lexus hummed through his iron-gated neighborhood on his way to work. His neighborhood was a guarded island, a safe and manicured sanctuary where he'd raised his child, where people kept expensive things in grandiose mansions. The enclave was protected by an electric fence at the perimeter and by private security men who patrolled with machine pistols in holsters. Real estate agents called the neighborhood number one in Moscow, a beautiful place where the rich could feel safe.

Outside the fence, beyond Victor's neighborhood-sized bubble, was the rest of Moscow. He and his Lexus crunched along streets littered with ground-up glass, the curbs decorated with Russian-made Vestas and Ladas disfigured by layers of vandalism. Victor passed rows of gargantuan apartment buildings, each one listless from the poverty inside. It looked like snow was coming. The fresh white would pretty up the frozen black stuck in the city's many orifices.

That afternoon, Victor had a meeting with his boss, the Russian President. I thought of something on the way to work, said Victor. The King of Saudi Arabia promised you a terrorist attack in America and never delivered. He should be ashamed.

The President agreed and decided to speak directly to the Saudi King, to pressure him. He would forego the usual preparation for a call—a planned performance monitored and recorded on both ends. He called the old man on his mobile and the King answered.

Your Highness, did you think I forgot? he asked.

The King sucked in some air. He offered no denials. I'll make it happen, Mr. President, he said.

Yes, said the President, you'd better.

It was only a day later when the Canadian woman's story began to spark, to smoke and to flame; it did so on a stage raised by forces unseen. Russian bloggers posting on Muslim websites began a debate.

They professed to be traditional scholars of Islam and were incensed that vile filth had paraded through pure and holy Mecca. The men responsible should be beaten and hanged, they argued. God knows better than anyone that depravity will destroy society, they argued.

Other Russians, posting to social media and pretending to be progressive Muslims, shrieked with outrage. Humanity cannot maintain perfect purity at all times and God knew this when he created us, they said. And who but an idiot would suggest we interfere with police arresting sorcerers?

Neither side gave ground and each looked desperate to win out. God is Perfect and God is Wise held one another in contempt. Each declared the other hopelessly naïve. They exchanged threats of violence.

Real people joined in.

Analysts and editors and clerics and gravediggers argued and spat at each other. The ground shifted just enough to inflame an old fault line. Pictures and accounts of the naked Canadian ran on televisions in airports, in cafés. Saudi men argued over tea and tobacco. Fights broke out, and some riots.

Saudi officials banned domestic media from posting pictures and descriptions of the nudity in Mecca, but it hardly helped. People had seen all they needed to. Nearly everyone in Saudi Arabia condemned the offensive and riotous statements coming from the other half of Islam, the half that was blasphemous and venal.

Outspoken Saudi clergy hid at home, afraid of armed mobs. There were violent scenes at public events where crowds burned two royal Saudi buildings.

The Saudi academics, Saudi young people and many wealthy Saudis were asking difficult questions: Was the Mutaween a lost cause? Had it lost the decency needed to defend morality?

Nassir Saud, head of the Saudi Security Directorate, the man responsible for the Mutaween, rushed with his driver to his King's palace in central Mecca. On the way, he wrote a letter. At the palace, he inserted it into an envelope that, in front of four pairs of eyes, was licked, closed, taped over and sent two floors upstairs to his King. Nassir asked for a private meeting and for the King's benefit, there could be no record of it. The King accepted and invited Nassir upstairs.

You're right, the violence is a problem, said the King. Where's it coming from?

This is the Russians, said Nassir. Probably they think we're driving down prices for Russian oil by pumping too much of ours.

The Russian President takes himself so seriously, said the King. He thinks he's the lion. He wants everyone to give way, like he's entitled to decide for the rest of us.

We can't let the Russian President get away with this, said Nassir. We need to put these people down.

Nassir, said the King, I need your help. I need a destructive explosion in America. In downtown Washington. It has to be an event that terrorizes Americans.

You need this? asked Nassir. You?

The Russian President needs it, said the King. Somehow it benefits him. The unrest will continue until you make an explosion happen in Washington. It has to be in February.

Why didn't I know this?

The King rubbed his eyes as though they were burning. Just do it and don't ask questions, he said.

I can make it happen, said Nassir.

After Nassir left, the King called the Russian President. You made your point, said the King. You'll get your explosion. You want it in February? Fine. Will you leave me alone now?

* * *

It was late at night, quiet. Homeless mongrels curled under parked cars. Ibrahim, in bed, was cocooned in a dream: his brown legs, downy and lean, bathing in extra-warm salt water, a glass filled with cola on ice. European women wandered the beach, dressed in spaghetti straps and triangle patches. Sly looks, pubic mounds, curtains of long hair.

Then came excessive light and Ibrahim shielded his eyes. A yank on an arm, then a leg. He inhaled something volatile and foul, something mixed with alcohol, and the world disappeared. When he awoke, a sack was coming off his head and Ibrahim had pissed himself. He was in a windowless room with two men looking like they'd caged an animal. One wore a familiar khaki uniform with epaulets with gold stars embroidered on them. The other was a beast with eyes that would not gleam, his black heart hidden under robes of white. His hands were claws, one spread on each knee. A bristly Van Dyke defined his otherwise square chin.

The beast asked Ibrahim if he'd insulted God, if he'd been blasphemous.

Nassir, of course not, said Ibrahim, as sober as a judge.

Under a crown of golden cords, Nassir crossed his arms. Mustafa said you favored a sorcerer, a woman who worshiped idols, he said. You asked Mustafa to let her go.

Ibrahim shook his head and sounded curious. Mustafa must have misunderstood, he said. Did you ask him to explain the parts of his story that were hard to believe?

Nassir gestured and the man in the uniform raised a wooden truncheon and *down* came the weapon on Ibrahim's skull. Ibrahim screamed, fell off his chair, cowered, raised a hand in defense, then *down* it came again and it opened a hole in the flesh of his forearm. Exposed, reeking of urine, he curled on the floor and wept like a man who understood that his life was over.

Nassir crossed his legs at the knee, lay his claws in his lap. You interfered with a sorcerer's arrest. Isn't that correct?

Ibrahim sat up and looked to Nassir and to the violent man in the commander's uniform. Ibrahim and every recruit to the Mutaween had received training in coercive interrogation and would have an idea where this was going. What do you want? he demanded.

Admit your sin, said Nassir. Start there.

In coarse Arabic, Ibrahim told Nassir to get to the point. If I admit sin, then blasphemy and death. If I deny sin when you're sure I'm guilty, same thing. Your goal is to kill me? Kill me. Every sin there could ever be—I admit and I deny. There, I'm dead twice.

The man in khaki shoved against Ibrahim's shoulders. Ibrahim's head fell back. The uniform thunked the truncheon on the floor next to Ibrahim's head and Ibrahim cried out. *Mustafa is a Saud!* screamed Nassir. Do you hear?

You should shoot me in the back of the head, said Ibrahim. Just do it.

The man in khaki seized Ibrahim's wrists, held them firm and Nassir took a metal tool and put its blades at the base of a middle finger and squeezed. The digit popped like a cork from a bottle and Ibrahim screamed as if he'd been shot. Rivulets of red ran down his wrist and smeared on his chest where he cradled his injury.

Do you know the pain I can cause you? demanded Nassir.

Ibrahim, in agony, rocked himself. Why can't you tell me what you want? he screamed.

Nassir sneered. You'll travel to America and you'll destroy yourself, he said. You'll do it someplace crowded. That's what I want.

Maybe I'll go to America and escape you, said Ibrahim. Maybe I'll start a new life.

Nassir revealed a tired smile. Why do you say idiot things? he asked.

You would turn me into your slave, you would send me on a suicide mission and leave me an out? asked Ibrahim, sarcastic. No, he said. You would never.

No harm comes to your sister, said Nassir. For her life, I will make sure. If you go to America and do as you're told, I promise safety for Alitha.

You are a liar and a cheat, Nassir. There's no reason to believe you.

You are completely odd, young man, said Nassir. I can do things and you act like it's nothing to be afraid of. You ignore the death threat to your sister. You forget what I could do to your cousins.

It's not odd to be curious, even now, said Ibrahim. It's not odd to wonder why I should be afraid of you. I know everything you can do—and so what? I've decided not to be afraid of you.

Nassir seized a handful of Ibrahim's hair and punched him in the teeth. Ibrahim's head lolled. Nassir kneeled and put his face close to Ibrahim's. I'll convince Alitha you're evil, that you want to kill her, he said. I'll help her to kill you. I'll give her weapons and I'll help her find you and after she's done, I'll tell her she killed the wrong brother—that the dead brother cherished her. I'll give her tools to end herself when her misery gets unbearable. Or, Ibrahim, you could go to America and end yourself.

Nassir had put countless souls to waste, was proud to have it known. He'd commandeered whole lives, had done it to squads of men like they were racehorses, animals to be created through insemination, to be warehoused, cultivated and trained, put down if they could not win. He was endlessly imaginative about cruelty and looked pleased to discover ways to inflict hurt. Nassir was known to triangulate between people and events in faraway places, to bring down the pain of hell on people who had no reason to suspect it was coming.

Ibrahim was silent, didn't move.

Nassir motioned. Put him in a cell, he ordered.

The man in khaki seized Ibrahim by the neck and lifted him.

This is quite a moment for you, Nassir, said Ibrahim. No matter what, you win and I lose. You must be very pleased.

Omar complied when Nassir ordered him to the interrogation room and Omar waited to be spoken to. Nassir pointed to a folding chair, told him to sit. Omar did that, too. With the pair was a third, Nassir's sometime bodyguard and khaki fixer, a man with ham-hock forearms. He slammed the room's metal door and shoved home the deadbolt. Nassir, his dark eyes and his triangle of chin whiskers leaned across the table. Omar, thick-bellied, his face half-hidden by a formless black beard, tried to swallow and could not.

Nassir asked Omar if he knew that his little brother, Ibrahim, had admitted to a capital offense. While Omar's mouth hung open, Nassir shocked him. I think your brother has you to blame for his situation, said Nassir.

Omar's neck jerked.

Ibrahim does what Omar tells him, said Nassir. You said that. I hired him on your recommendation.

There was no reason to expect this, Omar said.

I can forgive, said Nassir.

Omar covered his face and wept. He pleaded for mercy. He swore continued loyalty. I am sorry for my brother and I am sorry for myself, he said. I beg you, Nassir.

You ask forgiveness without admitting sin? That's no apology.

I confess, Nassir. I pledged that Ibrahim was pure and he was not.

Stiff-wristed, Nassir planted the tip of an index finger on the tabletop. You and Ibrahim will go to America where you will meet someone. You'll be given a mission. You'll explain to Ibrahim that unless he goes along, you and your sister will be ended. Omar and Alitha will be dead. When you get to America, a person there will give you everything you need.

America?

You will die and become holy. You will be washed of sin. You and Ibrahim.

Omar squeezed his eyes shut, held them tight to wring out the excess. America?

America.

Omar had a question and opened his mouth to utter it. Nassir responded, as if he knew what the question would have been. You will ascend to heaven, you and Ibrahim. You are martyrs. And I will protect your sister. If you do as you're told, I will ensure that Alitha is always safe. Otherwise, she dies and so do you.

You would ruin her? asked Omar.

Ask Ibrahim, said Nassir.

Ibrahim might refuse, said Omar. What then?

Your problem—not mine, said Nassir.

The medieval echo of big brass keys stirred Ibrahim. He was laid out on a bunk of stainless-steel sheet metal. The jangling got closer and someone shoved a key, turned a bolt and slid open the metal panel door, fast and noisy, in a track coated with sandy grit. Omar, a boulder of a man, filled the room and he sat the only place he could, on the toilet. The cell door slammed.

Omar clutched the back of his neck, eyes closed, and radiated silent condemnation. You'd be dead now if not for me, he said. Enforce Sharia. A simple job. You didn't have the sense to shut your mouth.

Omar, look at me, said Ibrahim. You think I had any idea this was coming? I couldn't go on being an ordinary cop. I had to be a *special* policeman, like you. I am here because of you, Omar. You and Nassir Saud have me here.

Omar stood, rediscovered he had no place to go, and sat back down. He banged a helpless fist on the concrete wall. I am insulted, said Omar. Ibi, they're making me responsible for you. With my own hands, I would love to kill you. You don't live right now if not for my mercy.

Kill me, said Ibrahim. I'm dead no matter what, so get it over with. Eliminate your sins by eliminating me—and burn in hell, Omar. You don't even ask what happened and already I am responsible. You are that loyal. You will agree with something that is so terrible without asking whether it's true. You're eager to believe what they tell you. And don't you wonder about the wisdom of your choices? You have become afraid, exactly how they want, Omar. You consume their fear like it's your food. They control you.

Omar's face seemed to expand from the pressure behind it. Do you know what this does to me? Omar began screaming. To know my life is over because you should have known better?

If they are serious to kill me then kill me, said Ibrahim. Why bother to involve you?

With beefsteak hands, Omar covered his face.

Whatever they're saying to convince you to go to America, it's a lie, said Ibrahim. They have a plan so spectacular it kills not one policeman, but two.

You are such a child, Ibrahim, said Omar. How is it you are even alive?

You are afraid of those to whom you pledge loyalty, said Ibrahim. They can't be serious. A Canadian sorcerer?

These are the authorities! yelled Omar. This is Sharia!

Ibrahim's eyes drew tight. You don't see it, do you? he asked. You don't see that you're here to make something happen they could not.

We'll be taking on a mission in America for our King, said Omar. We will be leaving on a ship as soon as you can travel.

Ibrahim got out one more syllable—a self-righteous syllable that would have begun a diatribe against the evils of cooperating with evil.

Don't pretend to be blind about this, Omar yelled.

Ibrahim sat up, leaned close and whispered, as quiet as he could, through lips that were white from dehydration. They are watching and listening? He asked. You want to appear obedient?

Omar slapped his brother across his eyes. Could you pretend to appreciate what I am doing for you? Could you please?

* * *

From the Suez Canal to Maryland was sixteen days and seventeen nights across open ocean—time enough for Omar and Ibrahim to grow weary of the iron groan of the oil tanker that ferried them. Rusty particles, some greasy, fell from bulkheads into their hair and their bedsheets. A diesel haze flavored their toothbrushes. In heavy seas, the swells taller and wider than city buildings, the gargantuan ship often seemed ready to fall sideways and sink. Boiling nausea came and went.

Skinny crewmen with dreadlocks and bloodshot eyes slipped between decks and gangways, tending oily machinery and fixing leaks in the ship's miles of pipe. They kept watch for pirates, their Russian AKs ready. When they relaxed at all, it was because they were smoking cannabis or playing games with folding knives. The crewmen wore the Liberian flag on their uniforms, spoke in a pidgin that sounded vaguely like French and slept in bunks above and around Omar and Ibrahim. They ate at the same tables and shit in the same toilets but never looked the brothers in the eye and never spoke to them. It was as if the crew wanted no recollection of either man.

The brothers' meals came from a deaf cook, a nervous man with a potbelly who made noises like a feral child. He had a puckered scar that ran through both eyebrows and he was prone to ducking away from people. Seven mornings every week he turned out platters of microwaved bacon, a food forbidden to Muslims, and tasteless scrambled eggs, always runny and served in heaps. Evenings, he often put out mounds of mushy pasta covered in a salty red sauce. His desserts commonly came from two-gallon tins of mixed fruit.

Every man on this ship scowls, said Ibrahim, as he and Omar lay in their bunks. From my lips to God's ear, this is putrid. The officers? In the clean uniforms? I've seen their nice rooms and they hate being here, too. This is the worst ever.

Omar growled. Right now, you should be hanging by your ankles with feces running down your face, he said. From his high bunk, Omar leaned over and with a hefty paw he pointed at the face of his younger brother. This is what you get for being an idiot.

Ibrahim swatted at him. He motioned. *This* doesn't have to be, he said. He pointed at somebody far away. Ibrahim's wiry forearm had a scabbed-over divot and there was a pink stub where his middle finger should have been. If we are dead, he has no reason to hurt our sister, he said. He cares about her only because she allows him to control us. He is obvious about being evil. And being on a ship that always smells of sewer makes me wish I was already dead. I should jump in the ocean and drown.

Omar's jowls quivered under a black bush without form, something he'd grown to appease the ones who enforced Sharia. With handcuffs, I will pull you to your holy end if I have to, said Omar. You have a duty—to God and to Alitha and to me.

Would it be awful to agree out of pity? asked Ibrahim. All I said was this ship is terrible.

From the high bunk came contempt. You're too stupid to deserve pity, said Omar.

Omar, can you be human? demanded Ibrahim. Will you ever learn compassion? Or will you die an ass?

By night, the oil tanker arrived in America and anchored miles south of the suspension bridges that crossed the Chesapeake Bay. The ship did not pass under, would not let itself be detected by video surveillance or transponders. Dark waters chopped under a three-quarter moon as the ship sat moored.

Two-thirds of the tanker's engines quit idling and the decks stopped vibrating for the first time since the Persian Gulf. Frigid outside air slipped around edges of metal hatches and brought in the acrid sweetness of burning North American hardwoods. Somewhere close, American people were living American lives—gathered by fireplaces, wrapped in woolens, simultaneously insulated and exposed.

The deaf cook burst in, oily handprints all over his kitchen pants, and he mouthed big, hurried words to Omar and Ibrahim: *Come now.* The cook touched their rucksacks, made a gathering motion and moved toward the deck above. In cotton shirtsleeves, the Saudi brothers—their entire lives had been spent between the equator and the Tropic of Cancer—sprinted topside where twenty-knot November winds caused miseries they'd never known: stinging skin, chattering teeth, runny noses.

A skiff approached. Except for pinpoints of red and green on the gunwales, the small craft was visible in the night only as a silhouette against the lights of shore. Omar leaned in so he could be heard. He'll have a firearm, Ibi. Be careful or you'll get us shot.

Ibrahim wasn't having it. If you want to be afraid of him, Omar, that's your choice, he said.

Kicking and falling on fast swells, the smaller boat approached, piloted by a commanding figure in American blue jeans, a black knit cap and a parka—a figure as square and fight-ready as any man that Omar or Ibrahim had ever seen. The commander feathered the tiller and the throttle, kept the skiff hovering two feet away from fenders bolted low on the tanker's side. Bags on shoulders, the brothers climbed down a rope ladder. After measuring the skiff's erratic ups and downs, they hopped across. The commander pointed at a tarpaulin on deck and in Arabic told them to hide if they wanted to live.

Side by side, the brothers lay awkwardly inside the hull and covered up. The skiff's twin outboards whined like scared cats and launched the boat over whitecaps. Under the tarp, the brothers' rib cages slapped down again and again. In the dark of late November, their necks and fingers stiffened, turned cold and painful, and they shivered. Their heads whiplashed and they complained of an urge to vomit that continued even after the boat tied off in a cove.

On shaky knees, dragging bags, the brothers followed their commander across a dock to a Toyota minivan. They stowed their gear under bench seats, buckled in, rode thirty minutes to Capitol Heights, on the eastern edge of Washington, DC, a neighborhood of two-bedroom brick boxes with carports, dead vines tangled in chain-link fences, dented metal bars on doors and windows.

They came to a plain house, square and low, went inside, down to a carpeted basement where it was warm and nicely lit, and the brown-skinned commander pulled off the parka and the knit cap, ran fingers through hair and told Omar and Ibrahim the house had been prepared for their comfort. They were to relax, to rest, to eat, said the commander. Nobody knew their location and they were safe.

Comfort be damned, the brothers eyed the commander, the neck veins like wires, her nails raw and ragged, a jersey revealing the outline of muscles and breasts. Masculine wrists, muscular wrists with no hair, wrists like handles on forged tools, and a square jaw that framed little pink lips. She was handsome and she was beautiful. Standing ramrod straight, she looked invulnerable, immoveable, and yet she was feminine.

Who are you? asked Ibrahim. What's your name?

I'm Norah, she said.

Two mouths gaped.

You've never had a woman give you orders, have you? she asked. The brothers shook heads and traded glances, each curious to see if the other might answer differently. Get used to it, she said. For ten weeks, I'll be teaching you how to act like Americans.

Norah told the brothers to stay in the basement as much as they could, out of sight, where there were cots and dressers with clean clothes. Upstairs was the house's one bathroom and its kitchen. She'd stocked the refrigerator with boxes containing premade Halal dinners built around veal and beef. There were paper cartons of hard-boiled eggs, bags of pita bread, salted hummus, pomegranates and mandarins, cups of yogurt sweetened with honey.

She gave each man a bolt bag. Inside was a counterfeit Turkish passport bearing his picture, an American visa and other essentials: a heavy wad of American dollars, paper maps, energy bars, bottled water, a flip phone and a packet of poison pills. The pills came with special prayers, written as poetry, to be recited if necessary. Norah's gifts to the brothers included a single firearm, a Luger-style Browning stashed in Omar's bag. The bullets were in Ibrahim's bag.

In the comfort of the basement of the safe house, they talked. Norah's accent and vocabulary suggested she had a formal education and, like the brothers, had grown up in the holy city of Mecca, Saudi Arabia. Norah said she would be giving the brothers their instructions, their direction. The brothers could not leave the house without consent; she would always be their chaperone. She would have to kill them if they did not obey.

Norah said she would leave the pair overnight to rest and to eat, would return the next evening, at dark, to begin their training. She became earnest, offered thanks to each of them for having come so far. A beep from the device on her wrist meant it was time for prayers. The trio kneeled, faces to the floor, recited ancient passages, sought blessings, and when they were done, Omar declared their mission was holy and would remain so as long as the brothers were obedient.

Ibrahim smirked at Omar, then turned to Norah. What is to stop us from escaping after you leave? he asked. We have passports and money. Couldn't we walk?

Norah spoke with confidence: Bars on the windows and doors. Did you see? They'll be locked behind me. And you don't have coats so the cold outside would probably kill you. My report says that Omar would beat you if necessary, to stop you from running. If you escaped from him, I would hunt you down and kill you. It would cost my life if I didn't. If there's nothing else to make you stay, think of me hunting you down and killing you.

Am I supposed to be afraid? Ibrahim sounded nearly cocky.

She didn't react.

Terrified? he asked.

Norah asked for his hand and Ibrahim gave it. With the grace of a ballerina, she bent his arm at the elbow and shoved the heel of his hand against the front of his throat, forced him backward, against a wall, and leveraged the heel where it could hardly be moved. With her free hand, she pushed a thumb into one of his eyelids and made it clear she could gouge. Ibrahim's face went red and bulged. He was facing a lethal fighter capable of mercy. He stopped resisting.

She released. I'm only offering a warning, she said. You must trust me and you must follow my orders, and then everything is fine.

I will follow, said Ibrahim, still red. I will do whatever you say.

Norah stared back, as hard as a hammer. Yes, she said. You'd better.

Ibrahim cleared his throat. This intimidation—you don't need it, he said.

Norah's face revealed confusion. What was Ibrahim suggesting?

When you told us to hide ourselves on your boat, to obey if we wanted to live, you established control, he said.

So why ask about escaping?

I wondered, said Ibrahim. I wanted to know.

You're odd, she blurted.

Not odd, he responded. Curious.

In the kitchen, under the glow of cobalt-blue pendant lamps, the brothers microwaved lamb kabobs and basmati rice. The atmosphere was cozy, and by design. Norah had scoured the sink and counters with lemon-scented cleaner and had created the feeling of home: a contemporary German coffeemaker, a line of greenish Mason jars, some with nuts and some with colored candies; herringbone-patterned area rugs in pastel blues. Corded window shades of natural jute and cotton paper blocked the view from outside. Checkered linoleum, decades old, looked vintage chic. The brothers were supposed to feel grateful for the comforts, and their first view of America was supposed to be pleasant.

It feels like we are still at sea, said Omar. The rolling in my head. He put a forkful of meat into his mouth.

I feel it too, said Ibrahim. I hope it stops. Ibrahim swallowed a morsel of grilled lamb that had been marinated in saffron and salt. With his fork, he stabbed another, held it up to examine it. This is my first decent food in weeks. I am appreciating beautiful Norah. She is feeding us well. He put the meat between his molars and chewed. He moaned, eyes closed. Oh, this is good, he said.

Food is food, said Omar. Don't act like you have entered paradise.

Ibrahim held up a hand while he swallowed, looked eager to speak.

Omar halted him with a heavy glare. Don't get comfortable, he said. We're here only a short while.

Ibrahim rolled brown eyes in disbelief. Will you permit one pleasant moment? he asked. One? Can you relax that much? We're almost at the end of our lives. Are you afraid of the beauty of a good meal? Then came sarcasm: Oh, no, he said. Maybe Norah's wish for us to enjoy our food will ruin us.

Omar's eyes narrowed. She is shameless, he said. How can we ignore a Muslim woman who abandons the rules of her faith? She does not cover herself. And what she did to you? Downstairs, thirty minutes ago? She should be whipped. His tone turned brotherly. Her breasts are obvious under her thin shirt.

Such a surprise, said Ibrahim. A woman with breasts.

By looking, anyone can see how big. He cupped his hands on his chest.

Omar, we're in America for two hours. What do we know?

We know Islam and so does she, said Omar.

You are somebody's useful idiot, said Ibrahim.

You do as you are told, said Omar. Don't forget. I am watching and so is Norah.

Ibrahim pointed at his older brother with his fork. Don't be an ass. That would be good for us both. He tapped. Eat, he ordered. You're ugly when you're hungry.

From a corner of the kitchen, a hidden webcam captured and transmitted the image and sound of the brothers. In her minivan, parked in the dark a mile away, Norah Saud, the only child of Nassir Saud, sat with her smart phone, watching, listening, nodding. And on a night when her van windows had frosted over, she was sweating out anxiety. She'd retrieved the brothers, established control, didn't get caught. Everything was fine and yet it felt like something horrible was happening, something nauseating.

Father had been correct. Omar was controlling and rigid. He would be easy. He attached himself to authority and damned those who didn't. He'd threaten and try to dominate a free thinker like Ibrahim. He would serve the mission in ways Norah feared she couldn't.

Ibrahim followed a fool's code, Father had said. Father said he was loyal to people who offered no value. He was scrawny and didn't make himself look like a threat. He ignored opportunity, got stepped on by those who didn't. He was exploitable and obviously so. Norah was still concerned. Was he scared enough? she wondered. He might bend rather than break, or he might be devious. Was he lying in wait? Was he hoping for an out? His question about escape was reason to worry.

The situation exhausted Norah, left her spent and morose; so much to do, so many preparations, too many places for things to go wrong, too many ways to make Father angry. She couldn't help but fear his anger, could only hope she would escape harm. If the police or the FBI swept in, the rest of her short life would be spent on death row. Americans would never forget the Saudi woman who ran a terrorist cell that attacked Washington, DC, who incited hatred. They might never know she'd been the asset of a family business that claimed her only when it was advantageous to do so.

She went straight home, haggard, hungry and a little ornery. All she wanted was to fall asleep and feel better.

THREE

Father's friends all liked to kiss me. Once on the right, once on the left. They came close enough to hear my teeth grinding. They would reach from behind and take my hand. They'd hold it while we walked garden paths. They had gardens, most of them. The gardens were quiet places to gather information and to make important decisions. If it was time for a man to die, the word often came while walking a garden.

Father's friends could know right away if your hands shook or were sweaty. I was afraid they'd smell my period. They came close and stayed there because they were considering my status and my value. They did it with everyone. Were you a threat? An asset? Maybe you were an idiot or maybe the man would accuse you of betrayal. You could be one of those boys who was somebody else's spy. A cunning boy would hold out for rewards. If he showed judgment and intelligence, he might be kept close and could learn how some men intimidated, how fortunes were made and preserved.

I never stopped being afraid of what would happen if Father's friends found me out. Sometimes it made my heart pound and I would breathe like I'd been running. How could I forget that the man holding my hand might murder me if he knew I was not male? Anybody would be afraid of that and stay afraid. If you were just a little off, they'd find out and they'd mutilate you. Every murder was a useful message to the ones still alive: Give me loyalty or your life is ended.

Being around Father's friends taught me how to act normal. Like, if you're holding hands with a man who'd kill you, better to relax. Don't stutter. Don't tremble. If you look afraid, it's probably over. If you act relaxed, you can get through. Constant pretending. You need to hold hands with death while you walk through gardens and keep coming up with pleasant things to say about the blood lilies and orchids.

Almost everything about me traces back to Father. I have his face and some of his traits. He taught me the importance of all the little things a person says or does, that all actions have meaning. A man who stands and talks to you with his feet pointed away is interested in something else. A person who sits with his head resting against the back of his chair is too much at ease, has his guard down. Father taught me engineering— how lateral bracing in the massive tankers prevents ships from breaking apart.

Almost everything I know about guns comes from him. Holding your breath and squeezing slow when aiming through a scope is crucial. Keep your magazine separate so if somebody steals your gun they can't kill you with your own weapon. He taught me to read and write in English. He hired a guard from the Japanese embassy to teach me judo—how to disable a man with two hands, how to kill him.

Did you know he named me? He said he chose Norah because it was a Muslim name that would seem normal to Americans. The day I was born, he did this. Twenty-eight years ago, he began to use me. He saw a newborn as an asset, an investment.

I've never said these words to anyone. Sorry. This is upsetting.

He disposed of my mother after the hard work of raising an infant was done. He put her in the prison cell where she died. When I was old enough to ask about her, he told me some women are called home by God as soon as they deliver a baby. I grew up mourning my mother. I thought she died giving birth to me. I wanted forgiveness. I was lonely for her. After I learned the truth, my hate for Father controlled me. I wanted him to suffer.

Some days the only thing that stopped me from killing him was fear that his people would kill me. His people were loyal and they kept secrets. They'd be dead otherwise. He made this known, it was his trump card. He would take new acquaintances to watch the religious police, his Mutaween, as they marched with weapons. Father would have the Mutaween captain salute him and offer respects and Father would give speeches about how his men were the best anywhere, that they were committed to him. People got the message. I doubt anyone in Saudi Arabia dared to talk about harming Father.

Father said his work with the Saudi Security Directorate allowed him to know everything about everybody. People at the Directorate listened to any phone conversation they chose and Father saw every e-mail he ever wanted. His friends, they spied for him. Who was in debt and needed rescue? Who'd been caught with prostitutes? With homosexuals? Who had influence in Russia? In America? Who boasted, was too eager for admiration? He knew if you were weak and couldn't run. He knew what time of day you'd be alone, when you were vulnerable. He knew what you needed most and it always seemed like he controlled people who could provide it. He was vigilant and he expected people to be vigilant for him.

His religious police—the Mutaween, the ones in the khaki uniforms with black berets? They killed and tortured for him. They would run electricity through a woman's vagina after they tied up her husband and told him if he didn't watch they would kill her. They would dig out a man's eyes if he kept looking away, but only after he listened to them kill his wife. The Mutaween would do anything for Father, as long as it served God.

Father believed people had to be vigilant, everyone vigilant always, and as long as you had that, you would be fine. Father said some people want to pretend the world isn't dangerous and as soon as someone points a gun at them, they lose all sense. He said that's when they should realize they've been worrying about the wrong thing, except most people are too stupid even to learn that much. He despised stupid, my Father. He liked to tell people they'd been reading too many books.

Father was my hero for a long time. He protected me and he taught me to be like him. He told me what to hate and why. I told him every thought I had.

Things changed when I found out about Mother. When I came to America, things changed more. Who could have imagined one country was so much less anxious than another? Most Americans are pleasant and not desperate. They don't treat you as a possible threat. They're happy to help you and happy if you do well. They're not trying to win by making you lose.

* * *

Norah's side of the bed was uncomfortably cold when she crawled in. Thirty inches away was a reliable source of heat, but one she liked to avoid: husband Dirk, snoring, squared up like a box turtle with a Glock under his pillow. Long ago, he'd harped when Norah demanded that he engage the safety before bed and he'd called her a ninny. Oh, mister burglar, gimme a sec while I unlock, Dirk had said, a girly voice coming out of his nose.

With an armed burglar, if you're asleep, you're dead, she'd responded. The safety is to protect *us*.

Dirk was stupefied. You're naïve as hell, you know that? he said.

In the dark, in the quiet, Norah settled under the cold covers, closed her eyes, let her warmth accumulate. Tomorrow, she'd brief Father about the brothers' arrival and he'd have questions, and he wouldn't stop with his questions until he found errors and exploited her vulnerability—until he pricked at her skin and made her bleed. Ignorant Dirk copied Father. He would pick at the same things and she'd bleed a little more.

Poor Dirk was witless. He had a compulsion to dominate and most of the world refused to bow. Fairly often, people told him to shut the hell up.

A great many people will stop and wonder if they become aware of gaps between their self-image and the world's view of them. Some might seek self-knowledge and adjust for the difference. Dirk found it easier to emulate an egregiously selfish man whose talent for dominance was the alleged source of fantastic wealth. Nassir was his hero. Dirk walked where Nassir had walked, said he could find safety along the man's path, the way infantrymen on patrol march in the shadow of armored tanks.

Dirk said he took comfort from Nassir's position, from the protection it offered. He'd been loyal to Nassir, had admired the man's superiority. He avoided any mention of the wealth Nassir had been born into. The same was true for his membership in the Saud family, as if those could be taken for granted.

Tomorrow, Norah would have to get in and get out of the safe house without being seen. She'd have to notify the Saudi embassy, her itinerary, her timing, so the embassy's security man, Bandar Zarkawi, could follow if he wanted. She thought it best not to wait, picked up her phone from the nightstand, typed in a message, sent it, let her head flop. Tomorrow's work would begin in less than five hours. Had she forgotten anything? Could the brothers escape? Could they mutiny? Father would be murderous. Always with Father—the threats.

So? Dirk spoke through a throatful of loose phlegm.

She lifted her head and nearly wheezed with surprise. You're awake?

I'm talking, right? he said. Brief me.

Picking up and delivering, all as planned, she said. No problems. Everything smooth. No worries. Norah reached, found Dirk's naked shoulder in the dark and stroked him. I'm going back tomorrow to begin training, as planned.

You didn't give them bolt bags, did you?

Leave it to Dirk to find fault; Father would be proud. I assessed them, she said. They pose no threat.

Dirk clicked on the light, sat up. Shirtless, his hairy heft was undeniable. You've known them for two hours and you hand over a gun, cash and passports? he demanded. They could've killed you and stolen your van. How is it you're even sitting here?

Father's known these men for years, said Norah. They just gave full control to an unfamiliar Muslim female. They took orders, no questions. This is a difficult foreign environment. If I give comfort and security, they trust me. That's how humans work. Father says that all the time.

Dirk's face went square at the corners and Norah could tell he was ready to say something born from ignorance. Darling, please, she said. You run a defense contractor. You think up reasons for people to buy your nukes. You know how this works.

Norah, I said not to give them the bolt bags, Dirk complained.

She sat up and faced her husband. She put her hands around her loose, black hair and gathered it. She lay it in front of one shoulder, a badge of femininity. Managing these assets is my responsibility and you've decided you can't let them see you, she said. You don't want to get caught, remember? You'll have to trust my judgment.

Dirk's naked torso kept sagging. The fingertips of a meaty hand scratched through his golden buzz cut. Our lives depend on you doing your job and this mission turning out right. Our whole lives depend on that one thing.

Dirk?

Yes?

That's two things.

He squeaked like a wheel that needed grease. Holy Christ, he said. You know what I mean. Look, Norah, it's your first mission. Don't screw it up. I don't know what your father would do to us. He reached, took her hand away from her ponytail, squeezed until it hurt, didn't let go.

She grabbed two of his fingers and bent them and would have broken them. He released. She turned on the motherly voice, the one that got Dirk to obey. If you give someone a complicated job within their expertise, you should expect them to use their judgment, she said. My job is evaluating people. I'm better at it than you are, we both know. And you don't know the men. They are Saudis, Muslims—you don't understand them.

Your father said Muslim women obeyed. Where's the obedience?

Norah whispered, mindful that Father seemed to have ears everywhere. Father doesn't understand women, she said. He's afraid of them.

Nassir is the smartest man I ever met, said Dirk. Like, next-level brilliant. He's not scared of anything.

Father is complicated, she said. You'd need to study him carefully and for a long time.

Five years I've known Nassir, said Dirk.

Norah had never told Dirk that Father had dressed her in men's robes, about the driving, about the extremes Father used to avoid women. She hadn't told him of Father's access to Russian intel, of Father's reliance on the Mutaween. Dirk knew nothing of the murder of Norah's mother, that Father was gay. She'd never told Dirk that his fears about Father had been put there by Father, that Father used the fear as a control knob.

It was better that Dirk didn't know, that he habitually discounted her views in favor of Nassir's. She wasn't going to fight him unless there was an upside.

Dirk's fingers made a V and pointed at his eyes, then he pointed the V at Norah. I don't trust it if I don't see it, he said. Nassir told me that's how it should be.

Norah had long ago discovered the impossibility of correcting Dirk's misconceptions and despaired over being bound to him. Father saw fit to marry her to this lump of coal, to embed her in America where her mission included steering Dirk away from his worst instincts, protecting Father's investment, all the while lacking resources needed for independence. She had no bank account. Her income came as little packets of money her husband issued. Her passport gave her diplomatic travel privileges but was hidden away. The two men in her life dictated her schedule, her opportunities and her duties. Dirk gave her a minivan, bought her all the guns she wanted, let her pilot his boats, kept her on a string.

She rolled away from her husband, hugged her pillows, wanted sleep to erase her irritation. Dirk was a man on a mission. He pulled off his underpants, slid up against her, poked her. I woke up with this, he said.

She resisted, got angry. He demanded, wasn't going away. She ordered him to turn out the lights and, in the dark, she gave him the business and kept working and it didn't take any longer than usual. He did as he'd been told and he whimpered like a little boy when he was almost there so Norah wouldn't get any in her mouth.

* * *

Was the entire world hungry for the company of the Russian President or did it only seem that way? Admiration was universal. It never stopped coming. The flow of requests for visits overwhelmed the government office whose only job was to tell people their president was too busy. Film stars admired the man whose words became law the moment he uttered them. Business owners, hockey players and lottery winners made him their hero. People gave him things—expensive things. They mailed him presents, all of which went into a warehouse to be appraised and liquidated. Government employees sold it all and the proceeds went into an account with the name of the Russian President's wife on it, which was nice because it meant that she rarely had to ask him for money.

People said every room the President entered was his. His focal point, whatever item got his attention, became holy. In the middle of sentences, the President turned away from those who couldn't keep him interested. Nobody complained about the man believed to be richer than any other person alive and who controlled one of the world's most lethal complexes of military might. Visitors never complained about a man who came of age as a spymaster, whose control and command were more important than the lives of ordinary citizens—the apartment dwellers and the newspapermen, the foreign diplomats and the rivals.

If a person wanted to visit with the Russian President they had to give him something he wanted. You want a picture with the President? Of course, you help the President and everybody is good.

Once, when the owner of an American football team arrived, there were hugs and laughs and the President was joyful and he was laughing and laughing until everybody else was laughing, too. You win and you win, always you are the winner, says the President. You keep winning. You and that terrific quarterback.

Yes, says the owner, laughing. We win a lot.

The Russian President points at the owner's hand. Your Super Bowl ring? Can I try it on?

Of course you can try it on, says the owner, flattered.

The President puts on the ring, hugs the owner, wishes for him to keep on winning and he leaves the room and nobody says a word about the theft of an irreplaceable ring of extraordinary value because the Russian President is accountable only when he agrees to be. Nothing he says is true, everything he thinks is possible and everybody understands.

* * *

During their first week in America, Norah took Omar and Ibrahim to get winter clothes and boots. She took them to a salty lunch at a noisy Chipotle, made them place orders, pay for their food. She took them to an organic grocer in Annapolis, found out which foods they liked. They followed every order she issued, didn't stray, were always in sight. As brothers do, they irritated each other, but resisted bickering when company was around.

Norah remained aware that Ibrahim had conceded her dominance and had lightened her load. Regardless, on their walk to her minivan, arms laden with groceries, she reminded the brothers that escape would be foolish. In a country where they had no family and no friends, they would be unable to hide.

Again with this? asked Ibrahim. Really? He took the grocery bags from her hands so she could fish for her keys and open the minivan.

Days passed. She drove the brothers into downtown Washington. Together, they rode the subways, using the underground stations they would enter on the day of their mission, and she told them to study the stride and the cadence of American commuters. She showed them the street routes to their safe house and explained how to get back if they were lost. She told them to use paper maps. They were to interact with the Americans—to ask directions, to exchange news about the weather and to speak politely about ordinary things. She said it was essential to become comfortable with the surroundings. You have ten weeks to learn the art of being American, she said.

When Omar displayed contempt for the Americans, Norah scolded him. When he persisted, she grew stern and told him that if he wanted to serve God he would respect his hosts. He would not want conflict or confusion on what became known as *the day*. If you remain this angry, you will make someone else angry, she told him. They may try to fight you or they will suspect you of something and call the police. You can't afford angry. Always be ready with something nice to say, especially on the day, Norah said.

It was breakfast time at the safe house when Omar's intransigence, his refusal to give Norah his full attention, became an issue. She dug the tips of her fingers into the flesh of his face, almost hard enough to hurt. You need to look at me when I'm talking to you, she said.

Omar's head was turned, his face pointed at the kitchen floor. You are a Muslim woman, he said. A grown woman. You are not covered. Your hair and your face are naked. I can understand you without looking.

Norah pulled his chin until his head turned. Omar forced his eyes closed. We will be together for some weeks, she said. You must look at me.

Omar's jaw was frozen and he spoke in the smallest voice he had. Please stop, he said. It is enough that I am sacrificing myself.

You cannot walk among Americans unless you act like an American, she said. You have to understand America. You can't appear angry or uncomfortable. You will stand out. You threaten yourself and you threaten me, and everybody who supports you.

For my whole life, I don't look at a Muslim woman whose head is uncovered, said Omar.

Norah tightened and stopped tightening when she sensed pain had begun. Open your eyes, she ordered.

This is not reasonable, he said.

Open, she commanded. She squeezed harder, ignored Omar's begging, increased pressure until he grabbed her wrist with both of his hands, tried to pry open her grip but could not overcome her strength.

Please, no, he pleaded. The pressure and the pain remained. He fought, gave up when the pain worsened, opened his eyes and stared at Norah. Better? he asked.

Norah released and stood taller. God, you are exhausting, she said. She put her face close to his, close enough so that Omar could feel her breath. He retreated, but kept looking at her. This is what I expect, she said. You need to look women in the eye, exactly the same as with the men.

Ibrahim chewed on a fig as he'd watched the scene unfold. Big brother, he said, everything's changed. Everything and always.

* * *

Nassir Saud sucked sweat from the nape of Victor Ivanov's neck, pulled on Victor's hair, forced his face to come partway around and shoved an awkward half kiss on him. They combined in a nude fetal curl, breathing hard, dripping, triumphant. A cloud of masculine heat above them, satisfaction within. When they got too cool, they pulled up the covers and brought in pillows from the edges of the bed.

Outside the hotel room, in the wood-floored corridor, two people walked, one wearing pumps with clicky heels. Nassir held his breath until the sound of them was gone. Victor was disbelieving. So much worry? he asked.

You wish to be dead? asked Nassir.

Anyone with your money is extorted, said Victor. Only a fool would kill a man who offered so much.

Nassir snorted. Of course. You lived in Paris for two years and now you have full knowledge of the universe, he said.

My president tells me I should give him a blow job, said Victor. He whispers it so I'm the only one who hears. He threatens to tell my secrets. He does this to keep me obedient.

He's crude and he thinks you're feminine, said Nassir. He's testing you.

Victor was undeterred. The man knows, he said. If he knows about me, he knows about you.

We'd know if he knew, said Nassir. His hatred for men like us? He doesn't hide it.

He hates us only because that is useful for him, said Victor. Every fag is an asset. We have to live in constant fear of him. If you don't see that, you aren't paying attention.

In the land of Saud, it is death, said Nassir. They do it quickly and everybody knows why. If I'm alive it's because nobody knows.

My president says the Saudis don't know value, said Victor. He says the dogma of religion blinds the Saudis. They do expensive things on principle.

Nassir stuttered, then ordered Victor not to be an ass—and not to tell. Victor, you can't let yourself be tricked into admitting, he said.

Victor sneered at the naïveté. Your king waits like a crocodile waits for a meal, he said. Only after you're dead would he tell everyone who you were because then the information is useless—unless your family wants to keep it quiet and then it has value again.

They'd come to an impasse—they pushed competing versions of reality and neither would yield. Neither spoke until the silence became uncomfortable.

My offer to your president, said Nassir. Does he find it acceptable?

Yes, said Victor. As you requested, the two Shia boys are in Baltimore. They have bombs planned for the New York City bridges and an anonymous tip will get them spotted at the appropriate time. The Americans will shift their attention away from Washington. The Russian President wants your promise the Washington attack will happen in late February. One of his companies will be signing contracts to purchase Washington real estate in March. The timing is important.

Late February, said Nassir. So it shall be.

FOUR
MANY YEARS BEFORE

A person who could hold a child's attention was one of the strongest people alive. Ghadia preached this and she lived it. At the Saudi Arabian Security Directorate Headquarters Nursery and Day Care Center, Ghadia took on the children who made problems—the ones who learned early to spot the weak and make them cry, the ones who made messes and ran away. Each of the problem children was impressionable and could be sent in directions that would make them happier and better. As their minds expanded, crevices opened and would fill with influence. Ghadia said those were places she could insert sweetness and generosity disguised as prayers and poems.

Because children learned language before they knew what it meant to be judged, they had a long phase when they were open and honest about themselves. They'd reveal beliefs free of anxiety or fear. This was when a person could discover their nature.

Ghadia observed that the shy ones made friendships if she grouped them together. They learned the value of kindness, didn't seek unfair advantage.

In the basement of Saudi Arabia's Security Directorate, she cared for and taught dozens of boys and girls whose mothers did secret things for national protection. Women were permitted to become linguists, code breakers and secretaries and Ghadia supposed that they spied on people who did not speak Arabic or that they questioned foreigners arrested for terrible things. When the working mothers collected children after work, they spoke with a practiced mildness, a tone that could not offend. They gave no hints about their occupations and none were ever asked for. If work taught them about a world that was alarming, they kept it hidden.

One afternoon, a chronically restless boy named Rafiq refused Ghadia's suggestion that he sit with his classmates and listen to a storyteller. Rafiq flung a shelf of books onto the floor. When Ghadia reached for his arm, he swung a fist, hit her on the point of her hipbone and ran, disappearing down a hallway. Ghadia clutched herself. The boy entered what the adults understood to be a dead end—a staircase leading up to a set of locked doors. Behind the doors was a gymnasium, long ago taken out of service.

Ghadia didn't chase fleeing children, didn't want to encourage runaways. She walked and stopped when she got close.

At the bottom of the staircase she called for Rafiq and waited. Two silent minutes passed. At the top of the stairs, she wrung her fingers when she found the doors to the gymnasium unlocked and the gym lights blazing. She searched under bleachers, found only empty cans, dead and dusty, that had once contained fruity Italian soda. In a timid voice, she called for the boy, breaking silence in an expansive space, an echo chamber designed for a crowd. She scanned the room, as silent as a tomb, and saw no clues to the boy's hiding place.

Ghadia walked the gym's perimeter and the wood floor issued brittle creaks, the sound of disuse. Her steps echoed as she tested doors. One closet was held fast by a keyed deadbolt. The doors to a set of rear stairs were chained closed. She quivered when she pulled on the door to the men's locker room and it yielded. Into the dark she stepped, a hurried rustling coming from within. Rafiq? she whispered. The rustling stopped. Then came whispering. The room sounded like it had a low ceiling and it reeked of Pine-Sol. She found the light switch. Rafiq? she queried. With the lights on, she stopped breathing when she caught sight of swollen, purplish genitals and two naked males. She lost her sense of space and time and nearly lost balance when she recognized one as Nassir Saud, the boss of every person in this twelve-story building. He was sweaty and crazed from homosexual congress.

Nassir's partner was a young man, one Ghadia had seen. He was a Directorate driver who ferried the agency's VIPs about town.

Beyond the door to the room, in the gymnasium, Ghadia heard footsteps, heard a boy cough. She killed the lights in the confines of the locker room, slammed the door and closed the hasp on the outside, temporarily trapping the males. She ran, grabbing Rafiq's hand on the way. She hurried downstairs with the boy, left him in the playroom with the storyteller, the other children, the other adults, grabbed her purse and fled. She skittered four blocks straight home where she found her husband and daughter in the kitchen, and was relieved that both of her boys, Omar and Ibrahim, were safe at school, playing soccer.

Ghadia screamed: *We have to go! We have to leave!* She turned off the stove where the daughter was cooking lunch. Ghadia grabbed the car keys, put them into her husband's hands, pulled at his shirt and slapped at him. Get up. Go. Drive. I'll explain later. She flung open drawers, grabbing essentials: passports, money, pictures.

The husband and the daughter stared at Ghadia with amusement; she was wild with trembling fear. She ranted and appeared ready to cry. She screamed and stomped a foot. *Nassir*, she shrilled. Nassir is coming. He'll kill us. All of us. Hurry.

Ghadia's husband made her sit, asked her to breathe slowly and said she should slow down. Ghadia became more agitated, fought against him, screamed more, then she stopped making any sense, flopped forward, her face in her hands. Her weeping became a pelting rainstorm and she pleaded for her husband to understand something she couldn't seem to explain.

It didn't matter.

In the time that Ghadia and her husband and her daughter would have needed to gather a few things, to begin racing away in the family's Volkswagen, Nassir's men would have come upon them and shot them anyway.

FIVE

I learned so much from Father, some of it for the good. Father's chief talents were pretending that he was never afraid, making people believe that he knew everything about everyone, making sure he was at the center of everything. Those things were leverage for everything he ever gained. If you put him in a flower garden, he acted like the flowers were calling his name, were worshipping him. He acted like a man who was adored. A garden would put him in a mood to convince people he was too mighty to be bothered by anything. He would throw out grand ideas, as if everything he wanted were possible, even what obviously was not. He pretended to be so brilliant he wasn't limited by the things he could not do. He claimed abilities nobody else had. His thinking was magical. He believed himself better and smarter than all the others and he liked those who believed it too. Walking in the garden, he kept his chest out and he stared at people, like you could fire bullets and he wouldn't care because he could command them to go around. He acted like the killer shark, a predator. But he was more afraid than anyone. I lived with him for twenty-three years and took his orders every day. I saw him when it was private, him and me. The FBI's records probably don't show his fear of women. He was so vulnerable. Inside he was fighting and losing a great battle. He was terrified and people had no idea.

* * *

Omar pressed a hairy slab of cheek against the inside of the minivan window. The vehicle inched along in traffic. He looked up and pointed up—at a monolith high on a hill. That tower is Egyptian, he said. Why is it in Virginia?

That's the Masonic Temple, said Norah. It honors the first American president. He embraced the history and art of Islam.

Sidewalk commuters with umbrellas and galoshes race-walked to the nearby subway station. Busy morning traffic took small steps. A viscous rain smeared the view of everything.

Omar, still staring at the Egyptian-style tower, squeezed out a groan. Americans hate Muslims and they want to end us, he said. Really, they want what we have. They're stealing it.

Ibrahim's head swung. That is severe, even for you, he said. When we were learning English, did you think we were stealing from America?

Look with your two eyes, Omar said. In front of you, right now. Theft of Islam. They put it on a hill, like a trophy. America wants people to think it won the war.

Ibrahim was curious, and fundamentally so. What have we ever lost to the Americans? he asked.

Omar pointed, aggressively. We lost that monument. Open your eyes, he said. The Americans are thieves. They don't hide the fact that they lure away observant Muslims. Our people and our society are corrupted by American thievery.

America has people who respect Islam, Omar. Just like there are Christians who choose to live in Saudi Arabia. Is that so hard to understand?

Omar plugged his fingers in his ears. You refuse to listen, Ibrahim. You ignore the facts, he said. It's a waste of time talking to people like you.

Ibrahim waited until his brother's fingertips came out. You can offer me all the anger you want, he said. I won't take any.

You hate people because they don't agree with you about what is holy, Omar charged. That makes you an ass.

Tension made Ibrahim's lips grow thin. You want me to lose my temper? he asked. Get angry? I should be like you, Omar?

Norah pulled the van to a curb. She would divert Omar, wouldn't challenge him. She'd always taken pleasure when the path of least resistance happened to be the wise one. Omar, look over there, she said. King Street Station. See where people are going in?

The busy space laid out beneath the elevated commuter train was shaped like a funnel. It pushed together one and all—big-city wingtips, muddy boots, professors of theory and metalworkers with their ballpeen hammers, their paths peacefully aligned, if only briefly.

I walk alone among the ugly Americans, said Omar. At last.

Remember what I said, Omar, Norah warned. Behave. Be pleasant.

Behave? Omar sneered. Am I a child?

Norah's voice revealed the anger that came from being under Father's heavy thumb. Her words came out loud, hostile and from deep within. Should I kill you now? she asked. She pulled a nine-millimeter from her ski coat and displayed it to Omar. Should I eliminate the man whose temper might get us arrested? Then, quieter: You need to calm down.

Norah thought she might get traction if she offered a few kind words. Before she could, Ibrahim motioned for her to put the gun away. Omar, she means that sometimes people are difficult because it's a bad day for them and it has nothing to do with you, he said. Don't be so harsh. He gave Norah a sign. This was under control.

See how I'm looking you in the eye? Omar asked Norah. Since I'm in America, I do what you say. You've noticed? Stop speaking from on high. You're no better than anyone else. He slammed open the minivan's sliding door.

When Norah imagined them side by side, Omar and Dirk were so much alike. Both favored provocative declarations that could make people angry, declarations that begged for confrontation. Often their declarations announced a claim of superiority. Just as often, their declarations were insults thrown at those they wanted to be superior to. They could provoke people who were otherwise peaceful and often drew mild spirits into a violent arena where they could be beaten and humiliated.

They both chest-puffed, made damn sure they wouldn't get stepped on. They made heroes of the famously superior, men faithful to a mercenary code, men who commanded wealth and armies that could threaten and inflict despicable forms of hurt. And both were preoccupied with the bottom rung of life's ladder—as if the worst thing ever was to be looked down upon.

For the several years of her marriage, Norah had suffered through Dirk's outbursts, through periodic crises of the faith he'd invested in Nassir. She'd looked in vain for an opening with him, to affect him, but he'd pledged loyalty to a titanic man who insulted, threatened and condemned all who refused subservience. Men like Father followed a mantra. They'd never apologize to a lesser man. To do so was to reveal the capacity for shame, to flag an obvious weakness that would become a tool for someone wanting to diminish them, or worse, to terminate them.

Dirk had wrapped himself in Nassir's armor, had picked a piece of ground at Nassir's feet and he stood it. Dirk and the armor had kept a vigilant watch over a single spot for so long that rust had fused the armor's pieces, made them a rigid whole that cocooned the occupant. He believed in protection from above, from the one to whom he'd pledged faith. The way he talked, Dirk must have felt he was part of the ground he'd stood. Dirk had the comfort of his guns, his ingenuity and his eagerness to project deadly force. By God, he would not be ignored and would not be stepped on. He would be a venomous serpent if threatened.

What began as a defensive crouch became Dirk's life and his view of everything. Dirk sheltered in his inflexible surround, protected from a world of cutthroats, a dangerous world controlled by every man's inherent need for superiority. Escaping the confines of his armor was hardly an option. Many had dared to venture away from protection and were never heard from again.

Who would dare emerge from their armor into that world? Who would walk without protection, knowing the risks? A vigilant man would never be so stupid.

Dirk, she'd decided, couldn't be moved. Omar was not so different, probably was stuck too, but still she would try. Why so angry, Omar? she asked. Be careful or you'll get us in trouble. The rain, cold and bothersome, blew in through the open panel.

You're not so smart, he said. You only needed to wish me good luck and this conversation would be over. I'll find my way back to the safe house, as you have ordered, master. I'll prove I've learned your lessons.

He stepped out, slammed the door and bent low enough to see Norah through the window. From behind his jagged black beard he displayed a durable plastic smile, disturbing because it was so obviously false. He headed for the subway entrance with no umbrella, rain blowing straight in his face.

Ibrahim, as lithe as a jaguar, unbuckled from the bench seat and twisted himself into the front. With his brother gone, there would be no argument over it. Omar will behave, he said. On the Mutaween, he always followed orders, even ridiculous ones.

He'd better, said Norah, if he wants to live until tomorrow.

Ibrahim tensed. *What?* he asked.

That man with the black hair and the tan coat? said Norah. That's Mr. Zarkawi, from the embassy. He can shoot Omar with his silent gun and, if he gets close, he can inject poison. He might also approach Omar and share holy words of encouragement. The ones who make decisions for us sent him. She looked Ibrahim in the face and only after he looked back did she give a warning: Be advised. We do not want attention from police or the FBI. When I drop you at the station in Tysons Corner, a man like Mr. Zarkawi will follow. In America, we're almost never alone.

Zarkawi and his immaculate black hair mixed into the funneling subway crowd, close behind Omar.

Something stung Ibrahim. You would tell me and not Omar? he asked.

Norah lifted her chin and squinted at him. She'd assessed Ibrahim, thought she'd seen through him. She didn't say what she was thinking—that Ibrahim was more stable, more deserving of trust than his older brother. She liked that he might also be naïve; it made him easier to manage. The minivan's dashboard almost certainly concealed a microphone and a camera, so Norah had to stay in character. Father could listen and watch any time he wanted and Ibrahim didn't seem to understand. I was concerned what Omar might do if I told him, said Norah. Did something happen? I've never seen him this way.

He thinks everybody is trying to climb over him, trying to beat him down, said Ibrahim. Sometimes it's too much and it makes him ugly. He wasn't so much like this before our parents were killed.

It was Norah's turn to be stung. Killed? she asked.

Murdered, said Ibrahim. Yes.

For her entire adult life, Norah had nursed the hurt of learning Father had condemned Mother to a prison death. Here was someone else nursing the same hurt. Her wounded expression begged for, and got, an explanation. We were walking home from soccer, said Ibrahim. We were met at the smoking remains of our home by Mutaween, who said our mother and father were dead from a fire. Our older sister, Alitha, was in a hospital. So they said. Relatives who offered to care for us were refused. We went into an orphanage that was horrible. We've never seen Alitha, but she sends letters. One day, I met this boy at the orphanage school—from the old neighborhood. He told me our parents didn't die in a fire but were shot by the Mutaween and the house was burned with them inside. He watched it happen. That day, while I was playing soccer? Blowing on the field was foul smoke. It was my house and my parents. They were burning.

Alitha is alive? asked Norah.

I hope, he said. Sometimes I hope for things even though there's no reason to. I hold out faith I know is false. Nassir knows that's what people do and he takes advantage.

Norah dared to lay her palm on Ibrahim's forearm, an offer of comfort. He lay his free hand on top of hers and she was pleased he took the gesture appropriately. Many Saudi men would have seen it as rude or sexual. Ibrahim seemed warmed by it.

No one told me, she said. She stopped, had probably said too much. Why would anyone have told her? And who else would know? I feel sorry for you, she said. She stopped again, knew she had stumbled. I don't mean that I pity you, I just mean…. She trailed off and restarted. I'm sorry for your loss, she said. She blinked and blinked, clasped her hands and stared at them because doing so might conceal her bewilderment over a startling discovery—that the brothers' parents hadn't simply died, as Father had told her, but that Father had had them killed. Alive, they must have been a threat to Father and he'd lied to Norah about it. He didn't want her to know. Was Father afraid of her judgment? Was he afraid she'd find sympathy for the brothers?

Ibrahim gave up waiting for her to look directly at him. So Alitha really is dead? he asked.

Norah must have stared at her hands too long because by the time she looked away, a milestone was apparent. For the first time, she'd been unable to project mastery over Ibrahim's circumstances. Her humanity was obvious. Norah reached for her ponytail, for her a source of feminine strength, and stroked it. She answered the question with a question. Have you found peace? she asked.

Omar is bitter, he said. Sometimes he gets enraged and it seems like that's how he likes to be. Angry makes him feel powerful. He wants to hate and he thinks his misfortune is always somebody else's fault. Whatever it was our parents did to earn their execution, he hates them for it. They did it to themselves.

Norah stared at her hands again. I didn't ask about Omar, she said. I asked about you.

Mostly I keep my balance, he said. If I start to feel sorry for myself or if I feel angry, I let it pass. That's how I cope. Omar is more dangerous and more complicated. You should be asking about him. He is proud of himself for growing up as an orphan and being devout, said Ibrahim. He thinks he's made holy sacrifices and that makes him better than you. He's possibly dangerous to you.

Norah bit down. Omar, a man who imagined himself far superior, called her out for looking down upon him. Perhaps his anger should not have been a surprise.

He hates and he hates, said Ibrahim. He hates anything that is not completely Muslim, like that is the only way a person could ever be. He is afraid that if he stops hating, God will punish him. He will become something less than he is now.

He said this?

Ibrahim nodded emphatically. You didn't observe this in him? he asked.

Her jaw tensed. Does he plan to hurt me?

No, said Ibrahim. For now, he's focused on Americans. This is the perfect mission for a man who hates Americans.

Her short nails scratched against the grain of her blue Levi's. Father had not properly vetted these men. There was a constant risk of conflict that would threaten any mission. Had Father been desperate? Did he think she wouldn't notice? He was getting a good show in either case. She gave him every reason to have confidence in her, to believe her loyal.

She was neck deep in Father's pit and, as if she could forget, here was Ibrahim, just as deep. Ibrahim seemed philosophical about it. He hadn't shown the desperation typical of someone soon to die. Norah was miles away from balanced or comfortable. Often grinding her teeth, she lived in perpetual fear of sinking deeper, of foundering. She shook her head—uncontrollably—at odd moments because the image of the pit was repulsive enough that it had to be gotten rid of. Her one salvation was Father's worldview. If she did as he demanded, if she was loyal, she'd survive. The gruesome tales he permitted to be known and the intimidating reputation he maintained worked for her benefit almost as much as his. Anyone who knew of Father would understand the consequences that would come from harm to his daughter. He often won battles because intimidation led his enemies to work around him, to avoid conflict.

Father's protection was welcome but came with an obvious price. Because Father was both protector and tormentor, Norah could never enjoy the feeling of being safe. Inside Father's circle were Father's threats and a swirling combination of vulnerability and self-awareness that had been known to paralyze otherwise intelligent people.

Before her was a man undeserving of the death sentence Father had issued and he showed empathy, he demonstrated grace. Father's dominance and selfishness hadn't turned Ibrahim inward, hadn't inspired wrath. How was that even possible?

And then there was this: He had such a fine ass.

And you, Ibrahim, why are you here? asked Norah.

Ibrahim turned away, stared at King Street Station, at the elevated train filling with passengers. I'm here because Omar requires it, he said. He is my older, bigger brother. He helped raise me after our family was gone. He made sure the orphanage didn't ignore Ibrahim, the skinny and fearful one, and that we didn't get sent to separate places. He made sure the mean boys left me alone, that I got medical attention when I almost died from a bad appendix. He saved my life. Right now, I should be in a tiny cell in the basement of the Security Directorate, captive of the Mutaween. The rest of my days, I'd be alone and starved to my ribs. The only way out of jail was self-destruction in some way that served the needs of someone terrible. Omar got me released. I'm here because of him. He refused to let me die slowly and to do that, he had to agree that he would die with me. Puffy half-moons surfaced. We each have something that's bigger than everything else, said Ibrahim. For me, that's Omar.

And Nassir, he said. Nassir Saud. I'm here because of him. His Mutaween killed my parents. He ordered it, I'm sure. When we were boys, he sent presents and money, and he made sure Alitha's letters got to us. When we were grown, he gave us jobs with the police and later the Mutaween. Ibrahim shifted in his seat, faced Norah. How well do you know him? he asked.

Norah cleared her throat, mindful that Father might be in the audience. If you admitted your father was the one who murdered a man's family and his sister, if you rid him of the last hope of life for someone who was beloved, how would he react? With anger? Violence? And if you showed him compassion, what then? Would your handlers doubt you? Would they kill you?

I know Nassir, said Norah. Of course, I do. He's dangerous. He has eyes and ears everywhere. He can hurt you and the ones you love in ways you'd never think of. However bad you think he is, it's not bad enough.

She put the minivan in drive and, preparing to pull into traffic, looked over her right shoulder, putting her mouth two inches from Ibrahim's ear. Do as I say, she whispered, and everything will be better. I promise. She found a break in traffic, turned forward and pulled the van from the curb.

Buckle up, she barked. The police might pull us over. She didn't look away from the road ahead. She was all business. She had to assume that Father was watching.

Except that today, he wasn't.

* * *

Silver-haired Louis Irons, Director of the Federal Bureau of Investigation's Counter-Terrorism Division, reclined on the government-issue sofa in his office. He was shoeless, one ankle resting on the other. He was smoking a Marlboro and he was thinking. Marlboros were a habit he'd acquired while serving in Vietnam, and for the most logical of reasons—it was healthier than not smoking. The smoke helped keep away mosquitoes; mosquitoes carried malaria; and, malaria was commonly fatal.

Fresh out of the U.S. Naval Academy, Marine Second Lieutenant Louis Irons had led an infantry platoon through the jungles of Quang Tri Province and discovered that a lit cigarette could cauterize minor wounds. He led his men through lands notorious for North Vietnamese ambushes, land mines, trip wires and venomous vipers. Under fire, Louis displayed the guts of a burglar. He'd never lost his composure. He gave the credit to the calming effects of nicotine. Cigarettes, he said, were underappreciated.

Remaining addicted to tobacco was unavoidable, but still sensible. The nicotine in cigarettes brought a focus unavailable anywhere else. Smoking got him through law school—helped him find meaning in textbooks written by long-winded Englishmen who were enamored of their own intellects. He'd grown up as an average student. But after Vietnam, at Georgetown Law, he finished twelfth out of a class of two hundred. Louis said Marlboros deserved much of the credit.

Louis looked out of his office window, facing E Street NW, sitting in the J. Edgar Hoover Building, five blocks from the White House. The exterior of the window hadn't been washed in decades and the city's gutters, below, were full of filthy snow. His Marlboro released a slow-unfurling ribbon that stretched sixteen inches, curled into a tumbling pillow, then pixilated into a carcinogenic haze, to be inhaled by anyone whose job required they visit Louis's office. When a 1997 Presidential Order made it unlawful to smoke in U.S. Government buildings worldwide, it was widely understood, even in the Executive Mansion, that national security required an unwritten exception. The wise man, the mensch, the Marines' goddamnedest Jew, Louis Irons, required one cigarette every waking hour to maintain his edge.

Without Louis at his best, America was likely to suffer grave and irreparable harm. So, Louis smoked at work and nobody complained.

In came Eve Coman, director of an FBI counter-terrorism team, cradling an overfull three-ring binder and she laid it open on the coffee table. Louis sat up as Eve walked him through a parade of images—pictures of a pair of Muslim brothers believed to be from somewhere near the Mediterranean, probably Saudi Arabia. The brothers lived in a Maryland safe house and met daily with their handler, she said. They'd visited landmarks and spent hours on public transportation. They were planning two simultaneous suicide attacks, probably in a major city, Eve explained. Agents had inserted electronic surveillance inside the house. The date of their planned attack was a few weeks away. Eve had enough evidence to convict, but she'd postponed arrest because the movements and the communications of the suspects promised valuable intel.

Eve had to keep shifting the binder as she switched it back and forth between herself and Louis. This would be easier if you'd learn to use a computer, she said. She turned to a page that displayed a plan for continuous surveillance of the safe house, a plan calling for FBI agents to be staked 24/7 in a perimeter three hundred yards from the house. She opened a spreadsheet, pointed at the place for Louis to sign. Her plan required advance approval of the overtime hours expected for dozens of field agents and for their daily expenses. Some other FBI team in some other city would see its budget shrink, and for reasons it could never know.

Let's keep a lid on costs, Louis told Eve. Schedule me for field duty. Every third day until the mission is over.

Nobody expects that, Lou.

I expect it, he said, and the mission requires it.

She closed the binder and took possession. Tomorrow morning? she asked. We need a team to report at four thirty.

He didn't hesitate. That would be fine, he said. He spoke again, before Eve could: You think I'm too old for field duty, don't you?

Do you think you're too old? she asked.

Sometimes a man can't tell if he's too old. He needs people to be honest.

Most people don't want to be told they're too old, said Eve.

I'm not most people, he said. Do you remember once when I said you weren't composed enough to be an FBI agent? Where would you be now if I hadn't been honest?

You're making too much of that, Lou.

Lou pointed at the three-ring binder. If these Muslim brothers came along fifteen years ago, you'd have been terrified. You'd push to arrest them and you'd miss good intel. When you first came here, you looked like a dog at a fireworks show. You wanted to pee right where you were standing.

Ease up, Lou.

Lots of people said you'd never make it here.

All right then, she said. I think you're too old for field duty. Sitting next to him on the sofa, she put a hand on his shoulder. She smiled like a mother who knows her son better than he knows himself. We don't need your brawn, we need your brains, she said.

You're quoting Nadine, word for word, he said.

Nadine doesn't want you at home all day, recuperating from an injury you suffered in the field.

Louis put on a sideways smile. She who must be obeyed must be obeyed, he said.

Looks like, said Eve.

Will you be on field duty? he asked.

Of course, she said.

What about your family? asked Lou.

Eve shook him off. The mission requires it, she said.

* * *

For her family, Eve prepared an evening meal of roast salmon, mashed sweet potatoes and biscuits. Dessert was fresh blueberries and sliced mangoes. As husband Jaime cleaned dishes, she announced that a project at work would keep her away evenings and weekends for at least the next three weeks. Daughter Olivia let out a teenager's whine. She needed help shopping for a dress for the winter formal. Jaime stopped rinsing dishes. Charlie's working in the Tokyo branch until next month, he said. I can't manage the whole DC office by myself if you're not home in the evenings.

You'll have to do some work at home, she said.

Jaime dropped a heavy fork against the bottom of the sink. This is major, he said.

Don't give me crap, she protested. You've told me fifteen times you have half of Charlie's job plus all of yours. Do you think I'd bring this home if it wasn't important?

SIX

In a public plaza in Mecca: a semicircle of black-haired men and boys. At the center, a man in a khaki uniform with a burnished scimitar. He pointed it up, the tip held high, let the midday sun reflect into as many eyes as he could. He celebrated the blade and danced with it. He thrust it forward, made it look like it was part of him. High above, attached to skinny stems, the heads of phoenix palms cast tarantula shadows.

The Saudi crowd grew, quickly, drawn by some of the most breathtaking public theater in the world. There were regulars, many of them, people who came often to this repeat performance, people warm to the familiar, people who found comfort living under a predictable system of command and control. Quite a few carried boys on their shoulders—impressionable minds in need of impressions. The performance came on the same day and at the same time every month. Nearby businesses shuttered or risked fines; the Crown was not going to hide its executioner under a bushel.

The uniform slashed his weapon in unexpected directions, sometimes toward those gathered. He was a soldier-performer who gave his audience a good scare and who added color and clarity to the emerald line that marked the limit of the Crown's tolerance for immorality and disloyalty.

In the center of the plaza, two men kneeled side by side. Two pairs of naked brown feet with white bottoms. Two white jumpsuits that reflected fuzzy hues from the excessive sun. Two faces hidden inside black sacks cinched around their necks, their hands pinned under their hind ends, their wrists zip-tied. They were about to have their heads severed. Everybody knew, including the condemned.

The kneeling men were motionless, compliant. Neither looked inclined to rise or resist. They'd both been buggered with wooden handles until their asses bled and their backs had taken the shape of question marks. They were ready to leave this world, a place more painful than whatever hell might offer.

The soldier-executioner was known to most of his audience and was well-to-do. He lived in a desert house on a hill, visible from miles away, a fine house with five cars in a five-car garage and a swimming pool surrounded by an immense rectangle of Bermuda grass, a house with its own garden paths, with banks of flowers in luscious rows—irises, blood lilies and orchids. He spent his leisure hours in an oasis fed by mass quantities of a liquid commodity far more valuable than the oil that gushed from Saudi extraction towers: clean water. Against the sunburned flesh of the Arabian desert, the deep greens of the executioner's estate were obvious to anyone whose plane was on a path to Mecca's Ta'if Regional Airport.

The flock of men and boys—no women, no girls—knew their role. They encouraged the performer and his performance, gave him room enough. People exclaimed at appropriate moments, silenced themselves at others. The soldier dashed and darted and if ever his blade came close, part of the semicircle dissolved and, after the blade retreated, the semicircle re-formed. Some held smart phones, capturing the majesty of a committed authoritarian, a man whose certainty about God's magnificence made him the object of envy. His audacious confidence elevated him above his audience, satisfied his audience's compulsion to be lifted by a connection with supremacy. He was bold enough to make people guess he was perpetually righteous.

Moving images of the uniform and his scimitar would be posted and shared worldwide. The influence of the day's events would travel farther and faster than dreamed of by the kings of distant past, the founders of this family-run syndicate fond of making offers to people who knew not to refuse. The ancient kings' stories were written on parchment in calligraphic Arabic, brutal stories gracefully told. They would have rejoiced over the influence available in the twenty-first century, at the capacity granted by something as simple as a link between all the world's computers for inspiring fear and obedience, at the prospect for effortless victory.

The executioner called loudly for justice, louder for peace and was cheered. A team of assistants stood at attention, a short row of khaki under black berets. The sword-holder recited words of a holy man and brought his crowd to reverent silence. He straightened his arms, sword vertical, and approached the focal point of his assembly.

One of the kneeling men wailed in Farsi, cried like an infant, then rolled onto his side. The buggering had ruined his anus and he sprayed shit inside his jumpsuit.

High above the courtyard, on the side of a white palace: a grand inset balcony, guarded by minarets and Islamic symbols cut into marble. On the balcony sat the most royal member of the family of Saud, the Saudi King, protected from the sun's brutality by a night-blue awning and comforted by vents that filled his outdoor cove with conditioned air. The King was a man of some height, but age required him to bend when he stood; he could straighten himself, but slowly. The crescent curve of his spine pressed into his armchair. The Byzantine mass of angles and antiquarian symbols that were woven into the fabric of his chair bent in concert to accommodate him.

When announcement of Nassir's arrival came, the King rose and walked to an air-conditioned salon, one of many places in this palace designated for exchanging royal greetings and salutations. The men embraced and kissed twice, long kisses, first on one side and then the other. They held one another at the length of their forearms and exchanged an extravagant range of smiles and appreciation, two men who had known one another for the life of the one who was only sixty, each believing he would never receive a lie from the other, except that each would keep a safe distance from the truth when circumstances required.

The King reached from behind, took Nassir's hand. On the way back to the balcony, the old man stopped at a display of cut flowers. He leaned, inhaled and absorbed sweetness. He closed his eyes and it was as if he'd allowed his spirit to lay upon the delicate petals of pale blossoms.

A man who loves the garden is a blessed man, said Nassir. It's a holy feeling.

You know, don't you? said the King. How it can wash you clean?

The King pointed to the balcony, to the armchairs in shade, where the men could sit, talk and be entertained by events on the courtyard below. The King often scheduled public gatherings in the courtyard to coincide with Nassir's visit. There were spies about, people who watched and tried to interpret the old man's patterns. The King had taken his father's example, let people see their ruler in public with his chief of intelligence, his enforcer, a man happy to be known as a ruthless predator, and he let them live in fear of him.

The pair sat, a knee-high table in front of them. From a skinny decanter of hammered brass, a servant poured an arc of steaming tea into china cups and the aroma of mint suffused them.

The King pointed at the courtyard and shook his head. Our landscapers, he said. I didn't like the old stone and ordered it replaced, and now we have this. He pointed at a different spot. See the stains? I tell the men what I want and you'd think I was their sister, for all it does.

Perhaps a mobile platform? asked Nassir. Or sheets of vinyl?

Why couldn't the landscapers have suggested that? asked the King. That's why I pay them.

On the courtyard, one of the khaki uniforms had righted the wailing man and settled him back on his shins, where he looked like a begging dog.

What offenses? asked Nassir, pointing at the condemned. He crossed his long legs at the knee and let his body settle.

The one closest, sorcery, said the King. He was teaching magic to young people. Then, in a quieter voice: His father is an exile in Brussels. He thinks he has safe haven. He writes evil statements about our kingdom and he publishes images of God. We will speak about him again before you leave.

Nassir blew on his tea, tested it, set it down to cool. The other?

He is a cousin to the first man. Dreadful. A homosexual.

Only the one? Nassir speculated. There must be partners.

We are finding others, said the King. It is disappointing how many.

They watched as the soldier moved closer to the wailing man, gripping the sword, arms raised above the man's neck. Your fate is a blessing from God, he proclaimed.

I will pray for them, said Nassir, hands loose in his lap. I will pray that in death they find wisdom.

You are a kind man, said the King, grasping his companion by the forearm.

Thank you, Your Grace. I only follow your example.

You've no talent for flattery, Nassir. I've never prayed for an infidel in my life. They're too stupid to deserve prayers.

Nassir blew on his tea again, sipped, then smiled. I can't figure out if I'm being teased or appreciated.

The King slapped Nassir's arm again. You old lizard.

The executioner continued his dance.

I come with news, Your Grace.

The King waved at Taalib, his attendant. The man approached, bent at the waist and gave an ear to his King, who explained that privacy was required. The bodyguards and the attendant left the balcony. Taalib waited inside a window where he could see his King but could not hear.

After floating, without motion, for as long as most men could hold their breaths, the sword fell for the first time that day. It penetrated the flesh of the man's neck but stuck on the C4 vertebra long enough to pressure an artery before slicing. It powered a bloody spray onto the clean khaki worn by the executioner. The body went limp and flopped flat, bouncing once. A rigid edge of the man's temple popped hard against the pavers, then his head rolled some twenty inches away from its former host, spewing fluids that had fed oxygen to the dead man's brain moments before. The executioner produced a rectangle of terry-cloth and used it to restore the sheen of his sword.

The executioner faced the sun and pointed his tool at the sky. He smiled, his straight, white teeth framed by a pirate's black beard dotted with the blood of his victim. He sang a well-practiced doxology: *In my homeland lives the pride of Muslims.*

Nassir leaned closer to the King and hid his mouth behind his hand, a move that would prevent anyone with binoculars from reading lips. Amir from Jedda, he is trusted, tells me that Jamal, your grand-nephew's friend, is no longer a threat to you. The insurgent group was small. Amir killed most of them. He spared two. They are in prison and are being questioned.

Amir by himself?

Almost entirely, Your Grace. Your grand-nephew, who is devoted to the Crown, he killed Jamal as soon as he knew the man's intent. With his own two hands, he killed his friend because of his concern for you and your good health.

Can you leave their addresses with my secretary? I will have someone send them my prayers and appreciation.

Nassir agreed, didn't take his eyes off the courtyard.

Below, the swordsman motioned. A uniform stepped forward and yanked on the head of the homosexual, stretching his neck. The uniform smacked at the black sack on the man's head, on the place where his face must have been, commanded him to remain still, then backed away. The uniform's chin was tucked tight and he looked pained by the coming violence.

The kneeling man turned obedient and, after a brief interval, his head *chunked* and settled on a flat side. His torso fell to the pavement, neck-stub first, surrounded by a wandering oval of opaque red.

The King reached, grasped Nassir's hand and shook. Winners, he exclaimed. Always winners.

A man in the crowd unfurled an American flag on a stick. He flashed a lighter and the flag became a sheet of flames. There was militant chanting about America. The King motioned urgently to Taalib and the attendant came out from behind the closed door. Have someone tell the man with the flag that political displays are not permitted. Make a small example of him.

Taalib lifted a walkie-talkie from his belt and transmitted. On the ground, a man in a uniform tilted an ear toward a device hooked to his epaulet. He listened and responded. The uniform rushed the man holding the flag, screamed at him, hit him in the face with a hand-sized truncheon, knocked him down, hit him again, kicked the flag stick out of his hands. Two other uniforms stomped out the flames.

The King turned to his companion. Is your American project going well?

Nassir nodded. We have dramatic developments soon. It is an exciting time.

Norah blesses us with her devotion, said the King.

You will be pleased with her work, Your Grace.

How soon?

Plans are always subject to change, Your Grace, but I am hoping within two weeks.

The King's hand clapped Nassir's knee. Blessed are those who can smite our enemies.

With the executions done, the crowd lost its shape and thinned out. A bony mutt with long legs loped onto the courtyard. The animal sniffed at the bodies, licked at pools of human fluids.

Taalib disappeared, then reappeared and offered a slip of paper to the King. The King took it, scanned it, handed it to Nassir. This is the man in Brussels, said the King. Could you have someone visit with him? Leave clues so they know it was us.

So it shall be, said Nassir.

The King tested his tea, took a deep pull, then waved to a small group that cheered at having attracted a moment of his attention. Nassir, have I ever told you how much I admire you for raising such a wonderful daughter?

Your Grace, Norah has been a blessing.

Nassir, why is it that you never remarried? I have always wondered.

I never found a woman I could trust, he said.

The King stared at Nassir. He shifted his stare from one of Nassir's eyes to the other. An evaluation was occurring. Please tell Norah that I say prayers for her, he said. Do you worry? America can be a terrible influence for a Muslim.

Worry is a waste of time, Your Grace, said Nassir.

But Norah lives in the belly of the beast, said the King.

Norah is steadfast and faithful, said Nassir. She has talents far beyond ordinary. She is committed to God and country.

It must have been hard to find a Muslim man in America who was a suitable husband for her, said the King.

My American company is large and we hire many Muslims, said Nassir. All of them want to marry the boss's daughter. Norah's husband understands what it means to marry into the Saud family. He preserves our secrets. Nassir smiled. Saudi Arabia has friends in America, he said. Many depend upon me for their income and their safety.

* * *

Norah and Dirk fretted before each conference with Nassir. Often they bickered. Fear of Father was one of the only things Norah and Dirk had ever confessed to. Norah put on an abaya and checked herself to ensure only her eyes showed. When the specially encrypted Skype with Father was close, she studied her notes, counted the items on fingertips that she wanted to remember. She often knew what Father would ask and she prepared. She reviewed dates and the order of events. She rehearsed. Dirk hovered and directed, as if he could control what Norah would say. He kept lists of triumphant talking points—problems he'd cleverly resolved—and planned to parade them before the man who had decided him worthy of superior wealth, the man who could take it all away.

Nassir's face appeared. His face and his voice filled the room. The mission, he said in English, for Dirk's benefit. How soon?

It's lovely to see you Father, said Norah. She wanted badly not to shrink. Regardless, she found herself tucking her shoulders inward.

The left side of Nassir's face compressed under the weight of irritation. How soon? he repeated. Listen to my questions before you open your mouth.

Dirk jumped in, seemingly without having listened. Nassir, I made two suicide vests. I crammed two dozen Semtex mini-bricks into each one. I even sewed them. I stole det cord and primers from a construction site so they couldn't be traced. You should see. Perfect symmetry.

Nassir sighed. The girl-child wants compliments, he said.

Dirk apologized and changed direction. I have the vests in a storage locker—the one here at home, he said. They're ready. Soon as you want.

Norah? asked Nassir. The volunteers? You've had nine weeks.

Norah, bothered, chewed on her lip and the abaya kept anyone from noticing. Omar and Ibrahim weren't volunteers by any definition—they'd been coerced. Father must have known she'd find out. Hadn't he heard her exchange with Ibrahim when they dropped Omar at King Street Station? His comments were a reminder that he always stuck to his narrative, facts be damned. He seemed to believe that by saying something, he made it so. He also made a hobby of interweaving lies because it confused people; they'd call him out for one obvious lie and two less obvious ones became true. And mother of heaven, she'd been training the brothers for only *eight* weeks. Father knew exactly how long it had been.

Regardless, she displayed her usual compliance. Training is almost complete, Father. We've had trouble finding burner phones that provide reliable communications between the different subway stations. When that's solved, we can go as soon as weather permits. She was pleased with how plausible her story sounded.

The electronic infrastructure inside the chosen stations is adequate?

Of course, she said. That's not the problem.

How long to get phones? he asked.

Three days. Faster if we're lucky.

Nassir sounded shocked: Three whole days to find phones?

How many times can we walk the length of a subway platform in one day without getting stopped? We have to test the phones.

He grimaced; some facts could not be ignored. The date? The date for the mission?

We need to go on a very cold day, a workday when the subway is busy and everyone has to wear coats. Dirk says the explosive vests are bulky. We need coats to conceal them.

Nassir, impatient, stroked his triangle beard with a fingertip. Just tell me the day, he said.

Norah checked her phone. Wednesday, next week, the morning is supposed to be well below freezing, she said. If the forecast holds, we can go.

Wednesday morning, next week, said Nassir. I'll send a diplomatic pouch to the ambassador in Washington so the embassy will know to be prepared for something. Make it happen.

Many Saudi women used abayas to hide contraband and to hide themselves. Many Saudi women moved about anonymously and were pleased to do so. Norah used her abaya to hide her lies to Father. Ibrahim and Omar could have gone the next day. They were ready and so was the necessary equipment. Whatever expressions might have revealed her lie were concealed within opaque fabric. And now that the suicide vests were in the storage locker—and access was assured— she needed time to execute her own plan.

She pivoted quickly, didn't want to give Nassir time to doubt her. Father, have we been exposed? she asked. I won't get captured, will I? I'm worried. She'd deliberately injected her emotions into the conversation. The most reliable player on Father's team was sounding shaky. Father would be annoyed at the unnecessary display and would see it as a threat to the mission. He'd feel compelled to tamp it down, typically done by revealing things that would comfort Norah.

We have the Russians' stream of live digital from the FBI, he said. An algorithm analyzes it constantly. Whatever the FBI knows, we know. There is a diversionary cell in Baltimore that the FBI is tracking, as we expected. They've got half of their agents pulled away from counter-terrorism duty in Washington.

Diversionary cell? asked Norah, not hiding her surprise. What's that about?

He held up a hand. The subject was not open. My work here is done, he said.

Nassir reached for his computer and he was gone, but something of him remained. Much of what Nassir accomplished was by the little voice he put into heads. People imagined they heard his threats. From the other side of the planet, he could control people, have them plan and arrange the horrific. They would kill for him, and at great risk. He had people who raced to contact him if misfortune approached. He had assassins who could find and kill nearly any soul alive. He could convince people to die violently in service of his needs, and all because of their fear.

But some things were beyond him—would never have occurred to him. He'd devoted his life to monetizing every relationship. With each new person who came along, including the ones who posed a threat, he'd ask whether this man could grow Nassir's influence or whether the person was a worker bee—whether they could perform tasks for him. The world behaved as he wanted, allowed him to stand tall. If he bent in service to another man, it was only because doing so would someday allow him to stand taller.

Nassir was so concerned about manipulating Norah's fears that he gave little thought to other portions of her conscious self: Was she tormented? Empty? Had misery given her an incentive to escape?

Nassir had seen Dirk's gawky attempts at dominance, could surely see he'd intimidated a lesser man, a dolt. He was probably proud of how easy it had been to get control of Dirk's life. But Nassir could not have imagined that most of America was nowhere near as self-interested as Dirk or Nassir, that Dirk's transparent nature would repel friends and neighbors. Nassir couldn't have foreseen that marriage to Dirk would leave Norah lonely enough to be needy. In Nassir's Saudi Arabia, the women were content to remain at home, servile and essential to the men, the ruling class. Nassir, no doubt, expected Norah to follow the model.

Norah despaired. She'd seen what life was like for a man and knew what it meant to be included, to learn. She knew how it felt to have someone cultivate your acquaintance, to value you for your talents and resources.

People told Nassir it was an honor to serve him and said it so often it must have seemed true. He fed anxieties that consumed common sense and made compassionate self-interest impossible. Nassir's agents were preoccupied—vigilant—about the need to *survive*, to avoid his judgment and his punishment. He'd have expected the same from Norah.

But no one knew Nassir like Norah. No one else had received his advice on how to be male, on the need to avoid displays of femininity. No one else knew he'd long insisted on parading his daughter as a man.

Nassir was drawn to men who subscribed to a code, one centered upon the pursuit of dominance. It was easy to decipher a person's meaning and his purpose if his goal was domination. Eye contact and a lift of the chin was an affront. To confess a lack of knowledge was to confess defeat. A confident adversary would respond to accusations in kind and in excess.

Nassir's code meant he would never guess that Norah had become lonely and resentful of her husband, that she'd hidden her urge to rebel against daily directives from her man-child husband. Norah was politely submissive and didn't dare contradict Father. Nassir wouldn't suspect she'd been searching for a way out, for money to support herself, for a place where she wouldn't be found.

Nassir couldn't have seen the shield she kept between herself and Saudi embassy personnel out of her concern over what he'd learn. He hadn't seen her stiff smiles. He didn't know what it meant to her to make a connection with a couple from her gun club, Annie and Jack, or how she agonized when Annie and Jack left Maryland and retired to the woods of Maine.

In America, Norah kept occupied, productive, but was rarely content. When Dirk went to work, she went running, swimming or lifting weights. When possible, she used Father's back door to view the Russian stream of data from FBI computers. She became politely acquainted with women she met at mosque. Anything more seemed impossible. They had families and tended to small children; she had an IUD and a gun collection. She read biographies and history, went target shooting at the First Precinct Pistol and Archery Club in David-sonville, the place she'd met Annie and Jack.

The flash-bang of pistols, the Zen of breathing slowly and squeezing smoothly, ripping bullet holes into paper targets shaped like fat criminals brought her to life. They relieved her ennui, reduced the despair of a self-aware woman who was anchored to a soggy loaf of a man. The stinging smell of burnt black powder and the ring of brass shells on concrete brought memories of the afternoon after her wedding, when dozens of men fired automatics randomly into the air, the day when Father declared that her life's work would be to help Dirk grow Douglas-American Aerospace. She could ensure her own prosperity, Father said. He would pray for her, that she would rise above the Americans.

In America, she found small talk at embassy parties, at gatherings of executives and undersecretaries, making connections with those who would exchange promises. She lived in a house, large and luxurious, that was supposed to insulate her from want.

On their wedding day, before Norah and Dirk boarded Father's Airbus headed toward Baltimore, Father gave her names and numbers of cousins at the Saudi embassy in Washington. These are good people who will guide you, who will protect you, he said.

She turned to Dirk. You know most of them already. Yes?

Norah bowed her covered head and spoke as she always did at moments Father considered relevant—as a protégé, grateful to be given wisdom, to receive the tools for prosperity and dominance. Thank you, Father, she said. I am indebted. And she kissed his hand.

Nassir would have watched his silver-skinned Airbus fade into heat shimmers, taking his daughter and her new husband to America. He would have felt something resembling happiness; he had things as he'd long wanted them to be. His trusted daughter, his closest ally, had control of an American door, could hold it open just far enough to let Nassir infect America with worries about security and to take in profit from America's fear, as it emptied its pockets in pursuit of better defenses. With Norah at Dirk's elbow, the man could be safely managed. The back door, a classic soft spot, became a stronghold.

Defense technology and defense profits that Nassir imported would feed the Saudi billionaires who owned the Saudi factories and the Saudi millionaires who ran them, the classes of people who employed and influenced the Saudi masses. Control of the vital defense sector would allow him to keep control of the Security Directorate and his access to impeccable intel about the shifting of the sands on which he and his country stood.

Norah observed all of these things. She heard it in the voice he used to interrupt Dirk, to call up the man's demons, to fertilize the roots that fed Dirk's fear of failure. She heard it in his conspicuous talk of the King and in his narcissistic demand for loyalty. She saw it in his devotion to American Internet news channels, in his celebration anytime events revealed America's looming sense of vulnerability.

For most of her life, Norah would not have dared to spy on Father. He was her hero, her protector. By the time she left for America, she'd installed hidden apps on Father's favorite devices, put covert electronic monitors in his homes and in his cars. She had learned more than Father would have wanted, and all because Abdullah, a close cousin, another of the King's grandchildren, had given Norah copies of a report Father had once ordered destroyed. The report confirmed that her birth mother had not bled out at the hospital after labor and delivery, but that she'd endured a year in a Yemeni prison. Rather than be kept as a possible tool for her powerful husband, Norah's mother took matters into her own hands. She starved herself, intent on quick death, intent on controlling her own end.

And years later, she became Norah's hero.

In the darkest hours, the owls hooted. Dirk snored. Norah woke. She sat up, put her feet on the floor and, ever so slowly, lifted herself from the marital bed. The rhythm and timbre of Dirk's breathing kept on, didn't change. She exhaled easily, pleased not to have disturbed him. In an unlit bathroom, she hauled the waist of her man-cut jeans around her hips and zipped, pulled on a sweatshirt and a pair of socks.

Smoother than Egyptian cotton, she slipped down into the kitchen. She pressed a panel on the wall. It clicked open, revealed the door of a safe and she entered an eight-digit code that Dirk thought only he knew. Bolts slid, the door opened. LEDs lit the interior where there were pistols, memos, a handful of thumb drives, passports, miscellaneous other items. Norah reached inside and snatched the one thing she wanted: a key to the steel storage shed attached to their boathouse.

In cotton socks, her heels going numb against the frigid concrete of the garage floor, she retrieved a weighty canvas shoulder bag from her minivan. Indoors again, where it was warm, she stepped into clogs and wrapped herself in a wool coat before passing the French doors at the back of her house into the razor-sharp freeze of February, across the fieldstone patio, past the evil-man shadows of topiaries under an unreal moon, past the tennis court and the fruit trees wrapped to protect them from winter, and to the steel locker on the back of their boathouse. Norah pushed in the thickset key and turned. The metal door swung silently on hinges with rubber bushings. Inside, she clicked a switch.

On the floor, under a cone of incandescence, two suicide vests. Armless and pudgy, they looked like royal-blue life preservers. She began mouth-breathing to avoid the bitter almond stink of Semtex. Norah said a short prayer, asking God to permit her to go undiscovered. She also begged for permission to live, to safely handle bricks of explosive putty that could detonate. Before her was enough Semtex to extinguish thousands of humans, to pulverize two subway tunnels, to shred structural steel. It would detonate in a flash fury if touched by the pulse of ignition.

Norah kneeled, slipped on latex gloves, tore at Velcro closures on one vest, opening its sewn-on pockets. From each, she slid out a rectangular two-kilo brick of explosive Semtex, pulled out the tip of det cord and plucked out the pea-sized primers the cord led to. From her leather bag, she took bricks of modeling clay. Each was sized, weighted, colored and labeled to precisely duplicate Semtex mini-bricks. Each had an authentic Semtex label. She poked a two-penny nail into each of the clay bricks, created tiny pits into which went the pea-sized primers, followed by tips of det cord. She inserted the phony clay bricks into pockets, portions of the original black wires still visible, and resealed the Velcro. She reached the last two pockets and gasped. There were twenty-six bricks in each vest; Dirk had said there were two dozen. She couldn't even complete the first half of her effort.

So stupid not to have checked first. So stupid to assume Dirk knew what he was talking about. So stupid not to have made more bricks than seemed necessary, just to be safe. So damn stupid.

She confirmed the number of bricks she needed to replace—she would require twenty-eight more—and, as planned, would return the next night to finish. She would leave both vests inert, filled with clay; she would deny Omar and Ibrahim the opportunity to become murderers. They would emerge, unharmed, from the subway, and would walk the long path back to the safe house, confused.

Norah rose, turned, reached for the switch, and was arrested by a sight: a mountain of army-green duffels, stacked high against a wall.

She tilted the hanging lamp, cast light at the bags and counted twenty duffels, every one clean, unscuffed, most of them attached to paper tags from Sunny's Surplus. Twenty canvas bags she'd never seen, bags kept under lock and key at her own home, without her knowledge, bags secured behind steel walls and an industrial deadbolt, bags stored where Dirk believed only he had access.

More Semtex? she wondered. Bags and bags of it?

She tugged at a zipper. Inside, a thicket of American money. She pulled open the wide-mouthed bag and found scads of bank-banded stacks of US currency—hundred-dollar bills, all of them. She counted. Inside the first bag, there were one hundred stacks, and another hundred stacks in the second. She opened a third, a fourth and confirmed: the same, inside every one. Twenty bags. Each full of Benjamin Franklins. Each with a hundred stacks of a hundred bills. This was twenty million dollars.

Her face seemed to expand and her imagination was warmed, aroused—a hot-air balloon began to fill, to rise from hard ground, a vehicle that, once filled, could depart under its own power and might forever be gone, might put infinite distance between Norah and the source of all fears.

She had an image of her friends Jack and Annie who had retired to Maine. She saw a house in the woods, privacy, safety, companionship. Now, she had a way to get there.

Her heartbeat pulsed in her ears. She checked the timer on her phone. Nine minutes she'd been out of bed. Every minute was another chance for Dirk to discover her missing.

He must've gathered cash in case he had to flee his home, his job and bank accounts, she thought. Fear had urged him to be prepared for failure.

The dark was absolute. Norah felt for the end of the sturdy wooden dock next to the boathouse and settled on her knees. Two at a time, she took Semtex bricks from her bag. Like a release of fishes, she let go, let the pieces sink into the muck at the bottom of Broad Creek. Each one descended, squirming against brackish water on the way down, to a place where blue crabs scavenged for things that were dead, where layers of sodden leaves descended in the fall and concealed everything, where things decayed, became soft and turned to soil. It was a place, God willing, that mini-bricks of explosive Semtex wouldn't be found, couldn't cause hurt.

Norah returned to the steel shed and, from each of the twenty duffels, she took ten stacks of bills. Dirk would worry about weapons and wiring. He'd been afraid enough to spy on his own wife, to make sure she wasn't disloyal. But he'd never count his bundles, not until it was too late. Ten stacks removed from each bag of a hundred? Ten percent was too little to be noticed by volume or weight. And Dirk would expect any thief to be as greedy as he was. If his money were stolen, it would all be stolen.

The stolen stacks, each two fingers thick, overfilled her shoulder bag but fit nicely in the under-floor compartment in her minivan. She backtracked, made sure she'd not dropped anything, rechecked the lock on the storage shed, wiped it clean of fingerprints and returned to the warmth of her house.

Anxious, fearful, hands shaking, Norah replaced the key in Dirk's kitchen safe and changed back into pajamas. Under the covers, she settled, eyes closed, and her imagination leapt from the tiny space she occupied, her body-sized compartment under a layer of down, to the wide open of someplace free, a place in Maine where a woman could spring from bed in the morning hoping to do something lovely that day.

Dirk stirred and mumbled like he was dreaming. Honey, where?

Here.

But where?

It's always been right here, she whispered. Dirk, you're dreaming. Go to sleep, my darling.

The next morning, as soon as Dirk left for work, Norah drove to the Best Buy store in Annapolis and went to the department where they had Lenovo and HP laptops on display. She signed into a g-mail account with a nonsensical address and a twelve-digit password, and she typed an e-mail and she sent it: *God's blessings upon you, Abdullah. I write with more news from America. Father has lost control of a terrible plan. My husband is running it and he's made mistakes that will leave our family exposed. Neither he nor Father know what is coming. They're hoping for loud noise with people dying and terrified. Everybody will know the Saudis were responsible. Please help.* To avoid detection by any algorithm searching through e-mail traffic, she used no words likely to draw attention—nothing about attacks, bombs, violence, meeting places or the names likely to show up on terrorist watch lists.

She confirmed the e-mail had been sent and she logged out of g-mail and took the browser to a website that would infect the computer with a virus designed to displace every bit of data with Chinese characters. Father had told Norah about the website and what it was good for, including the fact that the code had been written as a class project by Chinese computer students. For their amazing work, they got paid by a man who was married to a niece of the Russian President.

SEVEN

T minus forty-three hours and in the basement of the safe house Ibrahim kneeled on the prayer rug that he'd long ago plucked from the smoldering remains of his boyhood. The rug was a Bokhara rectangle of blacks and deep reds. He put his face into the wiry wool and kept it there. It still smelled like the *bakhoor* Mother made, burning incense that made the indoors smell like the white flowers in Mother's garden, the fragrance that was unique to his family, the fragrance that meant comfort and home. It was the smell that, as a boy, Ibrahim took with him everywhere, on his clothes, in his hair. The smell was between pages of books that his sister, Alitha, used to read him.

After prayers, the brothers rose, made their beds, straightened the room and continued one of their irreconcilable feuds. Omar said it pleased him to hate his dead parents, to stand above ground and to look down on two who must have lived poorly. Their death was a punishment from God.

Ibrahim reminded him that it wasn't God who killed their parents. Their killer was certainly Nassir, a wicked man. God wouldn't kill your parents and leave you to wonder why, said Ibrahim. He wouldn't torture facts so he could label a man as a sinner, then use sin as a tool to compel the man's self-destruction.

Omar sneered, tiny bottom teeth visible through curled lips. Your whole life, you pray to God and you don't know the first thing about him, said Omar. I refuse to listen to an idiot.

Ibrahim squinted and his mouth turned small. He looked pained. I need to go outside, he said, fingertips to his temples. I need fresh air.

Not without Norah's permission, said Omar.

There's sunshine outside. I can see it. I need to feel better.

Norah heard and descended the stairs from the kitchen. There are children outside, she said. They're walking home from school. We move only when the neighborhood is still, preferably at dark.

Five minutes, said Ibrahim. That's all. I'll hide in the backyard.

Anybody who sees you coming out of this house is a threat to us all, she said.

Ibrahim shook his head and took a step up, ready to ignore Norah's order. Norah shoved him, grabbed one of his wrists, bent an arm behind him and pulled, far enough for it to hurt. He winced, pleaded for her to stop.

If you don't create conflict, there will be none, she said.

Ibrahim shook his hand and she released it and it wasn't clear if Ibrahim would obey. She pushed against his forehead until she'd backed him against the wall. The last thing I want is for you to get hurt, she said.

Omar passed them on his way upstairs, headed to the house's one bathroom. You have no reason to feel sorry for yourself, he said. Omar went through the kitchen and was heard walking, upstairs, to the far end of the house.

Ibrahim stopped resisting, peeled off Norah's hands. I'll be fine indoors, he said.

Norah put a flat hand on his chest and pushed closer. He'd looked and sounded anxious. For the first time that she could recall, his calm had been intruded upon. He didn't have peace or energy to share. He looked needy. She was unnerved. Would he grow angry? Violent? You're too tense, she said. She was so close that her breath landed in his face. You really have nothing to worry about.

How could you possibly think that? he asked. I have to explode myself.

She moved her lips close to his ear: If you need to, you can come back here on the day of the mission. After I've dropped you downtown, she said. You and Omar both. I will come and meet you here.

The toilet flushed. Heavy steps from upstairs.

I don't want anyone getting killed, she said. Certainly not you.

When Omar got to the bottom of the stairs, Ibrahim was putting away his prayer rug. Omar, Norah said, if anything goes wrong on the mission, you can come back here to the safe house. I'll meet you here, she said.

Why would you say that? he asked.

Just in case, she said. If something happens, if something goes wrong, and you aren't sure what to do, come back here.

What do you mean to say? he demanded.

In the darkest part of the night, Norah awoke, stole the key from Dirk's kitchen safe, and slipped out of the back of her house, carrying a shoulder bag laden with twenty-eight bricks of clay, each one wrapped in a Semtex label. She unlocked the steel door to the boathouse locker and clicked the switch. The incandescent bulb flashed on. Where there once had been suicide vests, there was bare concrete.

She searched in the dark corners and the high places where there were hooks for hanging things, in cabinets—anywhere the vests might be hiding. The bitter almond stink lingered, strong as ever. She looked beneath the bags of money. She kneeled, feeling for clues in the shadows, found none. Her fingers were hurried, palsied, out of control, as she secured the locker door on her way out. In vain, she searched the boathouse and the apartment upstairs, looked inside both of the boats, under tarps, inside engine housings, inside bench seats. She went to the garage and searched the trunk of Dirk's Lexus where she found only Dirk's golf clubs and the odor of bitter almond.

When Norah slid under the covers, back in bed, she was clutching her own shoulders, wishing for them not to be so tight. When she realized she was panting like a dog, she stopped, but she couldn't stop the sound of her breathing, heavy and fast through her nostrils. She had an urge to cry but didn't dare.

* * *

The black on the far eastern horizon became a pregnant deep purple before bursting like a blister into reds, yellows, pinks. This was the time, each day, two Muslim brothers in Maryland rose from cots in the basement of their safe house and readied for prayer.

Each morning, an FBI webcam captured the brothers' faces brought low, their rumps high, reciting holy Arabic. Five times daily they prayed on a schedule posted in Mecca by Muslim authorities for use by nearly two billion Muslims worldwide. The Bureau had planted webcams and microphones and monitored the brothers. It caught them snoring. It caught them pissing on the toilet seat and lying about it, bickering, meeting with handlers. Words and conduct were documented, patterns identified. Lawyers and psychologists studied the vocabulary, the data, the body language, the context and drew conclusions.

In a secure room at FBI headquarters in Washington, DC, FBI Field Agent Abd al-Rahmaan sat erect, watching and listening to the prayers on a computer screen, fingertips ready on a keyboard. Each time either of the brothers spoke, he typed. Every entry included a time and date stamp taken from the recorded video. If the brothers mentioned a person whose name was known, Abd entered an alpha-numeric code. If it was an unknown person, Abd created a new code and entered it. If it was a person of interest, he added an additional code. For each subject the brothers might discuss, he added a third. If the subject was on a list marked urgent, Abd's computer would alert someone at the FBI who could read the notes in real time, an early warning system for any approaching storm, a storm that got the attention of important people who had taken oaths to protect and defend the Constitution.

In came FBI Supervisor Eve Coman. She carried her expectations out front, in the open. An FBI identification badge swung on a lanyard around her neck when she leaned and placed a chewy raisin bagel, a coffee and a cup of mixed melon at Abd's elbow. He remained focused on his computer.

She spoke directly, simply, without a trace of self-doubt: Here. Breakfast. So, what's happening?

Abd grunted like an old man. He took a hand from the keyboard just long enough to chomp into his bagel.

Eve pointed at the screen. Anything overnight?

Abd chewed aggressively, forced down an overlarge piece. Nobody in, nobody out, no outside communications, no attempted communications, he said. Fifteen drive-bys, all neighbors. No walk-bys. No aerial traffic except ordinary commercial aircraft. He rubbed an eye. Eve, I know I'm not supposed to complain about work to the boss, but I'm toast. Isn't there another Arabic speaker who could take a turn? Three weeks now, it's twelve hours a day. An hour ago I was crying for no reason.

You're right, she said. You're not supposed to complain about work to the boss.

He slumped. She patted him on the back.

Be a stud for twenty more hours, until we raid, she said. What you're doing matters. Eve touched a button on her smart phone and called Lou Irons. The subjects have not changed the date of their planned attack, she said. No change to their targets. No contact from outside that might require some adjustment. Can we keep our schedule for Wednesday morning?

Fine, he said. He would trust her judgment, the same as always.

After she hung up, she told Abd she had a good feeling. This would end well.

I'm supposed to be happy, said Abd. It's just that I'm exhausted from keeping constant watch.

EIGHT

With Father, it was always a balancing act. You spent every day terrified because of what would happen if you didn't keep your balance.

You had to spot every danger before it was on you. That meant being vigilant, which meant always being afraid, but you couldn't look afraid and you had to act rational and you could never admit if you were exhausted from being vigilant all the time.

You know how Father liked violence—he talked about it and he practiced it—and you had to devote yourself to his protection. He was only interested in himself and he had to be your urgent priority. You had to stay vigilant not only for yourself, but for him. He would drop you in with the lions if it helped him, but you had to always protect him. He'd insult you, treat you as stupid, and yet you had to be polite and respectful. Don't ever be nasty to me, he'd say. He'd command impossible jobs and you were afraid you'd be killed if you doubted him. He told the truth only when it was convenient—but if he caught you in a lie?

He ran the Saudi Security Directorate. He was supposed to protect national security. What about the schools' security or people's security at home? Father didn't mention those. In his mind, they didn't matter and so they didn't exist.

Saudis don't feel safe, most of them. People in Saudi Arabia are afraid and that's how the heads of the Saud family want it. That's what they mean by national security. It means the family's security. Too many Saudis believe if they're not afraid, they're not secure. They're afraid of not being afraid. The King promises protection from all the threats, especially secret ones, and so people say he's a hero. There are people in Saudi Arabia who see through Father and our King, who don't believe what they say, but they're probably afraid to say. So, there's fear if you believe and there's fear if you don't. Either way, the strongmen win.

Being in Father's world seemed necessary. He'd convince you the world was dangerous. He always said he knew more than you. He said only he knew how dangerous and where danger was hiding. He said you needed his protection and as soon as he said that, it was true. He could threaten you and promise safety at the same time and it never occurred to some people how ridiculous that was.

Most of the men in Saudi Arabia believed as he did—and lots of women, too. The way they grew up would make it hard to change. A woman was not allowed to leave the house without a male escort because of the risks. You couldn't be out alone. You had to have a good man to protect you from all the bad ones. You couldn't show your face or your body in public because of the bad men. At the shopping mall, you stayed on the floor that was only for women, and you ate in a female section of restaurants, and a man would have to drive you to and from. Most places, women were forbidden by Sharia because it was all men. But nobody ever said that the reason it was all men was because of Sharia.

Father had me learn judo and said it would make me safer. I had weapons training since before I had my first period. I studied engineering so I could know if buildings and boats were safe. I learned how to act like a man and make other people afraid of me, how to keep them afraid. I learned how to intimidate and control, to threaten people and offer them safety at the same time. I learned to admire blood lilies while I was holding hands with death.

Father had me in mind for terrorism since forever, I know he did. All the training and all that pretending, it was no accident.

Eve, here's the reason I liked Ibrahim. When he admires flowers, it's because he admires flowers. He says safety is an illusion. The only way to enjoy your life, to be at peace, is to accept that. If you warn him something is dangerous, Ibrahim is curious and he wants to know how dangerous. If you pointed a gun at him, he'd ask you what's the caliber of your bullets and why do you like to use that kind of gun.

Before I met Ibrahim, Father warned me. He said Ibrahim was the biggest idiot he'd ever seen.

* * *

If he were summoned to his boss's office at DAA, Dirk became a frightened possum, rigid and still, perhaps hoping nobody would attack a dead animal. As with his days in the US Army infantry, he'd stand at attention. Yes sir, no sir, I think so sir, he'd say. Dirk's boss at DAA was fine with that. Dirk's boss was also fine with the fact that by raising his voice he could get Dirk to promise the impossible.

The reason Red Merrill became Dirk's boss at Douglas-American Aerospace is that Red Merrill overheard staff project engineer Dirk Johnson declare that the world would be safer if every nation everywhere had nukes. Nobody would launch a nuke if everybody had one, he said. Who would be stupid enough to fire a nuke on somebody if he was afraid one was coming right back? Name one country.

Naysayers in the ranks at DAA gave him a nickname: Hilly Nukabilly. They e-mailed him memes about North Korean madmen and Afghani bandits.

Their contempt only bolstered Dirk's confidence and goaded him into advocacy for what he said was a neglected school of thought. Dirk would preach his gospel anytime, anywhere. He was as passionate about it as a father whose son was a star athlete.

People are too scared to even think about what I'm saying, Dirk told nonbelievers. People should just try it once and it would stay that way forever because it would work. Give everybody one missile, he urged. Ten kilotons, max. Issue a replacement every five years, so everybody is always ready to fire. Then, boom. Permanent world peace.

Before Dirk got promoted—before his boss became Red Merrill—Dirk had been one of Douglas-American Aerospace's most reliable worker bees. He supported DAA weapons enhancement projects, looking for ways to get more destruction at less cost. He'd spend a week with a caliper, going over the fuselage and nose cone of a tactical nuke, manually confirming dimensions on somebody else's CADD project. He studied VHS video of exploding weapons to confirm analyses done twenty years before. How many pieces of shrapnel were typically thrown off? How big were the pieces? Did the shrapnel tend to fly horizontally or vertically? How close did people have to be to a brick of exploding Semtex to get killed? Injured? Would you get more shrapnel—or less—if the Semtex were encased?

Life changed when Red became his boss. In his new job, Dirk marketed and sold weapons systems to foreign governments—global positioning munitions, bunker busters, hypersonic drones. Dirk sold people on the idea that possession of the threat of mass destruction meant safety. He traveled on DAA's private jets to attend dinners with defense ministers from totalitarian countries. He dined with defense ministers from countries neighboring the totalitarians. He knew which countries' weapons were superior to other countries' weapons and he knew the reasons why. He knew which countries' systems would soon become superior. He knew which countries were close to getting nukes, knew who would be most afraid of this. DAA clients knew that he knew. Red taught Dirk to use what he'd learned, to use what people knew about him without sounding disloyal. Dirk learned to sow seeds of fear by dropping incendiary hints, the kind of hints that made presidents fear dictators.

He worked with DAA lobbyists and wrote reports for them, reports supplied to members of Congress who had to approve weapons sales to foreign governments. Dirk was an earnest storyteller. His stories got retold. He put faces on the dog-ugly threats facing American allies, sounded the alarm for struggling democracies in desperate need of self-defense. He told of rogue nations threatening countries that could become American allies, described the benefits of keeping connections with monarchies that could become democracies, that could be swayed by the opportunity to cooperate with America. He described the hopes and dreams of tiny nations that would be overrun by better-armed neighbors—tiny nations that could become threats to America if they couldn't defend themselves.

Only in private did Dirk ever speak of the opportunities for profit that came from delivery of DAA weapons to faraway governments, how the sale of DAA weapons to one African nation would encourage purchases by its neighbors. Curiously, people rarely pressed him to prove his statements—not the DoD bureaucrats, not the senators from states with square corners and not the journalists who quoted from his reports.

You're good at this, Red told him. Dirk became unreasonably wealthy and saw the promise of more money. You need to meet the man who owns our company, said Red, and he took Dirk to Riyadh to meet Nassir Saud. The first thing when they met, Nassir held hands with Dirk and they walked in Nassir's garden. While his hands sweated, Dirk dutifully answered every question Nassir posed, and Dirk never asked why the inquiry was so personal. He said he was flattered by the questions. Also, Red had told Dirk that it would have been rude to question Nassir, that Nassir would see it as a sign of distrust.

On Dirk's second visit to Riyadh, Nassir offered his daughter— asked Dirk to take Norah as his wife. Red told Dirk it would happen and said it was a high honor. Dirk accepted without delay.

So it was that a day before *the day*, Dirk stood ramrod straight and promised Red that everything was on track. Things were moving as expected, he said. Precautions in place. The volunteers' destruction was guaranteed. Detection impossible.

The night before *the day*, Dirk could only sleep ten minutes at a time. Head on his pillow, he shifted about and fidgeted in the dark and woke Norah, annoyed her, made her snap at him. He got out of bed several times, fretted, wandered the shadows of his five bedrooms and four baths, his basement beer cave, his media room and his metal shop, and he stared out his windows at his seven landscaped acres, the guest quarters above his boathouse and his four hundred feet of frontage on picturesque Broad Creek. When he got to a window where he could see his steel storage shed, where the tools for mass murder had once been stashed away, he muttered about the ways *the day* might lead to a lethal injection. Too many people nowadays were afraid of burglars and robbers and killers, so their homes had security cameras. If criminal investigators went looking for pictures or video, they had a rich range of options. A detective could splice images from different sources, could find where you'd been. He could trace your steps, every day, all day. If you carried a mobile phone, you made it easy for him.

And those were the people you knew to watch for. Other threats were everywhere. Your own bombs might trigger too soon or at the wrong place. A loyal man could flip on you—it happens. Cops who stare. Nosy passersby. Accidental reveals: A zipper catches and pulls, falls open and people see a suicide vest underneath a coat. A man, top-heavy with bricks of Semtex, might fall down and slam his head on the sidewalk and right there, in a package no larger than a lone human, was every bit of evidence a prosecutor needed to get a large-bore needle pushing poison into your forearm.

Your own people and your own tools could end you. From all angles there was risk. Dirk could bail out. There was time. Sitting on twenty extra-large, stacked in bags in his storage locker, he could make that happen. Buy a beach house in Panama for cash and live small for as long as he wanted.

A parade of horribles danced. Escape options scrolled. The weight of expectations pressed down. His gut churned. Acid vapors rose through his nostrils and made his eyes tear up. He gave up all hope for sleep, felt desperate.

He wandered more, went room to room in the dark. He lay on a guest bed and put his face against the cool of a fresh pillow. He couldn't settle, couldn't lie still, went to the kitchen for pie and milk. He used his paw, bear-like, ate right out of the pie pan and while he was licking off, he scared himself with the thought of getting raped in prison and bit into a finger. He punctured the flesh deep enough to get flowing blood. In frustration, he smacked himself on both sides of the face and flung a line of crimson droplets on the wall. He put his hands on the counter, bowed his head and looked ready for prayer. Dear Jesus, he said. Let's do this thing.

When Norah woke, it was dark. She turned on her bedside lamp and there was Dirk, sitting in the bedroom chair, solid elbows on chunky knees. He began insisting on things. He unfolded a manly finger with the mention of each item on his long list and he ran through the list in haste, as if he might forget something critical he'd first thought of two hours ago and now that he'd unloaded, it was obvious that Norah had damn well better remember.

Norah hissed at him. What is *with* you? she said. I haven't even peed yet.

When she exited the bathroom, Dirk explained the suicide vests were in a car he'd borrowed without permission, parked two miles away, and he would drive the borrowed car and the vests to the safe house and then he would lug the vests inside and once they were inside, he'd touch the wires with a voltage meter. He would lay his hands on the bricks. He kept saying he wanted to put his hands on them, to put his hands on the bricks. It sounded like he wanted to bless them.

Norah saw a man who was afraid of the promises he'd made—afraid to keep them, afraid not to. He was panicked, bouncing among options, giving meaningless orders—prone to do anything that mania demanded. He was dangerous and needed comfort. She knew what to do. A fearful man is a follower, Father had told her. He'll pay any price that a confident leader wants him to pay if it brings a moment of relief.

You don't need to be so anxious, Norah told Dirk. It's under control. She pushed up her sleeves, revealed the sinew in her forearms. She gathered her hair over one shoulder and stroked it. We've rehearsed and tested. We've trained for almost all of the ten weeks that Father gave us. We're ready. The one most loyal to you—she tapped her breastbone—handled it.

Before Dirk and Norah arrived in separate vehicles at the safe house, Dirk demanded that she go in first, that she corral Ibrahim and Omar in the basement. He wanted to bring in the vests, to confirm integrity of their electronic systems without being seen. That was when Norah had to resist doing anything to reveal her satisfaction that the dread and the disquiet that Father had inserted into Dirk's brain was working to her advantage. Really—if the brothers were to die, would it matter if they saw Dirk?

Norah's charges kneeled with her in the basement for prayers while Dirk checked vests upstairs. When Dirk was done, he sprinted out to the borrowed Chevrolet, leaving too soon to be seen. His heavy breathing cast a mist that settled inside his windshield and froze.

Minutes after Dirk had escaped to his vehicle, Norah returned upstairs and left the brothers downstairs. Nobody saw her kneeling next to the vests and nobody saw her open the actuators, remove the fresh Duracells and replace them with dead Duracells. They didn't see her reinsert the actuators back into slots that had been made for them.

She called the brothers for breakfast—toasted Pakistani bread with cheeses and olives, stewed apricots, black tea with honey. While she finished putting out food, Omar waddled to the far end of the house for his morning piss. No one saw Ibrahim next to the vests, kneeling, extracting tips of wires from bricks of Semtex, cutting wires in places that the cuts wouldn't be seen and adjusting wires so they'd look undisturbed.

In the kitchen, Omar's eyes looked so empty as to be without life. He tried to eat but couldn't; he complained that his stomach had clamped closed. Ibrahim went slowly and tolerated small bites.

When it came time, Norah helped them into their leaden vests and their overcoats. Each man looked startled when he realized the load he'd have to carry. She spoke slowly, pleasantly, got some conversation out of each, decided that each remembered what he needed to.

When Norah's minivan left the safe house, Dirk followed at a distance—toward downtown Washington, where the morning rush would soon crescendo, where throngs would cram into subway cars and glide at highway speed through subterranean concrete hollows, a place where two properly sized explosive charges could force a collapse at both ends of a tube hundreds of yards long. It was an ideal scenario if one wanted to capture thousands of damnable Americans in a hardened capsule, to starve them of oxygen and leave them scratching, scratching at concrete, desperate for escape, until they bloodied their fingers. When rescue teams reached the victims, exposure would have turned their eyeballs a sticky white that had attracted particles of ash and filth. Final notes to children, husbands, wives, lovers would be scrawled on grocery receipts, on palms in blue ink.

Cable news would linger over descriptions of carnage: middle-school teachers and kids on field trips—mutilated and dead. Polite Canadian tourists. Mothers, infants, strollers and diaper bags. Overpaid functionaries. Law students. Newlyweds. Mail clerks. Unpaid interns.

Spidery Internet mad-mouths would put blood in a bowl, whisk until it was foamy and formed peaks, would fling it in all directions and describe the stains they'd left, would wonder what dangers were still hiding, would leave irrational, indelible fear in the hearts of suburbanites, senators, surrealists, Sensenbrenners. The violence would be forever linked to the sphere known as public transit, a place where Americans routinely sat listless, a place so ordinary that boredom and safety had become unspoken and priceless presumptions.

Policy wonks. Short-order cooks. A family from Iowa needing big-city treatments for their terminally ill son. A Labrador retriever in a harness, the handle held by a blind girl in a coat that didn't fit. A nurse's assistant, born in Cameroon, coming home from the hospital night shift.

And the value of commercial real estate in downtown Washington would plummet.

Standing by her minivan, Norah said goodbye to the brothers and offered comforting assurances. From a distance, Dirk could see Norah's head and shoulders, but he could not hear her as she sent them and their suicide vests into the urban tangle. From his car four hundred feet away, Dirk couldn't possibly have known what Norah was telling the brothers and couldn't have recognized the significance of a Muslim woman touching hands with Muslim men. He couldn't have heard Norah's words: If anything goes wrong on the subway, remember the house. It's safe there.

* * *

Eve Coman stood on a chair and addressed a room of US Marines, eighteen men, not one over the age of thirty, dressed from their boots to the top of their body armor in matte black, guns holstered, ready for a mission. Some had certification as snipers and some had fifteen years' training in the fighting arts. Some were roughneck door busters with biceps as big as grapefruits. They'd been requisitioned by the FBI and each had been briefed on the tiny Maryland house that was their target, including the Saudi Arabian brothers who were inside.

I want to remind you gentlemen that we're in capture mode, she said. Your lethal weapons shouldn't be lethal today.

What if they shoot us? asked one.

What these men know could prevent the next 9/11, said Eve. Our prime objectives are capture and interrogation.

There was a nonresponse from all the men in the room.

The ride to the safe house was thirty minutes in ordinary minivans, all of the vans dirty and scuffed on the outside. They showed nothing that would make neighbors or spies suspect the FBI was on its way to capture Saudi Arabian suicide bombers. The commanding officer in the group, sitting in the lead vehicle, leaned toward the ear of the armored man sitting next to him and whispered: If either one of those sand pigeons aims a gun at us, you make his head explode.

Roger that, said the seatmate. He shared code words with his comrades via helmet-mounted communications.

Minutes before the light of the first sun, in air that turned to cold vapors when exhaled, the vans parked and emptied and the men in black secured their chinstraps so helmets wouldn't bounce off when they ran. They picked up rifles from a rack in the back of their van, clicked off the safeties, and the team flew at sprint speed to all four corners of the tiny suburban house. There were bars on the doors and windows, a yard of weeds, an empty carport. Steam and smoke from a basement furnace escaped from a roof vent. With a crowbar as long as a broomstick, they bent the bars on a side door, bashed the door with one slam from a ramrod and swarmed like hornets inside the house.

As they'd hoped, they'd come upon the brothers while they were still asleep, still in their beds. The brothers begged for mercy from the men standing over them with automatic rifles. The brothers offered up their wrists and hands, made no threats and gave no resistance. Eve and her team sat half a mile away and heard everything on an Internet connection.

The suspected terrorists put on pants, were wrapped in blankets and closed into the backseat of a Chevrolet Suburban, inside a retro-fitted steel cage. The commander of the men in black pulled out his mobile phone and called Eve, buckled into an FBI vehicle. Capture complete, he reported. No shots fired. No casualties. Eve offered him thanks and praise. When people hear of what you've done just now, they'll be reassured, she said.

Eve called Louis at home, woke him up, gave him the news. With Eve on the line, he called the director of the FBI and they briefed him and he said he would call the President immediately and they should remain ready for conference calls with the White House's national security personnel for the next several hours.

There would be a press conference at FBI headquarters and the director felt it best if Eve spoke for the Bureau. Eve hung up and signaled the driver to get downtown, to headquarters. As fast as you can, she said.

* * *

Before and after the brothers came to America, Omar preached the virtues of inspiring dread among lesser people. In Mecca, working for the Mutaween, the worst of all were the queer whores and their customers—men who cried like girls when they got arrested. Nearly as bad were the Americans. Their godlessness came attractively packaged, looking like something joyful. He told Ibrahim the Americans had lured Muslims away from faith with promises of sexual ease, alcohol, of faggotry, all the pleasures of those who celebrated immorality and sin. The Americans were blithe, pretended not to see their impact. Omar said they could laugh in hell.

Norah overheard and demanded that Omar pretend to like Americans, made him promise. If they hear you talk like that, Norah said, American police will find a reason to arrest you. They pick up Muslim men who have light-brown skin and let them sit in jail, she said. The Americans had to be treated respectfully. You might not like them, but you shouldn't forget what they could do to you. You have to play their game.

Her words quieted him, made him stop spitting bile—at least they accomplished that.

After ten weeks of being obedient, of hiding his contempt, Omar and his suicide vest stomp-walked along a DC sidewalk during the frigid morning rush. Now was now. His steps were robust and certain. He looked eager for something. In his case, that meant to enter the buzzing underground subway station called Farragut North, to trap the Americans in the heat of their own oven, to punish their childish attitudes, the elitist naïveté that fed an abject selfishness. The Americans thought they set an example for the world? Disgusting.

Each bang of Omar's boot was another quarter ounce of disgust turned hard and cast against a black country, against its millions of deplorables. Every glancing blow against a stranger's shoulder along the crowded sidewalk must have warmed him. He refused to yield to the timid, made them go around. He and his suicide vest were ready to leave an oozing wound that might not heal in a dozen generations.

A hefty man, a scowler who hid his acne scars under a tangle of black beard, he sucked on the longer half of his unbalanced mustache as he strode. His energy took him into an intersection without looking. He jumped to avoid a moving car with a blaring horn that kept blaring until he finished his awkward struggle to avoid falling and possibly exploding.

He spoke to himself, said he did not dare fall. He'd told Ibrahim of terrorists from Mecca and Jedda. They liked their explosives cheap, which meant they were dangerously unstable. A man would detonate if he fell or if he were struck hard enough. Whatever you do, don't fall and don't slam into anything, he told Ibrahim before they parted.

Norah assured them the vests would explode only if exposed to an ignition source. Omar told Ibrahim he shouldn't believe her. Anybody who acts that smart is stupid, he said.

Bearing the weight of his vest under his overcoat, Omar stood, watched and listened, pretending to be a sidewalk commuter among the many, waiting for a walk signal. In a coat pocket, his hand pink from the cold, he cradled a nine-millimeter Browning. It was supposed to get him to his target if he were challenged.

A woman standing next to him told her side of a pointless story into her mobile phone. On the sidewalk across the street and all around him were young men in ties and nice overcoats walking fast and eager on their way to work, hands deep in their own pockets, men who never looked at other faces. Loud box trucks and luxury sedans bounded past and made unsafe lane changes. Two sirens sounded from the same location blocks away and the noises separated, bounced between buildings and arrived from different directions. Swirls of air, colder than the ice clogging the gutters, pushed loose wrappers and loose hair, stung open skin. Late February was ruthless. Despite it, Omar's sweat flowed in buckets. Under the shelf of black hair that covered his overcoat's collar, drops coalesced, rolled over bulbs of his flesh and down his spine. His exhales condensed, came back and crystallized on his eyelashes. He froze and he burned at the same time.

Ahead, soon, he'd end himself without any suffering. There would be roaring hell and a jackhammer shockwave and the Americans would atomize into a red mist. Their remains would be flung against crumbling subway walls, absorbed by dirt, lost forever.

His teeth were clenched, tight as Vise-Grips.

The walk signal lit. Omar wobbled but crossed anyway and couldn't keep to a straight line. Back on the sidewalk, he grabbed a metal post and dropped to one knee, took shaky breaths. His naked hand kept a stinging grasp on the post and he sucked for air. An unsmiling woman with dreadlocks hanging loose from under her winter hat bent down in front of him, her face even with his. I saw you stumble, she said. She pulled a helping hand out of a glove, touched his elbow, explained that she was a nurse.

Do you want help? she asked.

He told her in English to leave him alone, that he could be trusted to be responsible for himself and then he spoke in Arabic and called her a cunt.

The woman responded in Arabic. I served in the American Peace Corps, she said. Sudan for two years and Ethiopia for two more. I've been beaten and raped. I know a cunt when I see one. A cunt is someone who offers insults to a person that offers help. She lifted her hand from Omar's elbow and walked.

Omar sucked until his lungs filled halfway, exhaled, then did it again and stood steady on two feet. He moved forward, inhaled more deeply, and kept on with apparent purpose, occasionally putting down a stomp. Around him were so many other feet, shuffling on concrete. Strangers' stray syllables bounced around. Car horns. White noise from a silver airliner flying miles above.

He arrived at a place on the sidewalk where the crowd funneled on its approach to the escalator that led deep underground to the subway station known as Farragut North. His eyes watered, the world blurred. He braced himself against a parking meter and squeezed out tears, wiped them away with a sleeve and when the remnants froze on puffy parts of his cheeks, his eyes watered again. He flipped open his Motorola and pressed with his fingers, stiff and uncooperative. He held the phone, ready to talk with the only person alive with whom he claimed kinship: his brother, Ibrahim. The phone rang and rang and kept ringing until it stopped and Omar hung up and waited.

On noisy G Street, the centers of his feet painful from the cold, Ibrahim's steps were slow and regular. The weight of the Semtex bricks was serious; if you're walking on a busy street with fifty-two pounds of Semtex and around you are curious faces, fresh air and a path to freedom, the only thing you'll be able to think about is the Semtex. The station called Metro Center was blocks away and to get there he merged into a processional too concerned with the need to earn, with the need to be on time, to take notice of a lean brown man with a runny nose wearing an excessively bulky coat.

The hustling population came in colors. Scads of young women with flaming lipstick and nice teeth skimmed along, powered by music on earbuds. Bellies pushing, from the inside, against the buttons of long coats. Shoulder bags, handbags, black bags, briefcases, knapsacks. Mukluks, duck boots, wingtips. A trio of gray-hairs blocked the sidewalk's flow, studying a paper map. Black men in impeccable suits offered leaflets. An aluminum cart released steam with the unnaturally wholesome aroma of boiling hot dogs. Manhole covers spewed super-heated plumes.

Ibrahim exhaled mist. It settled back on his face and stole heat from a nose that dribbled. It was enough to make one wonder: What kind of a country could simultaneously be frozen and dotted with pockets of fire?

He checked his watch. Omar would call soon. He poked a thumb inside his overcoat and adjusted a shoulder strap where it was rubbing his skin raw. Visible from a block away: a brownish obelisk with three colored stripes and the words *Metro Center* in a thin typeface connoting an excess of politeness.

In an alcove at the top of a subway escalator, a woman played a guitar where she could be warmed by the atmosphere seeping from underground. Coins and dollar bills accumulated in her open instrument case. She filled the street with her sound. Heads bobbed as people walked. Ibrahim stopped. He balanced his extra-heavy torso against a concrete corner and felt himself grow lighter as the woman played a lilting melody and sang about fixing a hole that let the rain come in and stopped her mind from wandering. People disagreed, would never win, wondered why they don't get in her door.

Ibrahim fumbled for something that had been buzzing.

Hello, Omar, he said.

Are you ready?

I am starting down now.

Call me back if we get disconnected.

Ibrahim settled his feet on the escalator at Metro Center and the machinery took him deep underground. He turned sideways to make himself small, avoiding impact with hurried people dashing down. Twice that morning, Omar had warned him not to fall, told him he would explode if he did, that he would waste himself. Ibrahim sucked in his gut and held on for dear life.

Deeper he went, into a world defined by dim light cast onto panels of dystopian concrete powdered with grime. From somewhere far below came the fearsome rumbling of fast trains pushing billows of an urban funk that was moist and warm. It tasted of mildew and urine.

Are you still there? asked Omar.

I am here, said Ibrahim. His staircase disappeared and pushed his feet onto the terra cotta floor.

Ibrahim, call me back if we get disconnected.

The electronic subway gates at Metro Center grumbled open and closed, again and again. Columns of insulated commuters snuffled at loose mucus and moved at a practiced clip. A recorded announcement seemed to be all around and nowhere, a stern voice speaking words so vaguely that they begged to be ignored. Ibrahim moved through, kept rhythm, as he'd practiced. He approached a second escalator, this one short, and descended again. An LED sign showed scheduled train arrivals.

I have three minutes until my train, said Ibrahim.

Don't take it. The timing will be wrong, said Omar. I have one coming in right now and then in six minutes.

Omar?

Yes?

If anything happens....

What? I can't hear.

Deep underground, Ibrahim took a seat on a granite bench and kept his phone to his ear. Across the tracks was a light brown man who stared. The man had ordinary black hair, a lean face and a trim, American-style beard. It was Zarkawi, the man who had followed Omar into King Street Station. The man walked the length of his platform and rose above it on an escalator. He crossed over the tracks and escalatored down to Ibrahim's platform. Zarkawi slowed when passing. Do not be afraid, he said. There is no God but God and Muhammad is the messenger of God. They watch over you and so do I.

Ibrahim held still, as if Zarkawi were not there, didn't give away any suggestion that the two men had a connection.

He checked the LED display. I have a train available now. I can go, he said.

No, wait, said Omar. I can't.

A woman with a strappy handbag on her elbow and a mobile phone in her hand approached Omar. You're getting service in here? she asked.

Omar, disagreeable as ever, looked her in the eye. Yes, he said. Some phones get service in here.

Ibrahim listened from his end and seemed confused. What did you say?

Nothing. A woman asked me something. I had to look at her and talk to her. I had to act normal.

Acting normal? That must have been very difficult for you.

Shut up, Ibi. Pay attention.

Omar, before your life is over, can you laugh? Can you take one look at everything that's rotten and laugh?

Trains came and went, timed incorrectly. One approached Omar at Farragut North with a side-mounted LED display: GLENMONT. At nearly the same moment, a train entered Metro Center heading opposite: SHADY GROVE.

I can enter now, moving toward you, said Omar.

I can go too, said Ibrahim. Then, after a pause: Omar, have you forgiven me for using my mouth too much?

Shut up. Pay attention.

The incoming trains stopped, opened. Passengers exited, headed up and out. The seats and spaces refilled with people standing and grabbing poles. Omar entered the rear doors on the last car. If the plan worked, the passengers forward would be confined and starved of air. Those closest would be the luckiest. They'd feel no pain.

A uniformed transit officer stood before him, walkie-talkie on a belt that squawked in bursts. The officer was in a bronze-brown parka with his surname—Lincoln—on a breast nameplate.

People rubbed fingers and ears that hurt from the freeze. Omar inhaled by mouth and cool air settled fresh against the back of his throat. Compression somewhere inside was relieved. He inhaled another cool stream, long and slow. The fast pound of his heartbeat in his ears. A chime. A woman's voice, expressionless: *This is a red line train to Glenmont. Next station is Metro Center.* The subway doors thunked closed. The train popped forward, stopped, then popped again, and passengers swayed. A man lost his balance, spooned Omar from behind, pushed off and apologized.

In a side pocket, his fingers encased a yellow cylinder about as thick as a nice cigar. Omar flipped its plastic cap, exposing a black button. He waited for the transit officer to return his vicious stare. The officer seemed to be checking passengers, one by one, working in an arc across his field of view, a path that would soon lead him to Omar.

Omar's train traveled southeast from Farragut North, past the lights of the station, into a tunnel where fast-moving wheels pounded—*ba-boom*—against seams in metal rails. The car went faster, faster, and its ride smoothed. The car sped past cables mounted at eye level that appeared to be wiggling along the walls of the tunnel.

Omar brought the cylinder out of his pocket, into the light. Inside the actuator were supposed to be good batteries and the tips of two wires that were supposed to run to the mud-colored bricks of explosives wrapped around him. He unzipped his coat, revealed himself. Wrapped across his middle were dozens of chunky rectangular packets, each one held on with royal-blue Velcro and connected to all the other chunky rectangles with black wires.

Omar held the switch fourteen inches away from the eyes of the transit officer. The officer turned, looked. Omar glanced past the man's face at a red signal light as it flew past outside the window.

Now was now.

Omar's face went loose, except that the corners of his mouth turned up. He locked eyes with the officer. You are hated and now you die, Omar said. He pressed the button until he felt a click and he pushed a millimeter further. Inside the actuator, the tip of a stiff wire flicked against a stamp of durable foil. The circuit for an electrical charge should have opened.

The officer leapt. Omar ducked and the officer's face slammed into the pole that separated them. Omar touched his own face and stared at the lights. Shock, fear and disbelief at being alive, until the officer sidestepped the pole and, with a fist, broke Omar's nose. Blood streamed.

He's got a bomb! yelled the officer. Get away! Run! *Get away!*

Omar and the officer reached for weapons. Omar was faster. Two shots and the cop's shoulder and chest burst open and spewed red. The officer, jolted while his service revolver was aimed at Omar's middle, squeezed his trigger. His one shot hit dead center on a brick of Semtex under Omar's chin, and that was all it took.

A concussive thunderball shot the length of the subway car, blasted out windows at the far end as if they weren't there and kept going. Then a second detonation shock wave, the result of expensive R&D by weapons experts who'd discovered that a two-stage explosive charge was far more destructive than a rudimentary one-stage charge. Clothing turned to dust, skin and muscle to vapor. Metal walls shredded, fell away. Concrete walls disintegrated, powderized, collapsed, led a smothering tsunami of soil, black and heavy with wormy moisture, filling gaps between teeth and gums, crushing lungs, stealing away sound, light and life.

Before some victims could begin to wonder what happened, they didn't exist. Their brains and lungs and bones were smithereens. Omar had been right. For those closest to the blast, it happened so quickly there couldn't have been any suffering. Agony was reserved for ones removed from the blast zone, people who had the air pressed out of them by the weight of leaden dirt and who were denied the space to suck anything in, people who could see only black and could taste nothing but the soil shoved into the backs of their mouths, people whose rib cages were pressed so flat by a force so ruthless that the impossibility of breathing in was the only thing that mattered.

When Omar stepped onto his train at Farragut North, Ibrahim was at Metro Center stepping onto his own. He pulled in lungfuls of cool air, deep and slow. Four seconds in, four seconds out. Again and again. When the car began to move, Ibrahim was trying to admire the face of a beautiful woman standing close.

A person watching security video, images taken from above, wouldn't have noticed him. He was a single and unremarkable pixel massed with too many others—a mass that liquefied, flowed through open car doors and filled every car, including the last car in a line of eight. The mass flowed into aisles, between seats, into corners and crevices. Orderly and polite, the mass packed itself into a metal container that would seal itself closed.

The mass crystallized and stilled, revealing faces, arms and legs, smart phones, bored faces, and it sent up tendrils, many dozens, the ends curling around metal handles. Ibrahim leaned against a glass partition, able to see his fellows, but from behind a window. In front of him, the lovely woman, wearing pearl earrings and a Burberry coat, talked into an earpiece, dictating rapid-fire childcare instructions before the train could leave the station and she risked losing reception. There was a twentyish guy in a garish yellow fast-food uniform with a screaming crimson chicken on the front. A herd of silent office workers took positions, leaned into corners, against the sides of seat mounts, one carrying a Magruder's bakery box by the strings. A man in a wheelchair accompanied by a caregiver. Impossibly red hair attached to a someone Ibrahim couldn't see. Hidden fans pushed hot air and made enough white noise to obscure conversation.

A female voice, from a speaker inches above: *This is the red line train to Shady Grove. Next station, Farragut North.* Chimes sounded. Doors closed. Outside the windows of the car, twelve feet away, there was Zarkawi and his black hair and when Ibrahim's eyes landed on him, Zarkawi mouthed words in Arabic: Peace be upon you.

Ibrahim gave the expected response, one that would convey assurances: And peace be upon you.

Zarkawi and the lights of Metro Center slid away as the train went forward—fast, faster, then even faster.

Twenty-one seconds into the tunnel, the train jerk-stopped, as sudden as a kick in the ribs. Big metal wheels screeched against metal rails. Heads, necks and arms flung and people collided. Bags and briefcases tumbled and spilled. The man in the wheelchair and his loose legs tumbled. Ibrahim avoided falling only because he'd set his feet wide and positioned himself against a partition, as he'd trained.

Every light extinguished, inside and out; except for the spaces in front of a few iPhones, the dark controlled. And there came a roaring white noise—a crushing rumble that was heard and felt, a rocket ship lifting off. Anxious mumbling between strangers.

Emergency lights clicked on. Newspapers rustled. The checking of watches. Impatient sighs. After a time, smoke filtered in. It was vile and acrid—burning plastics. People coughed and covered their mouths with sleeves, hats, tissues.

More smoke, gathering slowly.

Excess human warmth gathered. Ibrahim's burden dug in, made him sweat and squirm. Through his coat, he touched the outline of his suicide vest, traced its ridges north and south. He kept his hand away from the actuator in his pocket. Warmth kept mounting and oxygen seemed hard to find. Riders removed scarves, hats, gloves and opened their coats. Sociable strangers chatted about the worrisome wait. Loners grumbled. One man stood, stepped to an emergency intercom, mashed the button and demanded action. The driver explained he'd stopped as instructed. He couldn't move without permission. Maybe a problem in the tube ahead? Sorry for the inconvenience.

Yeah, well, this is *bullshit* screamed the man.

Ibrahim scanned the windows and stared into the black beyond the train's rear door. No light, no movement. Had law enforcement trapped him? Was it moving in? Should he dare to escape, to flee down the dark tunnel? Or would that make him a target? Better to remain calm. He touched his forehead with fingertips. His mouth was dry and tasted of something lethal.

Aren't you hot, bundled up like that? a woman asked him. He shrugged and removed his knit hat, releasing trickles of sweat that ran down, under his collar. He touched his perspiring forehead to the cool of the glass partition next to him.

The man who'd cursed at the intercom smashed his newspaper into a ball. We've been here for nearly half an hour, he exclaimed. This is inexcusable. Then a bump. The train crawled backward until it reentered Metro Center. The station was ghostly quiet and still. Chimes sounded. Doors swished open. The woman's penetrating voice again: *This train is out of service. This station is out of service. All persons must leave the train and must leave the station immediately. Please do not remain on this train.* The announcement repeated. On-board lights flicked off, on and then died. Then came a grateful buzzing as commuters gathered themselves and filed out.

The train's operator sprinted. Passengers watched as he shouldered and shoved his way past those content to stand while the escalator carried them up. Then another voice from above: *All persons are to exit the station immediately. This station is closed. Walk, do not run, to the nearest exit.*

Ibrahim occupied a slot on the up-moving escalator, laden with standing people. Their faces said they were trying to decide how worried to be. The train operator reached the top of the short escalator that led up from the platform and ran. Passengers were left to wonder: What does he know?

All persons are to exit the station immediately, said the recorded voice.

Ibrahim stuffed his hands into his coat pockets. One touched the yellow cylinder that housed and protected his actuator. It turned slippery against sweaty fingers. The beautiful woman in the Burberry coat stood next to him on the escalator. He lingered, taking in her face.

She realized he was staring and looked back. What? she demanded.

Your face is beautiful, he said. I was admiring it.

She cast a frown. You're creepy, she said.

Walk, do not run to the nearest exit, came the voice from above.

What is this? What's happened? asked a man who was kneading his fingers.

Public transit is closed, said an unshaven dude, pulling out his earbuds. My phone says they shut down every bus and every train in the whole freakin' city.

A scrum of full-face helmets carrying protective shields dashed down concrete stairs, against the flow of people. Behind them was a hurried parade of uniforms: rescue workers, EMTs, SWAT officers with heavy weapons, nurses and doctors in scrubs and running shoes.

Just beyond the top of the escalator, the subway escapees stepped into an alien street scene. A dozen emergency vehicles with flashing lights parked in a ring. Traffic stood in the center of the intersection, blocked, unable to move, horns blaring, fear and impatience come to life as urgency, confusion, noise. Clouds of chalky exhaust formed layers. Drivers screamed. Engines raced pointlessly. A police officer wearing a bulletproof vest held up a megaphone: Keep moving, he said. Clear the station area. The sidewalks were thick with columns of people eager to be somewhere else.

A helicopter hovered low, beat at the air and pushed around hair, scarves, loose papers, eddies of dust. Fumes were inhaled and coughed out. In the maelstrom, terrified people pushed, shoved, caused others to stumble and some to fall. Ibrahim stopped several times, reached for the fallen, helped them to their feet, guided them. Don't worry, he said. We'll be fine.

Ibrahim's ears turned red and then hot. Thin spit tasting of salted vinegar gathered and churned under his tongue. He unzipped his coat a few inches and let in some cold air. He swiped a ginger ale from an abandoned hot dog cart, clicked it open and sipped.

He shuffled, no faster than the crowd permitted, across a parking lot, past an audience of office workers who stared, wide-mouthed, from behind office windows, past the gleaming inside of an empty fire station that smelled of gasoline, past public sculptures; diagonally through intersections with cars stuck among other cars, past the Chinatown arch, then down a half set of steps, through the greasy, glass door of a restaurant that advertised FRIED CHICKEN & SZECHUAN in magenta neon. He slipped into a booth-sized men's room that reeked of Pine-Sol, closed the door and slid home the bolt so that he could be alone. He lurched, was able to make half of his yellow-white vomit land in the toilet. He retched again and heaved acid. Chewy particles settled between his teeth and his cheeks and he spit.

He closed the toilet lid, sat and sipped from his ginger ale, swished and spit, kept sipping until the nausea passed.

He stood, unzipped and plucked apart the plastic buckles down his front. The hefty vest slipped from his grip and slapped hard on the tile floor. He recoiled. Dear God, he pleaded.

He pushed on the tap water, splashed his face and wiped with paper towels. He stared at himself in the mirror, could see he was living and breathing.

He pressed fingertips into his skin, held open his eyes, stared into the cinnamon fibers at the centers. He ran brown fingers through black hair and clenched white, white teeth. An involuntary groan rose, a slow burp tasting of olives.

Had Omar detonated? Was he gone?

He rinsed vomit from the sleeve of his coat, dried it with paper, slipped the coat back on. He rolled up his suicide vest, pulled open the hinged lid from a waste can and shoved the vest inside. He pulled the can to the edge of the sink and filled the can with water. He concealed the vest under mounds of paper towels, replaced the lid. He reentered the outdoor frenzy. His strides became smooth, easy. He moved due east, in the direction of the safe house, boxed in by humanity, walking slow when he had to, trotting when he could.

He took his phone from his pocket, opened it, pressed Omar's number and listened. Ringing. A woman's voice said too many callers were using the system, try again later.

Shoulder to shoulder, side by side, Ibrahim and the refugees flowed. Unable to use public transit, alone among the many, Ibrahim sauntered among a crowd that wanted to hurry, to get away.

East on G Street. North briefly on 4th Street, following the directions of the cop who was directing people and ignoring columns of cars unable to move. East on Massachusetts Avenue, where the flow was so heavy that people trampled on winter hats and mobile phones that had fallen and couldn't be retrieved. Around Columbus Circle, where travelers exited Union Station lugging carry-ons and suitcases. Across the green of Stanton Park, where a brief opening let him walk freely for two hundred yards.

He tried calling Omar. Ringing and ringing. He called again. Ringing and ringing. No answer, no *answer*. He pocketed the phone, chewed on his lip, moved on.

At Lincoln Park, he stood on a bench, above the crowd, scanning faces. Was he being followed? Was Omar anywhere? He gave up, walked more. It was breakfast time when he crossed the Anacostia River Bridge, where the crowd thinned and became a curiosity that turned heads, then to Prince George's County in Maryland and District Heights. He turned right on Opus Avenue, then to a brick house with bad yellow paint on the trim. Ibrahim hopped a low fence and kneeled by a basement window to look inside where two cots were strewn with pillows and blankets and on the floor was his Bokhara prayer rug.

He moved to a window on the side of the house. In the kitchen, counters cluttered with the residue of a failed breakfast, sitting as when he'd left.

Ibrahim stepped through scrubby growth, dead from winter, into the backyard, felt beneath the corner of a rusty shed, found a key that he used to open the safe house. Inside, he found his bolt bag and stashed it in the kitchen, where it would be easy to snag during an escape. He grabbed at food in the refrigerator: soft cheeses, orange juice, yogurt with honey, granola bars. Like a ravenous zoo animal, he downed whole mouthfuls.

He clicked on the radio. A newsman's baritone, tense and urgent, reported a devastating underground explosion near Farragut North, that the subway tunnel had collapsed, that a sinkhole had opened on 16th Street and threatened to drag in the St. Regis Hotel. Bomb threats all over the city. Desperate police were evacuating downtown. Rescuers couldn't reach the site of the explosion because of toxic smoke from an underground fire and because the tunnel was dangerously unstable for dozens of yards in each direction. Witnesses wept, could barely speak. Stay-at-home spouses and day-care centers were making desperate phone calls and keeping children away from televisions and computers. The President was being kept apprised. The White House was surrounded by a US Army battalion that had riot gear, anti-aircraft guns and orders to shoot anybody who made the President nervous.

A line of subway cars, jammed full, appeared to have been obliterated, said the voice on the radio. The number of dead had to be at least five hundred. The newsman paused and nearly cried. I ride through Farragut North every day, he said.

Ibrahim silenced the radio, retreated to his cot. Checked his watch. Breathed in slowly, then released. He clutched his pillow, discovered a sheet of paper beneath. *I will come for you*, it said, in lovely female script. He touched the words. I've seen this handwriting, he said.

He checked Omar's pillow. Same note, same handwriting.

Ibrahim flopped on his bunk, a hand loose across his face, and he drifted into sleep. For the moment, at least, he could feel safe.

* * *

The FBI's Eve Coman couldn't take the glare of the reporters' klieg lights. She wanted to shield her eyes with her hand but, before the television cameras began to broadcast, an FBI press officer stopped her.

You've never done this before, have you? asked the officer.

Eve confirmed she had not.

The press officer warned her not to shield her face from the glare, that it would make her look suspicious and afraid. If the lights were too much, the press officer recommended that Eve not look any higher than the first row of reporters. The press officer kept reminding Eve to look and sound confident, to inspire confidence. She pointed at the FBI logo on the shield hung behind the lectern. There has to be confidence, she said again.

There's plenty of that available right now, said Eve. She beamed. A euphoric wave looked to be washing over her.

When the time came, she read a statement to dozens of journalists: This morning, the FBI stormed a Maryland house and arrested two terrorists, she announced from the podium. Two men. Two brothers. Both from—she hesitated, read from her notes—Al Amaaria, Saudi Arabia.

She correctly pronounced their hyphenated Muslim names. Scads of cameras kept clicking and made so much noise that Eve could hardly be heard. She tried looking at the reporters directly and found she couldn't. She had to shield her eyes again as she read more from her statement and her notes. The brothers came to the US illegally and, while here, communicated with domestic handlers and planned bombings at two New York City landmarks, she said. They possessed explosives and electronic detonators. They possessed unlicensed firearms.

A journalist asked if the suspects had attempted any attacks or set a date for any attacks.

Our surveillance caught them discussing specific plans for bombing specific targets, Eve said. She didn't disclose that the men had discussed destroying two major bridges leading into New York City because details like that would scare the crap out of people. The FBI uncovered their plan and stopped it, she said. The terrorists are in federal custody. America will never need to fear them.

Eve turned, startled, when an aide tapped her on the shoulder and offered a note. She dismissed the aide, kept talking. The aide insisted. Eve took the note, turned silent and read: Terrorists have bombed the subway in downtown Washington, collapsing a tunnel and killing at least five hundred people. Eve turned to the aide, incredulous. The aide nodded at her boss. Yes, whispered the younger woman, her voice colored with grief. This just happened.

Eve didn't move and her eyes, visible to every camera in the room, briefly rolled back. She held the podium, apparently in danger of falling, then stood straight and leaned into the microphone. I have to go, she squeaked.

* * *

Twenty-four hours later, at a home computer, Nassir Saud watched a replay of Eve Coman's television appearance. He froze the video when Eve turned to her aide after reading the note. She kept the same stern expression she'd had moments before, but in less time than it would take to inflict a flesh wound, she'd lost something of herself and had to toss away her tether to the beliefs and instincts that anchored her. An urgent thing on her mind was suddenly displaced by another thing, far more urgent, one she shouldn't have missed.

Nassir studied Eve's expression, her posture. He touched the video screen, tried to touch her face. That's the look, he said. That's the look of a person who just discovered she's been afraid of all the wrong things.

NINE

Once, when I was sixteen, I was surrounded by Father's friends at a gathering, and I had a serious feeling of emotions, how dangerous it would be if I were found to be a girl. They would kill me, probably with the curved sword. What would it be like to have a blade sever your neck? Right after the cut, probably there are some seconds you can see and hear because your brain has some oxygen. How much pain? Would you panic? How would it feel to realize you couldn't scream because your lungs were three feet away? I could see and feel the bindings that they would put on my hands and I almost cried. My heart pounded, like a rubber hammer. I thought I was going to faint and maybe hit my face on something. I sat and sipped from a cold glass of water. I thought if I choked on the water and fainted, an ambulance would come and the medical men would try to revive me and pull open my robes. When I woke up, I would be doomed. I didn't dare reveal myself. I had to be always hidden.

I told Father that night that I had to stop going out as a boy. I cried and I begged. He refused. He said there was so much more to learn. Did that make me suspect?

He said it was my fault that I'd panicked. I'd kill myself if I couldn't learn to act calm, he said. Father took no excuses. Slavery is the inability to act unafraid, he said. If a man knows you're afraid of him, he controls you. In Father's eyes, you were constantly proving to people that you were not afraid.

* * *

The Somali nurse was young, inexperienced and brand new to Saudi Arabia; she acted as if none of these was true. She led the patient—she knew him only as an elderly man—and his attendant into the examining room and put him on a chair. She shoved a thermometer under the old man's tongue, wouldn't let him put it there himself. She held up a hand to quiet him when he tried to say something. She held his wrist with a fingertip and counted the seconds on her watch. Fluorescent white everywhere, even whiter from the smell of rubbing alcohol. She ordered him onto a scale, asked questions, made notes. She told him to remove his clothes, except for his underpants.

He stared at her.

Not now, she insisted. She curled a lip. After I leave.

She laid out a paper gown and left. The man lifted his keffiyeh and his cords and handed them to his attendant, Taalib. Out came two protruding ears never before seen in public. He unbuttoned two light layers of robes, fresh and fragrant, and exposed a brown belly that hung like a parasite. He pulled on the paper gown and took his place on the examining table. His naked feet dangled.

I am ready, he declared.

Taalib left. A handsome man, much younger, entered. He wore a spotless white physician's coat and, visible above the coat's collar, a dress shirt and a silk tie—royal blue with happy yellow spots. His black beard and his white teeth were perfect. He opened a folder, scanned the nurse's notes, set it aside. Grandfather, he said, everything is stable in your test results, except for your A1C, your blood sugars. I'm concerned.

God will reward you for your concern, said the old man.

That thought would make me feel better if God had been to medical school, the doctor said. If your blood sugars stay high, you'll lose feeling in your feet and lose energy. You'll lose eyesight. Grandfather, are you still eating chocolates and candies?

The patient waved his hand and dismissed the question.

Abdullah Saud, M.D., brought his face even with his patient's. You may not pretend we haven't had this conversation, he said. Most Saudis wish for you to have a long and healthy life. Health is more valuable than anything else and the sugar will ruin your body.

The old man sighed with intolerance. You persist?

Grandfather, you are our King. Your life is not only yours.

I can do with my health what I want. That's my right.

Abdullah smirked like a teacher ready to match wits with an unprepared student. How many treaties work because people know you'll honor them? he asked. How many companies invest here because foreigners know you value peace? You're not the only one who matters.

The King sighed again, with resignation. There's no hiding from you, is there? he asked. You know what matters.

Come back in a month after another blood test, said Abdullah. If you're eating sugar, I'll be able to tell. What questions do you bring this time?

I pee so often and it takes so long to start, said the King. Then it dribbles. For years, it comes and goes. Now, it feels like it wants to stay.

Abdullah motioned for his patient to lie on his side, to face the wall. He put on a pair of exam gloves, slathered two digits with medicinal goo, pulled down the elastic waist of the old man's underpants and, with the heel of one hand, held up a cold buttock. He bent so he could see in the crevice and located his target. He slid two joints of his index finger inside his grandfather's anus and probed. Your prostate is smooth but is slightly enlarged, he said. No change from before, he said. Your PSA numbers are low and stable. He removed his fingertip, snapped off the gloves and dropped them into a waste bin. Your symptoms are probably not a sign of anything that threatens your health. Your prostate is enlarged, which explains why you have trouble urinating. Your rising blood sugars explain why you go more often. He put guiding hands on the man's frail shoulders to help him sit. God will reward you if you eat less sugar. You will urinate less often. I can give you medicine to make your prostate smaller.

His King appeared confused, possibly unhappy, and wagged a finger in front of his own face. These places, they are sinking in, he said. Around my eyes. This is new.

You're eighty-one. It happens.

The King was impatient. I know it happens, Abdullah. Tell me what it means.

Abdullah couldn't help but look amused. The old fellow hadn't lost his wits. The layer of fat around your face and eyes is disappearing, he said. With age, this happens.

His patient was unmoved. He held one eye open very wide.

How much life do you have left? You want to know?

The old man nodded.

Abdullah touched the medical file. Except for the sugar, your numbers are good. You will probably get to see the children of your great-grandchildren. Kamila has been married two years. Maybe soon?

How much time, Abdullah? You want me to forget my question?

How long is a piece of string? said the doctor. We get vague answers with big questions.

The old man groaned. As if a medical education from Stanford makes simple answers impossible, he said.

Terrible things can happen if I'm wrong or if people misinterpret, he said. I've seen you speak with caution.

I have seen, Abdullah, that you speak respectfully to people who are not educated, said the King. He touched himself with a bony brown arm. Just because we didn't go to college doesn't mean that we're idiots.

Grandfather, please.

At your fourth birthday party, my daughter told me you were the calmest and happiest child she'd ever seen. She told me the same thing on your twenty-fifth. You never started fights and you never got bullied. You convinced people to respect you without threats. You have a talent for convincing fools to be less foolish. That's important. It matters.

On his rolling stool, Abdullah crossed his legs at the knee and leaned in. His King's story looked like it might keep bouncing along, not uncommon with elderly patients.

My knowledge of you runs deep, said the old man. I know who you are. I know you've cursed me and some of my decisions. You think you could do better—you've told people. You're not strict with Sharia. I know you and Norah fornicated when you were teenagers. I know that you almost didn't go to America for medical school because you didn't want to leave Norah. Do you still lust for her?

Abdullah was panting. How?

I know everything about everybody. I would be dead otherwise. My life is a parade of threats.

The physician's tone turned demanding. How do you know?

One of your cousins talks too much.

Nassir? Does he know? That Norah and I had sex?

The King didn't respond.

Grandfather, please. Does Nassir know?

The King shook his head. The one person who knew had the good judgment not to tell anybody else but me. I threatened her with punishment if she told.

You weren't angry? asked Abdullah. You didn't want to have us whipped?

Young people are predictable, said the King. I did unholy things when I was a young man, and half of my friends. You can't hope to stop it. So, you discourage.

Am I hearing right?

We make certain things sound awful to keep our children safe, said the King. We hope a bit of fear will make them obey. You tailor the truth for your children. Every parent does.

The physician's chest heaved, twice. In all my life, I never thought I'd hear this kind of talk from you.

I distracted myself from my own question, said the King. How long do I have, Abdullah? I need to know.

The old man had a knack for moving people past reluctance. Abdullah stroked his neat beard like a man ready to make an awful mistake that would leave him wiser. Maybe three years, he said. Maybe nine. Probably no more. You could get a virus next week and go quickly, or you might find inspiration and live long.

The King didn't seem able to find words.

Your father had the sunken places when he was eighty, said Abdullah. I saw them in pictures from the conference in Switzerland with Reagan. That was nine years before he died. You could probably live past ninety, if you listen to your physician. He placed a hand on his heart. That's the best I can do.

Why not tell me that before?

Grandfather, people don't like to disappoint you. If you get angry, lives are lost.

Abdullah, you don't think....

110

People don't want to tell you truths that are unpleasant, said Abdullah. Even your relatives are afraid. Often it seems you would ignore the facts anyway.

The world doesn't know that a king's choices are always ugly and the best he can ever hope is to pick the options that are less ugly. A leader never gets credit for that.

Your choices are designed to make people afraid of the Crown, said Abdullah. The fear, it affects their behavior. That's why the Crown holds public executions. You're not denying that, are you?

You remember Mr. Khadafi? Killed by his own people. They lost fear. It was almost the same for Mr. Mubarak. People without fear do dangerous things. They're unstable. People without fear threaten the rest of us.

It doesn't have to be that way, said the younger man.

Perhaps you are naïve, Abdullah. You see the world as a place to play, not to live.

Perhaps we just have different views on human nature, Grandfather. Do you know what life is like in Canada? In Portugal? People are not afraid and they're respectful.

The King took Abdullah's hand. We disagree on fundamentals, Abdullah, and yet I admire you. I trust you and I respect you. You can be this honest with me and it says something. Everyone who wants my attention comes to me. They repeat to me what they have heard me say. They don't want to disagree. They bow when addressing me. They color the truth. But Abdullah, if I want to be your patient, I have to come to your office. Your young nurse—a female—gives me orders so I won't be disobedient. I am just another patient. I have to accept your terms if I want to benefit from your skill.

Everyone has their way, Grandfather, said Abdullah.

You set a good example. The King's eyes teared up. When a man becomes aged, this kind of beauty is too much to bear.

Grandfather, what is happening? You're not yourself today.

The nurse knocked on the door. Doctor Saud, there is a phone call. Mrs. Dajani. She says chest pains and it's urgent.

The King wiped his eyes with a corner of his paper gown.

Abdullah whispered to his King, This nurse is new. I'm sorry for the interruption. Then, loud enough to be heard by the nurse, Tell Mrs. Dajani you are calling an ambulance for her and if she doesn't refuse, then that's what you do. Keep her on the phone, talk with her until the ambulance comes. Otherwise, tell her I will call in forty minutes.

The King sobered himself. Fatma Dajani? That's her? Go ahead. He pointed to a phone on the wall.

Please tell no one. The nurse should not have spoken her name.

An emergency? asked the King. Talk to her.

Mrs. Dajani often calls to say terrible things are happening but refuses treatment if it is bothersome or expensive, said Abdullah. If I take her call, she'll worry about a failing heart, which is imaginary. If she admits she doesn't need an ambulance, she'll calm down.

She is not well?

Her life is lonely. It's ending poorly and she knows it.

She is dying?

Abdullah Saud, M.D., folded his arms and backed away. Grandfather, I shouldn't say more. There are laws.

I am the law, Abdullah. I *am* the law.

Abdullah nodded. Her health problems might be improved if she wasn't afraid of changes, he said. I see her dying at home, alone, unhappy.

You can see how her life will end? asked the King.

She's never at peace, said Abdullah. Every time we speak, she's afraid of this or afraid of that. She'll spend years alone at home when she could have been doing something pleasant.

How will my life end? What do you see?

Abdullah searched all corners of the old man's face. Most people prefer not to think about that, he said.

I am not most people.

Abdullah took a fortifying inhale, slow and deep. Fine, he said. You will likely die from something chronic. It will make you waste away slowly. Your high blood sugars may have damaged an organ system. Maybe your liver can't keep up or your intestines get slow. At some point, the weakness makes everything feel so heavy that you have trouble keeping your head up. When the weight becomes too much, we try to keep you comfortable while we wait for you to die. Your body will labor. Breathing will be a burden until your body is exhausted and gives up.

That's how my father died.

Abdullah nodded. I saw it, he said.

Before the worst part comes, can you help me end it?

Sharia makes this conversation illegal, Grandfather. You realize?

Abdullah, you keep forgetting. I am Sharia.

Abdullah patted a hand against his pocket and something in a bottle rattled. I have pills, he said. After an hour you fall asleep and stop breathing. It's the most humane death I've ever seen. If you want that from me, you'll have to tell your sons. Otherwise, they'll think I murdered you.

When I tell them Abdullah will help me, they'll be fine. They trust you. The King adjusted himself and blinked four or five times, which is what he often did when he wanted a change of subject. I still want you to replace me, said the King. If I ask you again to become our next king, will you say yes?

I am only a physician. I'm not meant to be a national leader.

That's not an answer.

Grandfather....

You said you could do better than I have and you hoped for the chance, said the old man. Does it embarrass you that I know, Abdullah? Millions of people say they want to be king. I coveted the crown. I said I could do better. What modest person would ever take this on? Who with any humility?

Abdullah pinched the bridge of his nose. Some things you do seem very wrong, Grandfather. That's just an opinion. I honor you and I love you no matter what.

You have guile, Abdullah, but you never use it for selfish reasons. That one thing is enough to make your family love you. You appear so decent that many presume you are unselfish. They think you have no desire for control, for superiority.

I don't want those things.

Then why do you want to be king? Why do you think you could do better than I have?

The doctor scooted forward, ready to protest.

Why did you go to Stanford for medical school when you could have stayed home and become a doctor? asked the King. The old man pointed at Abdullah's white medical coat, to his breast where there was embroidered, in authoritative Arabic script: *Abdullah Saud, M.D.* You do many things to ensure you stand taller than others. He reached for Abdullah's wrist. A Rolex? Good watches are available for much cheaper.

Abdullah snatched back his hand.

I was like you, said the King. I learned. The old man put on his clothes and, before he left, told Abdullah one more thing: Please give Norah my thanks for the messages she sends.

I have another message from her, said Abdullah. Norah said Nassir's big mission would fall apart. He will embarrass you. She told me this before the explosion in Washington. I think Nassir is connected.

The King was silent.

If you knew of a threat to Norah, you would tell me? asked Abdullah.

Yes, said the King. But for Norah's sake, it's better if you become king. You can always know what's happening with her.

TEN

Eve, the day of the explosion, on the edge of downtown when I said goodbye to Omar and Ibrahim, something pulled. Like blocks of lead, that's how heavy. The brothers were leaving. Was this final? The end? They were walking hand grenades. That little bit of Semtex in Ibrahim's coat—two bricks—could destroy him. With all the pulling, I thought I would come apart.

It pulled on me because Ibrahim showed me things. Father had killed Ibrahim's parents, beaten him bloody and told Omar to bully him into suicide. All that violence and those threats, and Ibrahim kept his decency. The idea of losing him was bigger than anything else.

Father pretended he wasn't afraid. We both knew it wasn't real. Ibrahim never pretended. Until Ibrahim, it never occurred to me that fear was just an option. You don't want to be desperate? Don't want to be afraid? Don't be.

If you want to control a man without using violence, you have to study his fears. If you don't know what he's afraid of, you don't understand him. You're stuck with him. He'll ignore every truth you tell him. He'll say he's mightier and stronger than you and he'll keep talking like you're not there. He acts like being louder is the same thing as being right.

If you know what he's afraid of? If you call on his fear of the ones he answers to? He bows to you.

Father was right. If you make a man afraid, you control him.

* * *

After Norah left the brothers in downtown DC, she went straightaway to Annapolis. She parked near a surveillance camera in an above-ground garage next to the organic grocer. She shopped in spots where the store's video surveillance could capture images of her. She chatted with the man at the deli counter: When would he get his next shipment of Halal beef? Norah needed the freshest possible. She realized she was talking faster than she should and waving her hands around.

She struggled to calm herself. Easily and slowly, she said she would come back to the store the next morning if she needed to. She wanted to come and buy Halal meat the minute it came off the truck, she told the man. She didn't tell him that the thing she wanted most was a witness who had a reason to remember she'd been there, who could testify without doubt that she was grocery shopping if the men with suicide vests were arrested on the subway.

If she got pulled over and had to explain where she'd been on this particular Wednesday morning, she wanted a cover story. She'd been at the market. She'd have objective proof and so would the store.

In twelve minutes, she'd collected that evening's dinner: ground lamb, cumin, parsley, unflavored yogurt, rice and saffron, a pomegranate. And just for Dirk, a bag of chewy cookies with Paul Newman on the front.

It was as if she'd been caressing smooth stones in a clear stream. Once she had the evidence she came for, she was relieved. It seemed like everything might be fine.

The store had been its usual bustling self. Nobody seemed alarmed or on edge, and no one seemed to be concerned about anything but the ordinary parts of the everyday. Had both brothers escaped the subway? Would she see them again at the safe house?

She paid and drove south, toward home, not listening to the radio and not wanting to know if anything had happened thirty miles away.

She returned home to Dirk. With him, she'd maintain appearances, wouldn't let on that she was on the cusp of escaping. She'd fly away on her two million dollars, would land in Maine where she couldn't be found.

Inside, Dirk was attached to the special report on television. There were moving pictures of smoke pouring out of the Farragut North escalators, of witnesses who told of what they'd seen, people whose tears dissolved the soot that coated their faces, revealing pale skin and frantic vulnerability.

Dirk yelled for Norah. It just happened, he announced. She sat and watched, stunned. FBI agents had swarmed in, police cars were parked in rings around subway stops, pedestrians clogged streets because mass transit was shut down. People screaming and making no sense. People were so laden with fear that they sat on sidewalks and on the floors of coffee shops, silent, eyes wide, hugging legs tucked up in front of them. Police officers looked unsure of what to do or how to do it. There were talking heads, each with an analysis of what must have happened, who must have done it and why—none of them suspecting the Russian President had pressured the Saudi King who pressured Nassir Saud who pressured Norah and Ibrahim and Omar. Emergency vehicles moving fast, flashing lights, people getting the hell out of the way.

The injured were being brought above ground on stretchers, on strong backs, dragged by their armpits, some hopping on one good leg. Some of the injured turned out to be dead. They were taken to a loading dock and stacked.

Helicopters. Missile alerts. Bomb threats. Checkpoints. Armored vehicles on city streets. Condolences from far away and offers to assist. Interceptions of communications. Blood donations. Sheltering in place. Thoughts and prayers.

Norah was stunned. Neither of the vests had batteries. The actuators were useless. What the hell happened? she wondered to herself. Was Omar dead? Was Ibrahim?

Dirk was furious. Only one detonation? he said. Did I tell you Ibrahim was no good? Find him. Take him out.

Calm down, said Norah. Wait until we know the facts.

Fuck the facts, said Dirk. Nassir will kill us. Literally, he will kill us.

If he wanted to kill us, we'd be dead already, said Norah. He won't want to kill us if he knows we followed orders and we're loyal. She leaned and whispered, as quick as she could, and reminded him that Father was probably listening.

Norah turned to the television: There'd been one explosion at Farragut North and she wondered if Omar was dead. Ibrahim wouldn't have gone to Farragut North with him. Would he?

* * *

At Farragut North, there was a hole in the ground filled with two impossibly long escalators. They connected the sidewalk with an underground puncture wound that was two days old. At the base of the motionless escalators—staircases now—the rank taint of cold smoke. Echoes of construction from deep inside. On the subway platform, a layer of ash bore footprints of an army of frustrated first responders. The hazy atmosphere had a flavor that was vaguely toxic.

Anyone going southeast from the platform, into the train tunnel, would encounter increasing concentrations of floating ash. Eventually, they would wander blindly and couldn't breathe without a respirator. Robot cameras banged into walls and train rails, were useless for securing images. Engineers and fabricators labored on design and cautious assembly of a bolted-together network of steel shoring. Ten-foot segments of rolled I-beams with flanges of heavy armor plate. Without the incremental advances of the iron workers, safe access to the blast scene was impossible. Forty-eight hours' work remained.

Above ground, the loudest voices cast doubt on explanations for why, two days after one of the worst terrorist attacks in American history, the crime scene should still be inaccessible. What in hell was government hiding? The public deserved the truth.

The loudest voices disbelieved engineers who claimed steel shoring was required for six hundred yards in both directions from the collapsed section of tunnel. The loud voices denied that the subway tube was too fragile and too dangerous to enter otherwise. The absence of photographs from the blast site was proof positive of subterfuge that could serve only to shield the guilty. America faced a grave threat, they yelled, made graver because the American government was afraid to tell people what they should be afraid of.

The President didn't trust what the civil servants told him; he was too afraid to trust anyone. He commanded them to tell him what they didn't know. He threatened people with their jobs, demanded an immediate reopening of the subway tunnel, publicly promised the system would be rebuilt and operational in an impossible three months. Conspirators and traitors stood in the way of the President's wishes, he said. People needed to unite in opposition, he said.

The anger mills were working overtime; the noise was deafening. Never in the history of the republic had so many people found reason to fear so much from so few, screamed one famous voice. Cooler heads, preaching patience, were hard to hear and kept on anyway. Families disagreed, took sides, argued, split into factions that stopped talking.

Two days after the collapse of the subway tunnel at Farragut North, Washington offices and stores and roads had reopened, but the lack of subway service made commuting unendurable. Acres of automobiles inched into the city by morning light, then back out at evening. Car horns and middle fingers were common at bottlenecks. People, afraid of other people, began taking guns to work. Police stood watch at key intersections out of fear for public safety.

* * *

Eve Coman's coworkers could see her coming from far away; her uniform was a patterned dress and sensible pumps. She wore no jewelry because it got in the way. Always concealed were her law degree and her Glock 17M. Underground, on the tracks of the red line near Farragut North, she looked like an Arctic demon, sealed from her hair to her hands to her feet in a Tyvek suit, crinkly and white.

Her respirator fed her oxygen as she watched a construction team join steel members. The team maneuvered I-beams down the escalator, then deep into the shaft that got ever more foul the deeper one went. The construction process was awkward and obviously so.

Above ground, respirators came off and Eve could talk directly to the FBI's site director Tasha Grey. What had DCFD said when Tasha called? There must have been some reason their confined spaces rescue team wasn't on site and hadn't accessed the crime scene.

Tasha was shocked and it took one second to understand why: Nobody'd thought of the idea. Tasha was terse and self-condemning. She gave a sober apology.

There's a lot of things I'm afraid of right now, said Eve. Do I have to add the fear that somebody inside the FBI is screwing with me?

In the bathroom of the mobile command center, a box that shook with every hard step, Eve peeled off the Tyvek, down to her underwear, and began putting on her clothes. She was shivering, searching for pantyhose when her mobile rang. It was Lou, so she answered right away and on the line with him was the director of the FBI, who demanded to know why the effort to reach the site of the blast was taking so long. There'd better be a faster way or heads would roll, he said.

I just dressed down the site supervisor because of that, she said. I'm betting they'll reach the blast site in two hours. We're back on track.

Why let them get off track? asked the director. The President keeps mentioning my name and he keeps blaming me.

She called him Mr. Director and apologized. Despite good systems, good people and comprehensive planning, mistakes still happen, she said. She repeated herself. We're back on track, she said.

Mr. Director hung up. Lou stayed on the line.

Is he serious or just trying to shake me up? she asked.

I've been threatened by every president going back to Richard Nixon, said Lou. They need us too much to fire us. Coman, how long since you slept?

She said she'd had a two-hour nap just this morning.

Go home and sleep, he said. You need good rest and you shouldn't feel like you need permission. Your people, too. Some of them need to be told.

Eve had one leg of her pantyhose pulled up when her phone rang again. Mom, I need you home, said her daughter. Winter formal is six days away.

I have to be at work. There's a lot going on, said Eve.

The girl sounded unaffected. Mom. I'm not kidding here.

If you could hear yourself ten years from now, you'd die of embarrassment, said Eve. Go ask your father to help you.

He thinks I still buy my clothes at Gymboree, said the girl.

If you behave like a calm and rational adult, your father will treat you like one.

Eve's phone beeped with an incoming call. I have to go, she said. Love you. She hit a button on the face of her phone. And just like that, she was back in the game.

Traffic noise bled into her ear from the other call. Eve? said a man's voice. I sent you a text with a picture. This is a restaurant in Chinatown right now.

She held the phone away, touched a photo, made it large. The picture showed a royal-blue suicide vest on a bathroom floor, next to a toilet and a trash can. Tyler, you just found this now? Eve demanded.

We've been going store to store, one at a time, said Tyler.

Holy mother, she said. Back away. Clear the restaurant. The owner, the waiters and customers. Everybody. Call DCPD, get the block cordoned, get the bomb squad. Call from where people can't hear you. Understand?

Affirmative, he said.

Be polite, be calm, said. Eve. Don't tell people there's a bomb until the area is clear. A crowd of scared people is the single most dangerous thing ever.

She ended the call, pulled off the pantyhose rolled onto one leg and stuffed it into a pocket. She put on shoes and left the bathroom. She called Tasha and told her there was a second crime scene in China-town—a suicide vest in a restaurant bathroom. Call Tyler and get his location, she said. We need a site supervisor there now.

She got into an FBI Suburban, lay down on the back seat and asked the driver to please take her home.

Eve was unconscious, in bed, when her mobile rang. She answered without opening her eyes. It was Lab Director Clea Koff. The Semtex that blew up at Farragut North had the same markers as the Semtex in the vest Tyler found in Chinatown, Clea said.

Eve interrupted her, her voice dry from sleep. Conclusions please, not data, she said. It's too early. She propped herself on an elbow, flipped hair out of her face.

The intact vest you found and the explosive residue at the blast site very likely came from the same lot and batch of Semtex, said Clea. The chemical markers in both were the same.

You're sure? asked Eve.

Science, sugar, said Clea. You can trust it.

Eve let her head and shoulder flop back to bed, put fingertips to eyelids. What else?

The recovered suicide vest contained almost no explosives, said Clea.

Eve tried to stifle a yawn with brute force and lost the battle. Almost none?

Twenty-six bricks total, mostly modeling clay, said Clea. Only two made from Semtex. The clay bricks were shaped and sized like bricks of Semtex. The clay bricks and the Semtex bricks were weighted and sized the same. The clay bricks had real Semtex labels.

Weird, said Eve. Why?

That's your pay grade, doll, not mine.

What else?

The wiring between bricks had been severed in over a dozen locations, which might be tied into the fact that somebody embedded tips of the wire into the clay, maybe to make it look like it could explode. They even put primers in the clay. It looked so real.

Trigger type?

The vest came in without one. Maybe the trigger fell off. You want more?

I want more.

The intact suicide vest was stained with vomit and saliva from one person. A male of Middle Eastern origin.

Eve whistled low and long. Her husband, lying next to her, stirred and opened one eye. So, she said, there's at least one Middle Eastern terrorist running loose, and we got a conspiracy.

I have a report half done, said Clea. You and Lou can read it when you get in.

When *we* get in, you mean.

Lou's sleeping in his office, she said. He refuses to go home.

Eve flopped her mobile onto the nightstand. What the hell's going on? asked Jaime.

You have to forget what you just heard, she told him.

* * *

Norah dressed not to be seen: blue jeans, black turtleneck, dark coat. She announced she was leaving for the safe house. She said not one word about returning.

Her hidden webcam showed Ibrahim had returned to the safe house. She'd never told Dirk the house had interior surveillance and, curiously, he'd never suggested installing it.

Dirk wallowed in the comfort of the marital bed, covers up to his chin. I'm glad you listened and decided to go after midnight, he said. If the house is being surveilled, you can see the FBI before they see you.

Yes, that was a superior suggestion, she said. Please, let's not forget it was mine. She sighed at her own pettiness. Dirk's need for recognition was seemingly eternal, and there was no reason to deny him, except that it was annoying.

Dirk's neck and shoulders popped out from under the sheets. I came up with that, he said. It was me.

She scratched Dirk behind the ears, as if he were a basset hound, pulled the sheets back up to his chin. Relax, darling, she said.

Norah, this is your first real mission. Don't fuck it up. If either of the brothers has survived, you end them. One bullet to the head. Take a suppressor. I'll come later and help wrap up any bodies.

Norah sounded shocked. Are you kidding? she said.

They're an immediate threat, he railed. Do you want to find yourself on death row? Do you want to sit in a cell and wonder how many days you have left?

Norah stood, hands on hips. She'd pulled up her sleeves and displayed her ropy wrists. They know Father and they know me, she said. They know nothing about you. You're being ridiculous.

He snorted. We can't afford for you to screw this up, he said.

We need to gather and assess intel before we do anything, she said. A survivor might be useful for a different mission. He might have seen things. You don't dispose of an asset until you've gotten everything you can. Father's been saying that since I was fifteen. It's basic. She saw the argument as bulletproof and thought it would allow Dirk to better tolerate his lack of control.

He looked away from her, toward a wall that wouldn't argue back and ran his tongue along a tight lower lip. She turned out the bedroom lights as she left, knowing that his fear of failure would loom. Threats would hover. He had extreme fears, ones that Father had exploited, and had no answer for them. He'd be up half the night worrying about the terrorist who survived.

Her three-car garage was colder than a corpse and smelled vaguely of gasoline. Winter against skin made her face draw tight, made her shoulders hunker. She went to the garage windows, the ones that looked out to the moonlit road in front of the house. Fresh snow dusted the ground. No tire tracks meant no recent drive-by surveillance. She opened the garage door, listened for a drone, a helicopter, footsteps, a car engine. She heard only a frigid breeze. She peeled the toll-booth transponder from her windshield, set it aside, climbed into her minivan and drove.

Norah's return to the safe house was the only way the FBI could suspect, much less establish, a link between her and the slaughter of five hundred innocents. She'd never disclosed her full name or other details to Ibrahim or Omar, had only called or texted them with a burner phone. She'd had a lawyer, sworn to secrecy, buy the safe house for cash, and the former owner, deceased without heirs, was still on title.

If the FBI had identified Ibrahim, agents would be watching to see who came, who went, who communicated, whether Ibrahim traveled. They'd spy on any visitors until they found the visitor's associates, determined who they answered to, and figured out who issued the orders. But if the FBI believed an attack was imminent, they'd arrest anyone who entered. The Bureau would publicize the arrest to reassure a nervous public, to savor the satisfaction from their work and to improve in the eyes of the public.

If the FBI captured her, life was over. A member of the House of Saud with her fingerprints on five hundred dead? The Americans would love to hate her, wouldn't believe a word of her defense. Norah's sponsors would deny her and might assassinate her if she didn't agree to end herself.

She guided the minivan around unlit curves, past storefronts. Misery lurked on the wrong side of every decision, could take her without notice.

She kept going, shook off her worries, imagined the two million dollars in the back of her van as an off ramp from a turnpike that once appeared to have no end. It would be pleasant to have Father wondering how he'd missed the signs, became afraid of the wrong thing. He'd always been too certain of her loyalty.

A fresh start? No family sins to bear? A life without coercion?

She stopped at a blinking red light, a sentry at an intersection, silent and still, and looked both ways. A surveillance camera, mounted to the top of the signal, pointed at her. Seemingly every intersection had one, evidence that the world's biggest economy, the nation with the most massive fighting force on the planet, surveilled itself and held its breath, tense about what it might find; America feared everything and everyone. It didn't know who or what to be afraid of. Fright had become its normal, as had a preoccupation with survival, with self-protection. The intersection's red light kept on blinking.

The only reason for Norah to return to the safe house was her connection with Ibrahim. Was returning necessary? Wise? Would it be better to flee? He was a grown man, able to negotiate his own survival. He would know the door was open for his escape. She owed him nothing.

Ibrahim had performed every task Norah had ever asked of him and he'd walked her away from her own panic, given her reasons to be circumspect and curious. He'd received her threatening overtures without becoming resentful. He gave no hint of a grudge. He'd kept his eyes on what mattered. He'd been deliberate and logical when faced with mortal threats. He'd never sought unfair advantage, had never given half-truths, had never wished harm upon anyone, never cursed any person, living or dead. Had she ever known anyone more admirable?

She turned, accelerated and put the blinking red light behind her.

There, on the screen of Norah's secret phone, video from the safe house: a brother unarmed, a decent Muslim man who seemed to understand Norah's signals, a fellow pawn.

He could have run. Instead, he stayed put, made himself vulnerable. He sat in the one place where he knew he could easily be found and killed. At great risk, he had come back. But for a lack of options? For her? Or was he giving false clues? Did he want her to lower her guard? He could be lying about his loyalties—could be Father's spy.

He'd probably know she'd sabotaged his vest, that she was responsible for the failure of his mission. If Ibrahim had hidden loyalties to Father, he was an urgent threat. Killing Norah was likely his mission.

She slapped her own cheek and startled herself, hoping for a reset. She was worrying too much. There was no reason to doubt Ibrahim's sincerity. Going to him was the single best thing she could do, even if it came with risk.

She parked in an unlit place, three-quarters of a mile from the safe house, next to a paupers' cemetery, where no one would call police because someone with brown skin walked at night. She knew, from Dirk's maps, no government surveillance cameras were close. She locked her minivan manually—quietly.

She entered a patch of woods that bisected Opus Avenue and at the base of an oak she sorted through cantaloupe-sized rocks and found one less weighty than the rest. She twisted and it opened. In went her wallet and evidence of her identity, her car keys. Out came a Smith & Wesson with a short-barreled suppressor, two ammunition clips and a carbon steel knife in a switchblade grip. She twisted the rock closed and set it back, then shoved home a full clip.

Her gut quivered when she breathed out. Perspiration on her forehead. This could go so wrong.

She circled the safe house from two blocks away, scanning for drones, for FBI agents on stakeout, studying windows, garden sheds, dark places under porches. A light layer of snow decorated it. Before the neighborhood had bedded down, it had sealed out the rude forces of February: plaid blankets duct-taped inside of bedroom windows; storm doors with deadbolts and metal bars; wood stoves churning.

The rubber of Norah's ASICS on pavement made hardly a noise. Cold air stung the tip of her nose and ran deep into her lungs. The aroma of smoldering oak. House-mounted halogens blasted light onto side-yard trash cans. Before hopping the safe-house fence, she saw the front gate was held closed with the same stick that was in place the morning before the bombing. The deadbolt on the side door was locked, necessarily from the inside.

With her key, she unlocked the deadbolt, turned the doorknob and, noiselessly, pushed. In the dark of the kitchen, she removed her coat, rubbed her hands, grateful for the house's gas-fired furnace.

She tiptoed across the checkerboard linoleum, took cat-like steps down a carpeted staircase to a basement warmer than fresh bread and into a corner where she knew there was a cot. Lying there would be Ibrahim, a man whose leanness and balance made her wonder if he was part panther. She felt for his scruff and placed her cheek against his, warmth on warmth, followed by his startled awakening and breaths exchanged. She shushed him. It's me, she said.

He clicked on the floor lamp and sat up.

Ibrahim leaned on an elbow, bare-chested, smiled at what he saw. He spoke in a voice that teased: Four days? You couldn't get here for four days? He rubbed the dry bits out of one eye.

Three and a half, she said. Police are everywhere.

I was afraid something happened to you, he said.

The waiting was terrible, she said. I didn't think it was safe. She unlaced her ASICS, slipped out of them, pulled the pistol out of her waistband and shoved it into a shoe. I have to use the bathroom, she said, and dashed upstairs.

Soon came a flushing sound and she returned, holding her breath. Her gun and clip were untouched. If he was loyal to Father, Ibrahim would have turned the gun on her. Wouldn't he?

You left me alone with your gun, said Ibrahim in his pajama pants, standing, stretching every nerve. Outside, the wind was blowing; time stood still. Do you feel comfortable trusting me now? he asked. Yes? So, tell me the plan.

She hunted for subtle signs of deception—fingers moving too quickly, rapid blinking, tightness in the voice box. He lifted his chin, exposed his underbelly.

How could anyone be so vulnerable and so relaxed at the same time? she wondered. What are your thoughts, dear friend? she asked him.

My thoughts? he asked.

She nodded.

I'll leave my things and go, anywhere you say. If there are risks, I'll take them. If you tell me we have no choice but to let ourselves be captured, that's what I'll do. You seem so decent that trusting you is not hard. It helps that I don't have any better options. Also, I find you beautifully attractive and that makes me want to be close to you. He paused, studied Norah's reaction. Is that too much all at once? he asked.

Her question had been about logistics—how, when, whether to flee. She'd not expected an expression of affection rooted in trust. Her face warmed, took on color. There were dimples on her cheeks—rarely visible—from so much smiling. I think we might become excellent friends, she said.

She asked him if she could kiss him, and he said I think so, yes. They spooned for an hour, which wasn't long enough for two adult Muslims with fervent and unmet needs for compassionate touch.

Norah pulled the blankets up to their necks and settled her head on his chest, closed her eyes and expelled everything that had ever troubled her. Silence, as each searched for a starting point on a journey across alien ground; neither had ever initiated a conversation about mass murder.

I didn't push the button, said Ibrahim. I always planned not to. I sabotaged Omar's vest to prevent him from exploding. I cut the connections. I don't know what happened.

She covered her face with both hands and groaned. She pulled her hands away as if she was going to say something, then didn't. There were tears coming from a woman who knew how to make herself look hard-hearted.

I was ready to die if that meant I wouldn't hurt anybody else, he said. It feels like I failed somehow. I wanted for both of us to survive.

Ibrahim, she exclaimed, cutting him off. I disabled Omar's vest. Yours too. She shifted and faced him and the sheets made white noise. Your vest, I replaced almost all of the explosive packs with clay bricks. On the morning of the attack I replaced the good batteries in both vests with dead ones.

They pondered the impossible reality that both of them had failed to prevent death, that Omar, a lumbering zealot, had outfoxed them. The long list of plausible explanations included the possibility that Omar had fled and was alive. Norah thought it unlikely. If Omar had survived, she said, he'd be at the safe house asking for orders, she said. He was a man in need of a commander.

Ibrahim agreed, nodded. Why not remove explosives from both? he asked.

I was in a hurry, she said. I swapped out most bricks on your vest because I didn't bring enough the first time. A different time, I came back to finish, and Dirk had moved the vests.

You expected us to survive? he asked. He took her hand, held it to his cheek so it wouldn't leave. Omar complained because you don't cover yourself, said Ibrahim. You gave orders to men and touched us on the arms. Omar said you were damned by God. He wanted to punish you. Ibrahim's breathing turned into a wheezing. A tear dripped into one ear. Omar is where he has always wanted to be. That's better for him, maybe. He spoke with hints of a grief hard to keep in check. Is there a plan? he asked.

Your mission is being run by a woman, said Norah. Of course there's a plan.

He grinned. Does your plan include telling me your name?

You know my name, said Norah.

Not your family name, said Ibrahim.

She spoke without an ounce of affect. My family name is Saud.

Saud? You're a princess?

Neither one of us needs to act is if there is anything special about that, she said. Norah flopped her head on a pillow, seemed exasperated.

I promise I won't make a big embarrassing deal about this.

You'd better not.

Ibrahim touched Norah on the chin, seemed to be readying her for something. Or what? he asked. His voice included notes of pushback. Omar did that to me all the time, he said. He would threaten me if I didn't behave. If I didn't protect our honor, he would berate me. He would make my life difficult with threats. No more, please. I won't live with that.

I've been ordering Dirk around and ordering you around and Omar, too, said Norah. What you said before, about being with a princess, it was not good. Don't think of me that way, that's all I meant.

Ibrahim planted a wet kiss on her neck. Forget princess, he said. The Americans would call you a badass.

Norah held Ibrahim's face with both hands.

So, what's next? he asked.

We escape. Us. Together. I have money and I have a place. The people who give me orders will want me to kill you soon if it looks like you have no value to them.

Ibrahim motioned. Let's go. I'm ready.

I need to make some arrangements, she said. I'll be back.

She got up, got dressed, readied herself to leave. She pulled the Smith & Wesson from her shoe and set it on a dresser with a full clip she took from her pocket. Keep this close, she said. If you see anybody but me come up to the house, it probably means I'm dead and they're here to kill you. She kissed him. She promised to bring more food right away.

Norah lingered at an iPhone display in an Apple store in Annapolis, where she opened the browser and typed in a web address. She entered a user name, a password, and responded correctly to three security questions. A window containing Arabic script appeared on the screen.

A list of menu items appeared; she accessed a Saudi portal into Russian computers containing data the Russians had captured from FBI computers in America. She scanned for six minutes, long enough for a salesman to approach and to have his offer of assistance politely declined.

Norah exited the Saudi website, signed into a g-mail account she kept secret and wrote an e-mail to her cousin Abdullah: *There were supposed to be two events close together. The American bureau knows, but doesn't know who. They will soon find out about Father and his involvement. Because of him, America will blame us. Should you warn Grandfather? Yes, I still love you.*

She sent the message, signed out of g-mail, cleared the browser history, the cookies and the cache. She went to the computer's registry and wiped clean the memory.

A few hours later, physician Abdullah Saud, in his office near Mecca, read Norah's message. He copied the text and, using his own e-mail account, forwarded it to a royal address where it would be retrieved then ferried to his King.

He responded to Norah, without using her name or his: *Your last message was received and forwarded. Thank you and I still love you too.*

* * *

A tassel of unruly silver hair, the badge of a man who could have retired already, splayed on an office couch. Attached to the tassel was a body, hidden under a garish crocheted throw of red, white and blue that displayed the logo for the American Bicentennial. In her blue-black business outfit, Eve Coman stood above the body, pulled down the cover to reveal puffy half-moons under the eyes of FBI Division Director Louis Irons.

His eyes opened and he inhaled, as if frightened, before he saw his desk, his family pictures and Eve's face. Bad dreams, he said.

Eve laid Clea's report and a cup of coffee on the nearby table. Read this, she said. The executive summary is all you need.

Louis turned vertical and took the report. He gestured. Go get two more cups, he said. He sipped and read. When Eve returned, the report sat closed on the table. His Styrofoam cup was empty. On Lou's desk, the business end of a toothbrush leaned on a tube of Pepsodent. He'd combed his hair and tucked his shirttails. He was ready for duty.

The President believes that if the FBI was any good, this would never have happened, Lou told Eve. He says we're lazy bureaucrats. He ordered the attorney general to call me at midnight to tell me that. Lou sucked on his second coffee. Jackass. He flipped through pages of the report. Do you think there's enough in here to get me sleeping back at home?

Eve shook her head, took a seat. It tells us we probably have a conspiracy, that one of those involved is Middle Eastern. It says somebody probably didn't want the found vest to explode. We're not much closer to identifying suspects.

Lou stared at nothing in particular while he tapped a fingertip on his chin. This was a signal—acknowledged throughout the Bureau—that unpleasant insight had been formed.

You don't think we can release this, do you? asked Eve.

If we had proof of progress to make public, I could get rid of a lot of pressure, said Lou. But if people know there's a terrorist running loose? He stared into space again. People would panic. The gun factories couldn't keep up with demand.

He pushed a button on his desk phone and a young woman appeared. He gave her a ten-dollar bill and sent her downstairs to a sidewalk café for his usual breakfast order—scrambled eggs and ketchup on white toast. He turned to Eve. What's next? he asked. Tell me your thinking. He settled back on the sofa.

I was hoping we could talk, said Eve. It always helps.

He gulped the remainder of his second cup, reached for the third. Let's see if we can rule out stray possibilities, he said. Do you think the surviving bomber duped a different bomber into blowing himself up? Did one lure the other? Maybe the faker was focused on saving himself.

That doesn't feel right, said Eve. An attack on a highly visible, densely occupied target in a national capital? That's classic state-sponsored terrorism. Somebody wants an entire country running in circles like ninnies. Bombing a subway? You do that and you have politicians feeling threatened. They're screaming for justice and national security.

Then you have a guy going in with a vest that wasn't likely to do serious damage. It's inconsistent with everything. And have you heard of that happening? Ever?

For every weird something, there was a first time it happened, said Lou.

But does it fit with the rest of the evidence? asked Eve.

It doesn't fit, said Lou. Loose strands of white floated above his scalp like tiny ghosts. Okay, try this, he said. Is the recovered vest a red herring? Is it supposed to lead us away from what matters?

Why go to the trouble of inventing weird evidence and why risk getting caught planting it? asked Eve. Why dunk it in water? It's not a plant—not for us, at least. It doesn't send a clear message. I keep coming back to the water. This was somebody who thought the vest was a danger and didn't want it to be. He thought water would prevent it from exploding. So why was he involved in a terrorist conspiracy?

Eve, who would care? said Lou. Who? I always like going there first.

Who would put on a suicide vest but didn't want other people to get hurt? she asked. A suicide vest with only enough Semtex to kill anyone standing close. He ducked into the men's room so he wouldn't be seen removing it. A vest he thought was lethal. Eve tugged on an earlobe. Lou, did this guy chicken out?

Of course, that leaves us to wonder why his vest was nearly harmless and why the wires were cut, said Lou. If you had one, why the other?

Excessive measures taken by somebody excessively afraid? said Eve. Or too many cooks in the kitchen. Maybe different people worked on the vest and nobody knew what the others had done.

Lou cradled his half-empty third cup. The fact that our suspect abandoned the vest and soaked it in water—he wanted to live, he said. He was afraid of his vest, believed it was loaded. He didn't know it contained fake Semtex.

Eve rocked back and forth, eyes closed. Did somebody send him on his mission with a fake suicide vest that he thought was real? Did somebody want him to survive?

Maybe my first stupid question wasn't completely stupid, said Lou. Maybe our survivor was the one who got duped. Somebody handed out a real vest and a fake one. Somebody wanted one guy to survive.

But two bricks of explosive? asked Eve. Just two? Out of twenty-six?

Lou gestured at somebody far away. My cousin Igor runs a crematory in Hoboken, he said. Even he would admit that's weird.

ELEVEN

Norah's black hair was smooth and pretty under a white headband as she spooned pure sugar into her chai. The steam rising from her cup was all cloves and black pepper. It was early morning; she hadn't brushed the loose hair that had bent crooked overnight.

In an unbelted bathrobe, jowly and lumpy, Dirk entered the kitchen and recoiled. Blinding sunlight reflected from the snow outside onto the ceiling and lit the room. He squinted and shielded his eyes. Well? he asked. What's the story?

Norah clicked on the AM/FM on the counter and out came the sound of an angry man, ideal cover for people with secrets to discuss. She approached Dirk and whispered. Ibrahim survived, she said. He's at the safe house. The safe house is still safe. We're safe.

Didn't I say it was Ibrahim? exclaimed Dirk. Didn't I say?

Norah brought her chai close, inhaled steam. Some of it settled on her button nose. She was feeling patient enough to feed an insatiable narcissist. I guess you did, she said. She took her first sip and made a show of enjoying it. Dirk could be a high-strung ass if he wanted. It didn't mean she had to follow suit.

So what happened? he asked

She gave her answer without hesitation, didn't want to look deceptive: He pressed the actuator and he got nothing. Malfunction. Darling, it's not your fault. I'm sure there's a reason.

Lying sack of shit, said Dirk. I volt-tested the circuit and the batteries the morning of the mission. That puppy was armed and ready.

Dirk, things happen that we can't explain, said Eve. Did he break the actuator? Did he bang it and the batteries came loose?

The batteries were duct-taped. There's no way.

He could have pulled out wires without realizing, if he bent or fell. A hundred and twelve different things could have happened.

Dirk tucked in his chin. He looked ready to utter something in anger.

Norah was faster on the draw. Ibrahim says he'll go again, she said. Right now. He's eager. He's apologizing to me for being alive. He prays for us to find him a mission. We get two missions for the cost of one. When we speak to Father, we talk options. She put a hand on his shoulder and offered reassurances. Five days. It's nothing.

She knew the simplicity of her story would appeal to Dirk. Her narrative would plant him in a garden of insecurities and he would flounder: Had the weapons expert failed? His value and his position might be in question.

It would be just enough to prevent Dirk from debating whether to keep or kill the man. She liked that the core of her story was unverifiable and also made Dirk likely to worry about the wrong things.

Have you examined the vest? asked Dirk. Did you bring it?

She shook her head. He abandoned it, she said. He needed to escape and was afraid that he might get stopped.

Christ. Where?

Chinatown, said Norah. A trash can in a restaurant bathroom. I know the street and it's a miracle he chose it. The only public video on the block is straight overhead. I doubt his face was recorded. Norah sipped from her chai, swallowed, sank her teeth into a raisin bagel and savored the feeling of a plan headed in the right direction.

The police haven't found any vest, said Dirk. This would have been on the news. They would say if they found a vest. Right? So the police have no clues. They don't know there was a second man. We might be in the clear.

A dagger of ice came loose outside, fell from one corner of the roof and smashed on a garden statue. A covey of doves took off, fluttering. Dirk shuddered, turned, looked out the window. When he turned back, something in his face was different.

You need to take care of this man, he said. Ibrahim could take us down. With all he knows? He filled a cup with coffee, hot and black. It scares the living crap out of me that he's even alive. He made a gun with his thumb and finger. Boom—and we have peace.

She took another crunch of her bagel, chewed thoroughly, swallowed, wouldn't be hurried. She had superior knowledge, dominance, could control the pace. Patience is our ally, she said. We'll give the world time to calm down. Ibrahim doesn't know anything about you or me, except my first name. The FBI and the police are on edge. Their sky is falling. They're stopping random vehicles and, she pointed at herself, questioning people with brown skin. Now is not the time to move an asset on public roads near Washington. We'll speak with Father to get advice. He has missions in mind, certainly.

Dirk closed his eyes, pinched the bridge of his nose. Do you realize what Ibrahim could do to us? he said. Just by talking?

Norah was direct and she appealed to Dirk's self-interest. Dirk, do you want Father to be hostile? she asked. We could make the wrong choice. I don't like thinking about what he'd do to us. I'm talking about waiting less than one week.

A week my ass, said Dirk. The longer you wait, the more likely something happens. He's the only thing between us and a lethal injection. This one guy.

Our next step comes when it can be done safely, said Norah. No sooner. You have to relax. It's under control.

Dirk pushed into Norah, chest first. Waiting is stupid, he said. Kill him. Bag him up. We move him next week.

Dirk, this is an asset with tremendous value, she said. Think of what he's willing to do for us. Does Father want him questioned? Norah didn't directly oppose his attempt at intimidation and instead put a hand on his arm and held. She needed him nervous, afraid, but not excessively. She needed to appear as the source of reason, stability. She spoke slowly, gave Dirk all of her attention. Father would be furious if we did anything without his knowledge, she said. Ibrahim poses no risk. He can't leave the safe house. He can't call or e-mail anybody. Your imagination is running away.

Have you seen the TV? asked Dirk. I can't stand what they're saying.

I'm not killing him now and I'm not moving him, she said. If one of us tried to move him now, he would know something was wrong. He might fight or run.

Fight?

I gave him a gun, she admitted.

Dirk yelled: How damn stupid can one person be?

Norah shushed him, didn't want him making more noise than the angry man on the radio. We don't want him taken alive, she said. Without a weapon, he surrenders if law enforcement comes knocking. With a weapon, he's killed in a shootout. I have this planned out, like with everything. Her lie fit all the evidence; it was a nice feeling.

Norah, he could kill you, said Dirk.

He would have already, she said. Look, I've taken all the big risks because you're afraid to. If Father orders it, I will end Ibrahim. Boom. She snapped her fingers.

Norah didn't blink and her stare made Dirk retreat and look away. His lips pursed. He'd been forced back a step and he didn't like it, she knew. He'd been diminished and would be feeling the burn. It would have been too irritating for Norah to listen to the passive-aggressive threat that was certain to come next. I have a plan, she said. I'm patiently waiting for the right time to execute. Don't make a mistake that causes Father to mistrust you. Tell him it was my decision to wait. It's on me.

Dirk had been beaten back, forced to withdraw. Here was another case when his younger and smaller wife knew answers he didn't. He had to reckon with his shortcomings, his inability to interpret context. Norah had seen his anxiety build in cases like this, had seen him explode and she opened a relief valve, just in case. My doctor prescribed me a new bottle of Xanax, she said. In the medicine cabinet. Take one.

Dirk was spewing drivel, making a mess of things. He kept a stranglehold on the steering wheel of his Lexus as he drove to meet his boss, Red Merrill, on the man's motor yacht. He was vigilant, eyes darting as he drove, checking mirrors for hazards, for police cars with blinking lights. He chewed, fast and noisy, on a stick of Doublemint. In the passenger seat, Norah was irritated by the mastication of a man breathing through his mouth.

Norah turned on classical music radio. She leaned toward her husband's ear. Calm down, she whispered.

Red is pissed, said Dirk. For months before the event, he was all about two bombs—coordinating, *coordinating*. He was all over me about the plan to collapse the subway tunnel and capture people inside. Now he won't respond to e-mails or calls. We pass by at work and he stares. Dirk tapped his crown. Inside Red's head, he's mad. A fucking malfunction, is all. You said. This is nobody's fault.

Dirk didn't look away from the road when he opened the armrest, plucked out a miniature Beretta and let the lid jam closed. He shoved the gun into the breast pocket of his sport coat. I do not have a good feeling. He rapped a knuckle against the packet of hardened steel hiding near his left pectoral. Don't tread on me, baby, or I'll bite you with my fangs. I will kill you dead.

Norah suppressed an urge to whine. Dirk had become a paranoiac monster with scissor hands. An image of Nassir, his protector and boss, hung like a ghost. Dirk's restless dread was out of control and with a concealed carry, he was a danger to everyone. Dirk always said a warm gun was happiness, that he felt safe with one in his pocket. It was the feeling that he could put a finger on his trigger and nobody could do him no harm.

She massaged her wrists where it felt like the shackles were binding. She would, yet again, be performing Father's bidding. He was thousands of miles away and yet always present, perhaps watching and listening now. Dirk's reactions were commonly extreme. Father knew Norah would need to protect Dirk from himself, to preserve harmony on his team of mass murderers. If nothing else, Norah knew father counted on self-interest to protect him. Her essential want for self-protection would further Father's plan.

Sometimes it seemed that Father did know everything about everyone, including parts of the future.

Norah began by speaking kindly of things that Dirk ran on about when he'd had some drinks: the need to teach young men to work with their hands, the poverty–laziness dichotomy, society's devaluation of honesty. And you are always ready, always watching, she said. I've never known a man so vigilant. That's your grandmother's influence. Such a good woman.

Dirk nodded and reminisced about the grandmother who'd housed and fed him through middle school and high school, who'd taught him what safety felt like. The woman was Dirk's shield against an abusive drinker father. Dirk put a fingertip into the dent on the back of his head that his father had put there with a clawed hammer. We had American firearms locked and loaded, he said. One by her bed, one by mine.

Those thoughts would comfort him, leave him feeling less vulnerable, Norah hoped. They would calm him enough to permit a change in his thinking.

Father had told Norah the week she married Dirk that she'd have no problems with her new husband, as long as she respected his talents and spoke his language. It's not a difficult language, he assured her. If he does not obey, steer him toward his fears. If he becomes irrational, steer him away.

Father's words were prophetic. Dirk was a brilliant engineer whose concerns excluded everything that didn't affect him directly. Dirk had been the workhorse in a Douglas-American Aerospace division that reverse engineered nearly every guided missile made by DAA. Dirk had modified a line of projectiles, making them twice as lethal and only half as expensive to manufacture. In a lab with room-sized 3-D printers, Dirk hand-fabricated prototypes. With his fingertips, he could compare machined parts and detect differences as small as three one-thousandths of an inch. He had an architect's talent for spatial relations and could conceive effective designs for flying explosives on the power of imagination alone.

Out of high school, Dirk did as his grandmother had urged and enlisted in the United States Army. Aptitude testing qualified him for a division that fired and serviced howitzers and mortars that hadn't been used for anything other than war games in twenty-plus years. He machined oft-needed replacement parts that Uncle Sam refused to buy in bulk. One of his Army mates was Jesus, a Hispanic kid from East LA who always said exactly what he was thinking. Jesus told Dirk the Army wasn't good enough for him, that he was smart enough to go to college on a scholarship, that it would be stupid if he stayed in the Army.

Dirk commanded Jesus to shut up; the Army had been better to him than his own father.

Jesus was unbothered. You have to be a special kind of idiot to threaten a man who says you're smart enough to be somebody, said Jesus. To hell with you and the horse you rode in on, hillbilly boy.

The Department of Engineering at the University of Oklahoma was where Dirk first embraced an idea rejected out of hand by every academic who ever heard it—that all objects came in four dimensions, not just three. Material composition was the first of what should have been the four dimensions, more important than height, width or depth. The primary relevance of physical properties was an essential part of determining dimension, one of many things that the so-called fathers of engineering hadn't recognized.

The PhD eggheads had been allowed to choose the world's points of reference and, as usual, they'd mucked it up.

There are places I tell people this and they see the sense, Dirk once told Norah. But talk to a university professor, a man whose function and duties haven't changed since the fifteenth century. A man like that got his position because he believed the same as the other eggheads. His mind is a stone. He's stopped asking questions, can't learn.

Norah learned that appreciation for his self-proclaimed intellect was what he most yearned for. She could go to the same well repeatedly and keep her husband on target.

The Beretta in Dirk's pocket could be removed. Of course, it could. Managing Dirk was as easy as opening a safe when you knew the combination.

Red has always been a sensible man, said Norah.

He's been my boss for eight years. You don't know him like I know him.

I've never heard of him killing anybody who didn't deserve it—
and without first getting permission from Father.

You don't know everything that Red does.

I've known Red since I was old enough to talk, said Norah. He
and Father have known each other longer than I've been alive. Father
knows Red's secrets.

I repeat, said Dirk. You don't know everything he does.

Father is Saudi Arabia's chief spy, said Norah. He knows everything about everybody. He told me all about Red.

You don't know jack shit, said Dirk. You know what Nassir told you
and so you think you know better than me.

Norah quickly recognized the unique discomfort that accompanied contempt. Rather than let it sap her strength, she let it pass
through, let it go. Ibrahim was right. Don't hang on to anything that
might poison you, he'd said.

Do you know what the human spirit is made of? she asked Dirk.
Do you know its physical composition? Its most important dimension?
Self-interest is the primal force in all animal life. If a man gives money
to charity, it's out of self-interest. The donation gives him a good
feeling inside. That's what he's buying. What Red wants is the feeling
he gets from making money and keeping Father happy. She dropped
a fist on his thigh, only hard enough to keep his attention. Red would
only kill a colleague who posed a direct threat, she said. You're not
aiming a gun at him and you're not going to tell the FBI about him.
You've misread his signals, Dirk. You've grown fearful and lost your
perspective. You're the most valuable man he's got.

Dirk kept driving. You don't know him like I do, he said. How
many times do I have to say?

Dirk, you're being an *idiot*, she declared. You can't take that gun
in. She decided to be direct and bold with her criticism. She'd never
before revealed her annoyance at his lack of intuition or his inability to
understand human complexities. She'd displayed tolerance if ever they
disagreed, had never yielded to the temptation to criticize his thickness.

Dirk's voice took on a tremolo. He spoke of dreadful worries. He
crisscrossed the valley of the shadow of death. Red is one of the most

dangerous people I deal with, he said. I never told you the worst things he's done.

Norah comforted him, told him she had his interests at heart as well as her own, that they were in this together, that he couldn't afford to be wrong. She could see things he could not and she knew which of them mattered. He had to trust. She told Dirk that Father had enlisted Red because the man was monk-like in his focus. He'd directed missions. Some failed completely. He's been through exactly what you're going through, said Norah.

He's acting weird, said Dirk. Not regular weird either.

Dirk, five hundred people just got bombed to death and a subway tunnel collapsed, said Norah. It was your bomb and his bomb and the FBI is suddenly sniffing. It's affecting him, she said. Look how nervous you are. It's affecting you, too. She touched the top of Dirk's thigh and let her hand slide up. Everything's fine. I wouldn't be going in otherwise. Red only wants to debrief us. You're loyal. You're productive. Killing you is last on his list.

Dirk drummed his fingertips on the wheel, kept driving.

Dirk, he's not going to murder us, she said. Not on his yacht, not with his crew and his cooks and servers.

Not us. Not you. *Me.*

She turned urgent, commanding. Unless you go in with a better frame of mind, you're going to do something stupid. She softened her tone, became feminine. He hasn't e-mailed or called because he doesn't want a trail of communications. He wants it to look like business as usual. He chose his yacht because it's safe. It's hard for the feds to do surveillance on the water. This is a chance to talk freely.

I'm not a fool, he barked. He banged the heel of a hand against the steering wheel and the dashboard shook. Red is not a nice guy, not like you think. There are truths you can't handle.

Father chose you for your job because Red recommended you, said Norah. Red is the one who told Father you were a good one to marry his daughter.

He kept driving and kept checking his mirrors for hazards, for dangers, for lights that flashed blue and red. He took his eyes off the road and tilted at Norah. They both knew the tilt. That was Dirk's tell: *You're not superior just because you're right. So screw you.*

She reached across, slid her hand inside his jacket and—he would not try to stop her, she knew—removed the Beretta. This will go better without guns, she said.

On the dashboard of Dirk's Lexus, a gift from Nassir, there were tiny recesses spaced, on center, three and one-quarter inches apart, each recess big enough to receive and hold a screw that secured the dashboard. One recess housed a tiny fish-eye lens and a microphone attached to a mobile phone mounted secretly in the trunk. It allowed Nassir to sit with a laptop in Mecca, Saudi Arabia, and listen to Dirk in his Lexus.

Victor, are you seeing this? said Nassir.

I'm glad Norah is working for us, said Victor, settled close to Nassir on a banquette. He spoke with rigid lips, the closed-mouth vowels of a Slav. She will live long, he said. She will win. Again and again. You are proud?

I raised her right, said Nassir.

This is your son-in-law? This is really him?

His whole world is the cowboys fighting Indians, said Nassir.

He is dangerous?

No, said Nassir. Not with Norah around.

Red Merrill motioned for the butler to leave his yacht's salon, to close the door behind him, but only after the man had popped and poured the Veuve Clicquot. We bring out the worst in our enemies and that's how we get them to defeat themselves, said Red, raising his glass. We celebrate. Red and Dirk toasted one another. Norah did not touch the crystal flute poured for her.

Red took her glass from the bar and pushed it at her. Norah, please, he urged. Take this. It's a great day. His voice contained suggestions of lightness that seemed conjured for the occasion. His face was colorless and his eyes were as heavy-lidded as ever. Norah had never seen him offer anything but a plain expression. She'd never known how to read him and was sure that's how he wanted it.

She tightened. You know that I am a Muslim, that I don't drink, she said.

Red maneuvered the glass so close it seemed she would have to accept. God won't get mad for one glass of champagne, he said.

No one knows what God's judgment might be, she said. That's why I use my own.

Outside the windows of Red's yacht, *Defiance*, the Severn River slid by under an overcast sky, the water flat gray, still and dotted with plate-sized islands of floating slush. A seagull alighted on a railing by the window and seemed to be staring into the salon.

Any religion that says you can't drink champagne isn't worth the paper it's written on, said Red. He turned his back on his compatriots, sipped from his flute and admired the passing scenery. Gargantuan diesel engines labored far below their feet, burning a gallon of fuel every two minutes.

Red raised his glass, became courtly, strolled past the discontent. Today, America is alert and prepared for danger, he said. People are not relying on a false sense of security. We make the world safer without anyone knowing who we are. Let's drink to our success. He and Dirk sipped, then he appeared to remember something. And let's toast Dirk and Norah, he said. You're the tip of our spear.

Red took the unclaimed glass and poured most of its contents into his own, filling it nearly to the brim. He guzzled the teaspoonful that wouldn't fit. Any rewards you refuse will go to somebody, he said. Why not me?

The motor yacht continued to glide. The seagull took flight and disappeared.

Boss, are we okay? asked Dirk. I thought you'd be upset because only one vest exploded.

One bomb is probably just as good as two, said Red. What the hell happened?

He's too big of a pussy, is what I think. Nassir sent us a dud.

Father is an impeccable judge of character, said Norah, pleased for the chance to sound like a loyalist. Our man wanted this to work. There was a malfunction. He pushed the button and nothing happened. She touched her husband's arm. Dirk, it's not your fault. The man begged me for forgiveness. He wants a mission.

Red took a hasty swallow of champagne. Does Nassir know?

Dirk and I have a call scheduled the day after tomorrow, said Norah. He swore us to silence until then.

Whack him, said Red. If he's alive he's a danger. Most of all to you, his handler. Nassir has other volunteers coming soon.

That's what I said, blurted Dirk. His head popped up, he stood straighter. If he gets captured and he talks, we go down.

Norah remained stock-still, arms crossed, unmoved. I'm not doing anything until Father and I speak, she said. We agreed to wait. Ibrahim is an asset and he has value. There's no sign of detection, so we have time. She pointed at them. You men relax. Drink your champagne.

She kept her arms folded, hiding her hands; they were trembling and she didn't want anyone to see.

* * *

Ibrahim was fetal-curled under flannel sheets that Norah had bought for him, snoring just enough to be heard. He was warm and still, covers up to his chin. Kneeling, Norah reached inside and mixed her cold fingers with his. He didn't stir, was unaware, until Norah called him by name. He lifted his head and Norah said his name again and he clung to Norah's hand, she to his.

I went to sleep hoping you would wake me, he said.

It was dark. Norah could tell by his voice he was smiling. She touched him, found his mouth, and gave him a succulent kiss. His morning breath was surprisingly tolerable.

A minute later, the bedside lamp was on and Ibrahim was sitting up, the covers hiding only the space between his hips. Norah was side-legged on the carpet, hand on ankle, glancing when she could; his body was beautiful.

She'd brought food, she said. All things he liked. She was happy for the chance to see him and had something important to discuss. While she was talking, her eyes went all the way up one of his legs and she found a gap in the covers near the top of his thigh. She tilted so she could see better. Ibrahim caught her and she turned coy. She pretended it hadn't happened, kept talking until she got to the end of saying something and she tacked on how nice it would be if she had time to be with him today. She played with his toes.

He was overjoyed to see her, curious about her plans, ready to go where she told him, to do what she said must be done.

She stopped, cleared her throat. Her tone changed. I have terrible news, she said. I will have to kill you and destroy your body so it won't be found. I'll be getting orders, probably in less than two days. She bit a lip. We have to get you out of here.

Ibrahim smirked and pumped a fist. So, how will you kill me, commander? he wondered. I hope it's something exciting. He chuckled.

Norah was disbelieving.

We can make it dramatic and memorable, said Ibrahim. You could release spitting cobras into my sleeping quarters.

She blinked twice, astounded.

He wagged a hand at her. If Nassir Saud wanted me dead, I'd be dead, he declared. I've been living with that for twenty years. Again, now, he wants to kill me. So what? I can't control it, so I don't try.

You're to be murdered and mutilated, said Norah. They'll shoot me if I don't give them pictures showing you're dead and buried. Get serious.

I shouldn't make jokes? asked Ibrahim, playing the devil's advocate. I should be absolutely terrified? He lifted his eyebrows in mock surprise.

You're being odd again, said Norah. Do you care whether you survive? You'd joke about something like that? The only reason you're not already dead is that I bought you time. I made up a story. Your life hangs on that story and here you are joking, like there's no reason to worry. I could have run away from you and I'd be safe now. This is not some joking around.

Ibrahim leaned forward, closer to her, and he didn't blink. I'm being serious, he said. I want to know how you're going to kill me.

There, said Norah. Odd again.

Not odd, he said. Curious.

Who acts this way? she asked. There's a threat of death from people who could launch a shoulder missile from ten miles away. She snapped her fingers. Like that. Wake up.

How many times does a gun get shoved in your face before you stop being afraid of the gun? asked Ibrahim. How much torture is enough so you don't fear pain?

Before she could say anything she might regret, he stopped her.

Nassir Saud could have killed me so many times, he said. He could have killed me when I was a boy, the day I came home and found my family dead. He's the one who put me into the orphanage that couldn't always afford food. He could have got me any time. He didn't and it was only because I had value. When he hired me for the Mutaween, Nassir said he remembered me from when my parents died. He wanted me to think he was nice, but he'd had plans for me since I was eight. He'd kill me and ruin my soul if I didn't become his terrorist and kill myself. And Omar? He's threatened me my whole life. I would suffer and die if I didn't believe, if I didn't pray, if I didn't join him on the Mutaween. My death would be eternal. Being dead for me would be so much worse than for other people.

Ibrahim measured his words. It feels like I can't be afraid anymore, Norah, which is better, he said. Fear makes me desperate and dangerous, it makes me want to hate people. Fear kills common sense and trust. It prevents kindness and contentment. It doesn't make me want to smell flowers, it makes me want to hide in them. Ibrahim shook his head. It's not like extreme fear makes you live better or longer, he added.

Norah pointed at her ASICS, twelve inches away, pistol stuffed inside. You're not afraid of being killed? So fine, I kill you now.

Maybe you've lived too long believing fear is your only option, said Ibrahim. Why do couples get married and have children? Why do people decide to study a foreign language? Because every day we should be afraid of an asteroid falling out of the sky or mass murderers finding us. We should be afraid of viruses hiding in the dirt in our garden and breathing air in elevators where there's ten other people. We should know when we're sitting at a red light that a cement truck could lose control and slam into us. Somebody in a Russian submarine could push one wrong button and here comes a nuclear missile. The inspector who approved your house didn't see the loose wires that can cause a fire. Your dog licks you on the face and you catch a bacterial infection. The mailman has a flu bad enough to kill people and he sneezes on your letters before you get them. If people were as afraid as they were supposed to be, they would never be happy.

Where did you come from, Ibrahim Mohammed? queried Norah. How could a man get so beaten down and come up with something like this?

When I said I was serious, I meant it, said Ibrahim. How will you kill me? You need a plan. You need a cover story.

She squinted.

This is me being curious, he said. He banged the cot's frame. What's your plan?

I still think you're a little odd, she said. Okay, fine. I will lead you into a state forest in Massachusetts by telling you we need to move to a new safe house. When we get there, I'll tell you to look at the black bear wandering past and when you're turned away, I'll pull my nine-millimeter from my waist. Two hollow points fired into your brain stem. I'll dig a hole and bury you where nobody ever will find you. I'll take pictures of the bloody mess where your face used to be and I'll send them to my people.

He looked shocked. Wait, he said. Massachusetts?

It's four hundred miles to get there, said Norah. If people found your body, they wouldn't connect it to terrorist murders on the DC subway. Really, I chose the location because I have friends who can come there and pick you up. You'll live with them. They're coming from Maine.

Can't Nassir's people still find me in Maine?

First, those people will think you're dead, said Norah. Second, they don't know I have friends in Maine. I've never given any clues.

Then what? he asked. What comes after?

She squirmed. If they both escaped, she'd feared a need for constant vigilance, constant monitoring for threats, frequent moves, contingency plans always ready. She'd planned for possible escape from Maine to a farm in Nova Scotia where there were cabins for field workers. Alternatively, she'd priced sailboats with a boat broker in Boston. In case anything happened to her, she'd already written a note to Ibrahim. Her fingertips touched her eyelids. She made no sound, seemed to stop breathing.

You haven't thought that far ahead, have you? he asked.

Always, she said, I've lived for somebody else. I've lived behind a mask. I'm married to a man who humps me like a gorilla and I have to take his orders. I pretended I want to help suicide bombers destroy people. I grew up lying to everybody. I lied about my name and I told people I was a boy. Every decision is what somebody else expects. I don't own my life. I am always vigilant, every day, because of threats from all over. Whatever comes next has to be ordinary and boring. I want to live like a normal person in a small house with a garden and a dog.

She slowed, seemed weary. I've known people who looked content, she said. I want what they have. They have babies and pets and they have dinner parties and talk about good books and never worry if they'll get shot in the head. I'm exhausted from my life. Forever I've been exhausted. I want ordinary.

We have served the same master and found the same complaints, said Ibrahim. We want to find out what it feels like for life to be easy. He leaned, took her hand. If the best way for you to get what you want is to leave me behind, then you should leave, he said.

The reason I'm still here is because I don't want to leave you, said Norah. Whatever comes next would probably be better if we're together.

He kissed her hand and moved to kiss her face, but she wouldn't let him. Ibi, there is more, she said. You need to know some things. She pushed ahead. My father—you know him. He is Nassir Saud.

Ibrahim's head bobbed. His expression did not change.

You knew?

Suspected, he said. You look just like him and when I asked if you knew Nassir, you avoided the question. It made me wonder.

Are you mad? she asked.

Angry is a waste of time.

All the terrible things Father did and I'm his daughter. You're not upset?

He shrugged. I'm alive, he said. Nobody's shooting at me. Dinner will be excellent because you brought fresh food. Can we enjoy time together? That's all I want to think about right now.

I could learn to love you for being so odd, she said. Norah had dreaded confessing her connection with Father. Her confidence rose. There's something more, she said. Your sister, Alitha?

He held up a hand and stopped her. You wrote letters to Omar and to me, pretending to be Alitha, he said. You made us believe she was still alive. Nassir used you so he could use me.

How could you possibly know? she asked.

The note you put under my pillow—it was your handwriting, said Ibrahim. It was the same on Alitha's letters. I thought that was your way of telling me. He wheezed but did not cry. Your letters captured her spirit, her best parts. It was like you knew her.

I'm sorry, Ibi, said Norah. So sorry.

You did what you had to, he said.

She embraced him, kissed him. I have to leave, she said. I hope you're still here in forty-eight hours when I come back. She reached for her coat and pulled out an envelope. This is a hundred thousand dollars. If you decide to leave on your own, you'll need it. She put the envelope on Ibrahim's dresser.

Keep the money, he said.

You have two days to see if you feel like changing your mind. She touched the money. This is yours to keep. She looked around. Fill your pack with whatever you want. Wipe down the house. Clean the bathroom. You can't afford to leave behind hair or fingernail samples. You need to be ready to roll.

He put her hand on his chest. I'm excited, he said. Feel it? My heart's going boom, boom, boom.

Grab your things when I come to take you home, she said.

He beamed. I don't have to tell you what this smile on my face means, he said.

TWELVE

Annie liked the games she could play with her Marlin Golden. It was, after all, designed for creative feats of marksmanship. Also, it was perfect for shooting varmints that nested in the big barn attached to her house in the cold woods of Maine.

She put the rifle barrel on her shoulder, pointed backwards, and held up a hand mirror so she could aim behind her, at the far side of her barn where a paper target hung on a wall of cinderblocks packed with sand. She breathed out slowly, cold mist floating. With her thumb, she slow-pulled the trigger and hit the bull's-eye, but missed dead center by an inch.

Hockeysticks, she shouted.

She was readying her next shot when the timer on her mobile phone sounded. It was time to pull dinner out of the oven. She took her shot, hit dead center and brightened; it was an excellent time to quit the day's practice.

Annie passed through the door that divided the freeze of her barn from the glow of her kitchen. She clicked the door tight, locked it and yanked once to make sure. Inside was the extra-friendly, ketchup-y aroma of baking meatloaf. She set her rifle upright in a rack in the kitchen—behind a corner where it couldn't be seen by anyone looking through the barn door's glass panel. It sat, always in the same spot, unless Annie was using it. If an attacker came, she'd be ready.

Annie's guns were pampered pets, each with a name. She'd married a gunsmith who was the son of a gunsmith and her guns got oiled and calibrated and cleaned better and more often than nearly any guns anywhere.

From the blacks and browns of his basement workshop, beneath pine joists hewn and laid before Teddy Roosevelt was born, husband Jack called for his wife. When Annie came down, he motioned for her to sit across from him at his workbench. On one end of the stained wooden surface was a village of skinny condiment jars filled with differently colored oils. Next to the jars sat Jack and a halogen lamp that shed an unreal light. A volatile gun-cleaning solvent perfumed the air.

Jack lifted Annie's favorite target pistol, a Sig Sauer nine-millimeter, and pointed it at her right eye. The business end was close enough to Annie that the smell of burnt black powder would have stung. The weapon's hammer was pulled back and it was without ammunition, so the barrel was full of the harsh light cast by the lamp on Jack's end. Inside were carbon deposits that had accumulated in rocky lumps.

Oh, that's bad, said Annie.

Why didn't you come to me with this sooner? asked Jack.

That's enough, said Annie. She pushed the weapon away. Every gun is a loaded gun, she said.

Not this one, said Jack. Even the firing pin is out. Jack lowered the weapon, no longer blocking her view of his perfectly trimmed silver scruff. He stared at her through his reading glasses, which made his green irises look like martini olives. The inside of this barrel is uglier than an oyster's ass, he said. This is an hour of scraping.

What will it cost? she asked.

Sweet potato pie, he declared. With hot sugared pecans and Cool Whip. Vanilla ice cream on the side. Stone Fox Farms. Not that Hannaford crap.

Easy peasy, she said. Her fingertips prowled his Hemingway whiskers and she leaned across the workbench and kissed him. I thought you'd ask for a blow job.

My birthday's coming, he said. His left eyebrow rose.

The target competition is tomorrow morning, she said. I have to leave at eight.

He looked at a swan-necked brontosaurus on a Sinclair wall clock. Time enough, he said.

She gestured toward the kitchen. There was a black scar on her thumbnail where she'd hit it with a hammer two weeks ago. Dinner's ready, she said.

Upstairs, Jack washed his hands of gun oil at the kitchen sink. As he dried off, he stood tall and cracked his back, loosening joints that had been sitting the whole day in their rock-wall basement. Guess who called me this morning? he said. Completely out of the blue. Norah. She's leaving Dirk and she has a young man. She's bringing him to stay with us and she'll come back later.

Annie's face lit up.

Jack turned stern. Don't tell, he said. Nobody. They're hiding. She said don't e-mail or text or call because Dirk is spying on her.

I don't know how a girl as sweet as her could get married to a water buffalo like him, she said.

I'm going to Massachusetts with the Subaru at zero-dark-thirty, day after tomorrow. I'll meet her and pick up her young man. You coming?

You bet. I'll make sammiches.

She needs me to kill an animal when we get there.

Annie stopped and turned. Wicked weird, she said. Why?

I'm sure she'll tell us when she's able, he said.

She patted the sidearm on her belt. Me and Margie are ready, she said.

* * *

At Red Merrill's waterfront home: Seventeen squealing kindergartners in Disney birthday hats, every one bursting with noise and ricocheting around the mezzanine porch. Parents sipping whiskey sours. A bank of windows gave view to a noonday sun and the mouth of the Magothy River where it emptied into the Chesapeake. A woman in a maid's uniform lit candles on a birthday cake.

A young woman hidden inside a Mickey Mouse suit clapped a pair of four-fingered hands and embraced the birthday boy when he blew out his candles. Applause by the mothers and fathers. At least one member of each couple worked for Douglas-American Aerospace.

Then came laughing approval by grandfather Red Merrill, DAA's executive vice president, and his lieutenant, Dirk Johnson.

You want to talk operations? asked Dirk. Here? Dirk put his hands over his ears. The noise is why I'll never have kids.

You can't get better cover, said Red. It's impossible to pick one voice out of this many. Red smiled and waved across the room at a man from IT whose job it was to keep company computers buttoned up. Who would ever suspect we'd plan an operation at a child's birthday party?

The maid cut the Disney cake into wallet-sized squares, lifting and centering each piece onto a Disney plate. Then came a squealing maelstrom of sugar joy.

Dirk spoke into Red's ear, reminded him that Nassir's next recruits were scheduled to arrive soon. Dirk suggested the two newcomers roam landmark locations and randomly assassinate. Two assassinations in each of five huge cities, two in each of five rural areas, he said. People would piss themselves. They would never leave their homes. The country would unite in a demand for security. Did you know ninety percent of civilian surveillance units in the US are at least fourteen years old? I researched it, he said. That market could be thirty billion a year.

Children scraped cake and icing from their plates, guzzled excessively red punch from Pocahontas cups. A Bluetooth speaker played "Skinna Marinka Dinky Dink." The woman in the Mickey costume danced between tables and, in a display of glee, clasped her hands and held them near Mickey's heart.

Two guys and a car shooting people? asked Red. It's been done. They got caught, remember?

That was a successful mission, said Dirk. We made billions. And nobody knows it was us.

A maid handed Red a square of white cake bearing a cobalt-blue portion of Mickey Mouse's skateboard. He turned his nose. Here, eat this, he said. He shoved it into Dirk's hands.

In one motion, Dirk mouthed half of the cake Red had forced on him. With evident difficulty, he swallowed. Blue dye stained his upper lip. He turned back to the boss, undeterred. In a span of four weeks, we can have random events in all ten areas, he said. They go back in random order, do it again. If a place has weak political support for military spending, we go. Berkeley and San Francisco—we can do both in one day. California will be a lock for military appropriations. Then Ann Arbor, Chapel Hill, Austin.

Red pointed at the cake in Dirk's hand. You're going to eat that whole thing, right? he asked. Red shook his head, looked back at the children. We need a single, dramatic event and we need our volunteers to die. We need a venue that hasn't been tried, where people expect safety, where lots of people are watching, where it will be recorded so people can watch it over and over.

Red, work with me, said Dirk. I've got this planned out.

What happened to suicide bombers at the Fourth of July concert on the Mall? asked Red. A live, nationally televised event wrapped in a big old American flag.

We can do better, said Dirk.

Red shook his head forcefully. Bullshit, he said. The Fourth of July is a defense contractor's dream date.

What if we put shooters in one city? asked Dirk. Just DC. A test.

You're a genius at weapon design, Dirk. Stick to what you know or you'll make people worry more than is good for you. Let's talk about the man who survived his mission. How soon until he's dead?

Norah and I will talk to Nassir, said Dirk. If he wants the man dead, Norah will leave immediately. She's got a plan to take him out of state and bury him.

What about Zarkawi? Red snapped his fingers. One and done.

What if Nassir wants him alive? asked Dirk, repeating Norah's view. What then? Dirk folded his big arms and stood pat.

Norah pulled sharp knives out of the dishwasher first. Clearing hazards before entering a field of operations was SOP and favored safety.

She inserted the clean blades into the knife block on the counter in her kitchen, handles pointing toward the wall. She could gain a moment's advantage on an assailant if weapons were hidden from view. She put in the knives with the sharp edges facing up, which would permit her to take an overhand grip, the stronger position. Also, the arrangement would let her grab and throw in one motion.

A system for almost everything. Attention to details that might save her life. She invested herself in a state of high alert, didn't feel she could afford to let down her guard. Everyone was a potential threat—had to be analyzed. A threat could come at any time and from any direction. So, she kept safeguards in multiple forms, all close at hand. Kitchen knives stacked just so. Always a weapon clipped onto an ankle, out of sight. She made sure the couple's two boats were always gassed up and ready for a fast escape. She was vigilant.

Silverware done, Norah pulled out the dishwasher's top rack and moved on to glasses, but then came the unexpected noise of footsteps—on the stairs—and *snap*, constriction in her gut. She was wound up, hadn't realized Dirk was awake, was coming downstairs. She laid a hand on the knife block, weapons at the ready, put herself in position to see the kitchen's entry door and—yes, of course, it was Dirk. No attacker, no worries.

So? asked Dirk. How'd it go? Dirk entered the kitchen wrapped in a white robe, reams of cotton loose around his girth. Two of his oversized digits overfilled the delicate handle on the coffee carafe, requiring him to pour awkwardly.

Norah turned on Dirk's countertop radio and out came hostile male voices that sounded damn sure of something. All fine, she said. Our conference with Father in eighteen hours is a go. In case he wants to terminate, I'm ready. I have everything in place to take the man out of state and bury him. I thought that might reassure you. And if Father wants, I have two missions in mind for Ibrahim.

She pivoted, began discussing options for using Ibrahim if Father approved. Imagine the terror if a Saudi walked into a police station and started shooting, she said. If police aren't safe, nobody's safe.

That would be stupid, he said. A defense contractor makes money protecting national security. Local police are a different market entirely. You don't know anything about marketing, do you?

Dirk didn't ask about Norah's night at the safe house, about inter-actions with Ibrahim. So far, Norah thought, the conversation was a success.

He drew close, towered over her, spoke so that only she might hear him. You can't just pop him? he asked. Drive over? And *pop*? He knocked a knuckle on the counter. You could zip him into a body bag and be home in an hour. We retrieve and dispose when it's convenient. Bing, bang, boom.

We talk to Father first, she said. You can wait.

It would save everybody a lot of trouble. I'm just saying.

Fine, she said. You do it. She went back to stacking juice glasses.

He turned grim and sucked on his coffee.

Their eyes reconnected and she went to a tried-and-true strategy for draining tension: She stroked him. You're under lots of stress, Dirk. You have so much on your shoulders. When this is over, let's take a vacation and relax.

Dirk raised his coffee cup, gulped again, time enough for the air to grow both clear and heavy. How will you end him?

The asset is prepared to cooperate in his own death, she said. Obviously, he doesn't know what's planned.

How exactly?

She thought of Ibrahim's odd brand of curiosity, his questions about how he was to be killed, and resisted the urge to smile. I told him we might need to relocate him. I have a cover story for taking him four hundred miles away.

Dirk drew a shade closer. Irritation seemed to have accumu-lated. Tell me the goddamn plan, he said. I don't want to ask a thousand questions.

She threatened his gullet with the heel of her hand and he backed away. Western Massachusetts, she said, feeling good that her husband was disoriented by emotion. He was unlikely to stray from the subject. It's dense forest rarely used outside of hunting season, she said. They have some fire towers, that's all. It's so far away, we won't be linked to the body if it's found. I chose the location working with your paper maps, the ones you bought so we wouldn't have to search the Internet and leave an electronic trail, she said. Your low-tech plan to avoid detection is perfect. Massachusetts is perfect.

What else are you telling him?

He was drawing close to the uncomfortable subject of Norah's night at the safe house. She'd try to steer him in a different direction. I told him if we didn't have a mission for him, he might lose his life, she said.

Dirk's thick neck jerked. What a bullshit thing to tell him, he said. He can't possibly trust you. Right now, he's probably running.

She didn't tell him she'd left open the door to Ibrahim's iron cage and had given him a pile of money. The house is locked, she said. He can't get out. He thinks I told him about losing his life because I want to help protect him. Norah pulled one of Dirk's beer mugs out of the dishwasher and stretched to place it on a high shelf. He thinks I'm saving him from the bad guys, the ones who give us orders. I'm the good one, the honest one. The bad ones are waiting outside his door. A surprising number of people are comfortable in that arrangement. Just in case, she thought, more assurances. When a person is afraid enough, he gets desperate. He'll become loyal to anybody promising security, she said. We've talked about this. You know how this works.

He probably wants to tap you, said Dirk. Don't you think? He must've thought about it.

Norah settled a pair of coffee cups on a low shelf. The issue she didn't want to talk about had come forward.

He's tried, hasn't he? asked Dirk.

You're being ridiculous, she said. He submitted his entire life to someone else's control in pursuit of death, and he's observant Muslim. The last thing on his mind is sex.

Dirk stepped closer to Norah and leaned over her. His routine for testing a person's sincerity was to impose silence and see if they'd give themselves away.

Norah had seen it before and wasn't intimidated. She was direct, low frequency. He'll do as he's told, she said. He's obedient before he's anything else. Right now, he's sanitizing the safe house. He's on his hands and knees with a washing bucket, eliminating evidence.

Your asset is doing your job for you? Seriously?

When do I ever joke?

That's some serious psy-ops right there, said Dirk. The suicide trainer becomes a protector who says she might be a killer. He laughed.

Redirection complete, she thought. Objective obtained.

When she and Dirk talked with Father on Skype, Dirk would brag to Nassir that Norah was ready. He'd want credit for it, would want Father to think him essential. Dirk's want for supremacy, for wealth, for approval, would have him worrying about the wrong things. With her supposed plan to murder Ibrahim, she'd lit a gas lamp with a dancing flame and Dirk was crazed by the look of it.

In the length of a Skype call, she could have Nassir absorbed in questions about Ibrahim's value, whether to use him or to kill him. If Norah and Dirk zeroed in on Ibrahim, underscored their apparent division, the need for Father's advice, Father would go in, neck deep, immerse himself in an issue that might resolve all other issues. Do we kill Ibrahim? Or not? A second lamp would be lit. No one would wonder if Norah was harboring plans for her own escape.

She studied the block full of knives, close at hand, and indulged a vivid fantasy: She was staring down Dirk with a blade in her fist, plunged it into his center and watched as the blood drained, as he lost the ability to speak, to breathe. She felt a glow of hostility, then rid herself of violent images and saw the danger she created for herself by entertaining them. She had to avoid extremes to work effectively. The extremes were sometimes disabling and usually exhausting. And the practical side: Alive, Dirk was a useful tool. Norah could spoon-feed him fear and entice him with offers of more. She could lead him where she wanted to. He could be convinced to hide or eliminate certain problems for her. He might even eliminate himself, without knowing he was doing it.

In the hour before Nassir's face appeared on Secure Skype, Dirk showered, shaved, put on a shirt that he'd had dry cleaned three days ago. Norah put on her niqab, revealing only her eyes, as she always did for her conferences with Father. It was unnecessary for a Muslim woman to cover herself if the only ones present were members of her own family, but Nassir had always seemed to appreciate the gesture—likely because he was uncomfortable talking to someone who displayed femininity.

Nassir began the same as always. What do I need to know? he asked.

Norah began the same as always. It's lovely to see you, Father, she said. She silenced herself, knew Dirk was primed to set the agenda, knew Father would expect it. She would underline the urgency of the preferred issue after Dirk identified it.

Nassir, we have one who survived, said Dirk. Still in our control. I want to terminate, Dirk explained. Norah wants to use him again. I think the man's a danger.

How can he be alive? demanded Nassir. Whose fault is that?

Norah went to work and got right to the point: Malfunction, Father. Cause unknown. He pressed and it did not explode. He abandoned the vest on his escape. He returned to the safe house and remains cooperative. There are no signs of detection.

Are you convinced he is truthful?

Yes, said Norah. He pleads for another mission and he shows regret.

Which one? Which one survived?

Ibrahim, said Norah.

It would be better if he'd been the one who died, said Nassir. Do you have a use for him?

Two options, Father. First, a mass shooting in a police station. Second, a suicide bomb at a parade. Americans come out for Saint Patrick's Day when it's warmer. In two weeks.

Nassir's mouth bunched. He didn't believe he was being told everything—Norah knew. Doubtless he'd assume Norah had kept Dirk in the dark on something and he would demand an explanation the next time they spoke.

What are your wishes, Father?

Terminate, he said. Immediately.

Norah didn't want to look affected, didn't wait before turning to something else relevant, hoping to keep Father's attention away from other subjects. Father, did the FBI find the vest? Do we know?

The Russians' door into the FBI computers says the FBI found the vest and it's being analyzed, said Nassir. The test results, if they exist, have not been recorded.

Norah's gut churned. She had to worry about the discovery of cut wires and fake bricks of Semtex. How long until those facts got to Father? Norah fretted over how much time she had until the FBI put more data about the vest where Father could see it. Disclosure of cut wires and bricks of clay could happen easily and quickly. The FBI must already know, she thought. Norah was nearly woozy with anxiety. I'm eager to hear what their testing shows, she said.

As are we all, said Nassir.

So, the decoy operation was successful, she said. Her voice was steady, but barely.

The Baltimore operation worked as planned and still it is working, said Nassir. It consumes half of the area's terrorism resources. The FBI is too afraid of missing something to leave it alone. The need to protect the public requires them to think about such things. It gives us great advantage.

Dirk's throat cleared before Nassir finished talking and he readied himself. He would be jumping in as soon as he could, Norah knew. It was likely to be something contrary and seemingly urgent, something counterproductive. Would he call her out for not executing Ibrahim immediately? Norah pressed her foot on top of Dirk's, out of view of the laptop lens.

Ask Father about the impact, she interjected, with some sweetness. You were worried, I know. Was the result considered successful? She motioned forward.

Did we do okay, Nassir?

One detonation is excellent. Two would have been perfect. You've been praised.

Nassir secured a promise from Norah that she would notify him as soon as Ibrahim had been put down. He had no questions about how or when she would do it. He didn't care to know. The method, time and place—it appeared—were hers to choose, as she'd hoped. After an exchange of goodbyes, the laptop clapped closed.

Father would know that Norah had been protecting at least one of her men from certain facts. She'd never disappointed him and hadn't ever, as far as he knew, misled him for anything but noble purposes. He kept track of disloyal acts, large and small, considered them the most accurate barometer of a person's reliability. Norah knew this. And he knew she knew.

* * *

For several hours, Norah and Ibrahim rode north in the minivan. Early March was cold enough to fog car windows at the edges, to leave forests barren. Outside, banks of snow got deeper the farther north they traveled.

Ibrahim had planned to spend the eight hours playing a character that was mostly himself, talking only of subjects on a list Norah had prepared. The list of subjects included the day's schedule for prayer and the belief that a new mission would serve God and would honor Omar's spirit. What comforts would he find in the new safe house? Those things, he could discuss. If he needed to pee, he could ask her to stop.

Assume Father is watching and listening, she whispered before they boarded the van. Keep it polite. Don't talk of personal things.

On the peak of the Delaware Memorial Bridge, where the mass of suspension cables made some people uncomfortable, she offered assurances about the new safe house. You'll like it, she said. Our drive time should be about six more hours. She sounded like a flight attendant, and by design.

Norah turned her head, looked over her right shoulder, preparing to change lanes, and with her right eye, gave Ibrahim a wink, out of view of the camera she knew was on the dashboard. Everything was going fine.

Before leaving on their journey, she told him they'd park and leave the minivan, would head into deep woods where a mobile phone would get no signal, where they could not be monitored. They'd hike and meet Jack and Annie, Norah's old friends from gun club. Ibrahim would ride with Jack and Annie to Maine. The older couple would take him in and take care of him, for as long as he wanted.

The minivan hit a bump on the highway. A duffel sat behind one of Norah's bench seats. It clanked and sloshed. What's that? he asked.

Things we might need, said Norah. She cleared her throat, low and slow, and gave Ibrahim an unaffectionate glance. He went back to discussing subjects on her list.

In Massachusetts, the late-morning sky looked like a filthy cotton blanket. Norah parked, hung the large duffel on a shoulder, slammed the sliding door. Ibrahim grabbed a rucksack containing the few things that were his and they set out. We hike to your new home, she said aloud, wanting to be heard. Ahead were forty minutes of uphill climbing on an icy path. Along the way, lungs filled with piney dampness, mouths spewed mist. It was the kind of cold that made your jaw hurt, made it hard to talk. They spooked herds of deer, some foxes and one unhealthy looking black bear.

As they hiked, Norah was stuck on festering difficulties: threats from Dirk and Red and Father and Zarkawi and the FBI and the Saudi King and probably the Russians, too. If the FBI recorded details about the abandoned vest, Father and Dirk would know she'd been disloyal and they'd be terrified of what she might do. They'd end her. The Russians would fear discovery of their back door into FBI computers. The Saudi King would fear exposure, the backlash if people found out his Security Directorate orchestrated terrorist attacks against America. The Americans—if they knew of her at all—would presume she'd intended to murder and to incite terror.

She might survive, get caught by the FBI. She was a Saudi, a royal, and if they thought her a terrorist? Prison for life since—for now— there was no federal death penalty. Butchy girl gangs would target her once they knew she could fight. After that, what? Poison food? Nerve agent smeared on handles? It would be impossible not to worry. She had to hope the FBI would keep the vest's contents a secret for a little longer.

She would get Ibrahim to safety. That she could accomplish and she could ponder it with little tension. Hidden away, he'd be fine. There'd be no clue to his location, his life. He'd thrive, make friends and find work.

At a clearing, she found Annie and Jack—and he'd already shot a deer. Group hug—even Ibrahim was invited. Norah introduced them. These are two of the best people you will ever know, Norah told Ibrahim. They will care for you.

Norah had Ibrahim lie on the ground and look dead, took pictures of him with half his face covered in a mixture of mud and deer blood and red goo made for decorating cakes, red smears all over him, squeezed out of a plastic tube from Betty Crocker.

She cleaned him up with the soap and water and washcloths she'd brought. She pulled shovels out of her duffel and together, Norah and Ibrahim dug a cone-shaped hole under a rocky outcropping, a place shielded from ice and snow. They put in the deer's body and backfilled it with dirt. She took a quart bottle of bleach and sprinkled it all around, neutralizing sweat and hair that might have fallen during the dig. If anybody comes looking, they'll think that's your grave, she said. She put real kisses on him, holding him by the back of the head with one hand, holding his ass with the other. Annie and Jack had to turn away.

I'll meet you in Maine, she said. I have things to do in Maryland. She raised a finger before he could ask her anything. It's better if you don't know what they are, she said. She pulled an envelope out of her duffel, gave it to Ibrahim and told him not to open it. There was a note inside, she said, and he couldn't read it unless something happened to her. She turned and began her hike back to the minivan.

Hey, said Ibrahim. Thanks.

She turned back. For what? she asked.

For not killing me and burying me in the woods.

She stared back, confused and a little irritated.

Relax, he said. It's a joke.

She bowed her head, gave Ibrahim a girly little smirk, turned away and kept walking. She couldn't help it. It was hard to recognize humor and to smile if you were chronically afraid of getting murdered.

* * *

Jack turned his Subaru off a paved two-lane and *whomped* over a Waldo County mogul, past grimy mounts of hard-frozen mush built by snowplows, downhill on a dirt road, through stands of white pine and juniper, the trees coated at their ankles with lichen that glowed green in frigid humidity. The tires squeaked on frozen powder and pop-crushed bits of ice. They negotiated a tunnel of trees through the forest, white birch looking skinny against billows of balsam and then to a wide-open acre of clean white where hulks of granite poked through snow cover. A covey of wild turkeys milled about near one end of the yard. When they saw Jack's car, they squawked and scattered.

Annie turned her chubby cheeks toward Ibrahim and was a little too earnest: Our house is cozy, she said. Wait till ya see.

The Subaru plowed through a noisy square of pea gravel, its headlights illuminating the seam between two structures sewn together into something massive. Jack stopped Ibrahim, cautioned him as he prepared to open his door. Watch your step, young man, he said. Some spots out there are slicker'n owl shit.

Car doors opened, bags were hefted and slung over shoulders.

Black smoke from a basement oil furnace slipped from a roof vent and disappeared into a wind cold enough to sting bare skin. Skylights on the peaked metal roof were lit from within, warm and yellow.

This is your house? This whole thing? Ibrahim's arms were spread wide as he took in the magnificence.

This side, Jack pointed left, is all barn. He pointed right. This side is where we live. Mainers like their houses joined with their barns. The barn is warm enough in winter that you can dress a deer or chop wood.

Ibrahim saw white speckles bouncing off the arms of his Gore-Tex parka, bought that afternoon in Freeport. He pointed his face into the biting wind and beamed with watering eyes. Norah told me snow in Maine was beautiful, he said.

Jack touched Ibrahim's forearm, held it close, then lifted his chin so he could study the white spots through bifocals. Sugar snow, he said. It comes in little balls, not flakes. Makes everything pretty. Never falls heavy. It's Annie's favorite. Mine too. I won't have to plow.

Is it always so lovely? asked Ibrahim.

Is it *always*? Annie grabbed all of him, sank the side of her face into his chest. Oh son, she said, you'll make a great Mainer.

Ibrahim looked a little uncomfortable and turned his eyes to Jack with a face full of questions.

She's a hugger, Jack said. Better get used to it.

Dinner was a perfect homemade seafood stew with Pillsbury biscuits popped out of a tube and served at a pine table scarred from serving the fifteen thousand meals it took for Jack and Annie to raise their two sons. On the wall adjacent, a rugged cross, four inches tall. The cross's members were shellacked and adorned with tiny Maryland flags. At the base the artist had left a wooden knob and into it was carved the Boy Scout motto: Be Prepared.

Ibrahim slurped from his spoon, steaming with bits of cod, clam, corn and tomato, all local. After two bites, he turned to Annie. The pistol on your belt, is it loaded? he asked.

She hurried a swallow so she could answer. Call her by her name, said Annie. Her name's Margie. What kind of doodle-head would carry an unloaded sidearm? Annie took in another hot spoonful. She patted the metal strapped to her hip. The bad guys are out there and right here is a good woman, she said. Margie and I mean to stop any one of them who comes near. Bring it.

Annie, said Jack, waving a fork. That's enough.

Ibrahim looked at Jack. Do you wear a pistol?

It's a sore subject, young man. I keep my weapons in a gun safe, and when I want to use one, I unlock the safe and take it out. Jack faced Annie and turned the sarcasm dial up to full. That keeps people from getting shot by accident, ain't that right?

Annie's voice lost all sweetness. One time. Just *one time*, it goes off by mistake, mister man. You won't ever let it go, will ya?

You don't forget the day a round zings your earlobe on the way past your head. Jack got up and pointed at a nearby wall. See that, Ibrahim? That hole? That's where her bullet went. I never painted over it. I want her to remember the night she almost killed me sitting at this table. He sat back down. Secure your damn firearms. Common sense. You're worried about outside the front door. He banged the table and made the soup bowls jump. What about right here?

Annie dropped her spoon and it clanked against the rim of her bowl. If somebody breaks in and your guns are locked up, you have no protection, she said. Ibrahim? You were a cop. You know. Tell him.

Ibrahim's eyes darted back and forth between his hosts. He was the picture of a social dilemma.

Jack, see? He knows. That proves I'm right. Why have a gun if you can't use it when you need it? If the criminals break in and your guns are locked up, the only thing you can do is hope your teeth don't chatter and give away where you're hiding.

Jack sat taller, energized by conflict. The dopey teenager who breaks in while you're fast asleep can't get it, he said. Neither can your grandchildren.

The robbers come with guns, said Annie. That's how they work, ya nincompoop.

Ibrahim interrupted. Annie, may I have some more stew? he asked. It's delicious.

Jack leaned forward and ignored his guest, his words coming out like automatic weapons fire. Not once in your seventy-four years have you needed a gun to defend yourself. Nobody's ever threatened you with a gun. But once, Annie, you almost shot your husband dead. Then there's the times I know of that you fired a round without meaning to. Once you nearly killed somebody at gun club, and two more times you were lucky nobody was near. Those are facts.

Wrong question, she declared, guarding herself with a stubby index finger. How many times have I kept away problems because people didn't want to confront somebody who was carrying? If you have a gun, you have peace. See, I never have problems. Never, ever, mister snowflake. She patted Margie, the firearm she wore at home. Prevention.

I never have problems either and I don't carry, said Jack.

Prevention, shouted Annie.

Just saying it don't make it so.

Prevention. Prevention. Prevention. Prevention.

Ibrahim interrupted the argument by flopping his palms on the tabletop. The noise startled his hosts and shut them up. The most dangerous thing, he said, is when somebody has a gun and they're angry or scared. The mood didn't change. Jack and Annie appeared to be at a standoff. Annie, you've had weapons training?

She broke the mean stare she was giving Jack. Only a numbskull would carry a gun without knowing how to use it—and safely, she said. When we were in Maryland, Norah and I trained and tested newbies at gun club in safe handling.

The police in Mecca taught us you can't get angry if you have a gun, said Ibrahim. If you do, put it away. You have to keep calm.

I just said, Annie insisted.

I heard what you said. Do you understand why your guest might be afraid of you? Maybe your husband, too?

A flat hand over her heart and a moment of humility. I would never intentionally hurt anybody, said Annie. I'm calm.

Ibrahim held up his bowl again. More stew? Please?

Annie got up and refilled his bowl, then sat back down. It's so nice to have a man as handsome as you in the house, she said. She scooted back from the table, slapped her thighs. Would you come sit on my lap so I can hug you? Would you? Please?

Jack flew off the handle. *Annie!* He shouted.

Jack, you're always so dang serious, said Annie. She scooted up to the table, grinned like a child with a secret, turned back to Ibrahim. You know, you can sit in my lap any time you want.

Jack glared.

Annie cut him off before he could scold her again. Don't be like that, you old dust bunny, she said. Why can't you just relax?

* * *

In her minivan, Norah streaked south on an interstate highway, headed for the Maryland home she shared with Dirk. She was nursing a blister from all the digging she'd done in Massachusetts and it hurt like hell. Right inside her left thumb on the fleshy fold. It hurt every time she opened her hand. By dark, when she stopped to pay the toll at Baltimore Harbor Tunnel, her thoughts were focused on the jobs she had to do. The blister was just a thing.

At the wheel, Norah talked aloud to herself so that anyone watching and listening via electronic surveillance would know she was hungry enough to get cranky, that she was getting mad at ordinary things—drivers who left their blinkers on, people with one headlight. South of Baltimore, she visited a Halal grocer, got herself a meal in a paper box, then drove to a place, hidden and dark, where she could eat and see the moon on the Chesapeake. It was a place she knew. Twenty feet away was a mailbox.

She savored two kinds of olives, the texture of a correctly done hummus, cold cubes of marinated lamb coated in unflavored yogurt. For the benefit of anyone watching on the dashboard camera, she made herself sound satisfied and bagged up her trash. She clutched between her legs with a contrived look of surprise, grabbed the roll of toilet paper stashed in her duffel, pulled it out slowly enough that it could be identified on the rough feed of a pinhead camera, and beat a hasty exit into the dark. On her way out of the minivan, she grabbed a paper sack stashed under the edge of her seat. Inside was a handful of pre-addressed and pre-stamped envelopes. Each envelope bore a different name and each one was empty. She held the packet by the edges, leaving no fingerprints. She slid the envelopes into the mailbox, so fast that it hardly seemed to happen. Then she pulled her pants all the way down to her ankles, squatted behind the box and peed. She bunched a clutch of toilet paper, cleaned herself. Anyone who saw her would believe her cover story: She'd been in urgent need of relief.

When she arrived home, she went straight for her bedroom. She laid down her mobile, emptied her pockets, and announced to Dirk:

Target extinguished. No worries. She told him Ibrahim was dead and buried. She'd taken pictures after she'd killed him. On the iPhone. Look, if you want. Fright touched her throat and her vocal cords tightened for the length of two syllables and she gave her sternum a feminine tap with a flat hand. Norah breezed past it, said she was exhausted and was getting into bed, needed some rest. Killing people will suck the life out of you, she said.

* * *

Absorbing tropic pastels cast by the sun before it rose on the desert horizon, Nassir lingered in his garden—an artificial oasis fed by great quantities of scarce drinking water—and stroked a blood lily along its stem. He inhaled an orchid, brought the scent into him, as deep as it would go, a scent that a French visitor had once compared to champagne at breakfast. He'd spoken many times to Norah about the value of capturing beauty and keeping it close. He told her about finding and keeping songbirds and flowers. A few moments with birdsongs and blood lilies could bring a peace that made everything seem simple, he said. Beauty can turn a labyrinth into a stepping-stone. That kind of peace can make a person float like a water bug, nearly weightless, and glide on still waters, he said. It's necessary to have peace when it's time to do the hardest things.

The mobile phone in the pocket of his robes vibrated. He closed his eyes, kept the white petals touching his cheek. He let the phone vibrate twice more before he answered. It was Victor, the Russian. It's fine, the agreement, all of it, Victor said.

Everything I wanted? asked Nassir.

More than you asked for, said Victor. Our defense minister will visit your King, as soon as you say. He will speak in public for Russian-Saudi unity. He will insult America. In private, he will offer to sell our Russian fighter jets, discounted. European newspapers will report the offer as if they've uncovered an important secret. American voices will repeat the news many times. Our friends in America, the sponsors of the loud and angry voices, will have the critics complain that Russians are stealing America's influence. When DAA offers to sell better jets to

Saudi Arabia at no profit, the voices will say DAA is an American hero. People will believe DAA sacrificed for America. When America goes shopping for security, yes, perhaps DAA gets the contracts.

Nassir closed his eyes, leaned into a jasmine flower, inhaled. That would be more than perfect, he said.

Victor licked a pair of lips so thin they barely showed. He will decide the time and place of your next mission. He will want an incident with mass fatalities at a location of his choosing. Maybe four weeks away? He'll tell you the day.

Nassir resisted. Victor, he said. July four is the date. I told you it was set.

You do it on the day the President says, said Victor. Otherwise is unhealthy.

Nassir protested. This is unreasonable, he said.

Victor was unmoved. The ones who refuse my boss never live very long, he said. I told this to you before. If you give him an offer, you cannot refuse the part he accepts. If he ever wants you killed, I'm probably the one. I pull your trigger.

He'd never kill me, said Nassir. He counts too heavily on the intel I give you. And I am not his tool, said Nassir. My mission is my mission. He'll understand. He won't fight because he knows he can't win.

THIRTEEN

The twenty-two men and women were curious as hell. Each one was an employee in DAA's office in Fairfax, Virginia, and each was deep in conversation. An executive-level mandatory meeting without notice? Why the secrecy? The talk turned to less urgent subjects—tolerance testing, contract deliverables, subtleties of DAA's travel reimbursement policies. The patter would've been indecipherable to an outsider.

The hubbub quit when FBI Division Director Louis Irons, accompanied by Eve Coman, entered the conference room and put up a hand the gentlemanly way: elbow at ninety degrees, two fingers raised. All voices stopped, as if the lights had gone out.

Word of Louis usually arrived before he did. He was the warrior who'd gained from his battles. As a Marine Second Lieutenant in Vietnam, he'd discovered an efficient way to empty the underground tunnels that sheltered so many of the North Vietnamese. And he'd done it simply, with gasoline and matchbooks. If you are required to kill someone, he'd say, you have to do it right.

His career had been built on a persistent sense of calm that he seemed able to share—that and a gift for finding elegant resolutions for jagged dilemmas. In his early days as an FBI field agent, he'd profiled and identified an elusive serial killer, a man obsessed with Holden Caulfield, and divined the criminal's identity. Lou went to the man's apartment and spoke of adolescent things the killer understood. He spoke of an overwhelming urge to protect children. The serial killer gave himself up, saying he wanted to save his daughters the embarrassment of a public trial.

With quiet established in DAA's conference room, Louis lowered his hand, let it settle in his pants pocket. Anyone forget to leave their phone behind? he asked, looking around at the windowless space and his audience of DAA engineers and executives. It happens, he said. He queried people sitting at the long conference table. You? You? Heads shook.

He'd made contact with the faces in the room; it seemed understood, he'd taken control. He gestured with his readers. Even if CNN reports all of what I'm about to tell you, don't assume it's been declassified, he said.

Preston X. Douglas Jr., senior among all the DAA executives at the table, stood. Then Preston X. Douglas Jr. spoke of the company's respect for the needs of the federal government. He did not need to mention that the same government bought DAA's most expensive and most capable technologies and fed the company two-thirds of its income. He said DAA expected its employees to cooperate. Cooperation with the FBI was good for everybody involved, he insisted.

At a corner of the table, Dirk raised his eyebrows while looking at Red. Why had the FBI come to DAA? Red shook his head, enough to say that he didn't know either. This is a little close to home, Red whispered.

Let's begin, said Louis. Eve Coman touched a button on a projector that cast a picture on the wall: a business-sized envelope with a first-class stamp, a US Postal Service cancellation imprint, a name, and the address of the Saudi Arabian embassy in downtown Washington. On his pad of paper, Dirk drew a tiny exclamation point.

Red hushed him. Not now, he said.

The name of the addressee belonged to a former DAA computer engineer. The man had found some things. He'd tried and failed to blackmail Dirk. Dirk had talked to Red and Nassir about the man and he disappeared the same day. No body was found. No signs of foul play observed.

Lou touched his glasses against the wall, on the edge of the image of the envelope. Twenty envelopes just like this lit up the postal processing detectors at Brentwood Road, he said. The outside surface of each contains traces of TATP. Your TATP. We had hazmat crews and bomb squads at Brentwood for hours. There was no danger, but you couldn't have known without investigating. We collected twenty envelopes, each one with trace amounts of explosive TATP rubbed onto the outside.

Red leaned toward Dirk's ear and whispered: What the fuck have you got us into?

Lou continued: Ten envelopes were addressed to persons who have worked at DAA's Washington office. The other ten were addressed to the Saudi embassy, downtown. Each one empty. The sender knew TATP would set off alarms. Who? And why? Is a terrorist attack coming? Does someone have a grudge? Is this a scare? We could be looking at imminent mass murder or an asinine prank. Is there a connection with Farragut North? Today and tomorrow, we'll be interviewing each of you. Eve passed out sheets of paper. This is the schedule of interviews, he said. Note the time for yours and don't be late.

Louis motioned to Eve. Next, please. On the wall, the image of another envelope, this one addressed to a man named Bandar Zarkawi. Zarkawi was the one who kidnapped and murdered the missing computer engineer. He'd buried the remains in a forest in West Virginia. He regularly ended the lives of threatening people.

All the envelopes addressed to DAA listed the Saudi embassy for the return address, said Lou. All envelopes addressed to the Saudi embassy have DAA's Washington office as the return address. No fingerprints. None of the flaps and none of the stamps had been licked, so no DNA. The printing was from a plain-jane Hewlett-Packard. The envelopes are Office Depot store brand. We've examined these for stains, for imprints, for crimping. We've tested for spores and particles from a particular microenvironment and for sneeze spray. We've swabbed for biologicals and reactives. Teams have examined each envelope to see if the previous analysis missed anything. He was stock-still except for the readers he tapped against one palm. Louis shifted his posture, began looking down at his hands, seeming humble. Then he picked up his chin and started checking the faces around the room. Each of you we called here knows something about these names and addresses. That's only part of what we know about each of you.

Louis tapped at the wall and up came the image of a different envelope, addressed to a man whose office had shared a wall with Dirk's. Dirk had complained to Red that the man was a snoop. Dirk wanted to end him. Red said no. Dirk ended him anyway.

Some of the names on these envelopes are people the FBI has been monitoring, said Lou. One is on a terrorist watch list and got expelled from the country. All of them have security clearances in their home countries. Whoever sent these envelopes has knowledge and resources available to very few. They may have had time inside FBI, Saudi Arabia or maybe here.

Up flashed an envelope showing the name Susan A. Smith, who'd been secretary to several company executives, including Red. Susan and Red had slept together when they were married to other people. Red gave her herpes and she left the company soon after.

The next envelope: a former DAA clerk who'd seen things, a man who quit after a month. Then another name, operations manager at the Saudi embassy who was married to Nassir's half-sister, a man who'd worked under all of the last ten Saudi ambassadors.

Maybe it's a disgruntled employee, a former employee or an employee's ex-spouse, said Lou. Maybe it's a guy who wanted to work here and got denied. We have personnel over at the Saudi embassy conducting interviews right now. We're talking to everybody from the ambassador to the receptionist. At US consulates inside Saudi Arabia, we have investigators working.

Louis pointed at the door, locked and sealed, guarded from the outside. Our investigative work will be done away from other Bureau personnel, he said—away from Bureau computers to minimize the risk of exposure.

Is someone trying to intimidate us? asked one man. Everybody knows we sell to the Saudis.

Louis held up a hand, stopped the man. We'll talk individually, he said. Let's not give rumors a chance to start. Please don't talk about this until your interview.

The DAA lunchroom had happy yellow cabinets and vinyl flooring decorated with space-age rocket shapes in Crayola colors. Somebody had made cinnamon toast and the smell was heavenly. Red didn't give a flying fuck. He laid a palm on the Keurig as it grumbled and spewed oily black into his mug. He reached, sipped, swallowed, his eyes not focused on anything. Every living name on those envelopes could do us up the ass, he said.

Dirk was breathing like he'd been moving furniture. I could throw up right now if I wanted to, he said.

You're the only one I can think of who knows what those names mean, said Red. You talked to somebody.

This is not on me, Red. Don't even say that.

This is on you no matter what. You need to fix this, big man.

Help me figure this out. Somebody is screwing with us. Boss, think. One of your ex-wives? One of their friends?

Red refused the idea. Neither of my ex-wives knows squat outside of spa lunches and tennis, he said.

I saw Rita in divorce court, said Dirk. She knows things—and she despises you.

Red drew closer to Dirk, close enough to choke him. Do I tell the FBI what I know about these names? I have stories for every one. Or do I deny and get caught lying? Damn Zarkawi. The FBI's at the embassy now and I'm sure they want to question him. What'll he say?

Dirk wrapped his arms around his own middle and folded in half, until his face was almost to his knees. Red, dial it back, he said. I can't think.

Red didn't dial it back. Who did you tell that I slept with Susan? he demanded. She knows all about Nassir and can identify him.

Christ, calm down, said Dirk. Susan teaches high school math in New Zealand. *Smith*. She's a Smith. Half of the country is named Smith. He steadied himself against the counter.

Red went hot and red. Please tell me you have an answer, he said. Then the sound of shock: This is Norah, he accused.

Dirk leaned over the sink. No way, he said. Norah's locked tight.

What do we say about Zarkawi? asked Red. Can you keep a straight face and tell them you had no idea he was whacking people that you knew?

Dirk turned on the tap and let the water rush. He took a handful and splashed it across his face.

Turning on the water? You think there's surveillance at DAA? Really? Are you thick?

Dirk puked up a cupful of something.

Red asked him if he still had the bags of cash, and Dirk tilted and said of course he had the cash.

Time to bail out of this airplane, said Red. You've got our parachute.

Dirk sucked water out of his hand, swished and spit. I'm going home, he said.

* * *

Here's a clean white apron, said Jack. If it gets soiled, replace it. People won't buy wine from someone dirty.

The basement stock room for Camden Wine & Cheese was tidy and bright. Boxes of wine stacked by type. The smooth concrete floor looked nearly new. The ground-rock that made up the basement walls of the antique building had been painted matte gray. Ibrahim put a loop of fabric around his neck and spread the bleached cotton across his middle. He pulled the apron strings around front and tied.

Jack motioned for Ibrahim to follow him upstairs, to the display floor.

Ibrahim put up his hands. Jack, I'm in hiding, he said.

Dirk Johnson ain't within seven hundred miles of here, son. He'd never come to a place this cold. The only people on the coast of Maine in winter are Mainers.

Ibrahim followed Jack up the stairs and scanned the sales floor. Picture windows framed by Victorian beadboard gave a view to the street. Pegboard dividers held up utilitarian displays filled with wine bottles lined up like soldiers. Florescent tube lights hung close to the ceiling. A National Cash Register, an antique metal hulk as big as a tombstone with rows of red and white buttons, stood guard on an iron counter.

Jack flipped the sign, announced the shop was open and unlocked the door. He gave Ibrahim two lists of wines. The first list is bottles that have been sitting too long. You take them off these shelves, box 'em up and put 'em downstairs, he said. The second is bottles you bring up and put out for sale.

This is wine, said Ibrahim. All of it.

Jack said nothing.

Jack? said Ibrahim.

What?

I am Muslim.

Nobody's asking you to drink it, son. This is not lightning, it's a lightning bug. There's a difference.

Ibrahim would not handle bottles of wine. He wouldn't budge. So Jack bent a finger and led Ibrahim to an unheated back room, filled to the ceiling with empty boxes. He unlocked and rolled open an overhead door that revealed a back alley filled with greasy dumpsters and mounds of ice stained with unidentified substances of a disgusting nature. All this cardboard needs to be broken down and stuffed into recycling, said Jack. You're just the man for the job. There was wine in these boxes when they got here, but not now. That won't be a problem, will it?

No, said Ibrahim. Of course, I don't have a problem with that.

Jack kept on. If you get tired of working out here in the alley where it's dirty and cold, come see me. I got some clean boxes of wine that need to be moved from one warm room to another. Jack turned to leave and turned right back around. With the men in Bible study, I read the Quran all the way through, he said. The Quran disapproves of drinking alcohol. It doesn't say doodley-squat about moving bottles around.

It's not just religion, it's culture, said Ibrahim. We don't want to encourage alcohol. It's disapproved.

Do you disapprove of me for selling it? asked Jack.

No, said Ibrahim. The only person I ever disapprove of is myself.

* * *

Androscoggin Guns and Ammo of Aroostook, Maine, was typically empty on Tuesdays, or nearly so. On Tuesdays, the cost for time on the firing range was cheaper than dirt. On the Tuesday that Annie took Ibrahim to Androscoggin's range, Rocky French stood alone on the firing line. He pumped steady and fast, round after round, into a pockmarked, full-length poster of a hated female. He reached the end of another clip and kicked away spent brass. He slid an empty magazine from the handle of his American-made Smith & Wesson, shoved home a loaded replacement and fired some more.

When Annie and Ibrahim passed his station, Rocky reflexively flicked on his safety and set aside his weapon. He pulled spongy orange stoppers out of his ears and let them hang on a string that ran around the back of his neck. The metal building, as big as a bowling alley, filled with the hum of fluorescents. Annie, why don't you shoot with the ladies' club? Isn't that what ladies do?

I shouldn't be on the line right now because I'm a woman? asked Annie. Really? A smart guy like you couldn't think of a reason to swallow that thought? Annie squared up, ready to make something of it.

Rocky put his hands up and bought space. I'm saying what everybody thinks, he said.

Everybody? Rocky, it's only you that's here. She pointed at his target—a famous woman's picture with bullet holes all through it. I believe your mama raised you poorly, she said. That's the only way to explain a numbskull comment like yours.

Mama taught me to respect women, except not the ones who think they're better'n me. He pointed at the pockmarked poster of the ambitious wife of a former American president. Especially not the screamers and bitches who want my guns, he said.

Next time you see a dictionary, look up misogyny. Want me to spell it for you?

Damn it, Annie. I'm a man. All's I want is to live like one.

Annie lowered her chin. You're a little over the top today, she said. They got a Tampax machine in the bathroom. Give me a quarter and I'll run get you some.

He grimaced and grinned at the same time. You kill me, he said. He let go a laugh.

Annie wasn't kidding around. She pegged him in the chest with an index finger. Looky here, mister man, if you talk to women that way, you're mud wrestling with somebody who wants to strangle you by the jellybeans. That's a poor strategy for a man who complains about being lonely.

Rocky shrank. He lost a struggle for words.

Annie turned motherly, put a hand on his shoulder. Be nice to people, Rocky, she said. Women, men, everybody. The same way you expect people to be nice to you.

She turned to leave. You're not one of those causing the problems, he said.

Keep trying Rocky, she said. You have a long way to go. And stop leading with your chin, Popeye. Come for dinner. I'll make tuna noodle. Call me.

Rocky reinserted the stoppers in his ears and took dead aim. If he was surprised that Annie hadn't introduced her companion, he didn't look it.

Ibrahim obliterated the centers of over a dozen paper targets, back and forth, at distances of fifty yards, twenty-five yards and seventy-five yards. Annie approached him from behind and tapped the hard shell of his hearing protection. Startled, he pulled off his headgear.

Time's up, champ, she said. She put a gun case in front of him, flipped it open.

Ibrahim pulled and parked his bolt, ejecting a casing and exposing the chamber. He turned the grip toward Annie, barrel pointed away from anybody's feet or legs and offered it. Your friend Rocky—I don't understand, he said.

Understand what? Annie smiled. That I'm huggy with a gook like him?

Aren't you afraid of him? asked Ibrahim. He sounds angry enough to be violent.

I know his mother, she said. He's never had sweetness in his life.

I think he's violent. You should stay away.

He's one of them deplorables, said Annie. She wagged a finger. You have to always be nice. Every person you'll ever know has a life story that'll break your little heart.

Annie, how——?

Everybody except for Dirk Johnson. That man is a bag of moist turds.

How can you not be afraid of that guy?

People get screwy if they're angry, said Annie. Usually, that's the people God gives us. If we care about ourselves, we have to care about them.

Ibrahim looked confused.

Jesus says that, said Annie. Your Muslim God—him too, I bet.

Ibrahim waited until Annie had inserted her guns into their receptacles inside the gun case and then he closed the lid and locked it. I rarely see such caring in people, he said.

Annie grabbed his head like it was a melon and kissed the side of his face. You are one of the good guys, she said. Let's go home. I'll make us lunch. I'll heat up those homemade beans you like. And grilled cheese?

FOURTEEN

In his own guest room, in his own dark house, the alarm clock rang at three o'clock in the morning. Dirk sprang up, alone and frantic. There was a sore spot inside of his lip where he'd been chewing.

He lifted night-vision binoculars and, through the bedroom window, scanned his tennis courts, his backyard, his boathouse, the water, houses across Broad Creek. Sailboats bobbed on moorings in the dark. Everything looked ordinary, safe. It didn't matter; he breathed like he'd been sprinting.

On the floor below, in his windowless pantry, he pressed on a piece of wall. It clicked open and revealed a steel safe. He dialed, opened, put on gloves, pulled out two pistols and keys to a boat, put in his mobile phone, closed the safe and the panel. At the sink, he wiped down both guns with a wet paper towel, removing fingerprints and whatever miscellaneous fibers might have accumulated.

Outdoors was cold as death, windy enough to make his eyes water while he hunkered deep in his full-length coat. From his garden shed, he took a collapsible ladder and a drawstring sack. From a small patch of woods, he palmed a ten-pound rock, bigger than a softball, and shoved it in the sack.

A motorized pulley system in his boathouse lowered a twin-engine Boston Whaler into the water. Dirk and his dual outboards puttered slow and silent as they eased along Broad Creek. Out on the South River, he opened it up a little. On the broad waters of Chesapeake Bay, he gunned it, screaming across swells and landing with thuds. Bursts of a dank salt spray hit him in the teeth and made him hock and spit. Wind swirled, left him unable to hear anything else, so he watched over

184

his shoulders, above, ahead. He kept inside the squared-off windscreen, hid himself from the howl as best he could. He glided slow over shoals at the far west end of the Bay Bridge. At the ends of the bridge, passages were narrow, but there were no infrareds or transponders. Then he screamed across open water all the way to Gibson Island, where there was a three-story Tudor with English gardens next to a pier and where a man was inside, sleeping alone.

Four hundred yards offshore, Dirk killed his motor and scanned waters in all directions with binoculars. He looked to the sky for drones and found only stars. His destination was dark, motionless, and remained so when he tied up his boat two houses away.

With the collapsible ladder strung onto his back, he hopped fences and hid himself next to the house that was his target. Beneath a balcony, he set his ladder and climbed. With the blade of a pocket-knife, he released the thumb latch that held the balcony door. At the threshold, he waited and listened, then listened more. He stepped through and touched the door closed. He kneeled and panted like a frightened animal.

He crossed the quiet of wool carpet, passed a staircase, avoided contact with a tiny table that bore knick-knacks. He kneeled again and listened. The sounds of snorting and snoring came from down the hall. He peeked around a corner and crept, like a nun, past an enormous mahogany armoire. He put his gloved fingertips on the half-open bedroom door, tested it, and it opened without a creak; the snoring continued, the rhythm, the depth, the timbre unchanged.

At the man's bedside, Dirk reached across, Glock in his hand. As smooth and sudden as the fall of a judge's gavel, he placed the barrel in the man's mouth and used the man's thumb to pull the trigger. Dirk squinted, wasn't blinded by the flash of the explosion. The bang was as big as a bomb and made his ears hurt.

Brain matter and fluids spattered across half of the fabric-covered headboard. Bone fragments and blood combined into a chowder that saturated pillows. There were little white floaters, feathers from a pillow that had exploded.

The deceased hadn't said a word. He looked to have had no notice of his end and no fright. A bullet to the brain stem was quick and, by reputation, painless. For two centuries, that had been the traditional method of slaughter among cattle farmers in certain parts of Dirk's native Oklahoma.

Dirk left the gun in the man's left hand, his dominant hand, the front end of the barrel resting on his bottom teeth. One of the dead man's eyes hung open, revealing a vitreous orb, useless, unfocused, his bottom jaw hanging like a drawer someone had yanked open and left loose.

Dirk stood, stared, and sighed—exhausted, like he'd spent everything. The dead man couldn't ever manipulate Dirk. He couldn't ever stand in Dirk's way. He couldn't sacrifice Dirk to save his ass. He was all the way dead.

Back at his boat, Dirk unmoored and powered away from the murder scene, toward the center of the Chesapeake, toward deep waters, past the bridges, past Annapolis, back to the South River and Broad Creek. At the mouth of the creek, he stripped naked and shoved his clothes— underpants, everything—into the cloth sack with the ten-pound rock inside and let it slip underwater. Teeth chattering, he motored to the cove that was home to his boathouse. He set his motors at idle speed, kept the transmission engaged, inched the boat inside and closed the sliding door. He hosed down the interior of his skiff and bailed in some brackish water to dilute any fluids left behind. He raised the boat in its sling where it could dry, free of inconvenient fibers and fluids. In the boathouse apartment, he took a warm shower, washed away remnants of murder, clothed himself in jeans, a flannel jersey and a parka. He cantered across the hundred yards of cold and dark between his boathouse and his back door. Inside, he put on pajama pants and a T-shirt and crawled into the bed warmed by his sleeping wife. He woke her and she asked where he'd been and he told her the truth about the murder and told her she damn well better be his alibi if he needed one. He'd been home, in bed, all night. Dirk fell into a deep sleep, freed of certain worries.

The man who could easily be blamed for so many things was dead, seemingly by his own hand. Red Merrill would tell no tales.

Dirk's snoring woke Norah before the sun. She tried to sleep again and couldn't. Sitting on the toilet, she dared to tap a message onto her burner phone: *Husband is irrational. He ended his boss at the big company. This will lead back to the King. He should know. I still love you too.* She typed in an e-mail address for Abdullah and sent it.

She powered down the phone and, on the bathroom floor, she prayed until her heart stopped pounding. She didn't care if she wasn't facing Mecca. She guessed she had twelve hours to gather her things and fly.

* * *

In Camden, Maine, a young man, average height and weight, shoved into Jack's wine shop and pushed the door closed behind him, sealing out the frigid air. Outside, it was cold enough to make your lungs hurt. His naked hands were a hurtful shade of pink, his nose ran clear and he kept wiping it on the sleeve of his UMaine hoodie. His duck boots left a trail of crusted salt as he walked the store. He took a long while looking around, sometimes holding his hands under his armpits where they might get warmer. He didn't look like a wine buyer; he might have come in only because he needed to get warm, which was fine. It happened all the time.

After several minutes, he put his fist around the neck of a five-dollar bottle of Barefoot Moscato, an appropriate choice for a young man who couldn't afford a coat. He approached the sales counter, reached into his waistband and slid out a Colt Python .357 Magnum and its eight inches of hollow steel. The Python was a handheld cannon. It had earned its name because its barrel resembled a thick-bodied serpent.

With minor difficulty, the young man cocked the hammer, reached across the counter and pointed his gun at Ibrahim's face. Give me all your fuckin' money, he said.

The shop door opened and in walked a man off the street, an elderly fellow with a cane and a belly. He began surveying fine wines on the wall, looked unaware.

Jack stood twelve feet away from Ibrahim and the enormous National Cash Register. Do it, whispered Jack. Don't get shot. Do it and get him out of here.

Ibrahim examined the weapon, then considered the young man's face. He touched the end of the barrel with a fingertip, brought it up, pointed it at his right eye. The robber yanked back, waved the weapon at him again. Give me money or you die, he ordered.

From behind the robber's shoulder came the end of an oaken cane, flung from above, toward the hand that was holding the gun. Ibrahim took advantage of the moment. Just before the cane cracked against the young man's wrist, he grabbed the Python by the barrel and twisted. He stole it away, easily, and flipped it under the counter where it would not cause harm.

The pain and the excitement made the would-be robber drop his bottle of wine. It shattered and let loose a fruity flood. He grabbed for his injured wrist and screamed from the pain.

Ibrahim waved off the old man. Keep your cane to yourself, he said. He turned to the young man. You're an awful criminal, he said. With such a revolver, it's obvious if you don't have ammunition. I can see light through the barrel. Also, the inserts in your revolving cylinder are empty. And an eight-inch barrel at close range? Even half of that is too much.

The robber's face twisted, revealing a spot on his bottom jaw where two teeth were missing.

I was a policeman once, said Ibrahim. He pointed at the shelf in front of his knees, below the counter, where he'd thrown the Python. That gun would ruin your life if I let you keep it.

The robber stood still, tensed. He looked like he expected to be electrocuted.

Ibrahim banged the heel of his hand on the red CASH button and his register drawer dinged open. Are you even old enough to buy alcohol? he asked. He pulled out a pack of bank-fresh ten-dollar bills, counted out five onto the counter and slid them toward the man. You look hungry. Take this. He returned the rest of the bills to the drawer and shoved it closed. I'll wipe the fingerprints off your weapon before the police get here.

You want to give him money? You want to help him so he doesn't get caught? Jack pointed at the robber.

This man is no threat to anyone except himself, said Ibrahim. He faced the gunman. The longer you stand here, the more complicated your life gets. He waved toward the door.

That's my money! Jack approached, looked ready to take charge.

Ibrahim stiff-armed him. I have money, Jack, he said. I'll pay you.

You take every damn cake I ever saw, son, said Jack. That wicked boy should be chained up and whipped.

Ibrahim spoke to the gunman: Will you run away? Go. Ibrahim reached under the counter and pulled out a loaded Sig Sauer, displayed it, then slid it back, out of sight. You should know that I could have shot you, he said. It was my legal right.

The young man shoved the cash deep in his pocket. The cowbell rang hard when he yanked the door open and it rang again when the door closed behind him.

CAMDEN, Maine (AP) — A cool-as-a-cucumber wine store clerk stole a gun from an armed robber and gave money to the robber because the man looked hungry.

Knox County police report that Ibrahim Mohammed of Waldo County recognized that the robber's gun had no bullets. The clerk gave the would-be robber $50 and wished him well. The robber fled and has not been apprehended.

"What kind of idiot would give money to a robber who forgot his bullets?" said the owner of a nearby store, who spoke on condition of anonymity. "Who does that?"

Knox County Police Captain Lori Maclean says people should assume that anyone who is armed is also dangerous. "If somebody is pointing a gun at you, it's usually best to do as he says," said Captain Maclean. "If you try to be a hero, you'll probably be dead."

Police are investigating and are asking citizens with information to come forward. The robber is described as a male, approximately 20 years of age with brown hair and medium build. In Maine, armed robbery is a Class A felony, punishable by up to 30 years in prison and a fine of $50,000.

* * *

Hosni Madbouli was cultural attaché at the Saudi Consulate in Boston; it was his job to closely follow regional news in New England that would be of interest in Saudi Arabia. It was an easy job and he was good at it, partly because he was terrified of what would happen if he made mistakes.

Hosni's wife was one of the Saudi King's favored granddaughters. The old man had ninety-one grandkids and sixty great-grandkids and most got none of his attention. Hosni's wife, Sadia was her name, was one of the few people in the world who could have the King's attention any time she wanted. The King had taken measures to ensure that the world would always be kind to such a lovely young woman.

Somebody on Hosni's staff spotted a particular news story and told Hosni he should look at it. The story made the bottom half of the front page of The Portland Press-Herald.

Hosni wrote an e-mail to his wife's cousin, a staff supervisor within the Security Directorate in Mecca. His e-mail included a link to the article. The article included a photograph. The photograph showed a brown man at the front door of a Camden, Maine, wine store as he was leaving work. The name of the store and its street number were printed on the door. In the photo, the man looked shocked, like the camera had surprised him. The caption said his name was Ibrahim Mohammed.

A day later, the photograph landed on the desk of Nassir Saud's chief of staff with a note: *Are you interested in a story about a Muslim man selling alcohol?*

* * *

Dirk Johnson sat down at a DAA conference table with Eve Coman, expecting questions. Like virtually every other DAA conference room, this one had fake ficus trees and no windows. Dirk was on his third cup of coffee.

Mortar fire, incoming immediately. Have you heard from Red Merrill today? she asked. Eve Coman stared at the centers of Dirk's eyes and didn't let up. Dirk had to look away.

In a separate room, Louis Irons and two FBI newbies watched the conversation on a flat screen. You're recording, Reynolds? Lou asked.

Affirmative, said the young man.

Yesterday, when we left work, said Dirk. Not since then. He shifted, started again. No, nothing today.

Eve didn't respond, stayed quiet and stared.

After an uncomfortable interval, Dirk spoke again: I told you, nothing today. Nothing since yesterday afternoon. Nothing.

He's going to make this easy, said Louis.

We can't reach Mr. Merrill, said Eve. Do you know where he is?

Dirk shrugged, shook his head, didn't speak.

Do you know how we can reach him? she asked.

Dirk drew in deeply and pulled his hands from the tabletop. What's this about? he asked.

Eve repeated her question: Is there some way you know of that we can reach him?

Dirk responded slowly and sarcastically, his voice rising: Like, call him on his mobile?

Wouldn't you have guessed that we'd already tried that? asked Eve. We have people at his house this morning, looking for clues. They're crawling all over the place. She watched his face. Please listen carefully to the question. Do you know how we can reach Red Merrill?

Dirk shrugged. Under the table, he jiggled a leg.

Eve wrote something on her legal pad. Mr. Johnson, I'm writing down here that from the start of my questions, you appear fearful and evasive. She took her attention away from her legal pad and back to Dirk. So, fine. Different topic. Susan Smith. What can you tell me?

What do you want to know? said Dirk.

Everything you do, said Norah.

A woman by that name used to work here and I hardly knew her, Dirk said. People said she was super nice. I always thought so.

Where is she?

Dirk shook his head. Susan's been gone for several years, he said.

I didn't ask how long since she left, said Eve. I asked where she is.

How should I know?

She repeated her question: Do you know where she is? I'm looking for a yes or a no. Yes, you know, or no, you don't know.

So, you don't know where she is, said Dirk. Same as you don't know where Mr. Merrill is.

Eve went back to her legal pad and took notes. I'm writing here that on my second question I encountered more evasion, she said. I'm still looking for signs that you are being cooperative.

Dirk began to complain, then cut himself off.

Had you heard that she was teaching school? asked Eve.

Wait, what? Who are we talking about now? You're trying to confuse me.

Had you heard that Susan Smith was teaching school?

Dirk shook his head again. She'd be a good teacher, he said.

Had you heard she was teaching school? asked Eve. Has anybody ever told you that? Have you ever read it or learned that somewhere? Yes or no.

Dirk folded his arms, shrugged again.

Eve let the tip of her pencil hover above her pad. Are you telling me that no, you hadn't heard that?

Dirk shook his head, again. She's teaching school, he said. I get it.

Eve tightened the grip on her pencil and scratched on her yellow pad. Clear evasion, three occasions, she said. She sounded nearly angry. Mr. Johnson, did you have a housekeeper named Florence White? she asked.

He nodded. Yes. Florence still keeps house for us sometimes. I hired her through a service. I pay her taxes in full, in case you're wondering.

Wasn't Florence White also a housekeeper for Susan Smith? asked Eve.

Dirk shrugged again and didn't say a word.

Didn't Florence White tell you that Susan Smith had left the country and was teaching school somewhere else?

Maybe, he said. I'm not sure if I remember.

Haven't you asked Florence to get messages to Susan because they're still in touch?

I doubt it, said Dirk. I think I'd remember that.

Didn't Florence tell you that Susan was teaching school in New Zealand? asked Eve.

I'd probably remember that, if she did, he said. I don't really hardly know Florence, though.

Eve's pencil dug into the paper. More evasion, she said. Her lips went rigid and her hands turned into fists, one with a pencil poking out of it. Mr. Preston Douglas, president of your company, stood up at our meeting yesterday and told you to cooperate with law enforcement, she said. I'll be sure to tell Mr. Douglas how much of our time you wasted.

Louis sat up and talked to the flat screen, as if he could be heard: Don't get mad at your witness, Coman. Stick with what's relevant.

She put her legal pad between them, at the center of the table, let Dirk see that she'd been writing. I'm taking these notes, Mr. Johnson. People will use these notes to make important decisions. They'll use your comments to decide if you should be a suspect in any crimes. Can I write down that you did not know that Susan Smith was teaching school? Is that right? You did not know?

Dirk held open his hands. I just answered that, he said.

Eve made some notes. Why are you so uncomfortable with the question? she asked.

Dirk looked like he'd been poked with something sharp. I have no idea what you're talking about, he said. Absolutely no idea.

Some people lack the intelligence to understand when a person is looking for a simple yes or no. Are you one of those people?

Louis beamed. Coman, you're a sly one, he said.

Don't insult me, he barked. I'm not stupid.

You understand the difference between yes and no? she asked. Do you have that much intelligence?

Next question, please. He banged the table with a closed hand and his coffee splashed.

She asked him about Bandar Zarkawi and Nassir Saud, about Victor Ivanov, about embassy parties, about visits to Saudi Arabia, invitations to royal residences, about Norah and her loyalty.

He squirmed and his face said he was bothered, but he stuck to his script. He knew everything he would have to admit to and not one thing more. He frequently said he was confused. DAA sold weapons and weapons systems to the Saudis, he said. Of course, he knew Mr. Zarkawi and Mr. Saud. DAA marketed to people who might affect purchase decisions or who offered access to decision makers. He'd never heard of anybody named Ivanov, except maybe on television. He respected Nassir. Nassir's a good man, devoted to family. The Saudi royal family runs the country. Of course, people in palaces are involved in national defense. And DAA is a profitable company. It makes money and so does he.

Eve dropped her pen, looked up from her pad. When's the last time you saw Mr. Merrill?

I told you. Yesterday.

When's the last time you saw Mr. Merrill? she repeated, louder.

What is this? he asked.

How long since you've been to his house?

He pushed his chair away from the table and went for the door. I don't like your tone, he said. I'm not answering any more questions without my attorney.

Were you at Red Merrill's house last night?

I said I want an attorney. Don't you have to stop your questions when I say that?

Go get your lawyer, said Eve. I'll put in my notes here that Mr. Dirk Johnson turned defensive when confronted with questions about being at the Merrill residence yesterday. She scratched her pencil on the paper. So, what were you doing at Mr. Merrill's house the last time you went?

Dirk let his head bounce. Seriously?

How long has it been? she asked. Less than a month? A week?

Dirk hesitated on his way out of the room, looking tempted to defend himself.

Suppose a video system placed you next door to Red Merrill's house last night, she asked. Just suppose. What would you say to that?

I was home. I was in bed. You can ask my wife.

What will your wife tell me if I ask her where you were last night? she asked. What exactly?

I was at home, said Dirk.

Is that what you told her to say?

Dirk's neck seized and it made his head shake.

Do you feel all right, Mr. Johnson?

He opened the door, headed out.

Subject refused to answer questions about his whereabouts last night, said Eve, loudly, taking notes.

He took a half step back into the room. I was home, he declared. In bed. My wife will tell you. Call her. Ask her. I know exactly what she'll say.

Norah sat at a table at the Jasa Kebab restaurant in downtown Baltimore, forty miles from home, listening on white earbuds as Eve badgered her husband. Norah was linked into the iPhone in Dirk's pocket and she'd heard all of Eve Coman's questions and all of Dirk's answers. An hour before, she'd shoved clothes and shoes into suitcases, picked up two clean Glocks, boxes of ammunition, plucked her driver's license from her wallet, but left the rest of the wallet and her purse where she usually did—in a vestibule by the garage. Inside her purse was the iPhone that Father and Dirk knew about. She'd slid into her pocket one they didn't. She'd put the keys to the minivan on a hook in the kitchen, same as always, and left a Post-it note that Dirk would find on the refrigerator door when he came home from work: *Uncle Faisal and Aunt Rashida picked me up for dinner. Be home late.*

She set a timer to turn off the home surveillance system and turn it back on after a delay of eight minutes, and she dashed out the door of her garage, dragging a suitcase and a duffel. She punched the code into the gate at the bottom of the driveway, slid past when it opened, watched to make sure it closed.

Three hundred yards downhill and around a bend in the road—at a curb, in front of a stand of forest—Norah unlocked a used Mazda she'd bought for cash two days before.

She got in, pulled on the safety belt and drove due north.

* * *

In her cream silk blouse, Eve studied the wormy spread that used to be inside Red Merrill's skull. His forehead had degloved, and skin settled into layers around his nose. She observed a muzzle, resting on his bottom teeth, his dead left thumb inside a trigger guard. She kneeled next to his bed and looked through, on the trajectory of the barrel. Light was coming through the missing portion of the man's skull and revealed the insides of his sinus cavities.

Back from the mobile evidence trailer, a thick woman with an orange crew cut entered shaking mixed liquids in a vial. She held the vial up to the light of a window and looked satisfied with the result.

Are you O'Connell? asked Eve. Can you tell me what's going on?

O'Connell tucked the vial into a pocket. So, you're Eve Coman? she asked. Yeah, I sent you a text. This is a murder that's supposed to look like a suicide, and I haven't found any clues yet about who the murderer is. You could have saved yourself a trip.

Yes, I saw your message, said Eve. Walk me through your steps.

Steps?

Eve nodded.

Steps? asked O'Connell again.

What have you been doing here? Which forms of analysis have you completed so far? Which parts of the scene haven't been examined yet? What do you expect to know better in four hours after some testing? What seems likely to emerge from the evidence? So, steps. Tell me your steps. If I know your steps, I know what your work means.

The woman tucked in her chin. My steps? O'Connell clasped her hands in front of her gut. At my old job, she said, I filled out death certificates and put down cause of death.

Eve exhaled disbelief. How long have you been with the Bureau?

Two months, said O'Connell.

You're an FBI evidence tech? You're the one they assigned to me? I'm looking to solve one of the worst terrorist attacks ever and I have you on my team?

O'Connell shivered.

On the lane in front of Red Merrill's magnificent house, people walking with dogs stopped, asked questions of the officers standing guard—Why the emergency vehicles and a box truck with FBI markings? Was everybody okay?—and learned nothing. They were looking over their shoulders at Red Merrill's house as they walked away.

Upstairs in Red's bedroom, Eve studied the orange hair, the nose ring and the apparent insecurity. How did you get here? she asked.

They pulled me out of a classroom in Quantico and sent me here. They said it was because I scored high on the FBI evidence test. Also, I ran the evidence department for my county in North Carolina.

Your county? What county?

Canton County.

I know Canton County, said Eve. Population tiny. You must have been a one-person department.

O'Connell nodded.

The FBI evidence test—how high was your score? asked Eve.

Ninety-seventh percentile.

Eve raised her chin, sounded hopeful. That's a hard test.

O'Connell nodded again. Yes, ma'am, she said.

Where'd you learn evidence?

I learned anatomy when I got my nursing degree from ECU. I worked in the ER in Greenville for five years. I seen every kind of way there is to die, probably at least ten times. I know when somebody had an accidental overdose or if they did it on purpose. Don't ask me why. I just know.

So, you never documented investigations? You never measured out murder scenes? Took samples? Performed forensic exams?

O'Connell shook her head, her lips thin, closed tight. Every death, on my job, if there was foul play, I called state police, she said. The county can't afford investigations. Mostly it was old people who died in front of the TV. And suicides. You get a lot of suicides in a rural county.

How did you know if there was foul play? asked Eve.

You could tell, said O'Connell.

No one to teach you?

I filled out death certificates after I figured the likely cause of death and I gave them to a funeral director, said O'Connell. He's an M.D. They appointed him coroner. The county pays him ninety dollars every time he signs. Whatever I wrote, he just signed.

Sounds pretty Andy Griffith to me, said Eve.

Maybe, but it worked, said O'Connell.

I don't see how it could have. What's your clearance?

Top secret. No other trainee had that.

Eve folded her arms, her hands sheathed in bold blue nitrile gloves. Forward looked like the way out. Here's the drill, she said. We have a segregated office for just this case to protect our work. That's where you go in the daytime when you're not in class or on a crime scene. Every piece of evidence you look at, assume you'll testify about it. One day, a lawyer will cross-examine you in open court about every possible cause of death except for the one you believe in. He'll kick open every door you haven't locked up. If a case goes south because you cut corners, I'll make sure you hate your job and I'll keep making sure until you quit the FBI.

Should I be taking notes right now?

No, said Eve. Listen and remember.

I got the pitcher.

Picture. So, how do you know this is not a suicide? Explain.

O'Connell brightened. So, the first thing you see is this old man, curled up and holding a gun in his mouth. There's nothing, like, super obvious to take you away from suicide as the cause of death. Thing is, though, if you peel up the corner just a little, there's a different pitcher.

Picture.

That's what I said.

Just—keep going, said Eve.

Well, there are the basics, like the method and the kind of weapon. A gun is the most common way for the suicide of a man. This man is sixty-three. That's a typical age for a White man who is a suicide. The upward angle of the bullet is what you always see with a self-inflicted shot in the mouth, and that shot's very effective. It cuts the brain from the whole rest of the body. It matches the angle that is comfortable for a suicide victim's wrist. Again, you're thinking suicide.

Eve held up a hand. When you and I are done here, you are going to dictate all this into a computer? Right?

O'Connell's head bobbed. The victim's grip says suicide, she said. Mouth shots usually happen with a push on the trigger with a thumb—a backwards grip with the handle away, like you see here. But this kind of gun for this man? This one thing, this gun, makes me know this is a murder.

Really? Eve's voice was full of doubt.

Did you look around downstairs? asked O'Connell. Did you see guns?

He has glass gun cases downstairs, said Eve. He has a gun safe. He's a marksman. He's got awards. I saw.

You're a city girl. Your service weapon is your only gun, I bet.

What's that mean? Eve asked.

This man has target competitions with rich people and he's a collector, said O'Connell. His pistols, they're antiques or else they're precision machines. He blows his head off with a Glock 21? That gun is four hundred bucks. Private security firms buy boxes of Glocks. But look downstairs. There's not one weapon worth less than four thousand. A guy like him thinks this is a crappy little gun for crappy little people. No way is he using that to end himself.

Eve's mouth hung and her forehead wrinkled. Maybe he just didn't want to get his mess all over a nice gun, she said.

Puh-lease. I seen this guy twenty-seven times. He appeared to use the thumb from his dominant hand on the trigger. Typical for a suicide. The site of his suicide is also common. He's in bed. So far, the only fingerprints I found on the weapon come from the victim.

The shells?

None on the ejected shell, but that's not so weird. Lots of times, a shell gets in a gun without a print getting on it.

Suicide note?

O'Connell's head shook slowly.

Unusual? asked Eve.

Like, extreme. This man made himself mad stacks. Look at this big house. *Pictures* of himself everywhere with senators and famous people. He lived on the water with a big freaking boat in a neighborhood full of big freaking houses and big freaking boats. He thinks he's better than us and he wants people to know he's better. When a person like that kills himself, he leaves a suicide note. A rich White man is desperate to be heard. He thinks he knows it all and he has to tell everybody.

Drugs? asked Eve.

You ask good questions. Positive for a drug that is probably Ambien. She fished the vial out of her pocket, shook it in front of Eve's face. I don't know who takes Ambien before bed and kills himself in the middle of the night. That drug knocks you out.

When did he die?

About four a.m.

He took the drug at bedtime? asked Eve. You're sure?

I know it.

Eve went back to looking inside of Red's dead mouth. You'll find out about this weapon? Where it came from?

O'Connell was on a roll. Already did, she said. It was manufactured in Georgia fourteen months ago and the manufacturer has no records of it ever leaving the factory. It had to have been removed without permission. So why would a rich guy with tons of fancy guns all over his house be holding a cheap, stolen weapon? Weird, right?

How could you know about the gun? asked Eve.

O'Connell patted the phone in her pocket. One call to the factory, she said. I told them I was FBI and they didn't doubt it. Took ten minutes.

What else?

O'Connell pointed at the muzzle on Red's chin. The recoil of a gun this powerful will make it fling away from the victim. If a suicide is still holding this gun when you find him, it's in his lap.

Eve began to ask a question.

O'Connell answered before disbelief could take shape. The victim took a hollow-point shell at the base of the brain, she said. No way he could have held. It would have jerked away on firing. Plus, look at his shooting hand. See the spatter? Usually that hand jerks back with the gun and gets only light blowback. This guy has serious blood on his shooting hand and the blowback is missing in two spots, like it was shielded.

Like someone held the victim's hand on the gun and pulled the trigger? asked Eve.

O'Connell nodded with purpose. I think somebody studied suicide on the Internet before they did this, she said. They knew half of what they needed.

Clues to ID the murderer?

No fingerprints. No weird fibers or foreign sweat on the gun. At least not yet. Maybe we'll find more in the lab. In some ways, the murderer was smart. Or murderers. Maybe there's more than one.

Eve tallied the clues. So, this was staged to look like a suicide, and so far, clues from the murder scene don't tell us who, she said.

O'Connell was looking cocky. Didn't I already say that? she asked.

At home on his couch, Dirk's mouth had been left wide open. The flabby part of his soft palate vibrated when he breathed and he sounded like a garbage disposal. The TV was on and the sound was off. A phone call on his mobile phone woke him. He checked the screen and it was Nassir—which was odd because when Nassir called, it was almost always to Norah's number.

His voice was expectant: Where's my daughter? It's hours I've been calling.

Dirk tried to moisten an impossibly dry mouth. She's sleeping, he squeaked. He tried to swallow and it hurt. Upstairs, he said.

Right now, go wake her, said Nassir.

Dirk rose, crossed the kitchen, hit the light. Her purse is in the mud room, same as always, he said. Up the stairs, he hit the switch, then around a corner, hit another switch, light shining on an empty bed. Hold on, Nassir. Wrong room. He went down the hall and every bed was empty. Nassir, I'm telling you, she's here.

Dirk returned to his kitchen, bare heels pounding across cold ceramic, opened the door to the garage. The minivan is here, he said. She's home. She can't go anywhere without her car. He touched the hood. It's cold. She's here. She's sleeping.

I searched for her mobile and it appears to be at your home, said Nassir. Is this true?

Dirk closed the garage door, returned to the mudroom, unzipped her purse. Her phone is right here. It's turned on. It has plenty of charge left. She never leaves home without it. She's here, I'm telling you.

I need to discuss with her my belief that Ibrahim is alive, said Nassir.

You saw the pictures, Nassir. His skull was bashed.

Find Norah now and call me. Nassir hung up.

* * *

Every night at closing, Jack turned the dead bolt on the front door to the wine store, shook the handle and made the cowbell inside clang. Inside the shop window were sparkles from strings of LEDs wound between bottles of Italian and California reds. The seven o'clock bells started at the First Church tower, two blocks away. It's cold enough out here to kill a man, said Jack, blowing mist. That'll keep the riff-raff out of Maine.

Jack pushed a button on his key. His Subaru beeped and unlocked. He started the car, waited forty seconds to let engine oil circulate and warm. Up, along the coast, on Route 1, he drove in the dark. Past municipal islands of light, past shuttered antique stores where summer folks came looking for quaint, past coves choked with frozen chunks bigger than barges, then north on Beech Hill Road, past trailers, once abused, now dead, left open to the whistling meanness of winter, past private drives that tunneled into forest and led to the homes of those, some wealthy, who preferred the company of woodstoves to people. Down steep hills, frosted over and slick, stopping at crossroads with blinking red lights casting intermittent bursts of eerie onto volunteer fire departments and town halls.

A safety-minded man, Jack kept to the speed limit, slowing when it looked icy. A small line of vehicles followed, turn for turn, keeping to one of the few Waldo County arteries safe to drive after a heavy snow, a route where someone would be sure to come upon you if you turned over in a ditch. He went right and headed east on Route 3 and most of the cars kept going straight—all of them except for a Ford Focus of indeterminate color, coated in salt. In the driver's seat of the Ford was a lean man with a black beard, neatly trimmed. On the front seat next to him: a mobile phone, a paper map, a wool hat, fingerless gloves, and a short-barreled rifle with a scope. He followed Jack's Subaru at a distance.

* * *

Four whiskies was always better than three. Into his mug went two fingers of Canadian Club. He declared his wife was a winner, then louder, a goddamn *winner. He lifted his mug, loosened his lips and gulped.*

His chunky wife, hands on hips, told him he could go fuck himself if he could ever get his limp noodle to stand up.

He flung his cup of whiskey and hit her between the tits, flung her off the porch. She rose, looking murderous. She asked what his buddies at the barber shop would think when they found out that the only piece of ass he could get was his fourteen-year-old daughter. She said he had shriveled balls, balls no bigger than raisins.

He jumped up and chased, and she ran. She ran past her hedges, crazy like a fox, across an acre that never got mowed, and she jumped high and long across a dry well, a relic, four feet wide and two hundred feet deep, landed safely on her belly with a thud. Lumbering on the power of liquor, the husband plunged into the well, his fingertips catching a wooden lid that looked ancient and rotten. He saw her relief, saw her back away; no way was she saving him.

He was enraged. Oh, you better hope I don't get out of here, he said.

Jack pointed the remote control at the picture tube of his vintage Sony Trinitron, pushed pause. The man hanging over a dry well got to hang a little longer. Jack got up and moved for the kitchen, briefly blocking everybody's view of a blurry screen. I need another merlot. Anybody else?

Annie huffed. This is the best part of the movie, she said. This is where she finally gets him good. Norah and Ibrahim have never seen it.

Won't take a minute, said Jack. Ibrahim was drinking Moxie, Norah lemonade. Want some suds? Jack asked, pointing at Annie's empty beer can. She said no. Then, to Norah and Ibrahim: Want some merlot? Perhaps a chardonnay? You're sharing a house with a Christian wine merchant who has pledged to save souls. I'm a terrible influence.

Ibrahim got the joke and laughed.

Then came disorientation and an explosion. There were splinters of glass and splinters of wood and the sound of being shot at with a cannon, so close and so damn loud. The picture window behind the sofa shattered, big shards everywhere, bouncing off arms and legs. The first bullet put a bloody, harmless hole in the cartilage of Annie's left ear, kept going and blew up the television. Everybody dove. Jack, Ibrahim, Norah toward the kitchen and Annie opposite, toward the stairs, as the windy freeze of outdoors flowed in and there came more shells, one at a time, big ones that whummocked holes in the wall behind the TV. One sang through the sofa where Ibrahim had been sitting moments before. One hit the framing in a corner and plugged. Two more hit the outside wall, below the picture window, and blew out billows of plaster dust. From the floor, Jack unplugged a lamp then reached for wall switches and made the house dark. When he reached for the switch—high enough that his hand was visible from outside—two shots came near.

Jack ran for the kitchen. The projectiles kept coming, took out chunks of walls and windows.

Jack, where are you going? called Annie.

I'm calling the cops. He reached for the kitchen phone.

Mister Alzheimer's, we haven't had a home phone in almost a year. And besides, we're miles from town. The police never get anyplace until after somebody is dead, she said. Annie unsheathed Margie, clicked off the safety. I got this, she declared.

She kneeled, hidden behind a staircase, dressed in her aloha muumuu, blue palms on peach horizons, a holster around her waist, her uniform for evenings at home. Her two wrists had combined into one lethal extension, holding her protection in front of her. Who in holy hellfire? she asked no one in particular. She poked an eye outside of a pillar. You think you can take me out? Watch it, buster. I'm the rattlesnake you just stepped on.

Annie started up the stairs, called back to Jack: I'm going to an attic window. Wait thirty seconds and turn on the floodlights.

Already out of view of the attacker, Jack tipped the heavy kitchen table on its side and used it as a shield from gunfire that might come through the wall; Norah and Ibrahim crawled next to him.

Annie stole to the attic, stationed herself inside a dark gambrel and swung open a window. She scanned the black acre in front of her home where there was no noise, no movement, save for the swaying and creaking of tall trees in light winds. The volley of bullets had stopped. She kneeled, pointed her weapon past the driveway, toward a hulk of granite deposited centuries ago by a passing glacier, perfect cover for a sniper who wanted a view through the front window. She braced her elbows, readied herself, took her breaths smooth and slow.

At the house's waistline, brutalist halogens flashed to life.

Annie was poised, ready to take a safe shot as soon as she saw it. She heard chunky-snow footsteps from somewhere outside. She ducked in, went to a rear gambrel and leaned out. Along a narrow path between the frozen forest and the back side of her house, a single line of foreign footprints where nobody should have gone in the few hours since the last snow—footprints that ran toward a sliding barn door.

Annie pulled back into her attic, unlatched an insulated panel that gave entrance to the loft of the attached barn, swung it open, stepped through, right behind her Ruger Blackhawk. The barn loft was frigid enough to shock anyone not wearing a coat and it smelled like heating oil. She looked down, through slots in the rustic floor, and two stories below she saw the barn's big sliding door pulled open—only wide enough for a man to pass—and glimpsed a figure moving from light into dark, a sight that made her clap a hand over her mouth. Beneath her, straight below, next to the door leading from the barn to the kitchen, there was an evil man who'd come to kill.

Silent as a house cat she went, gripping her weapon, daring to settle her finger inside the trigger guard. In the dark of the barn's loft, she went across the rustic pine deck, past stacks of Christmas decorations, sets of antique chairs. Down a dark staircase to the shadows of the barn's second level, onto a platform that overlooked the barn floor where she did much of her target shooting, where there were stalls with stanchions, a yard tractor, last century's farm implements, lots of places a man could hide.

She spread her feet on the deck and, beneath her fuzzy house slippers in the amber glow of a sixty-watt bulb, something moved. She saw a wool cap covering the top of a head, and she saw part of a face surveying her kitchen through a window, studying the place where Jack and Norah and Ibrahim were hiding. Then she saw arms raise and point a short-barreled rifle at something inside her house.

Annie settled on her knees, put her muzzle into a crevice between the floorboards, aimed her weapon at the center of the knit cap and squeezed and squeezed again until her unprotected ears rang like faraway sirens and the peppery burn of spent gunpowder made her eyes water. She kept squeezing after she'd emptied her gun. The figure was akimbo on the barn floor, one side of his face planted on concrete. The upside of his skull was a shiny-wet mass of blood and bare teeth, a death mask.

She'd cleaned his clock.

Annie fell to her bottom, flopped on her back, hugging her weapon and hyperventilating, blood dripping from her torn ear. When Ibrahim and Norah and Jack reached her, she was muttering pleasant nonsense, eyes closed, curled like a fetus, laughing and panting and laughing more. Ibrahim and Norah reached for her, tried to lift her and she resisted. Annie, are you okay? pleaded Ibrahim. He pulled valiantly, trying to get her standing.

Jack stepped in, stopped him. You leave her be, he said.

Ibrahim was incredulous. We have to get her inside where it's warm and there is light, he said. We have to see if she's injured.

Back off, said Jack. Her whole life, this moment is what she's been waiting for.

Jack patted and searched his empty pockets, said he was heading inside to find his mobile, that he needed to call the police—and pronto.

Norah stopped him. Don't, she ordered. I know how we can use that body.

Two days later, Annie and Jack took the Subaru to Northport to see Robah Bumpass, a poet and defrocked priest who spent winters in his wheelchair by an iron stove, smoking Borkum Riff from a meerschaum. His Grundig, topped with rabbit ears, was always busy with eclectic vibes from a community radio station. Today it was a live 1980s recording of Talking Heads.

He had a notebook open in front of him, the page covered in wordy strings of blue ink.

Sure, you can use my van, said Robah. He covered his ears and closed his eyes. I don't want to know why you need it. I might worry, he said. With a ballpoint, he tapped on the pad of paper he'd been writing on. I can't talk right now, he said. Busy.

From behind him, Annie put her hands around his shoulders, touched her cheek to his ear and kissed. We'll bring chowder and biscuits for dinner if you'll read some bad poetry to us. Wednesday?

Key's on the hook, he said.

Inside Jack and Annie's barn, Norah and Ibrahim wrapped Zarkawi from end to end in an oily plastic sheet. They lifted him and plunked him into Robah's panel van. The task was easier because the man had frozen stiff as lumber in the two days since he'd died. A warm body is so floppy it sometimes takes three people to carry, said Ibrahim. With bungees, they secured Zarkawi. They covered him with a loose remnant of carpet and slammed the sliding door—after they'd helped Jack and Annie clean up their house. At Hammond Lumber, Norah paid for plywood panels and helped Jack put them where windows had been smashed. They swept broken glass and plugged bullet holes with putty. They hauled the ruined couch and the dead television and chucked them in a dumpster at the transfer station. With Norah's money, they went downtown to Macleod's and bought new.

Jack wouldn't let Norah offer an apology. Anyone who fixes a problem has said it all, he said. Deeds are what matter.

She kissed him, said she loved the feelings he gave her.

Norah and Ibrahim drove away with an icy body, a decrepit, ruinous thing. Norah promised Ibrahim, brimming with certainty, that the body would help save them.

Next came three hours on Maine highways, through acres of pointy pines and white birch, a tour through villages with clapboard churches that badly needed painting. She kept at it for eight hours and after dark she rolled into an over-bright Citgo at Nanuet, New York. She couldn't keep her eyes open, had to rest. She lay in the back of the van, two feet from the body of the would-be assassin and used a duffel as a pillow. Ibrahim took the wheel. She was too tired to have any fear left, dropped into a heavy sleep and didn't move once all the way to Maryland.

The former cop kept the van to the speed limit and signaled before lane changes. He was good at knowing what would not attract attention.

FIFTEEN

Dirk spent all the time he could in his comfort zone. He took target practice with fast-fire automatic weapons and easily obliterated pictures of famous elitists. He rode his Fat Boy to Chesapeake Beach and played pool at Tyler's. He streamed reruns of *The Six Million Dollar Man* on his bedroom television and drank light pilsner from brown bottles. That's where he was, in the dark of night, when his phone lit up with a message: *Go now to the Lady M.*

Dirk had been expecting the message. It meant that a pair of volunteers had arrived and needed to be retrieved. Dirk dressed in layers and escaped his back door—out of sight of anyone—and sprinted through the humid cold to his boathouse.

In his Boston Whaler, he motored out to the Chesapeake, away from eyes, from electronic surveillance, toward a hulking tanker anchored near a shipping channel. The cold made his nose run and he didn't wipe it. A frigid stream snaked inside his scarf and made his thick neck turn hard as wood.

The Oklahoman had trouble getting his skiff to hover near the ship's overwhelming mass; wind threatened to smash his tiny boat against the bigger one. His slow approach was shallow and without meaning to, he stuck his starboard gunwale beneath a rubber fender bolted to the side of the big ship, then decided it was a useful accident because it held him still. He squinted at the top edge of a steel wall high enough to hide the moon. He let go two short blasts from an air horn.

Dirk held his position, waited for his passengers to climb down. A line of swells swept through, faster than a flock of geese, and swamped him. Dirk was soaked to his ankles and spewed profanities. The back of his boat sank six inches. The exhaust ports on his idling outboards sounded like they were drowning.

A pair of men with shoulder bags descended a rope ladder. Hurry it up, Dirk demanded.

They jumped across and splashed into Dirk's small craft. Get down, he commanded. Cover yourselves. Hide. The men looked at him and then at each other. Dirk yelled, louder than before: Get down. Hide, goddammit. They crouched, not wanting to soak themselves in the frigid water.

Screw it. Don't get down. See if I care, said Dirk. He chunked his outboards into reverse, worked loose from the fender, then gunned forward and turned hard to port. The onboard water surged over the stern, back to the bay. Both passengers toppled. One slapped the gunwale as he fell out and the man who didn't began yelling in Arabic. Dirk idled, unclipped a twelve-foot-long boat hook and inched toward hands and arms slapping about desperately. The thrashing man grabbed the pole. When he got close, Dirk reached with one monstrous hand, grabbed the man by the belt and lifted.

Do I have to tell you again? he said. Get down.

We are from the desert, said the soaking-wet man. We don't know boats. The man's teeth chattered and the wind made a big noise.

Get down and stay down, Dirk repeated. He made a show of putting his hand on the throttle, of being ready to gun the engines.

The clothes at the safe house were dry, at least. Half of them were way too big in the waist. Dirk promised to get some properly sized, to bring fresh food, to supply them with all they needed.

I'm happy you're here, said Dirk, not asking for names, not offering his own. He gave each man a bolt bag. Inside each were photos of two targets to be killed, addresses, maps, an international driver's permit, ten thousand American dollars in a bank-banded packet, a fake Egyptian passport. Each included a reliable little Glock and sixteen rounds of ammunition.

Which one of you is the better shot? asked Dirk. He pointed to a slim case on a dresser. Inside was a Ruger Blackhawk Long Range, a rifle prized by snipers. It came new with a Nightforce Scope, but I put on a better one—a Nikon, said Dirk. I calibrated it for you.

He jingled a set of car keys. Go as soon as you can, he said.

On the lane in front of Dirk's house, three silent shots outed three streetlights. A pair in black approached his driveway and entered the code for the security gate and each lugged one end of a cumbersome burden up to Dirk's garage door and dumped it. They darted around to the back of the house, where one of the pair opened a back door with a key. Forty-five seconds later, they closed and locked the door behind them and fled on foot.

Upstairs, Dirk had been as still as a dead man for hours, mouth agape. He never stirred when his back door opened or when it closed, and he didn't hear footsteps. First light arrived and he put a pillow over his head, shifted and fell back to sleep. Perhaps an hour later, he sat bolt upright, listening to the urgent pounding on his front door. He grabbed his phone, tapped the app for his outside security cameras and the screen was blank. Holy hell, he said.

He raced downstairs, flung open the door, found two faces. Get off my property, he demanded. I have that security gate for a reason.

The two faces were wearing blue uniforms. Dirk Johnson? asked one of them. Can we come in?

I'm sleeping. He prepared to slam the door. A stiff arm stopped him.

Mr. Johnson, what can you tell us about the body in your driveway?

In bare feet and pajama pants, Dirk pushed past the officers and crossed the cold cement of his front porch. On his driveway he observed a figure—male, bloodied, missing half of a face. The half that remained was a hideous purple, the eye open like the ones at the fish market—unmistakable because it belonged to Bandar Zarkawi. Dirk grabbed his porch railing in both hands and didn't dare let go. Norah was rubbing failure in his face. There was no other way to explain it.

A yellow police ribbon was taut across the front of the perimeter fence and flipped in the breeze. A wave from a pear-shaped neighbor—Dirk had met the man once. The man had a collie on a leash and was standing in the road, watching. Dirk swayed, kept his grip on the railing.

How did this body get here? asked the officer.

How would I know? said Dirk.

You have video surveillance? asked one of the officers, pointing at a camera mounted on the front of the house. Can we come in and look?

He was silent.

Sir? asked the officer. Sir? Your video?

Am I being detained? Dirk asked.

Sir, I'd like to come in and look at your video, said the officer.

Dirk turned hostile: Am I being detained?

The officer drew back. All's we want is to look at your video and ask some questions, he said.

Dirk slammed the door, went straight for his mobile phone and called Nassir.

Fifteen miles away, an FBI agent sitting in a room crammed with electronics watched a computer screen scroll through phone numbers. It stopped on one. Next to it was the number for a phone in Mecca, Saudi Arabia, that was blinking. It was the same number that had repeatedly been calling Dirk. He clicked on it. A desperate voice came streaming in, urging Nassir to pick up.

Then a different voice, far away and veiled by white static: What do you have for me? Have you found Norah?

Nassir, Zarkawi is dead, said Dirk. Norah killed him. She dumped him right here on my driveway. Right here. The FBI is at my door. This is the end of my life. Do you know how fucked I am?

* * *

Under the extra-white brilliance of tungsten-halogen field kliegs, Esme O'Connell kneeled on Dirk Johnson's driveway, gathering data from Bandar Zarkawi's hands. She took photos of the front, the back, macro images of the tip of each finger. She pressed each finger against a print reader. She swabbed for chemical evidence on his fingers and his palms and took scrapings from under his fingernails. She drew close and sniffed at the back of one of his hands. She swabbed there, too. She opened the half of the man's jaw that remained, inserted a mold maker, pushed the stiff jaw into the closed position, then removed an imprint of slightly more than half of the man's teeth. By the time the sun was directly overhead, she knew the dead man was left-handed, that he was fastidious in his hygiene and was an aggressive nose-picker.

At lunchtime, Eve Coman pulled up in front of Dirk Johnson's house in a Bureau car, a gray-blue Ford, a family sedan with its windows blacked out. She waved O'Connell into the evidence trailer. Eve flopped an oversized Panera bag on a desk. It contained sandwiches and drinks for the crew working and guarding the site.

Is our dead man a Saudi?

Seems like.

Name?

O'Connell handed over a transparent evidence bag. Inside was a paper napkin, two inches square, taken from the dead man's pocket. On one side was printed an anthropomorphic piece of Interstate 95 with a head shaped like the state of Delaware. The character's legs were astride a Harley-Davidson. On the other side was a note, handwritten: *Call Nassir Saud at Saudi Security Directorate and tell him Bandar Zarkawi is dead.*

Eve saw it and licked her lips.

Does this mean something to you?

Yep, she said. She gestured in the direction of the body, wanted to know more.

He's brainless and gut-shot, said O'Connell. His core temp is twenty-five Fahrenheit and at the edges, he's soggy. Ali Baba got killed somewhere else and put into the deep freeze and he had several hours to thaw.

Frozen? asked Eve. Really?

He died eyes open, said O'Connell. Both corneas have freezer burn.

Eve peeked out a window of the evidence trailer, toward the house. Security video?

There's two people recorded at twelve minutes to four, both in black, when it was dark. They ran up and chucked the body, quick and dirty. Ba-boom. Then they ran out of frame. Two minutes later, house cams stop recording. We got uniforms going door to door. I thought, you know, because maybe somebody else with security video got pitchers? O'Connell whipped out an index finger. Everybody says it that way. Don't make me prove you wrong.

Eve didn't say a word.

The uniforms are babysitting the homeowner, said O'Connell. He is so dang nasty. Site security dangled handcuffs before he would stop screaming. His lawyer just got here.

I'm going in, said Eve and she moved for the door.

O'Connell grabbed her wrist and held. I got more. You need to know this. Like, one, in the boathouse—bags of money in a locked room. Eighteen extra-extra in fresh paper. Twenty army bags and each one's got nine hundred K inside. Like, who puts just nine hundred in a bag when there's room for more? And in the same room it smells like serious Semtex. We sent dust samples to the lab to see what kind of particles are present.

She stood, ready to head indoors, to confront Dirk Johnson. If you get positive results for Semtex, call me. That would give me enough to make an arrest.

A dead body on his driveway isn't enough?

You just told me he probably didn't kill this man or transport his body, said Eve. I need more.

SIXTEEN

Eve savored the feel of an office chair that had the perfect degree of firmness. The chair supported and balanced the nape of her neck, her spine, her arms. Her eyes ran the length of the streamlined, post-modern conference room. The space and the suite of offices that went with it were crown jewels in the career of a Buddhist interior designer, a West Coast legend, an old Thai man with a white ponytail who saw his life's mission as selecting and arranging fixtures and furnishings to induce calm, to put people in a mood to be reasonable.

In front of Eve was frothy, sweetened chai in a cup with a cork wafer on its bottom; the cup could be placed silently on any hard surface so as not to interrupt anyone's thinking. Six floors above busy K Street, dense Pakistani carpet and a barely audible white noise canceled the outside sounds that might distract or annoy. A magnificent view of Franklin Square, its massive, leafless oaks and sycamores dusted in new snow, gave Washington, DC, a look and feel that was orderly and moderate.

She sat for ten minutes and hardly moved. When she closed her eyes, she floated. The room had a way of making one's biggest problems seem like small objects that could be held in one's palm. When she opened her eyes, Eve looked refreshed, like she'd shed the dizziness that came from spending an entire winter being shoved forward so fast that the only thing she could do was steer—grab the wheel and don't look away—and hope she could hang on for as long as it took.

Her chest wasn't tight. She wasn't mindlessly squeezing like she had to go to the bathroom. She was aware of how slow and how deep and how purposefully she could breathe. She remembered a delicious afternoon on a long-ago vacation, reading an Annie Proulx novel, unaware of anyone or anything that hadn't been written on the pages.

Eve's host, DeAndre Green, made a graceful entrance. The thick file folder he brought seemed to weigh nothing at all. He had handsome gray streaks at his temples and was known to be deliberate in all things. He gave people his full attention and was quick to notice others who did too. He told Eve it was damn fine to see her. He'd heard stories of her successes. His smile was just for her.

You've done well pilgrim, Eve responded. She grabbed DeAndre by the hips and planted one side of her face against his chest. Between them was a comfort unique to former coworkers who'd been lovers, a pair that might still be sleeping together except that one had been promoted and become boss of the other, took the advice of FBI's ethics counsel, broken things off, and later married a boy she'd known in the fifth grade—and had birthed a daughter. And you're still as gorgeous as ever, she said.

They sipped more chai, sweet and peppery, poured from a matte black carafe, talked about mutual friends still at the Bureau, of modern office politics rooted in the long ago. They talked of extreme criminals, unheard-of combinations of creativity and greed. They segued into the forensics of human nature, analyzing the odd classes of hubris that had led so many to prison. It was a conversation they'd enjoyed across pillows as newbie agents—in the formative years of their working lives and their relationship with the law.

She tapped the table, and just like that, it got real. Tell me why I'm here, counselor, she said.

Eve, you can switch on the drama like an actor, said DeAndre. Ever considered trial work? You'd do well at a firm like this.

Eve jumped in and made him stop talking, as if doing so was absolutely necessary: If the Inspector General thought you'd tried to influence me? She shook her head.

DeAndre stammered, was in doubt.

Ethics is something I'm required to worry about, she said. She frowned and the idea left the room. So, what is it? Your mystery client has a proposal and your message said I knew her.

He didn't speak. Instead, he took her mobile and his mobile and closed them in a metal compartment in a drawer. He flipped the blinds. He didn't want someone with binoculars to read their lips, he said.

He sat and let the air settle, then started: You've been investigating Dirk Johnson? His wife, Norah Saud, hired me.

That's your client? she asked. Then, in a sisterly tone: What do you know about her?

She's a survivor, he said. A badass with a conscience.

She can rip out your guts with her bare hands. Did she tell you that?

He looked shaken. She's violent? he asked.

Eve retreated. Her background makes me fear it, she said. I don't know of it.

I spent three hours talking with Norah, he said. She gave me time enough to decide if she could be trusted, seemed to know it was expected. She told me her father raised her to become a terrorist. She didn't know until it was too late.

She admits to terrorism? asked Eve. That's a hell of a thing for a lawyer to say about his client.

She was duped and she was extorted, he cautioned. Her father and his type are devoted mercenaries. They have muscle. They get away with some shit. This woman tried to sabotage their work. She's not somebody I'd have prosecuted. No contempt, no anger, no entitlement. There's not an ounce of criminal spirit in this woman.

People like her are never innocent, said Eve. She's hired counsel and is secretly approaching the FBI. It doesn't feel so innocent.

You've got her wrong, DeAndre insisted.

Eve interrupted. For the sake of our conversation, I'll give her the benefit of the doubt, she said. Is this about Farragut North?

DeAndre spoke in a voice hardly loud enough for Eve to hear. She can give you names, dates and addresses. She knows the Saudis have developing terrorist plans. She knows of a Russian back door into FBI computers that might make you stop breathing. She knows about the envelopes you found with explosive residue. She knows you took pictures of envelopes to Douglas-American and did a slide show. She knows you're monitoring Dirk Johnson. DeAndre opened his file folder and pulled out a letter-sized piece of paper. This is a list of the names on those letters that nobody's supposed to know.

Eve read down the list. Norah sent the envelopes? she asked.

They were designed to cause problems for Dirk and his boss, to make them afraid so they'd get stupid and get caught, said DeAndre.

DeAndre, why now? Why not before five hundred people got slaughtered? And why the smoke and mirrors? She could have sent us an e-mail.

If her people knew what she was doing, she'd be dead—and she thought she could prevent the explosion, said DeAndre. She thought she'd crippled the Semtex that exploded.

Eve didn't look any less concerned. You are so outside your wheelhouse, she said.

This client's not in anybody's wheelhouse, he said. She came here knowing you were responsible for the Farragut North investigation, that you were the one to negotiate with. She looked for someone who could persuade you and she found me. She knows what the FBI uncovered during each of my background checks. Some of it comes from twenty years ago, he said. She knows our history. Everything. She's counting on our friendship to solve her problems. She hired me so she could appeal to you. She wanted this known so you wouldn't doubt her motives. She wants to tell you about the back door into FBI servers. The Saudis are using it. The Russians, too.

She's using naked honesty to get an edge, said Eve. Who knew life could be so simple? Eve's tone changed. Who knows what she's told you? she demanded. We've not disclosed what Norah seems to know, and for good reason.

Are you hearing me? he said. Eve, the Russians are draining your servers and sharing intel with their totalitarian homies all over. You have no secrets.

Let's get down to it, she said. What does Norah want?

She'll sit for interrogation, DeAndre said. She'll testify in court. In exchange, she wants immunity—for herself and for her partner. After she's testified, she wants a promise the FBI won't search for them and won't keep records on them. They want to be left alone.

A partner?

Norah and her partner know about recruitment, funding, operations, concealment, he said. Everything. He interrupted himself. Neither one caused harm at Farragut North and they haven't given away intel, he added. These are the good guys. Each of them survived getting planted in a hellhole.

We'll see about that, said Eve. Then she warned him: You can't repeat any of this. Not here at the firm and not to your dog. If people thought the FBI was vulnerable to hackers, the gutters couldn't hold all the blood.

You cute little thing, said DeAndre. You think people get their mellow from believing the FBI is keeping its secrets.

She turned up the volume a little too high. We *can't* have people thinking the FBI is vulnerable, she declared.

He smiled sideways. I think I just got you excited, he said.

Don't pretend this is funny, she said. I'll need your man's name.

Not yet, counselor. I'll tell you what you'd find if you knew his name. I'll lay it all out. If there's anything he fails to disclose? You can prosecute. We'll carve it out of the immunity agreement. If you commit to that in writing, you'll get his name.

If he's wanted in Saudi Arabia for a misdemeanor he forgot to disclose, we can arrest and extradite?

Not we. You. Eve Coman. You have to approve any action. DeAndre was resolute. My clients know of you, he said. I promised they could trust you.

She whispered: This is a huge ask.

Oh, bless your heart, he said. You're trying to bluff a man who knows all your cards.

She exhaled her pretentions, and all at once. DeAndre, don't play me, she said. Please. I would hate you.

He reached for her hand. My clients have been victimized by master manipulators, he said. All they want is out. When I told Norah she could trust you, she almost cried.

Eve drained her cup. Send it to me and I'll sign. She snapped her fingers. The deal was done and she wanted DeAndre to talk, and that's what he did. The trust between them—accumulated over two decades, little bits at a time—left them confident.

Norah's father is Nassir Saud, director of Saudi Arabia's FBI, he said. He secretly owns Douglas-American Aerospace. He sent Norah here and married her to Dirk Johnson, one of his puppets. Nassir extorts ordinary Saudis into terrorism and ships them here. His plan was for Norah to train them and march them into battle. He wants DAA to keep him rich. He uses the company to steal American intel, and he feeds it to Russia because the Russians give protection to Saudi Arabia. Eve, ordinary Saudis are being used as scaremeisters. Americans scream like children and DAA profits by selling us weapons to make us feel better. Saudi Arabia and Russia take it all to the bank.

How long has this been going on?

Farragut North was Norah's first job.

More missions? asked Eve. Upcoming?

Nassir Saud sent two Saudi men who are probably already here, he said. Likely, they're at a safe house in Maryland. From his folder, he pulled out a square of paper, placed it in front of her. The address, he said. Again, he placed his hand on Eve's. Norah thinks they're coming for you.

Eve darkened. You're not serious. You couldn't be, she said. You wouldn't have waited to tell me this.

If I'd told you up front, you wouldn't have believed me, he said. Your little slide show at DAA left Dirk Johnson unhinged. He killed Red Merrill to save himself. Norah will testify that Dirk confessed—if you can overcome the spousal objection. Dude's a murderer, straight up. He's also feeling desperate. He has no trouble killing people to save himself. Do you see how this adds up?

And what about Norah's partner? asked Eve.

Former Saudi cop, said DeAndre, speaking of Ibrahim without saying his name. He told of Ibrahim's family, his imprisonment, his torture, of threats to kill his sister. Norah and her partner each need a green card and an American passport, he said. The Bureau has to agree it won't put info about either one of them into any electronic database. Paper only. If they get found, they're dead.

There's no way, she said.

If the FBI's computers don't scare you, you're not paying attention, he said. You also have to promise the Bureau won't put me under surveillance and won't target me.

Eve clutched her pearls, shook her head. You're a lawyer, not a terrorist, she said. You're former FBI. We'd never spy on you.

Eve, the Bureau is in the hands of men who are sixty-plus years old. Lots of them can't tell shit from Shell Oil and all they want is to intimidate people. For them, that's the easiest way to get their job done. And those old men answer to a president and an attorney general who jump every time they see a shadow. They don't have time for due process if there's a *Negro* or a *Muslim* in those shadows. Eve, you have to promise.

Come off your soapbox.

DeAndre opened a nearby drawer and pulled out her phone. You need to call your husband. Now.

* * *

The best wins require no fighting, when the loser accepts inevitable defeat—when he doesn't want to waste the effort. Father often told me this and it was one of the few things he was right about. He lived for that kind of win. He wanted people to yield without being told to. Mostly, they did. People were afraid not to, including people who'd only heard of him, which in Saudi Arabia was almost everybody. He built a reputation by arresting people and severing hands and heads. He had his own army that burned families to death in their homes, that would shoot and kill people if they tried to escape the flames. So, people did whatever Father wanted. They took his hints as commands. They avoided anything that might anger him. He wanted to win and that's what he got.

Father once gave a gun to a prisoner who'd been in solitary confinement for three years. He told the man it was loaded with a single round. You'd think that was stupid. You'd think that somebody doomed to a cell for the rest of his life would be a threat. Father said he'd discovered that if you took away all of a person's hope—if you totally drained a man, if you denied him water, food and comfort, and left him convinced he'd never put another drink to his lips, that he'd never see the sun—you'd end up with someone who thought of no one but himself.

That kind of suffering always turns inward. A person that low will end himself if he can.

Victory by exhaustion or intimidation of an enemy would satisfy Father. It reaffirmed his beliefs. It fed him.

What should I think of a man whose life was devoted to controlling people like he owned them? He imagined himself as all-knowing, with no limit to his authority. He said he'd earned that, that he was entitled. I lived with Father for over twenty years. He never knew what it meant to be at ease. The face he wore was always for someone else. Every relationship was built on hidden motives, on his need to win. He never once had a friend, someone who would tell him what he needed to hear, someone who actually knew him. His entire life, he hid himself because of what people would think. I doubt anybody who was old and wise ever took Father under a wing and counseled him. If they did, Father would have been plotting for ways to take advantage.

He was a stranger to everyone. When I saw that, I stopped being angry. Eve, honestly, I pitied him.

* * *

Before physician Abdullah Saud could open his car door, it was opened for him by palace ushers wearing white cotton gloves and palace robes embroidered with the image of a scimitar. They greeted him with solemn words, as they always did: There is no God but God. Muhammad is the messenger of God. Then they guided him indoors, through a corridor decorated with travertine and gathers of silk, past individually lit portraits of ancient royalty. An elevator was open, waiting, and before he could push the correct button, a gloved hand pushed it for him. The doors closed. The mirrored car ascended—two levels, three, four—and glided open. There, a carpeted library, a lair for study and thought, a room gently illuminated, dotted with pairs of leather chairs, leather sofas, everywhere an ottoman, one of them occupied by the stocking feet of an old man who was relaxing with a book. Arched windows framed and tinted the early morning sunlight before allowing it in.

Inside the library, all was well.

Abdullah offered greetings to his grandfather. The old man rose and the two men kissed, enough to leave moist impressions on one another. I'm sorry it took me so long to get here, said Abdullah. Am I forgiven?

You're always welcome and it doesn't matter when you arrive, said the King. They sat close to one another on a sofa and the King clasped Abdullah's closest hand with both of his own. For the rest of your days, your behavior decides what's correct. You're always right, always on time. Few will argue with you. You are the rare person who learns power's gravity, the way it changes you and how it changes the way people treat you. You'll learn to live as *my* king, starting now.

Abdullah's face blanked, like a man whose lights had gone out and was left driving in the dark. You—are our King, he said. Abdullah lifted his free hand, ready to point at his grandfather, the world leader of Wahhabism, its infallible figurehead, its papal icon. He pulled his hand back fast enough that he did not offend, but he'd been thoughtless, and grievously so. Pointing at the Saudi King had gotten men whipped.

This is not what I told you I wanted to talk about, Abdullah said. I'm confused.

Your light already outshines mine, young man. Get used to it.

I'm still confused, he repeated.

The King kept going: When people around you, the old man pointed at himself, know that you are king or that you will become king, you become the brightest light in every room. Your attention becomes the most valuable commodity within our borders. People sometimes kill those you favor with attention and they do it out of naked jealousy. Some want to affect your understanding in ways that will benefit them. Others become obvious fools for your attention. Everyone wants to influence you. Every kindness, every compliment and every bow of a head is from a person who wants something from you. Every stern face is someone who wants you to feel pressure to appease them, or maybe to intimidate you. Some are greedy for what you have, some know that to be seen with you will improve their fortunes. Some of us are hoping you will succeed for selfish reasons—we want you to protect our legacy. Some just want to control people—to gain power in any form possible. Some will want to kill you and take your place. They all want to influence you or control you. Everyone. Everything they say and do has meaning. You need to understand the words I'm saying because you'll be living them. You'll have to grow accustomed to decisions where either way, people will die. You need to be comfortable with that. You need to live with the burden of threats you can't back away from. You have to do it all without any apparent fear. If you look weak or afraid? You'll ruin it for everybody. This starts now. Today.

You think everyone wants to influence you? asked Abdullah. Every single person you meet?

The old man affirmed.

Your friends? Your wives? Me? You think I want to influence you?

You don't like some of my choices, said the King. You feel certain enough in your beliefs that you want to replace me. Right now, you behave in a certain way because you don't want me to change my mind about your future. You want to preserve my view of you.

Abdullah released a burst of astonishment. You don't trust me, he said.

I know what it means to be human, said the King. This bothers you? I'm not trying to intimidate you, and I offer no threat. I'm offering you lessons in how to be me. My trust in you should be obvious.

Abdullah bowed his head. The surprise start of the King's campaign was not well-timed. Grandfather, the reason I came here is to tell you some things you won't like, he said.

You sound afraid of my judgment.

Not afraid, grandfather. Respectful.

Your respect sounds too much like fear, he said. You can't afford that.

Standing far, far away from the King's library at that moment was a man whose life would be affected by the news soon to reach the Saudi King, but the man didn't know it yet. He was poking his face into his refrigerator in a galley kitchen in Washington, DC—in a three-bedroom apartment in the Woodley Park neighborhood, four subway stops north from Farragut North. Behind a jug of milk, he'd just found his last bottle of Newcastle Brown Ale when the phone in his pocket rang. Eve Coman's husband, Jaime, answered immediately. Yes, he told Eve, he was at home and so was Olivia, their daughter. Jaime promised he would close their apartment's blinds and curtains. The dining room didn't have regular curtains, only sheer drapes, but he would close them in case it helped. He would keep Olivia away from the windows and would invent a reason that would not alarm her. He would turn on only the lights he needed and leave them on. He wouldn't do anything that would reveal movement if someone was watching from outside with binoculars.

Or with a scope on a rifle? he asked.

Eve didn't stop with her instructions: FBI agents—men that Jaime had already met—would be up to the apartment soon, and he shouldn't open the door to anyone else. Jaime didn't ask why. Eve always said if she was giving orders, it was best not to question them.

Jaime reached for a chair after Eve ended the call and only when the chair was well within his grasp did he sit down. He held the cold bottle of brown ale against his cheek.

Six thousand miles away from Jaime and his bottle of beer, Abdullah gave his King the message he'd brought: Norah says Zarkawi is dead—the security man from our Washington embassy. He tried to kill Norah and some others and they got him first. They dumped his body in front of a house where Nassir's American agent lives. Lots of things that Nassir wants secret are about to become public. It will lead back to here—to you.

The King denied it. If Zarkawi was dead, Waaqi at the embassy would have called me. That much I know for certain. Nassir would have beaten you here to tell me.

The embassy doesn't know.

How can you believe her?

Norah is honest always, said Abdullah. I am the same with her. I would trust her with my life.

The King still had doubts. She's telling you this because she wants to influence us, he said. If she tells you she killed one of ours, maybe she wants you to be afraid. What does she want? Ask yourself.

She wants to be safe. She wants us to leave her alone.

She wants more, said the King. She has to.

Abdullah was quick to interrupt. She wants for others as much as she wants for herself, he said. She's not like the people you know.

The King patted Abdullah's hand, kept it on his thigh. It was rare that anyone was so quick to reveal their judgment of him or was so direct about it. You're not afraid of my response to that? asked the King, with a half grin. That's good. Norah sounds resourceful and you have reason to trust her. She could become useful, said the King.

That's possible, Abdullah said.

You knew each other as children, when you could be open with each other, said the King. Anyone as resourceful as her, who you can trust, is someone you want to keep close. She might save your life one day.

Again, possible.

Just like you're saving hers now.

Am I? he asked.

Isn't that why you brought me this news?

To be fair, Grandfather, I also wanted you to benefit from the knowledge.

The King looked pleased. You're going to be good in this job, he said.

Not much later, while the sun still shone, a certain galley kitchen in Washington, DC, was back in action. Four floors above busy Connecticut Avenue, Eve Coman used a George Foreman griddle to make paninis for her family. Gooey cheese dripped from slices of brown bread and the kitchen floated on the aroma of basil. Eve and Jaime and Olivia sat in the living room, away from windows, plates on their laps. Before her first bite, Eve sank with a heavy sigh.

What? asked Jaime.

I hate the feeling of being sealed inside the only space that's safe, she said. This is not normal. We can't eat at our dining room table because it's dangerous near the window.

Jaime tried to lighten the mood. We'll live like rich Russians for a week, he said. We don't go out without bodyguards and we have our shopping done for us.

After they ate, they clicked on a flat-screen Samsung that sparkled with colored and well-defined images of people swirling about in a different time and place. They watched English-accented characters who were always subdued and reserved, except for when they weren't. One character, an old woman, was droll and got laughs.

Eve's daughter, Olivia, fiddled with her smart phone every few minutes. This show is boring, said Olivia.

This is the country we could have ended up in, said Jaime gesturing at the screen. This is your evening history lesson.

Eve told Olivia to put away her phone. Watch the program for twenty minutes and don't get distracted and see if maybe you like it, she said. Olivia protested. Eve snatched away the device.

Olivia squinted back, hatefully. You're such a bully, she said.

The characters on the screen waltzed at a party under a grand tent, touching only when necessary, and they sipped bubbly wine out of dainty crystal flutes. A woman wearing a crown ordered her sister not to marry a commoner. The sister swore like an English coal miner and stomped away.

Were they really that weird? asked Olivia.

Only the rich ones, honey, said Jaime. The working Brits, the ones who drove the Jags and the MGs, they were normal. They had fun.

* * *

A frigid wind rushed along DC's Duke Ellington Bridge, pushed dead leaves into piles, swirled and spread them out again where they could get stepped on. A woman in a pea coat and fuzzy mittens crunched along the sidewalk. She pulled off a mitten, fished her keys from her purse and approached the entry to her building. There, under the awning—two men, one with an oversized shoulder bag, both in burgundy and yellow caps. Repairmen? One was holding an intercom receiver, wired to the wall next to the front door, talking into it, apparently with a person inside. The woman inserted a key, pulled open the door and politely held it. I'll be right up, Michael, said the man into the phone, and he hung up. Anybody approaching probably would have assumed the man was talking to someone inside the building, which was, like nearly all American apartment buildings, home to several Michaels.

He thanked the woman and was formal about it and wouldn't look her in the eye. At the elevator, she pushed the button to go up. She turned and looked when the men refused to wait with her and they slid down the hall. She watched them enter the door to the building's central stairs.

Assholes, she said.

Robah Bumpass's forest-green panel van, now lighter by the weight of a man's body, sped north at interstate highway speed, toward Baltimore and beyond, Ibrahim at the wheel. I'm exhausted, he said. You must be, too. Can we stop and sleep?

Norah pointed at a billboard for a hotel that didn't look like part of any national chain. Two miles. They'll take cash and won't ask for ID.

They pulled in and she was exactly right.

The fake repairmen dropped the bills of their caps so their faces wouldn't be seen by security cameras on the way up. On their toes, they sprinted six flights up a naked concrete staircase, as quiet as owls, onto a flat roof, past decking and lounge chairs, past gas grills, and they crunched across pea gravel. They settled behind the building's elevator equipment. From his sack, one removed and opened an ordinary-looking black case. He extracted a rifle and unfolded its hinged stock, set it down gently, careful not to disturb calibration of its scope. He pulled out a yoga mat, a bath towel rolled up, waterproof tarps, wool blankets, a four-pack of Red Bull, a stack of Oreos in shiny, single-serving packets. He lay flat on the yoga mat; his partner covered him with a blanket and a tarp. The rifleman rolled the towel and lay it inside a gap on a parapet as a brace for his long barrel.

The companion kept watch, above and around, as the man with the rifle readied himself. By the light of an iPhone, he reviewed notes and pictures of the person they'd been assigned to assassinate. She was an elegant White woman. She had a bob that was layered and highlighted. On the ring finger of her left hand was a silver Claddagh band. She was right-handed. Her profile showed a patrician chin, a little-girl nose. She lived with a daughter and a husband and if they were collateral damage it was okay.

Together, from their elevated perch, the men spied over the canopy of Rock Creek Park—over the tops of the broadest and grandest sycamores anywhere, trees old enough to have shaded Abraham Lincoln when he rode horseback. The men studied a particular apartment building, half a mile away, one with the scope on his rifle, the other with 20 x 80 binoculars.

Apartments in the faraway building lit up, one here, one there. The lights never stopped blazing in an apartment of special interest and with one eye closed, the rifleman zeroed in. His scope revealed a dining room window shaded with sheer drapes. On the sill, a clay pot overflowed with ivy. The room contained a trestle-style dining table surrounded by round-back armchairs.

The assassin comforted himself, ready for a long wait. He bunched the yoga mat under himself and rested the side of his chin against his own shoulder.

Occasionally, shadows moved close enough to the sheers to make them look like they'd moved. One shadow approached the window and hovered. The assassin's finger curled, the soft flesh indented by pressure against the trigger. Both men held their breaths, ready for the shot. And then the shadow retreated. They exhaled together. The rifleman let go the trigger.

Above them, an odd buzz that lasted for a few moments, went away, came back. The one with binoculars looked up, saw nothing, and returned his focus to the target.

In the seven-story canyon below, car horns, screaming sirens in the distance, and the streetlights' shadows playing on federal-style impediments. Well past dinnertime, the city was wide awake. The hour for evening Muslim prayers had come and gone; in this city, that meant nothing.

The man with the binoculars grunted. Is there motion on that roof? he asked.

Some kind of security, said the rifleman.

Again came the buzz and the man with binoculars stood tall and looked up at a drone, hovering twenty feet above.

Through his scope, still trained on the faraway building, the rifleman saw a man's face, one eye planted against a scope on a rifle that was aimed back at him. Then a white flash, silent, that jumped from its muzzle. Get down! he yelled.

He hadn't yet finished the words when his companion's head exploded. His body flopped onto the gravel and stuck. Two other incoming shots exploded into dust, one against the bricks of the parapet wall that hid the assassin. Another came through the parapet gap where the rifleman had been aiming and smashed through a window in the rooftop booth that housed elevator equipment.

The would-be assassin lay face up, hidden behind the parapet. He aimed his rifle in the direction of the hovering drone and, with one shot, broke it into bits. He shoved his gun back into its case, dug into his companion's pockets for car keys and money, grabbed both bolt bags and ran—jumping down stairs, out a back door, into an alley, then along Ontario Street where there was more tree cover, keeping to places that a drone would have a hard time following. He ran until he was breathing like a racehorse, until the neck of his shirt was saturated with his sweat, and he kept running, kept running, didn't stop until the sound of all the sirens—so many sirens—couldn't be heard.

Olivia extended an open hand toward Eve. She wanted her phone back. It looked as if she expected it.

Eve looked to Jaime, who was full of ambivalence. She picked up the device, ready to return it. It's not normal to be on your phone all the time, said Eve. It's unhealthy.

Mom, okay. I get it. Olivia grabbed fast and missed; Eve had withdrawn, quickly enough to keep the phone from her daughter. Mom. Please.

Eve kept the phone out of Olivia's reach. One thing at a time, said Eve. One. If you stop and smell the flowers, the flowers have to be the one thing that matters. Olivia's eyes were on the phone, only the phone. You're thinking what I'm doing is BS. It may take a few years before it looks like wisdom.

The screen of Olivia's phone lit up. Mom, please, said the girl. Heather is texting me. It's something important. Probably homework.

I'm thinking you don't understand what I'm saying, said Eve. She took her eyes off Olivia only long enough to hold down the button that turned off the phone. I need you to pretend, until you wake up tomorrow morning, that your phone doesn't exist and that computers haven't been invented.

Olivia let her mouth hang wide open.

You have about twelve hours with no Internet, no phone. Think about what's happening right in front of your nose. Sleep without being interrupted by your phone buzzing. Maybe you could read a book before you go to bed.

Olivia cursed at her mother like an English coal miner and stomped away.

The assassin drove east, away from the center of Washington, DC. When he got to his own neighborhood, he turned his lights off, parked three blocks away and walked through dark streets. Through a gap between houses, he saw police cars and uniforms milling around the safe house. He retreated to the Nissan and drove away.

He texted Dirk: *Safe house discovered by police. Target one alive. She has security.*

Dirk responded immediately: *Target 2. Go.*

Ibrahim yanked closed the hotel curtains. He pulled off everything but his shorts and rolled under the covers of the hotel bed. He punched a pillow, made it right, and curled up like an infant.

Norah clicked a message into her phone and hit send. She waited, read a response, sent out another message, waited, read again, wrote some more. Once the phone was face down on the nightstand, she worried. Would the Americans burst in with guns? Would a killer from the embassy? Would Father discover Abdullah had been communicating with her? She paced, peeked through curtains, patted a hand on her chest, worried some more, couldn't relax.

Ibrahim turned his face so he wouldn't be talking into his pillow. You can put your problems in the drawer right there, next to the bed, he said. They'll be waiting for you when you wake up.

What do you know? she asked. So many things could happen to us right now. You don't know Father like I do.

I know you need some sleep, he said. He yawned. You must be exhausted from worrying so much. You should rest. He fell back into his pillows.

She curled sideways under the covers, her nose touching his, absorbing the biscuity breath of a man whose compass always pointed in the same good direction, who kept plenty of air inside the comfortable bubble that surrounded him, a man whose level of self-concern never rose above the reasonable.

You're wonderful, she said. She grabbed his hips and pulled him close.

* * *

Mr. Johnson, you're like a bad penny, said Eve. You keep showing up in the bottom of my purse. Why is that? Eve Coman settled into Dirk Johnson's living room sofa. An officer in uniform stood at attention, just inside the living room door. Dirk and his lawyer sat across from her. The whole room knew she was unwelcome.

Dirk opened his mouth. He uttered an angry syllable before his lawyer, Moe Howard, put a hand on his shoulder and squeezed hard enough to quiet him. My client is not here to answer questions, said Moe. He is invoking his right to counsel. He clicked on his courtroom voice: He's an innocent man who deserves to be left in peace.

It was an innocent question, said Eve.

Nothing about you is innocent, Ms. Coman, said Moe.

Mr. Howard, can you tell me why your client has all those bags of money in his boathouse? We counted eighteen million dollars.

The whites of Dirk's eyes became visible.

Did you hear me? said Moe. My client is not answering any questions. It's no crime to be wealthy and to keep cash. You must be a criminal to think the way you do. Are you a criminal? Should you be investigated? The FBI's inspector general might like to hear from me. Maybe you stole some of my client's money.

Eve pressed, never looking away from Dirk. I'm not asking him any questions, Mr. Howard, I'm asking you. Mr. Howard, have you asked your client how much money we should have found in his boathouse? Dirk squirmed. Mr. Howard, does your client have any idea who dumped this body on his driveway? Our review of video suggests that the perpetrators might have come inside his house before they left.

You are being instructed to leave, said Moe. If you don't, my client will have me sue you. Dirk Johnson has a Constitutional right to freedom of movement. Your officers threatened to arrest him if he left his house. They are despicable. They're ignorant of the law. They'll get you sued. And I repeat: Did you steal from my client? I notice you haven't answered the question. I'll make sure you're the one who pays to put it back. Your retirement accounts, your investments, the equity in your home, all gone. Dirk Johnson will take it. I'll make sure your name is all over the Internet. Poof, and suddenly you will hate your life.

Is Mr. Johnson hiding evidence from the feds? asked Eve. Did he destroy evidence? We could go after him for obstruction of justice. We could seize assets. In a murder case? Oh, he's headed to Supermax in Colorado. Concrete floors, slit windows and steel doors. He won't stay a virgin long. There's a muscleman in there who will make Dirk Johnson his bitch. Shower time, every day, is blow job time. How's your client's gag reflex? Eve snapped her fingers. Poof, and he's wishing he was never born. I don't like your game, Mr. Howard, but I can play it if I have to. Eve turned to the lawyer, who was speechless. Mr. Howard, I'm just a woman asking a few questions. Then, a pause. Oh, dear, are you intimidated? Because you look intimidated.

That's enough, Ms. Coman.

Mr. Howard, did either Norah Saud or Nassir Saud know the dead man? Was he Saudi?

Dirk whispered: Make her stop, Moe.

Mr. Howard, where is your client's wife? asked Eve. I'd like to speak with her. A minivan with her name on the title is in your client's garage. Our investigators found her purse and mobile phone on the kitchen table.

Dirk made two fists and squeezed.

Is Mr. Johnson tense? she asked. Does he know something he'd like to tell me? Can we set up an appointment at headquarters?

Leave, Ms. Coman, said Moe. On his attorney's instructions, he will not be answering any of your questions.

Will you have him seeking Fifth Amendment protections? asked Eve. It won't raise any of the FBI's suspicions if he admits that talking would reveal that he broke the law. You can think about that between now and the time Mr. Johnson starts to answer questions. Mr. Howard, could you ask your client who has the code to open his gate? His wife? A housekeeper? Any neighbors?

Moe put himself in front of Eve, close enough that their lips nearly touched. Leave, he said. Now.

Mr. Howard, has your client seen any signs of forced entry? I'm thinking this body must've been dumped by somebody he knows, somebody who had easy access to his house.

The lawyer pushed Eve's shoulder, shoved his belly against her, forced her two steps backward.

Are you assaulting a federal officer? asked Eve. Maybe you could join Mr. Johnson in Supermax. That's a pretty mouth you got there, boy.

The officer standing guard approached, ready with the butt of his rifle.

Moe backed far enough away that he wasn't touching her. The only thing I'm doing is telling you to leave, he said.

Mr. Howard, what does your client know about the suicide bomber who blew himself up at Farragut North last month?

Ms. Coman, I'm not going to ask again, said Moe. He kept his face in hers. He exhaled fumes of cigarettes and coffee.

He made her retreat. Your breath is disgusting, she said, waving a hand. We have reason to believe the suicide bomber at Farragut North was a Saudi citizen, she said. Your client's wife is a Saudi. We think the dead man is a Saudi. Your client sells arms to the Saudis. I understand that he travels often to Saudi Arabia and every day he talks on the phone with people in Saudi Arabia. All these connections with the Saudis—what do they mean?

The law says you cannot question my client once he invokes his right to counsel, said Moe.

Eve brightened, as if she'd just been complimented. I'm questioning *you*, Mr. Howard. Remember?

Moe opened the door. Leave, he commanded.

When's the last time your client spoke with Nassir Saud? she asked. Was it today?

Leave, said Moe.

She offered up an inauthentic smile. My work here is done, she said. She led the uniformed officer out of the house.

The door slammed. Dirk rose, red in the face. Norah stole two million from the boathouse, he accused. And she must have talked. This woman knows too much. Dirk stared through the window as Eve returned to the FBI's mobile evidence trailer. He pulled a phone out of his pocket. Nassir needs to know about her.

Moe stopped him from dialing out. They're listening, I'm sure, he said. Use mine.

* * *

The Saudi King held on to Abdullah's hand and didn't look likely to free it anytime soon. He held it high on his thigh, closer to the space between his legs than most men would have liked. Abdullah didn't squirm. In medical school, he'd made classmates laugh because he'd been humming mindlessly one day while his scalpel was carving open a cadaver's scrotum. His resolute calm was ever-present, an expanding force—a rising tide that could lift all boats.

Grandfather, I suspect that when Nassir calls, he'll have plans to kill several people high in the American government, said Abdullah. He'll want your permission to end what he claims is a threat to you.

I can tell a real threat from an imagined one, said the King. I do that every day.

Norah is talking with the FBI, which means Nassir is threatened. Saudi Arabia is threatened only if Nassir remains with your government.

That threat sounds real, said the King.

He wants to use you, Grandfather. He wants to kill people to keep his job.

He has done that quite a few times, said the old man. This is normal.

It shouldn't be normal, said Abdullah. If I take your position, it won't be.

You say that now, said the King.

Grandfather, did you know Norah's husband—the American—is not Muslim? asked Abdullah. Nassir lied to you. Abdullah looked into the King's eyes, as earnest as a schoolteacher. A Christian man, an American, knows our family business, he said.

This isn't something you'd normally worry about, said the King.

It worries you, said Abdullah. I know it does.

Nassir would never do what you say.

Norah's husband helps to run the aerospace company, said Abdullah. The husband organized the explosion in Washington, DC. He has poor judgment and Norah's job has been to keep him away from trouble. He was raised Christian in Oklahoma, one of the most Christian places in America. He knows nothing of Islam.

I would know this if it were true, said the King. Do you know how many spies work for me?

You think I'm a liar?

Be careful, Abdullah.

Did you know that Nassir used to dress Norah as a boy and told people she was male?

Maybe you are a liar, said the King.

Norah says he taught her how to act like a man. He paraded her to places dressed as a male. She pretended all the time. Nassir isolated her so he could be the only influence in her life. All the boys and girls were afraid of her.

You weren't afraid of her. You fornicated.

She was lonely and young, said Abdullah. We both were.

I represent all the people in our country, our tribe, said the King. I can't go believing things like that just because Norah says them.

Did you ever hear anybody say that Nassir had a nephew he favored?

Abdullah, he has dozens of nephews.

Ask him about Qurban. That's the name he gave to Norah when she dressed as a male. The name does not exist in Nassir's family. It would be easy to confirm.

The old man's face turned hot. I would know this, he said.

Abdullah spoke with the ease of a man who had it all figured out. Ask yourself if it's reasonable to take measure of what people tell you, to wonder what's truth and what is not. Someone told me that people will lie to their King to influence him.

You're afraid of Nassir, said the King. That's why you say what you do.

For me, Grandfather? Can you pretend to believe? Only for two minutes.

I have to change everything to believe you, said the old man.

Abdullah was steady and persistent. You only need to pretend that certain facts are true, he said. Why is it that Nassir never told you how his wife died? Grandfather, you told people about your wife who bled to death after childbirth. People asked and you told them.

Abdullah, Nassir's wife was a suicide. She left her family and she was ashamed.

Nassir kept his story simple and he repeated it until it seemed true, said Abdullah. It was easier that way.

Everybody knows her story, said the King. We all know.

Can I send you the Security Directorate's report on her? It's on my e-mail.

How do you think she died, Abdullah?

Abdullah put a hand on the old man's shoulder. This is good. You're being curious, said Abdullah. Nassir locked her in a cell by herself with nothing else. No books, no television. She refused food and water. It took three days before her heart stopped.

The old man stood, turned away and examined the books on the shelves of his library, the official record of speeches from Saudi kings of old, their expressions of faith, of loyalty to Sharia—a holy doctrine that, like quite a few holy doctrines, was known to shift with the installation of each new supreme leader. The bindings that held together their declarations were made of the brand of leather used to whip adulterers and prostitutes. After decades of sitting undisturbed, the leather was brittle, but retained a masculine aroma.

Norah says Nassir locked up her mother because he was afraid of women, said Abdullah. Also, he was angry that his firstborn was not a boy.

Are you accusing him of being homosexual? asked the King.

I'm saying he's afraid of women and girls, said Abdullah. Half of the world—he is afraid of it. He is desperately afraid people will find this out.

I've known Nassir since he was born, said the King. He has warned me of people who would have killed me. He has protected me. I would be dead if not for him.

He pretends to care because it's in his interest, said Abdullah. He is dangerous, even to you.

He would not dare to threaten me.

He keeps a plan to kill you. Norah knows the details. He's friends with a man named Tahir who is desperate to kill you.

I'm supposed to believe something that is impossible? That the man I've trusted with my life would murder me if it served his needs?

Any man who doesn't admit that he is sometimes a fool, said Abdullah, is twice a fool.

Abdullah hadn't been gone sixty seconds when the King's mobile rang. The King checked the name on the screen before he picked up. I suppose you heard that conversation, Mr. President, said the King.

The Russian President confirmed he had—and that Abdullah was right about Zarkawi being dead. Also, did the King know that Nassir Saud really was a homosexual?

Do you want something? asked the King. A man as busy as the Russian President must have a reason for calling.

Nassir refuses my directions, said the President. He says he knows better than I do.

You think you can tell me how to run every part of my country? asked the King.

You think I can't?

The King lit into him. Piss on your arrogance, he said.

You'd be doing the same thing if you could, said the Russian President.

No, said the King. I don't wish to own you. There's a limit to how much one man should have.

I need Nassir ended, said the President. This is not a request.

The King didn't hide his contempt. Will that be all, Mr. President?

I'm sure I'll need more later and when I do, I'll call, said the Russian.

SEVENTEEN

In tiny, ragged steps, the edges of Norah's front teeth bit clean through the nail on her littlest finger, almost all the way across. She captured the hanger between incisors, yanked it away and spit it on the floor of her carriage—a black, bulletproof Chevrolet Suburban. She was belted in, solid, couldn't go anywhere. In the front seats were two FBI agents, both in suits, who encouraged Norah's dread. When they responded to nervous backseat queries from Norah or Ibrahim, it was in a dialect that DeAndre could speak back to them, inflections included. DeAndre said not to worry. Eve Coman was running the show. She always did as she promised.

An interstate highway of white concrete sped by, so much faster than seemed safe. When the behemoth Chevy took corners or changed lanes, the leaning made it obvious the vehicle was prone to flipping.

Norah chose a spot on the nail of her ring finger and began biting.

The time was near to confess and to implicate. Vile acts and Old Testament cruelties to be admitted. She'd always done as Father ordered, had been a tool for a man who took pride in malicious creativity. She was one of the many afraid to say no to him, forced to choose between impossible alternatives—whether to inflict misery or to suffer it. Whether to whip a chained man or to be chained and whipped.

Norah hadn't fully disclosed herself to anybody, not for her entire life. She'd been vigilant, always hiding something, never daring to let others judge her. If they knew too much, the embassy people would tell Father on her. If Dirk had ever known her plans, he'd have choked her in her sleep. Would Ibrahim's feelings change if he knew of her violence? Would he walk away?

Would Abdullah change his opinion of her?

Would the Russians want her dead?

Upon Norah's reveal, Eve Coman and the FBI would be the first to know the full picture, the severity of it. A White American woman, someone sheltered, privileged, would no doubt harbor the kind of judgment that would make her eyes burn. And how different could the FBI be from Saudi Arabia's men in khaki? Each had a selfish definition of justice and an incentive to mutilate the accused.

Perhaps Norah's life would end with confinement, devoid of comfort—cold breakfast mashes of oversalted meat glopped onto trays—or getting assaulted by prison guards who used mop handles.

Yes, she'd been promised immunity, but agreements were often torn up. The bullies—and the Americans had them—would laugh if you called on them to honor a bargain they didn't like. Guarantees and safeguards were often lies and if you'd thought otherwise, you were an idiot. You can't hurt them, so to hell with you. Eve's army must have some of those. They might be hiding, but they were there.

People like Eve understood little of life and justice under Wahhabism and were quick to judge. If they'd ever studied Wahhabism, it was in a classroom, reading books lit by the lamp of due process, books written by people with the naïve expectations of those taught to play fair. They'd never imagined the anxiety that comes from living in a world where your father might condemn you to be flogged until dead because you'd been raped by your brother. It would be easy to blame a Saudi woman for going along with mass murder if you didn't understand where she came from. It was beyond human capacity to offer mercy to a person considered despicable.

Still, to confess: Did she have to? She chewed and chewed on a thumbnail, tried to get it to tear off.

Ibrahim, belted in next to Norah, touched her hand and stopped her. You're afraid? he asked in Arabic.

Her eyes hung and emotion oozed; she was scared as hell. We could have run away to hide—somewhere quiet, she said. We have two million.

Don't wonder what if, he said. You have to assume that you can trust, that things will be fine. We're past the point of no return.

Father's friends are everywhere, said Norah. What if even one person at the FBI is evil? We could be dead in an hour and then out comes the bone saw.

In poetic Arabic, he said he was praying for her to find peace. Desperate fear leads to poor choices, he said.

This doesn't scare you? she asked.

I know it's scary, he said.

From his seat just behind, DeAndre shushed them, warned them that they were being heard. It's not safe to talk here, he said. Stop it.

She held Ibrahim's hand tightly, pulled it into the valley between her knees. She said she was sorry and had no business being so needy. She kept one expression the rest of the trip. She could have let herself cry, but it seemed better if she didn't. With some things, it seemed like you had to keep on pretending.

* * *

Eve Coman crossed her arms and stared out of an FBI window at a plain-faced office building that never changed expression. She tapped a foot, paced, looked around the room for something to do, saw her notes, sat down with them, couldn't sit still, stood back up and paced some more.

Louis Irons interrupted his reading. There's no reason to be so nervous, he said.

The woman we're dealing with scares me, said Eve. She could be evil.

Eve went to her desk and pushed on the speakerphone. Lola? Isn't she here yet?

She's not due for half an hour, said Lola. Eve, relax.

What time is she due? demanded Eve. I need an ETA.

Silence.

Eve ranted into the speakerphone: Why was she in the dark about the time when interrogation was to begin? She'd only asked for an effing time. She scolded Lola for being a complainer. Still no response. Lola? Are you listening?

From a dozen offices away, Lola zipped over, stuck her head in the room and startled Eve. Boss, we are so almost there, said Lola. We'll have Dirk Johnson in custody by lunch.

Eve looked ready to attack. I have questions, Eve said. All I want are some damn answers.

Louis barked, raising his voice for the duration of one syllable. *Just* stop, he said. Nassir Saud isn't coming to the meeting. It's his daughter. With a tilt of his head, Louis told Lola to leave. Once they were alone, he scolded Eve. A good commanding officer never loses her head, he said. You are so much better than what I just saw.

Nassir Saud is the man who had us chasing ghosts in Baltimore, said Eve. What's going on while we're handling Norah? Are we being played? I'll bet it was Nassir's assassin aiming his rifle at my family. She pointed at her office window. He could be aiming at us right now, Lou.

Lou rose and put his face in hers. Sit down and calm down, he ordered. So much is riding on that.

Norah and Ibrahim sat next to each other at the FBI conference table. Across the table was Eve Coman. She settled against the back of her chair as DeAndre and Norah and Ibrahim conferred over the language of the immunity agreement the FBI had written. Norah and DeAndre signed it and Eve signed it and DeAndre said it was fine, that the meeting could begin. Six young FBI attorneys entered the room and when they sat down, they outnumbered Norah and they gave her the feeling of being surrounded.

Norah and Ibrahim were offered coffee and water and they asked for water and there was an awkward few minutes of no chit-chat while the woman who'd been seated closest to the door had to search a couple of FBI kitchenettes for a clean pair of tumblers because the FBI refused to stock bottled water.

One of the FBI attorneys wrote down an idea. She tore it off her legal pad and gave it to Eve. Eve liked it and nodded with thanks.

Norah felt like a small dog in a crowd of big ones. She unconsciously made herself look a little bigger by tightening her neck and her shoulders. Her mouth was dry as dirt.

When her water was set in front of her, Norah gulped, drank half of it in two swallows. Let's do this, she said.

Eve told Ibrahim she would have questions for Norah, but only after he left the conference room. Somebody rose, ready to escort him out. Norah refused. Ibrahim was not leaving the room, she said. He needed to hear what she had to say. She would not be denied.

That's not part of our agreement, said Eve.

It is now, said Norah. Hidden beneath the table, Norah's hands lay in her lap, one of them holding the other so it wouldn't shake.

Eve spoke into the ear of the attorney sitting next to her and the two of them nodded, having agreed upon something. He can stay until we begin questions about his conduct, said Eve.

DeAndre signaled his approval.

Eyes turned to Ibrahim. Fine, he said.

Norah's fingertip drew a couple of circles in the air. Let's go, she said. Her stomach cramped. She bent at the middle and grimaced; some things she couldn't hide.

Are you okay? asked Eve.

Just go.

Eve's opening move was predictable. Could Norah confirm that Dirk Johnson had confessed to murdering Red Merrill? she asked.

Yes, Norah said. She explained in detail Dirk's confession, the methods Dirk said he'd used to make it appear that Red had killed himself. She volunteered the date of Dirk's confession to her, the time, the place, the fact that only Dirk and Norah were present. She outlined Dirk's confessed motive and his methods. She was careful to say that she'd not known anything in advance and could not have prevented it, hadn't contributed to the crime in any way. It took forty seconds.

Holding Dirk's crimes up for the room to see offered Norah some relief, seemed like an easy way to get things started. Norah released the toes that she had curled up in her shoes. Maybe this wouldn't be so terrible, she thought.

You came prepared, said Eve. She looked at DeAndre and, wordlessly, she thanked him. His assurances about the witness's value were looking rock solid. It was apparent he'd given his client good lessons on how to avoid saying too much or too little; Norah had hit her mark.

A member of Eve's team slid a piece of paper and a pen across the table. The affidavit? Norah asked.

Eve confirmed. With your signature on that, we can arrest Dirk Johnson, she said. We'll have him in custody in an hour.

Norah offered it to DeAndre for his comment. I've seen it, he said. It's fine.

Norah read it anyway before signing. The affidavit was passed back and the woman who'd produced it left the room.

Eve restarted, and with some self-interest: What did Norah know about the attempt to kill Eve's family? Who was responsible?

Norah said it was almost certainly Dirk, but she had no personal knowledge, nothing that could be used in evidence. I listened in when you questioned Dirk about Red Merrill, she said. You had him cornered and I thought right away he might try to kill you. Dirk and Father are the same kind of person. They'll both kill to solve a problem. They see it as an ordinary part of doing business.

There came lots more questions about the attempt to assassinate Eve followed by denials of knowledge and wrongdoing. As soon as I suspected, I contacted DeAndre and had him tell you, said Norah. Do you doubt me on that?

Eve was slow to answer. No, she said. I don't suppose I do.

The questions segued into the subject of Farragut North—the planning, the logistics, the names, the dates, the reasons. Norah became cautious and then defensive, afraid of where her answers would lead. Her voice trailed off several times when she had to admit to certain things. Several times she was asked to repeat and she wormed about in her seat. She recounted her training of Ibrahim and Omar, the threats she'd made, intimidation used to keep them obedient, her physical assault of each one, of practice visits to Farragut North and Metro Center, of developing timelines for terrorists. She'd kept the brothers in a house-sized cage. She'd given instructions to them to maximize the number of fatalities they'd inflict. She'd hidden information from them when she felt it beneficial. She'd given updates on the brothers to Dirk and to Father. Whatever directives they gave her, she performed them.

Norah told of murders in Saudi Arabia she'd performed at Father's direction, of her cooperation in Father's extortion of people who didn't know any better. She interrupted herself: Everything I tell you, I'm immune?

Yes, said Eve. She tapped the paper the immunity agreement was printed on. Your excellent lawyer saw to that.

Norah continued: She'd lied to people for Father so he could take advantage. She'd learned to drive. She'd learned guns. She used her nice female handwriting to write fake letters to people when Father asked her.

The questions kept on and kept on. It felt like small arms fire coming from close range. Norah couldn't seem to sit still. Everything inside her was tight and she looked weakened by the questioning.

Norah's confession made her nauseous. She'd once shot a man on Father's orders, she said. In Riyadh, she'd kicked a pregnant woman in the belly. She'd spied on agitators, knowing they'd have their heads cut off.

Several times she stopped talking because she had to rearrange herself. Eventually, she let it flow. The pressure pushed down on her and she was too weary to push back. She wept, stood and pushed herself away from the table. She faced away from people, her cheek touching the wall. When she lost control of her weeping, she kneeled on the carpeted floor and used the wall to keep from falling over. Her peace of mind went completely missing.

Eve dismissed the other FBI people from the room, kneeled next to Norah and offered her tissues. Norah dabbed at her eyes and her sobs grew less severe.

You don't have to be afraid of me, said Eve.

It's not you, said Norah. She looked at Ibrahim and took his hand. Do you think less of me? she asked.

He hugged her and said no, that he was in love with her and hoped for it to stay that way. He was not fit to judge. God says we shouldn't judge, he said. Confess everything and you don't have to worry about it anymore, he said. Get it out.

I've never felt so exposed, she said.

Norah rose, took her seat again and tore several tissues from Eve's box. Now what was your question? she asked.

Eve's team returned to the room and took more notes. The young attorneys kept handing written suggestions to Eve.

The women talked for two more hours without a break. Eve's supporting actors occasionally had to excuse themselves for nonnegotiable visits to the bathroom. Neither of the principals seemed willing to interrupt things. When the questions got to Ibrahim's actions, Eve didn't ask him to leave the room. DeAndre had told Eve she had no reason to fear Ibrahim, no reason to worry that he and Norah contrived their stories to be consistent with one another; an hour with Norah was all it took to prove that he'd been right.

Will you testify in open court against your husband? asked Eve.

DeAndre had told Norah to expect the question; no criminal investigator would waste time on a case that could be defeated by the ability of one spouse to refuse to testify against the other. I'll testify, said Norah. I do not plan to assert the spousal privilege, using the phrase before Eve did.

Do you intend to assert the spousal privilege if Dirk Johnson wants to testify against you? Eve asked.

Absolutely not, said Norah. When Dirk knows that I'm planning on testifying against him, he'll invent crimes that I'm not guilty of. I know he will. But he's got no evidence to support anything. He'll say Farragut North was all my idea, that he was taking my instructions. Proving him wrong is easy.

How easy? asked Eve.

Jump into Broad Creek, said Norah. At our dock, under the water, you'll find bricks of Semtex. I put them there after I took them out of the suicide vest that Ibrahim was going to wear. Dirk still has no idea I replaced most of the bricks in Ibrahim's vest with clay.

The two women, each with an entourage, came back the next day and the questions and answers went for six more hours. Murder, dismemberment, extortion, said Norah. Mass murder, secrecy, egotist potentates and bags of money. Official lies that got people killed. The stories seemed like they would never end.

At the end of the day, Eve was chewing on the end of her Bic. You want me to believe you're innocent in all of this? she asked.

DeAndre inserted himself into the conversation: She doesn't care if you believe, he said. She only cares if you give her immunity. She doesn't want the FBI following her for the rest of her life.

* * *

Eve, my introduction to murder came at age fifteen. Father pointed into the desert and told me to drive. We were going to see a man we hated and we were going to kill him. We.

The man had accused the Saudi King of terrible things, homosexual things. Somebody heard and told Father, and he told the Mutaween to put the man in jail.

For his entire life, Father told me, the man refused any work and stole to support himself. Father hated thieves. Thieves kill society, he said. Businesses fail because people steal. People who are entitled to their wealth are made poor by people who don't want work and so they steal. A thief doesn't deserve luxury any more than a condemned man should have a vacation. We cut off their hands for a reason, he said. Father wanted me to fear thieves and hate them and I did both.

I kept driving the Range Rover until we were miles into nowhere, deep in the desert where heat killed almost everything. Along the desert road were animals, dead—some hyenas and other kinds I could not tell. The smell came in the car. Moistened death. There were clouds of bugs and ugly vultures hopping, taking turns.

Father knew his surroundings. He gave me directions off the paved road. We went to a place where it was scrub and sand and we waited outside the car, and just when the heat was too much, a van came and three men in khaki got out with a naked prisoner whose hands were zip-tied behind him and they shoved him down. He was hairy all over, especially near his penis, which I'd never seen one. I stared. He tried to stand and his legs wobbled and he gave up. He sat on his bare bottom, his arms held back by the zip ties. Then, snap. He was polite and pleasant. He talked to Father like somebody who knew him. He didn't sound like a thief.

My mouth tasted like metal and I thought I would spit up. This man would be dead in minutes. An insect buzzed my ear, close. I jumped sideways and I had to put both hands flat on the ground to keep from falling, and that's when I started seeing spots that weren't there. I was desperate for water, desperate to get away. One of Father's khaki men had a gallon jug and poured it. He coated the naked man in honey to encourage bugs and hyenas.

The man was saying things to Father and he knew Father's name. The man said he'd lost, it was obvious, and he had no reason to fight. He said, You won, Nassir. I admit. Good for you, Nassir. The victory, the congratulations, they're yours. He admired Father's determination and put him at ease. Father was feeling proud of himself and wasn't hiding it.

Then the man asks questions. Was Father pleased to inflict pain? Did Father's men know they would be killed if Father suspected them of disloyalty? Did they know Father was afraid of them? What if Father's men turned on him? Did the men know Father was queer? Had Father sucked any of their dicks? The man was smart. He was going to have somebody else kill Father, if he could.

Father was enraged, he was screaming nonsense. I'd never seen him lose his composure. He kicked the naked man in the face and all the questions stopped. The khakis put a sack on the man's head and Father kneeled next to him. People like you are stupid and don't know it, he said. You don't know your place. Father waved and a khaki man brought a machete. Father put it in my hands and shoved me. Be a man, Father said. Don't be anything less because then people think you're afraid. He went and stood with the uniforms. Three men plus Father, in a row, their arms crossed. I really was afraid. The most ever. The khaki men saw a male because I had on male robes. They expected me to behave like a man, to take orders. They stared, ready for me to murder the man. I stood as tall as I could. I needed to look like I was bigger than a girl. I walked up to the man and raised the blade. Father yelled at me to stop. No, no, he said. I was relieved because maybe he'd changed his mind. Not his head, Father said. The feet. Cut off the feet.

Father mocked him after I'd whacked through both his ankles. Father told him: Try and crawl away. That will give you false hope before you die and it will make sure your son never finds your body. Father said he would have somebody contact the man's son and tell him where to find him. Your son will come for you so he can bury you and he will see that Nassir Saud cut off your feet in the desert and left you to die and he will tell people how terrible I am. You and your son will end up helping me. Think about that while you're deciding whether to crawl away and keep your son from finding your body.

As I drove us away, Father was telling me that was how you could really beat a man. You take away every reason he has to live and you leave him wanting to die but having to wait for it. If people ever hear that story, Father said, they'll do anything I tell them to.

It was so hot that day. You would not believe.

* * *

The Saudi King maintained twelve palace estates in his home country, and he made it known that he spent almost all of his time at one or the other. He hated for people to think he was anything but a devoted family man. Every domestic palace had acres of lush gardens, each an extravagance that would have been as dead as the desert but for the heaps of royal wealth devoted to producing and piping in gushers of desalinated seawater clean enough to drink. From the air, against the background of desert sands, the gardens appeared unnatural: oblong islands of deep green, borders cut in by squads of Saud cousins who, like their fathers and uncles, were probably the world's highest-paid horticulturalists.

Inside the gardens were leafy trees casting shadows on paths of smooth stone, a place where pastel petals, blood lilies and mixed floral aromas could thrive in desert hell. English topiaries, boxwoods mostly, were trimmed to resemble predators and prey: panthers and tigers, chipmunks and baby rabbits that made children coo. Feeders and baths were havens for candy-colored songbirds brought from Costa Rica and uncaged in the gardens.

As Abdullah had predicted, Nassir went straight to his King, met the old man in his garden, and said it was urgent. Could they talk indoors? The King said he was glad Nassir had come. He had something important, too. He took Nassir's hand, except this time it was fingers between fingers, and he did not let Nassir lead and the King did not go inside. He stopped at a hedge that resembled the face of a lion and stroked it. Every animal lives at the mercy of the lion. And we're animals, Nassir. Every one of us. Hidden diffusers spewed conditioned air throughout the garden, keeping the atmosphere perfectly pleasant.

It was glorious.

The lion needs mercy, from somewhere, from someone, said Nassir. From the members of the tribe, he needs mercy to live. Who would protect him from eight jackals coming at once?

Most other animals hide if the lion comes near, said the King. Before any conflict, before anger or injury, most animals concede the battle to the lion. The King kept stroking the lion. They call this one *king* for a reason.

There is tremendous value in being able to avoid the damage that comes from conflict, said Nassir. Inspiring fear serves me well as I do your business, Your Grace.

Forty paces away, crossing the garden and drawing closer: two of the King's bodyguards, sidearms in holsters, each with strips of braided brass on the shoulders of their dark uniforms. The men were fighting soldiers who'd earned their way out of Saudi special forces and had a well-known mission: to keep themselves between their King and any threat to his safety. They formed the last ring of security around the King. The uniforms in the garden meant Nassir was considered a threat. Nassir knew. His King knew. The guards knew. Someone— someone trusted—had concerns about Nassir's loyalty and there'd been no one in the royal circle with the knowledge or the incentive required to overturn the leaden questions that pressed down on Nassir.

Is this the important thing you wanted to talk about, Your Grace? asked Nassir, referring to the uniforms.

The questions raised about Nassir must have been significant, must have been enough to cause damage when cast against the armor that Nassir had built around himself. The armor was the residue of never having been caught in a lie, of consistent loyalty from Nassir's field agents and assassins, of devotion to his role as protector and fixer. All that, and decades of accurate, life-saving intel about liars and traitors. Somehow, despite it, he was suspect.

You're here to tell me that trouble is coming our way from America? asked the King. With the tip of a brown finger that was too old to straighten, he lifted a blossom and kissed it as if it were the cheek of a girl-child. America has always been afraid to deny Saudi Arabia, and all because America has been afraid of what happens if we're no longer their backchannel to Moscow. I fear that could be changing.

With a palm, Nassir brought in a long-stemmed peony and inhaled its sugary scent. Before I leave, he said, there are things you should know. Norah killed the security man from our embassy in Washington. She dumped the body on her husband's doorstep, as if he was a murderer. The husband helps run Douglas-American. The body brought the FBI to his house. Our six-billion-dollar company could be lost, our path to controlling our defenses, our path to keeping the Americans willing to defend us. Our path to independence without oil. It could all be gone, just because of Norah. One person, one woman, stands in our way. She is your enemy, not me.

Norah's husband? asked the King. What mosque did he attend when he was growing up?

Nassir tucked in his chin—it looked like an involuntary motion. He spoke slowly: What is it you really wish to know?

Did you marry your daughter to a Christian and lie to me about it? asked the King. Did you bring an infidel into the royal tent?

I have lost your confidence because you think Norah's husband isn't Muslim?

He went to school in Oklahoma? asked the King.

I'm sure he did, said Nassir.

Blackwood High School, in particular. An American school. A public school.

I should know this?

You know everything about everybody, said the King. You say that sometimes.

Nassir cleared his throat.

Your daughter's husband is not loyal to Saudi Arabia, declared the King. He has no understanding of Islam, no idea who I am, and he wouldn't care if he damaged me. You gave our secrets to people who could never be counted upon. The King's eyes wandered. Tell me about your nephew, Qurban.

Who is behind these questions? asked Nassir.

The King answered with a stare. Do you remain friends with Karima's brother, Tahir—the one who hates me?

Nassir looked at the bodyguards. The men looked back, hands on hips, weapons on belts.

Are you still friends with Tahir? asked the King. We found e-mails on his computer. He told people that you offered to let him murder me. The King shifted bony shoulders under loose robes. When the Americans found Bandar Zarkawi dead on your son-in-law's driveway, did they find a note?

Nassir snorted and the only things that came out were fear and loathing. Did the King have a connection to Norah? he asked. Had he heard about Norah through the FBI? Through the Russians? Why would you hide that from me? he asked.

Call Nassir Saud and tell him that Bandar Zarkawi is dead, said the King. That's what the note said. Yes? Why does the Russian President say you let Victor Ivanov shove his penis in your mouth?

The Russian President wants something from you, said Nassir. He wants to separate you from those who would protect you.

I have chosen the one who will succeed me. He says he will not be needing you.

What does he want from you, this man?

The King did not look away from his flowers. The Americans know that Nassir Saud, head of Saudi Arabia's Security Directorate, is the secret owner of Douglas-American Aerospace, he said. They're going to seize the company. They say it's a criminal enterprise.

I make impossible choices so you aren't burdened with the truth, said Nassir. I turn enemies into allies with promises I'd never keep. I turn people who would kill you into people who don't know they're helping you. I've saved you from threats you never knew about. Even as he said the words, Nassir must have known his effort was wasted.

Before Nassir left, the King kissed him twice. The King's guards put Nassir into the back of a palace car, took him home and stood guard with their weapons, one outside each of the two gates that gave entry to the property surrounding his residence.

When Nassir awoke the next morning, guards were still there, but different ones. He tried his landline and it was dead. He tried his mobile and it was, too. No Internet. He took a burner phone out of a hidden drawer and called Victor. The phone rang and rang and went to voice mail and the only thing Nassir knew to do was to weep like some women he'd seen.

EIGHTEEN

Nadine? Nadine? Louis Irons, a Bureau division chief, a man who'd twice been short-listed for director of the FBI, a Marine Corps badass, clicked into his kitchen, barefoot, wearing only a pair of black suit pants with an open zipper. A marbled slab of fat hung over his waistband. Where did you put my dry cleaning? he asked. I need a clean shirt.

His wife looked up from The Washington Post spread across the breakfast table and stared at his layered middle. You look like something that melted, she said. And that clicking from your metal knee—it's annoying.

It's your imagination, said Louis. Nobody else says they hear anything.

I imagine things every time you walk near. Why is that, smart guy?

He stared, irked.

I put the shirts in your closet, she said. You didn't look. You never look.

I was just in my closet. I looked.

I can't reach the high bar anymore. I hung them low. That's how come I know I put them there. With the spots on her hand, she waved him away.

Louis disappeared. He returned with the calling cards of a career civil servant whose fashion sense coalesced during the Nixon Years: a white dress shirt and skinny brown-striped tie held in place with a shiny tac. You hung the shirts with my casual pants. Who would look there?

Do people know the reason you haven't retired is because your wife would murder you if you stayed home? she asked. In her lavender housecoat, Nadine rose, opened the refrigerator, poked a skinny wrist inside and retrieved a brown paper sack. Don't forget this. Do you know how much was on our credit card last month from you buying lunch?

I chase the terrorists, said Louis. I go where they go.

Name one place you can't take a ham sandwich and a can of Fresca, she demanded. She arched an eyebrow. She went to the front door of the apartment, opened it and spoke to the man standing watch in the hall—an agent for the US Secret Service, a beefy man who seemed capable and boyish at the same time. Ryan, are you ready? I need for him to go to work.

Ryan grinned and showed his straight teeth. Mrs. Irons, please tell Louis we're always ready.

She called at him: They're ready, Lou. Go.

He appeared and pulled on his topcoat. I'll be late. Will you be awake when I come home?

Nadine adjusted his coat at the shoulders, turned him around and pulled his chin until their faces were close. She kissed him long enough to taste him and looked at him once in each eye. If you're lucky, she said. She smiled and on his way out the door she patted him dead center on his behind.

Across Connecticut Avenue from the main entrance of Louis and Nadine's apartment building was another apartment building with an open window on the second floor. Despite the persistent cold of March and the morning mist, the window had been open for an hour. It connected to an apartment, unlit, drapes open. Four feet inside was a man, sitting on a bed, his long rifle and its Nikon scope balanced on a ladderback chair, aimed out the window. The man checked his watch and returned to his scope, which had its crosshairs centered on a strip of sidewalk between an idling Chevrolet SUV and the side door to the building that was home to a man marked for assassination.

Inside the lobby of Louis and Nadine's building, behind a wall of miniblinds, apartment dwellers and those who attended to them went about their morning: a super with a stepladder waited for an elevator; a red-uniformed doorman at the nearby main entrance gushed over an elderly couple. Louis stood within a vestibule by the side entrance and took orders from his escort. He waited for word it was safe to move, to be ushered into a waiting vehicle. The driver radioed he was behind the wheel. The motor was idling and a door was open for the passenger and his escort. The suits stationed outside had their firearms at the ready. They'd scanned the scene and spotted no threat.

When one of the suits got out of the SUV and pulled on the door to Louis's apartment building, the rifleman's finger curled and touched his trigger. He took a breath, slow and long, and held. A muscle above his dominant right eye spasmed and his eyelid quivered. The instant Louis and his escort emerged, he jerked. His gun jacked a pellet of lead that shattered a man's rib, ripped through a lung and nicked the anterior edge of an L5 vertebra before skipping off the sidewalk and plugging deep into the rump of an unfortunate Portuguese deliveryman who howled and urinated on himself.

The bodyguards who'd been stationed outside locked onto the gunshot's source—the open window was the obvious choice—and fired. One shot sideswiped the rifleman's temple and burnt his skin. A second and a third landed square in his chest and laid him flat, bleeding fast.

Louis and Ryan dove, heads first, into the backseat of the Suburban and the driver gunned it. Siren wailing, the SUV surged and dodged away, keeping to the yellow line in the middle of the street.

Gunshot wound. Upper right quadrant, said Louis. The driver radioed ahead, identified his destination as the emergency room at Howard U Hospital ER and asked for doctors to be ready.

As a second lieutenant in the Marine infantry, Louis had seen lots of shredded torsos. Muscle memory took over and he put pressure on the entry and exit wounds—both sides of the man—to limit blood loss. He sandwiched it between his hands, one pressing with his balled-up suitcoat and the other with a paper sack that carried oversized slices of seeded rye bread.

The bleeding bodyguard moaned like he was in labor and pleaded for more life, didn't want to die. Louis told him to stop his damn whining. A medic at a tent hospital in Vietnam had once told Louis to be stern with battlefield patients; he said no injured man would think he was dying if somebody scolded him for complaining about pain.

Ryan got to the ER within three minutes of being shot. Before Howard's doctors and nurses became his rescuers, he very nearly died.

* * *

In the Waldo County seat, at an iced-up car wash, Norah and Ibrahim had hosed out the back of the van before they returned it to its owner, Robah, the unpublished poet. They alternated efficiently between Norah's hose and Ibrahim's brushwork.

Norah had steeled herself for a walk into a liquor store and her purchase of a dark-green bottle of Irish whiskey. She felt compelled to offer an explanation to Ibrahim. It's for Robah, she said. Annie said it's his favorite.

You don't have to make excuses, not unless you're doing something you intend will hurt me, said Ibrahim.

I was afraid you'd judge me, she said. Sitting in the glow of neon beer signs, Norah took his hand. I hope I can learn to be as good for you as you are for me, she said.

After buying the whiskey, the couple drove to Robah's farm—Jack and Annie met them there—and stayed when Robah invited them to sit and enjoy a meal. Before they ate, Robah and his wheelchair rolled out to his barn with them and introduced them to Edna, St. Vincent and Millay, his three new calves. Edna wiggled like a big puppy and everybody hugged her. Ibrahim got cow shit on his shirt and had to borrow a clean one from his host. At dinner, Robah taught them about limericks. He'd written a limerick for each of his four guests. He made them promise to memorize the poems.

I'm not memorizing this, said Jack. My name doesn't rhyme with *dick*.

It does if you read it right, swore Robah. Look, you memorize one poem and then you're writing them.

Jack pulled out and read a poem by Robah with six long stanzas, each one describing stupid little children. He finished with two slaps on his own knee. He guffawed. What does that even mean, Robah?

I haven't decided, said Robah.

After dinner, Robah and Jack and Annie sipped on the Irish whiskey, which was made in a tiny Irish town by an Irish company that was home to Robah's great-grandfather in his boyhood. Ibrahim and Norah had diet ginger ale.

They turned on Robah's Grundig and listened to the community radio station playing a scratchy 1936 live recording of Louis Armstrong and the Hot Five performing *Muskrat Ramble* at Chicago's Bugsy Moran Ballroom. The music's speed hinted at a sweaty, orgiastic concert hall where people danced vigorously, sometimes with both feet off the ground. It was the sound of joyous abandon.

Robah ordered Ibrahim to give back his shirt before leaving; Ibrahim would have to ride home in the chill, bare-chested. As Ibrahim handed back the shirt, Robah slapped him on the arm and offered a steely grin. The night you went home with no shirt is the same night you started writing poetry, said Robah. You won't forget this for your whole life.

The younger man was on the verge of laughing. I think I like you, Robah, said Ibrahim, but you're a little weird.

Not weird, said Robah. Daring.

Annie had been staring at Ibrahim's bare chest while they stood inside Robah's front door, prepared to leave. You have such beautiful nipples, she said. Can I touch one? Norah and Ibrahim and Robah laughed it up, Annie laughing along with them, but the truth was that she'd sounded serious.

Jack looked bothered by it. He opened the door and announced it was time to go. The cold air was coming in and the movement toward the door stopped when Robah spoke in a belligerent tone: Don't ever come here if you didn't call first and get permission. I keep my guns close at all times. I don't intend ever to be victimized. Never ever. We clear?

Ibrahim was startled and looked to other faces in the room, and everybody else but Robah looked startled, too.

Jack's surprise looked the most severe of all of them. You feeling okay, old friend?

The old man slapped Ibrahim's arm again. I'm just kidding you, son. Look at me. I'm an old man without a wife living on a farm. You come to visit any damn time you want. You and your girlfriend both.

* * *

Nassir lay nearly naked on the table while, spider-like, the physician's brown fingertips crawled across the flesh of his abdomen, probing for abnormalities. Nassir's stomach growled.

You're hungry? asked the physician. He stood tall and perfectly handsome and wore a clean white cotton coat with his name, *Abdullah Saud, M.D.*, embroidered in Arabic script across his right breast.

I've had nothing since breakfast. Very little yesterday. Thank you for staying late to see me, Abdullah. I feel quite ill.

The doctor hovered over Nassir's face and flicked the beam of a penlight at his pupils, one eye at a time, back and forth. Scrutinizing Nassir's irises, the physician put his face close enough to Nassir's so that each man was inhaling breath given off by the other.

Your parents—they are well? asked Nassir. He held himself perfectly still, no doubt mindful of his examiner's expectations.

When he was done examining Nassir's eyes, the physician motioned for him to sit up and when he did, the younger man stationed himself between Nassir's knees, his hands wrapped around the older man's neck. He pressed his fingers into the soft spots and worked their way up to his jaw and to his temples. Father has designed a new kind of desalination plant being constructed by the sea near Dammam, said Abdullah. Very efficient. Two plants can support a city. Our King believes we can export the technology and profit from it. He believes it may replace the oil money. Father is like a boy with a toy.

He put the heel of a hand on Nassir's forehead. Push against this, he said.

And your mother? Nassir strained, then relaxed.

She has published a new version of her textbook. She talks of retirement. He held out a palm, facing down. Give me your left hand. Push up, push against this. Nassir pushed, then they switched and he pressed up with his right.

Your parents are people I have always admired, Abdullah. It is no surprise that you became our King's favorite grandson.

Abdullah scoped each of Nassir's ears, pressing inward, as deeply as his instrument would allow.

Our King talks of you often, said Nassir. Your successes? You would think they were his.

I honor our King with my loyalty and respect, but he is still a grandfather. Abdullah laughed. If I worked a delivery truck, he would declare I was the most valuable driver in the world. He scoped Nassir's nose, one nostril at a time. He removed his scope, swapped out one of the pieces, and used it to study the inside on his patient's mouth.

Nassir put a hand on the younger man's elbow and interrupted the examination. Abdullah, do you know what happens if you lose our King's trust?

We both know this, don't we? said the younger man.

You are blessed to know at a young age, said Nassir. You will live a long and happy life. Nassir held open his mouth again, let the doctor finish his examination.

Tell me about Norah, said Abdullah. She is living in Maine? Abdullah typed notes into a computer mounted on a metal stand, then turned back to Nassir. Follow my finger with your eyes, he said.

Nassir sat up straight and clenched his teeth. Maine? What do you know about Maine? he asked.

My finger, said Abdullah. Follow my finger.

A knock came on the door of the examining room. Doctor Saud, a phone call. Doctor Geschwind from San Francisco. He says it is urgent.

Please forgive me, said Abdullah. He removed his exam gloves and reached for the wall phone. Michael. Nice to hear from you. What do you need?

Nassir watched Abdullah on the phone, the simple drape of his white coat, the laugh lines on young skin, and the enviable comfort of a man whose circumstances were improving. Some doctor from a big city, far away, thought enough of Abdullah to call and ask his opinion.

You are always the joker, Michael, he said. Please. I have a patient. Tell me what you need right now, and I will call you later. My littlest one, Sultana, asks about you. You need to record some more video stories and send them. While he listened, Abdullah relaxed against the wall.

Abdullah spoke again into the phone: Michael, yes, she was my patient when I was at Stanford. I do not think she has CJD. I remember running genetic tests for her and I found no variants. She tended to imagine things worse than they really were. She needed lots of reassurance. When they finished, Abdullah hung up, apologized to Nassir for the interruption, gave his attention back to his patient.

It appears you are beloved even in California, said Nassir.

Life has blessed me with many good friends, said Abdullah. He put away the last of his instruments. You say you feel ill, but I see nothing wrong. He crossed his arms and waited for the older man to gather his thoughts.

The spirit of my life has left me, said Nassir.

Abdullah said he understood, that it happens. The first thing, your health is fine, Nassir, he said. Your blood test and your physical examination are ordinary. He looked at his own hands, then back at Nassir's eyes until Nassir closed them. You are anxious about what might happen to you?

Nassir opened his eyes, suddenly red and puffy, and he nodded. I will confess to you that I'm afraid, he said.

From one pocket of his white coat—like he'd been expecting the request—Abdullah produced a brown bottle with two pills. Take them both at the same time, said Abdullah. It takes an hour.

Nassir hugged and kissed Abdullah before leaving. You already live a bold life, without fear, said Nassir. You have discovered how and you are only thirty years old. I'm proud of you.

Thank you, said Abdullah.

Please tell Norah she is safe, said Nassir.

Abdullah nodded. Of course, he said. He did not tell Nassir that message had been delivered days ago.

Nassir left his physician's office and not one more word about Maine had been spoken. The guards from outside his front gate drove him home, saw him inside his front door and returned to their stations at Nassir's two gates.

* * *

The Russian President was gathering his things after a meeting with Victor Ivanov. He stopped himself. One more thing, he said. Your asset, Nassir Saud? I told the Saudi King he was no good. He'll be gone soon.

Victor looked like he'd been slapped. Gone? he asked.

The Russian President confirmed.

Do you want me to tell Nassir? asked Victor.

That might be for the best, said the President. Tell him also that his man, Dirk Johnson, is in jail and is talking with the FBI. Maybe if you are lucky you can get Nassir to suck your dick one more time before he's dead.

Victor huffed, ready to respond in anger, then relented. Is there something you want from Nassir? asked Victor. Maybe I could get it for you. He could help you.

What I want is for him to be gone, said the President. He knows too much about me and he is losing everything. He has the wrong incentives. He could profit from causing problems for me.

Victor sat back down and covered his face. He hasn't caused problems and he won't, said Victor.

You don't know all the things I do, said the President. A pause. You're wondering what this means for you? asked the President.

Victor nodded. Nassir is not just an asset, he's my friend, he said.

If you don't have Nassir as your asset, it means you're not very useful here. It means that people will find out you're a faggot, said the President. You won't be safe in Russia. We can't have people thinking there are faggots working with their President.

What do you want me to do? asked Victor.

If I were you, I'd go to America, said the President. Americans won't care who you are. Some of them will like you better, and you can serve me there.

What will you want?

You need to be useful to me, said the President. Find as many ways as you can. It's very bad for you if you can't.

For the rest of the afternoon, Victor tried e-mailing and calling Nassir and he got no answer. He couldn't concentrate and couldn't sit still and so he went home early and he lay down in a quiet room and tried taking a nap but couldn't fall asleep because his mind was racing, racing.

NINETEEN

This was the perimeter of the Federal Correctional Institute in Cumberland, Maryland: two layers of chain-link fence, each as tall as a line of telephone poles and topped with loops of razor wire spaced sixteen inches on center. Between the layers of fence was ten feet of ground covered with a threatening tangle of razor wire. New-prisoner orientation at Cumberland included a visit to the barrier and an advisory: No would-be escapee had ever reached the second fence. The few men with idiot luck enough to clear the first all died the death of a thousand cuts. They were allowed to lie, some for an hour, and to bleed out; a dying man afraid for himself is far more dangerous to remove from a field of razor wire than is his body, said the guard.

There are easier ways to become a suicide, said another of the guards. If that's what you want, ask around.

The prison library didn't have a single window. It did have books and an inmate education center. In rooms hardly bigger than closets, inmates could get a GED, learn to read or study the Bible. The building also contained at least as many threats as it did men. Lots of them sat around and competed for control. As with every group of animals, there was a pecking order, a chain of command. Everyone in the chain pledged loyalty to those above and they all protected the top man from harm. They worked in unison, in confidence, to repel dumbfuckery. They chewed up and spit out weaklings. They declared themselves a tribe.

This was Dirk's new home, at least until his lawyer negotiated a deal. At the end of his first day in prison, he'd done what all the new prisoners did, which was to lie on a bunk in the dark, in fear of waking up with his anus shredded. With every stray noise, he flinched. He lay under covers with his hands in the shape of fists so he'd be ready if someone came at him. He was desperate to fall asleep and desperate to stay awake. His breathing was fast and shallow, fast and shallow. He'd be on the sleepy edge and then he'd force himself to sit up and look around for a sneak attack.

God help me, he said. I don't deserve this.

On the bunk below was a sixty-year-old man named Rufus who was in for life. Shut up, you white pussy, he said.

On the three-hour drive up to Cumberland from Washington, Eve fretted about Moe Howard. Would Dirk take his cues from his lawyer and turn hostile? State Department and CIA lawyers were crawling over the case with questions: What other attacks were the Saudis planning? What did the Saudis want? Who was cooperating with them? With Moe Howard in the mix, this is an impossible job, she told DeAndre. His scare factor is crazy high. Her questions went everywhere and all at the same time. She sounded ill. If I could throw up, I'd probably feel better, she said.

For all of the ride, DeAndre listened from the passenger seat. I've had cases with Moe, he said. The man's dangerous. He'll give you twelve things he wants you to be afraid of and he'll threaten your entire life in case you're not afraid enough. It's a terrible thing when someone that resourceful has no humanity. The only way to beat him is to work around him. You have to communicate directly with the one he represents, the decision-maker. If you don't have to deal with Moe, he can't beat you.

Eve Coman stared down Dirk Johnson as he and his lawyer and a prison guard entered Cumberland's stark interrogation room. The room's tiny table was particle board covered in maple laminate. Because one of its legs was broken, it had been wedged into a corner to keep it from collapsing. As Dirk entered the room, Eve talked to DeAndre about their drive to Cumberland. She wanted it known that they planned and worked together. They had people and money behind them and were a joint force that would stop only if stopped.

The prison guard dropped Dirk on a folding metal chair. Dirk had his hands cuffed behind him and couldn't sit comfortably. He stood and tried to loop his hands under his feet, to get his hands in front. The oafish guard slapped him on the side of the head and yanked the neck of his prison scrubs and his hindquarters fell back into the chair. His hands got stuck under his thighs and he was forced to sit low, like a child, barely able to see the tabletop.

Eve showed her FBI badge to the guard and asked if the prisoner could be allowed to pull his hands in front. She would take responsibility for any harm he caused, she said.

Fine, said the guard, who made it clear he wasn't leaving. Dirk brought his cuffed hands into his lap and sat like an ordinary man who happened to be handcuffed.

I don't mind making your client's life a little easier, Mr. Howard, said Eve. My only reason for being here is to find out what he knows. That's my entire agenda. Can we talk about that without getting combative?

Moe Howard, lawyer, gunslinger, destroyer of adversaries, went straight to work. He said he would put Eve in jail. You are spiteful and vicious, pursuing a criminally sexist campaign against Dirk Johnson, he said. Norah Saud is actually guilty of something, and I notice she's not living in a prison cell. Moe reached into his leather satchel and slapped down a stack of paper. This is my petition for habeas corpus, he said. Then he slapped down another. And this is my motion for sanctions against you. When you come to court to argue these motions, you better bring your toothbrush and your pajamas because you won't be going home. The judge will be locking you up for contempt.

Eve didn't cower. You're such a little man, she said. You think you can convince me you're the one lawyer in this world who files stupid motions and wins? Mr. Howard, she said, I gave you a sworn affidavit from Norah Saud attesting to your client's terrorism. I have Dirk Johnson's e-mails and telephone intercepts to corroborate her. You want a judge to rule there's no basis for us holding him?

Eve sat close to Dirk, looking at the side of his head. It wasn't clear if he was listening. She slapped him once on the back of his shoulder. *Your man*, she said, is accused of international terrorism. There's not a black robe in Maryland who wants to go home and explain to his family why he let an accused terrorist walk, especially if the accused is rich and has the keys to the company plane. How's that judge going to look if Dirk Johnson flies away? Nobody wants to be known as one who got conned by a terrorist.

Dirk was expressionless and kept staring at his hands. Was he listening? You're giving your client false hopes, she said. Write all the motions you want. I have twelve young lawyers working for me, each of whom wants my job someday. Your two motions? Sanctions and habeas? We get those every week and have standard memos to oppose them. I can have oppositions filed by tomorrow morning without breaking a sweat. And then where are we? We wait for a month or two to get a hearing date and your motions get denied. You'll have postponed the date for your client's trial and guaranteed that he sits in a shitty little place called limbo for months longer than necessary. Her tone changed; she sounded like she might be mocking her adversary. Maybe I'm not supposed to be intimidated, she said. Maybe you're just churning. Are you charging him a high hourly because he's rich?

We're talking about the rest of a man's life, said Moe. I'd burn this place to the ground to protect that. He stuck out his chest and thumped a fist on it.

Nice hyperbole, Mr. Howard. Seriously, the rest of your client's life will be spent in jail. Have you told this to your client? Eve slapped Dirk on the shoulder again. That's you I'm talking about, fella. Will Dirk Johnson sit in isolation twenty-three hours a day at a supermax? Will he have to turn his ass to the shower wall if he drops his soap?

Your days as a bully are almost over, Ms. Coman. There is no federal death penalty and you have no case. Rock solid, I just proved it. Go ahead and read it. He banged a fist on the papers he'd slapped down and he had to save the table when it looked like it might fall in. Eve and DeAndre didn't move; they offered no help righting the table.

A man on death row always has to be afraid the next president will want to kill him, she said. Could happen any time. A man like Dirk thinks he's cozy in his little room and along comes somebody willing to trade his symbolic little life for votes in the swing states.

My man wants out, now, said Moe. He gets full immunity or he doesn't talk. Threaten all you want and we'll ignore you. This is Moe Howard you're talking to.

She picked up one of the motions as though it would dirty her fingers. You do know that when you sign up for e-filing, these go by e-mail? You send and receive instantly and don't have to wait three days for Mr. Postman to deliver. You know this, right? Because it seems like a guy as smart as you would jump at the chance to avoid falling behind all the other lawyers.

Moe pursed his lips, ready to blow, but hesitated. His heavy lids retracted, lifted by eyes that bulged like soft-boiled yolks. It took some time for him to get words out. It's not a secure system, he said finally.

She grabbed her coat and her bag on the way out. Mr. Howard, you could have told me on the phone that my request to negotiate was a waste of time. It would have saved Mr. Green and me the six hours' round-trip from Washington. You could have saved it for yourself, too. How much are you billing Dirk Johnson for this trip? When you and your client accept facts and are ready to deal, please call me. I promise never to waste your time.

Before she left, Eve bent low, brought her face even with Dirk's. Are you hearing the crap coming out of your lawyer's mouth? she asked him.

On the way out, DeAndre was shaking his head at Dirk's lawyer. Can you see why the FBI keeps promoting her? he asked Moe. She just screwed you to the wall.

* * *

It was the end of another gray Russian day. Lights clicked off downstairs at Victor Ivanov's house. The last one left on was in the den, next to Victor, who scrolled through his mobile phone. As he scrolled, he wrote selected e-mails and phone numbers onto a legal pad. Scrolling.

Stopping. Writing. Double-checking. His wife demanded to know what was going on. Victor said he was due to get a new phone at work and always when that happened, data went missing. No Russian with decent computer skills is programming phones, he said. That man becomes a spy because the money's fantastic. This will take a while. Go up to bed, he said.

When he was alone, Victor tried calling Nassir's number once more and got no answer. He called again. Same thing.

Later that night, Victor lay in bed for hours, eyes open. Before the sun rose, he got up and muscled two suitcases into the trunk of his car. He did it without disturbing the sleep of his wife or his daughter. Their still-new Lexus automobiles sat, cold and still, in the family's garage. Victor had put his wedding ring in a leather box on his dresser where he kept loose money. Soon enough, his wife would find it. He left no note.

Victor drove away from his white-pillared house with the Sistine-style fresco inside the entryway where his face and an impossible version of his body had been painted in the form of a fearsome, godlike figure. At the perimeter gate, he told the guard he didn't need an escort. He went, unprotected and unmonitored, into the decay of Moscow, toward the airport where the day's first international flights would soon start taking off and landing.

Victor's phone rang; it was Nassir calling from an unfamiliar number. Are you okay? asked Victor.

No, said Nassir. I'm under house arrest. No Internet and no phone. I couldn't be calling except I had a mobile hidden away. The King wants me dead. He gave me poison and he's hoping I take it.

Victor made a painful sound. The Russian President is the one who wants you dead, he said. He ordered your King to make it happen. Leave Saudi Arabia. Now. He whispered, as if he could prevent eaves-dropping: I'm moving to America. Meet me there.

Everything makes sense now, said Nassir. This is worse than I thought. Through a skinny gap in the drapes, he spied an armed man guarding one of the two gates that gave entrance to his yard. So, this is about your boss, he said. What did you say about me?

Victor's response was hasty and urgent. I might be the only person in this world who would cry at your funeral, he said. Nobody else cares.

Your boss wanted you to tell me he wanted me dead, said Nassir. He's making it clear I have no out.

Get to America, said Victor. Find a way. Nothing else makes sense.

I can't leave my house, said Nassir. I'm a prisoner. Guards with guns are at both entrances.

I'll send some men to kill your guards.

It's too much to fight against Vladimir. Every version of that game ends the same. Vladimir could come for you, too.

How many planes do you own? asked Victor. Get on one. Fly.

The Russian President always gets his way, said Nassir. I'd have to be a child not to see that.

You don't have to be afraid, said Victor, on the edge of outrage. Nassir, please. Try. With your money, you can hide.

It's out of my control, said Nassir. I give up.

The Russian President can't see everyone all the time, said Victor. He says he can, but he can't.

Victor, it's over, said Nassir. I'm done.

Road noise from Victor's Lexus flooded the phone. There was fear and hatred going in all different directions at the same time.

Please—can you find Dirk and kill him? asked Nassir.

This is his fault?

Completely, said Nassir. He can't keep secrets.

Anybody else? asked Victor.

No, not her. Just Dirk. People will look at her and they'll think of me, said Nassir. She's the proof of my life.

The lovers ended their call politely, as if it wouldn't be their last. Victor slowed when he crossed a bridge above the black waters of the Pakhra River. He opened the window and flung his state-issued Motorola at the water, like it was a flat rock. It skipped twice and sank.

* * *

A Friday evening in Mecca: The city withdrew, became quiet and introspective. In lots of neighborhoods there was the beautiful smell of grilling meat. Cab drivers with creased faces sat in urban parks smoking Parliaments, talking politics, making fun, avoiding mention of unhappiness connected to the King. Often enough, contempt was hinted at, but it had to be suppressed; the King's loyalists were embedded all over.

Street vendors and beggars were gone from downtown, which was still as an empty courtroom. The office workers had gone home to the women destined to be at home all day and every day, many of whom thought it best not to think too much what they might do if they'd been able to leave the house.

Nassir was alone at home and sounded entitled to something better. He talked to himself and lingered in self-pity. His abject hunger—his crying need for food and freedom and authority—made him violent. The mirror in his master bathroom shattered when he heaved a bottle of shampoo.

He kept reopening his refrigerator and rediscovering that he was out of meat and basmati and everything fresh. His cupboard was down to odd items: fava beans, colored condiments, dates, rice crackers, gherkins in clear jars and stacked-up six-packs of Coca-Cola in cans. There were skinny boxes of Napoleon bonbons, imported from Belgium. On the front of each was an unflattering rendering of a stern French statesman who, two centuries earlier, had waged wars by insisting that he was invincible and then made it obvious the idea was a sick joke.

One at a time, Nassir's housekeepers and cooks had approached Nassir's house. The guards sent each away and said not to return. The gardener, too. Mail wasn't allowed in. Garbage accumulated inside. Days' worth of dirty plates, each with a different oily residue, teetered on a counter.

He'd used up his tea and coffee and he acquired a severe headache that stayed for two days and put him in bed with a wet cloth on his forehead, muttering in distress. Hidden sprinklers set on timers kept watering his garden; he strolled there several times each day, searching for something that might magically return.

It was a rash move, but he was desperate: Nassir exited his front door and went to the nearest gate and its alloy bars attached by metal hinges to a concrete wall seven feet tall. He addressed the guard *sotto voce*, a voice lacking humility and revealing an urge to get his hands on someone or something he could command: I'm going for some dinner. He opened the latch on the gate and pushed.

The guard pressed himself against the outside of the gate and kept it from opening. You're not leaving, he said.

I need food, Nassir announced. I'm starving.

The guard muscled up.

Nassir stepped back. He pleaded. I need food, he said. I'm back in ten minutes.

It would be unhealthy for you to keep bothering me, said the guard. You can see my rifle, can't you?

Nassir retreated further and stopped pushing on the gate. Money? he whispered. You want money?

My orders are to keep you inside this fence and to kill you if you come outside. If you have money when you do, I'll kill you and I'll take it.

Nassir was as hostile as a narcissistic sociopath who'd been rudely refused what he thought was his entitlement. He became abusive and accusatory and it didn't take long until he'd nearly exhausted himself with his profanity. Afraid of the guard, Nassir had done all his foul-mouthing in his garden, directing his anger at a fig tree, but loud enough that he could be heard over the wall. *I deserve better*, he shouted.

He walked away and followed the inside edge of the high wall that bounded his city land, turned when he reached a corner, went to his second gate and talked to the second guard. I'm hungry. I need to go out for some food, he said. I'll be back. He released the latch on the gate and pushed. The guard shoved the business end of his gun through the bars. I can pull this trigger and then you won't be hungry, he said.

The guard kept his gun aimed at Nassir until the older man walked out of sight and he pushed closed the gate.

Inside a second-floor window, Nassir spied on a guard. Who do you think you are? he demanded. Nassir pointed at the man. You're suspect. You hear me?

The shouting was loud enough to be heard outside. It made the guard turn and look, but only long enough to see that he wasn't threatened.

Inside, Nassir wandered in stocking feet, heels pounding, sometimes smacking his hands on walls, as if the sheetrock would submit to him on the threat of pain. He cursed until spittle was flying. In his kitchen, he found the phone he usually carried in his pocket. He tried it, just in case, and it didn't work. He was infuriated. He threw it at the shiny marble floor and it smashed. He tried to force American curse words out of his gut but what came out was an unfulfilling combination of notes, a diminished minor chord.

Nassir stared at himself in a hall mirror. He saw the face of a man who was old and unwise, covered in an uncontrolled spread of white whiskers. The world has taken all from me that it can, he said.

On a counter in his bathroom was the brown bottle of pills from Dr. Abdullah Saud. Nassir took it to his bedside table along with a half-full glass of water. He lifted the lid and sniffed. Vinegar and vomit. He hurried the lid back on.

In his underpants and his black socks, he crawled under thin sheets, pulled his knees up to his chest and shivered because the air conditioning worked so well. Cradling the bottle of pills, he hovered there, long enough to warm himself, which was long enough to become absorbed with concern for a different discomfort—the chronic pain of hunger. He went to the kitchen cupboard and devoured handfuls of dates and he ate spoonfuls of a very nice chutney on crackers and poured effervescent Coke onto chips of ice and gulped. He opened one of the thin boxes, took out three Napoleon bonbons and while he was eating the third, he began weeping.

He'd been starving and now he wasn't. Did it even matter?

In his library he reached behind books and removed a Russian-made hunting knife, a weighty steel blade with dragon's teeth. The look of it could leave a man feeling cut. He pressed it under his chin, against his carotid, and held it. He wouldn't take his King's poison, wouldn't give the man the satisfaction. Because to hell with him.

He pulled the knife away from his neck and slipped downstairs, out his front door, to one of his gates where there was a guard, back turned. Nassir slipped through the gate, plunged the blade into the back of the guard and ravaged the man's spinal cord. The guard went limp and fell in a heap. There was a commotion; people scattered. Before Nassir could rise from his task and run to the second gate, the second guard shot him in the center of his chest. The guard didn't call anybody until all the blood leaked out of the old man and it was clear that he was utterly and absolutely dead.

Several Saudi news websites mentioned the incident. The Director of Security Directorate, Nassir Saud, was a sad little suicide, they said. The Crown Prince, Abdullah Saud, M.D., would announce a replacement.

TWENTY

Victor Ivanov was like many Russians in that he both idolized and despised America. America had teeth and muscle and brains enough to be the global alpha, an apex predator with unquestioned dominance, a keeper of holy powers. Instead, America was a lazy lioness, a jungle cunt.

America knew the score, knew it had bettered all others. It could crush and could keep crushing. The half of America with testicular heft had shamed the half without and made it obvious that the home of the brave, the nation with the most extraordinary concentration of weaponry in world history, would never use its position to take anything so valuable as an advantage. The Russians laughed at America for letting go of what should be kept. For the Americans, Victor believed, leverage was made to be given away and repurchased at a loss. America's feminizers wanted the nation in their own image. They wanted a country that was a virgin school mistress, a skirt that fed and cared for the witless and the scrawny as if poverty might ever be capable of offering rewards. Poverty? Poverty deserved no kindness; poor men deserved early deaths.

Victor marveled that America kept itself mortgaged so it could kill or destroy at any location on the planet on a moment's notice. America had stockpiles of nukes that could be hidden, moved underground and under oceans without detection. It had squadrons of jets able to fly halfway around the world, able to decimate and able to flee from enemies faster than the speed of sound. A US Navy pilot could have breakfast in his North Carolina kitchen, bomb Libya in the afternoon, and be home for dinner.

America had mastered the science and the art of spying on the entire world. The intelligence services could receive, synthesize and assess the world's entire flow of phone calls and e-mails and text messages and private messages. They could track the movements of nearly every person everywhere.

America had excesses of power and protection. It was a steel fortress with bulletproof windows and weapons good enough to be considered magic, but it took nothing more outrageous than a loud noise to make the populace scatter like poodles. The nation lacked the fortitude and common sense to pocket its winnings, to take benefit from its investment. America's fear left it nude, vulnerable to those who could only afford to covet what America had bought and paid for many times.

Dirk Johnson? He was an American bull moose—rich and privileged and plowing through china shops, as if that would vanquish his enemies. Behind him had been the full faith and credit of Nassir Saud, one of the world's keenest billionaires. A man too stupid to remain invulnerable sat in prison. Victor Ivanov saw Dirk Johnson as another American undone by his fear of fear, a man too stupid to realize his own weakness was his undoing.

Victor received the keys to a Cadillac Escalade at a rental desk at National Airport and followed American highways through Virginia and into a Maryland April. The thick of urban Montgomery County—home to office towers that held aloft the names of law firms—yielded to rural Frederick County and billboards wanting to cast the American psyche: ONE NATION UNDER GOD. He exited, pulled into Waffle House for breakfast and, unlike in Russia, didn't have to worry that highwaymen might rob him and burn his body in a junkyard, or that petty thieves would pry the chrome off his SUV.

Lots of Russian men savaged America, but even they had to admit it was home to enviable forms of peace and prosperity. America was safe strolls on public streets and clean water drunk straight from kitchen taps. America was where people waited politely if there was a line, but knew there usually wouldn't be. It was policemen who couldn't be bribed and drivers who yielded sometimes when they didn't have to and businesses that didn't pay protection and, somehow, never got torched. America was where an honest man could make and keep a fortune.

America was also a fantasyland. Democracy meant giving power to the weak. It was a repulsive idea and America was too proud of itself to see. America saw itself in a mirror and didn't hide its belief that the rest of the world should want to be just like it. America looked down its nose at the strongman and yet was saturated with the same brand of narcissism.

Victor sipped Waffle House coffee while waiting for his creamed chipped beef on toast. He worshipped his wait, his peace, the silence inside his head. He was overfull of abiding patience; his food could take an hour and that would be just fine. Moscow, dour and overcast, would remain forever removed by nine time zones.

Beyond the restaurant's oversized windows were empty fields to listen to, miles and miles of them. This was where the soybeans and corn grew in summer, where warm days, steady ones, could slip by gently, their numbers counted in sunsets and glasses of lemonade.

A steaming plate of food arrived in the hands of the waitress, a fleshy woman with Disney tattoos on short arms. She set the plate in front of Victor and spoke with an accent as tangy as grape jelly. When she asked Victor if he wanted more coffee, she touched him on the shoulder and called him sweet pea.

Victor swooned. I'm half in love with America, he said.

Most of us are too, hon, she said.

* * *

An overloud announcement on the Cumberland prison PA: *Dirk Johnson. Visitor.* Dirk went to central station, shoved his hands through a slot and offered himself for handcuffing. The guard who took him to the visitors' room put him and his orange jumpsuit into a chair within arm's reach of a slim gentleman in a spring-weight suit whose journey to this place had come at the vindictive request of his dead lover.

278

Victor was charming and oily at the same time. He took Dirk's hands briefly, said he was grateful to meet—happy to talk in private. He motioned and Dirk leaned closer. Victor removed a ring and twisted it. See the metal prick that comes out underneath? he whispered. I was ordered to use it on you and inject a nerve agent. They'd have found you with white foam spilling from your dead mouth.

Dirk was aghast. He swallowed wrong and could hardly stop coughing.

I'm not here to harm you, Victor assured. I'm here for your protection. I'm the only person you can depend on. You're in grave danger.

Dirk hadn't asked the visitor's name or the reason for the visit. He posed no questions about the man's agenda. The man offered intel and warned of danger and offered protection and camaraderie. He looked like someone who knew the value of vigilance. Lights were blinking red and green and all at the same time.

Dirk's appetite for dangerous detail, his constant need to be wary, were being fed. He opened his eyes, ears and mouth, ready to receive. In danger of what? he asked. From who?

Victor flicked his business card onto the table. It had only his name, a mobile phone number, a g-mail address and his position: Presidential Advisor. It bore an embossed golden eagle with two heads. The animal—its glittering body was protected by the white, blue and red flag of Russia—clutched weapons in its talons. The King of Saudi Arabia thinks you know too much, said Victor. He ordered me to kill you, which I refuse to do.

Dirk protested too loudly: I don't know anything about the King. Nothing. He shouldn't be afraid.

What matters is what the Saudi King believes, said Victor. The facts are what he says they are.

I think he's an excellent king, a terrific king, said Dirk. He fussed like a puppy that had to go outside. You have to tell him I don't know anything. Knowing about him wasn't part of my job. Can't you make him understand?

I'm alive because I escaped to America and I'm not leaving, said Victor. The only ones I'll ever speak to from now on are Americans— if I'm lucky.

Dirk's voice lost its gravity. What do I do? he said.

In this prison is a man you need to meet, said Victor. He is the one the inmates respect the most. Find him.

Dirk was confused and impatient: What are you talking about?

They call him El Aceillo. He ran the police in Mexico and got caught in America, killing people who might tell on him for running drugs. That's your man. If you make friends with him, he will protect you.

Dirk boiled over with questions: How soon might someone try to kill him? How could he protect himself?

Victor interrupted. All you need to know is that the Saudi King is your sworn enemy. He took Dirk's wrists, still in cuffs, and held. I'm your guardian. My loyal friend Nassir Saud told me about you.

Dirk was up from his chair, pacing, talking. I'm in prison, he said. How could the Saudi King kill me in here? As soon as his thought had formed, he turned it into an unfiltered question and demanded an answer, as if Victor would know the Saudi King's thinking.

This is what you're wondering? said Victor. You saw the answer with your own eyes. He pointed at his ring. Maybe he'll send another visitor like me. In this prison are men and they still want to protect their daughters and sisters outside. Someone might convince a prisoner the best way to protect his family is by harming you. That man might put poison in your food.

Dirk sounded warped. Is that what he's planning? he asked.

He thinks I'll kill you today, so probably he's not planning anything, said Victor. When he learns you're alive, maybe a guard in one of the towers will be asked to shoot you when you're outside for exercise. Maybe you're asleep and someone will throw a Molotov into your cell. He's clever, the King. Please be careful, for your sake. I'll visit and bring you information. He handed over a carton of Marlboros and a packet of twenty-dollar bills. Dirk grabbed for them, slipped them into his orange jumpsuit, as if they could be hidden from the cameras recording everything. I believe you can use these, said Victor. I'll bring more next time.

Dirk got suspicious. Why are you doing this? he asked. What do you get?

Victor stayed on key, rhythm unchanged. Since I was a college boy, I have been close with Nassir Saud. We were best friends. I'm sixty-two and for my whole life my best friend is Nassir, who's dead now. Did you know? He died because the Saudi King was afraid of him. Nassir told me about you. He said you were loyal, that you were a loyal, loyal man. I wanted to protect you. I thought you deserved it. A loyal man is a good man. Nassir would want this for you.

Dirk's head shook, his eyes closed. Please protect me, God, he said. I pray for protection. Eyes open again, looking at Victor: I won't be able to eat or sleep. I can't relax. I have to be on high alert all the time. His head wobbled. I am grateful to you, he said to Victor. You have opened my eyes.

I suppose I have, said Victor.

I'm in prison for the rest of my life, said Dirk. I don't know how I can do this.

I'm here to help, said Victor. I want to honor Nassir and your support for him. E-mail me or call if you need to. I can find out if there are threats. He patted Dirk on the shoulder like an empathetic old friend, then readied himself to leave. My work here is done, he said.

In the driver's seat of his Escalade, before he left Cumberland FCI's parking lot, Victor tapped a message into his phone and sent it to a former lover in Moscow who was head of staff at the Council of Ministers: Dirk Johnson is now an asset. I scared the shit out of him. He'll get deflowered by Aceillo. Tell Vladimir.

Careful, wrote back the envoy. You don't want a suicide.

You worry too much, wrote Victor. This man is terrified of death.

* * *

In the long unfurling of the year after the suicide bomber snuffed five hundred human lives at Farragut North, foolish consistency returned for most of Washington, DC. A large majority of people returned to their cages and took the same lead roles. Most people asked the same questions, got the same answers and fled the same hobgoblins.

For most, fundamental assumptions and fundamental habits were unchanged. It was as if they'd swept up the ashes of Farragut North, trucked them away and agreed not to speak of them. In the underground parking garages downtown, it was the same cars in the same spaces. Dinged-up aluminum lunch carts on the same corners, every damn morning at the same damn time. Mystics tickets. Parking tickets. Panhandlers who got ignored. Flu bugs. Zoloft. League softball.

Immediately after the bomb at Farragut North, nearly everyone had been top-heavy with fear, feeling on the verge of a disabling illness. People had been sickened by the shock of underground violence that had come so close. Stories of human skin gone crispy from the heat of obliteration had scarred them.

People were grateful for a return to what felt like default, for the comfort and reassurance of the familiar: the white smell of lit candles at Sunday Mass, baritone voices on news radio.

Underground reconstruction near Farragut North pounded hard enough to be felt and heard above ground. A tunnel borer opened a gargantuan subway tube where one used to be. Diesel exhaust flowed up and down 16th Street, spread by trucks on wheels as heavy as thunderstorms. To and from the construction site, they carried concrete, stacked pallets of rebar and big clods of red mud. People protested the mess and the smell and demanded it be solved and when they did, everybody knew it was okay to stop being reverent. They could demand their due; time to act normal again.

Some people announced they were not like everybody else and they kept a chokehold on Farragut North and proclaimed a need to remember the violence. They cultivated and fed discontent. Nobody would tread on them. They were proud of their vigilance.

Some moved out of the city, away from dangers. They found comfort in suburban spaces where maybe there wouldn't be criminals.

It was only a few weeks after the assassins were dead and Nassir Saud was gone and Dirk Johnson was put in jail forever and the threat of terrorism retreated that Eve and Jaime and Olivia were coming and going from their apartment as they pleased. They ate out in their own neighborhood and walked home after. They sat on their apartment balcony in broad daylight. Eve was the first to say how liberating it was to not need bodyguards and to not worry about getting assassinated. We don't have to live like the rich Russians, she said. She looked as energetic and as relieved as someone who'd been shot at without result, but at night she ground her teeth.

Daughter Olivia got her learner's permit and during their long drives together, Eve probed: How are you coping? Are you sleeping? We can talk if you need to.

She told her mom to leave her alone. Farragut North is so, like, over, she said.

Jaime praised Eve, said he was proud of his wife. If there was a Nobel Prize for law enforcement, you'd get it, he said.

DeAndre pleaded with Eve to come work for his firm. He promised she'd be happier working with a trusted friend, that she'd have more time for family. She could make more money, get more time off. She wouldn't have to stake out safe houses on Sunday nights. Nobody would throw her under a bus.

Are you begging? she asked.

We've known each other long enough, he said. I can beg and you'll still respect me.

Eve wouldn't think of it. Your clients scare me, she said.

She stayed true to the FBI and kept learning from Louis. She attended staff meetings, taught seminars to FBI newbies. She requested that NSA listen to certain phone calls and she took people in for questioning and threatened them with jail time. She came home after work and made family dinners and worried about Olivia. She mentored junior attorneys and evidence techs.

On the anniversary of Farragut North came bomb scares. At subway stations all over DC were brown paper grocery bags and a caller said some of them contained bombs. Eve managed twelve crime scenes, borrowing bomb squads from cities and big counties as far away as Wilmington, Delaware, monitoring developments and reporting them to Lou and the FBI director and the White House. She totally had it under control.

In the middle of the maelstrom came a phone call from Olivia's school. On learning of the bomb scare, the school had told students to return home. Olivia was terrified. She locked herself in a supply closet and refused to leave.

Lou told Eve he'd direct the response teams. Go—you have to go, he said.

At the sound of Eve's voice outside the closet door, Olivia emerged and held on to her mother like a baby animal in fear of getting eaten. She cried all the way home and pleaded with Eve to lie with her in bed. All I want to do is fall asleep and feel better, she said.

From the family's apartment, Eve and Olivia heard and felt the explosion of a real bomb at Woodley Park. Their windows rattled from the shock wave.

The very next day, Eve and her Volvo drove Olivia to a doctor's visit and on Chevy Chase Circle a guy with diplomatic plates who spoke only Russian ran full speed through a stop sign and broadsided them. The Russian man yanked Eve out of her car and screamed as if it was her fault. He seemed intent on provoking her—pushing her as if he wanted a fistfight—as the fast flow of impatient commuters, engines racing, horns honking, threatened them both. Eve finally pulled a gun on him.

A DC cop intervened, tried to arrest the Russian and couldn't; the man had a diplomatic passport. Another car with diplomatic plates picked him up minutes after the collision and he was gone. He'd left behind an aged Ford Explorer, key in the ignition—no key ring—in the middle of three busy lanes of traffic.

Eve went home and called the doctor and begged him to write prescriptions for Xanax, one for Olivia and one for herself.

The world had too many nuts, Eve told her daughter. It always had and it always would. Somehow we survive.

TWENTY-ONE

Jack and Annie got most of their daily exercise walking to and from the mailbox. From their front door, the round-trip was a mile. A gravel driveway led away from their home in the woods and the tidy rectangle of Canadian fescue that Jack kept trim with a push mower. Wrapped around was a broad acre of knee-high meadow and in summer it grew thick with coarse grasses, oxeye daisies and Queen Anne's lace. Insects hovered above the grasses, touched on the spots that looked wet, and often fell victim to swallows that swooped fast and low. Boulders pockmarked the meadow; only their noses were above ground. In the forest surround, living, breathing wildlife.

One warm morning, a North American porcupine meandered near the house and her two offspring followed. At the sound of Jack closing his front door, the frightened mother darted and hid, leaving the little ones confused and alarmed. Jack and Annie climbed the driveway, hands in pockets, with plans to retrieve the morning mail. Unseen, two barred owls kept asking the same question: *Who cooks for you?* Under a low ceiling of summer fog, the June morning offered the promise of goodness and mercy.

Despite age, Jack and Annie walked like they had somewhere to be and a time to be there. Annie raised a question that was presented as having been carefully considered. What rhymes with orange? she asked. Jack shot her a look. She said she wasn't joking. She was writing a poem. What rhymes with orange? she demanded.

You should read more books, he said. Nothing rhymes with orange. It's one of those words.

There's no such thing as a word without a rhyme, said Annie. If you can come up with a word, you can come up with a rhyme.

Holy mother of Waldo, the things you think.

The air was pure balsam. Crunchy gravel underfoot.

How could anybody get so irritated by the truth? asked Jack.

They reached the mailbox at the top of the driveway. On the two-lane, a logging truck heaved past at highway speed, louder than Niagara Falls, dragging a wall of wind that filled Annie's ears and battered her face. She flinched.

Porringe, declared Annie, when it was quiet again. She stood triumphant.

It's not a word.

I made it one, she said.

What does it mean?

It's breakfast food. Oatmeal plus fruit.

Knock yourself out, he said.

Jack brought home the stack of items he'd found in the mailbox. At his desk in the basement, he sorted through and found an envelope with no stamp and no marks, except the front had two words, handwritten in blue ink: *Norah Saud*. When he gave it to Norah, he dangled it from the end of his arm like it was dangerous. This came, he said. And it wasn't the postman delivered it.

He found Annie in the barn and told her. I got a scary little feeling, he said.

Don't matter what comes, Annie said. With Margie here, we're ready. She patted the pistol on her belt.

Norah didn't look startled when she realized the envelope held a note from Eve Coman. *Can we meet?* said the note. *It's urgent.* It listed an e-mail address where Norah could send a coded response. It showed a place and time for a rendezvous.

Norah despised the idea of talking to the FBI but gave Eve the benefit of every doubt. Eve had proven herself truthful and decent. The woman had never done anything that wasn't completely fair. She'd kept every promise she'd made. Norah e-mailed a single word— yes—which meant they'd meet at sunrise the next morning.

For much of the afternoon and evening, Norah fought off violent demon intrusions. At odd moments she'd shake her head, the way someone shakes a finger with a paper cut. She bit her nails for the first time in months. Eve wasn't a threat, but she was FBI. Her whole life was threats. No doubt she'd brought some with her.

Norah did spend part of her afternoon with Annie, searching on the Internet for rhyming words. She kept biting her nails and she didn't stop until Annie smacked one of her hands and scolded her.

Mama was a nail-biter, said Annie. Nasty little habit.

* * *

The Passy Trail ran three miles upriver from town on the abandoned bed of the Moosehead Lake Railroad. Under a canopy of hardwood foliage, the trail connected with a network of others that could take a hiker and her brown boots to New Hampshire, then all the way to Georgia. On a bend overlooking the Passagassawakeag River, sitting on a Passy Trail bench installed at the foot of a hill of sugar maples, Eve Coman and DeAndre Green could have been any couple who'd stopped to rest. There was no reason to guess they were waiting to deliver intel to a woman who'd spent her formative years dressing as a boy, training to be a terrorist, and had unwillingly served as queen on a strongman's chessboard.

Norah's footsteps announced her. She sat on the bench and took in the faces of her companions. I put distance between me and my fears, she said. I've been sleeping well. She held up all ten fingers. Until yesterday, no more biting. Life was ordinary. You're here to ruin that, aren't you?

When Eve told me what she knew, I agreed to bring her here, DeAndre said. I'm sorry for your sake, sister. You deserve better.

A man is coming to see you, said Eve. A Russian. He wants to use you. He wants to scare you into becoming his asset. We're here to warn you and we'd like you to be ours. We'll be completely open. No hidden motives.

Norah pinched an earlobe like it was a relief valve. Is there any escape from the strongman? she asked, very nearly angry.

The man coming to see you reports directly to the Russian President, Eve said. He knows what the President is interested in, knows his priorities. We need to know what questions the President is asking. Sometimes, we'll ask you to feed false intel to the Russians. I'm only asking because this is vital.

We? Norah pointed back and forth between DeAndre and Eve.

Eve laid it out. As soon as people at CIA knew this man had come to America, they hounded me, she said. They need me to work him. Norah, you're the best opportunity we've had in years. You can play the fearful survivor and he'll never suspect.

Is this Victor Ivanov? asked Norah. It feels like you're testing me to see if I'll tell you I already know who he is.

Would that be so bad?

So, I become your spy—your asset? asked Norah. If he finds out, he'll end me.

DeAndre jumped in. This is bigger than us, he said. The Russian President is rat-licker supreme. He's serving poison tea and political infections worldwide. He rigs elections in other countries and installs muscleheads. They do whatever he tells them.

Victor expects to own me and he's bragged about me to his president, said Norah. That's what I'm hearing?

He's not going away, said Eve. Sorry.

Norah saw a possible flaw in Eve's story. How could you know Victor's plans? she asked. He keeps himself secret. He was the Saudis' main source of Russian intel for years.

The Crown Prince—Abdullah Saud—said Eve. He has a friend in Russia and a CIA connection. I'm here because he wanted to warn you. This could mean you're on the Russian President's radar.

Norah never lost her composure, but her silence spoke volumes. A grandiose mass of pointlessness had roped itself to her, threatened to sink her. What incentive was there to match wits with a man who would quickly end you if you were too much trouble? Why fight with a man who always wins? In front of her dangled the lure of anger, of hate.

For all of her life there'd been orange-white lightning bolts that landed close by, each one powerful enough to kill with its sound alone. Father had tossed them at her like a vengeful god. And now came another, from overhead, a crack in the sky. She was nearly defeated by the thought of it. A generation of running, dodging and fretting about Father had burned up much of her supply of resilience. She wasn't sure how much was left.

The only thing worse than spying is not spying, said Norah. You're saying I have no choice. So, what do you need to know? she asked.

Happy to have you on board, said Eve, as earnest as ever.

Only until I can get rid of you, said Norah. Quickly, she added: Eve, you are lovely. I'll always feel indebted. It's the FBI. They scare me.

The FBI is home to imperfect people, the same as everyplace else, said Eve. We accomplish things you can never hear about. We're better than you think.

Victor was Father's lover, said Norah. They were close. Father was also Victor's main asset. Without a connection to Father, Victor is not very useful to Vladimir. Knowing the Russian President, he probably threatened to out Victor unless Victor found some way to become useful again. So, go ahead now. Your turn.

Since he's been in the US, Victor visits your husband in prison, said Eve. Dirk is his asset. Victor told him the Saudi King wants him dead and promised to protect him. He gave Dirk the name of a man in his prison—Aceillo—who he should use as protection, and Victor asks about the man every time he visits. Victor sends intel about your husband and Aceillo to the Russian President. We see and hear almost everything Victor does. We need to know whether Victor is gaslighting us—or does someone inside Cumberland Federal Prison have real value?

First thing, said Norah. Dirk's not my husband. Not anymore. Second, what has Victor told his president about me? How could I have value?

He says the Saudi Crown Prince knows you and trusts you. Vladimir understands that you have influence.

Norah sat still. Her eyes got puffy. Vladimir can't know that, she said. He can't. It's impossible. Her voice began to lose definition. I was careful, she said.

Eve looked confused.

With a wipe of a cotton sleeve, Norah cleared the corners of her eyes. Her composure took a little longer.

Wait. This is about Abdullah? Eve asked.

I love Abdullah, she said. We're in love from when we were children. I told him we had to hide how close we are. We know everything of each other. I'm vulnerable to him and him to me. When I was a girl, he was the only one I ever knew who had no agenda, who didn't want to use me. He loved me for me. If that makes me valuable to Russia, I have to stop talking with him. I love Ibrahim. Ibrahim is my partner, my equal, but Abdullah is always my best friend.

Eve touched Norah. In my business, this is a common problem, she said. There's a common solution. You tell Abdullah about Victor. Not just things you know, but things you suspect. Abdullah has to know this Russian man wants to enlist you and you have to let Abdullah use you. If you care for him, you'll do this.

I should spy on the spy? Oh, how simple.

Not simple, said Eve. *Simpler.* In the long run, it would be simpler.

What if the Russian finds out? asked Norah.

You know how to be careful, said Eve. That's why he won't.

Norah sagged. You didn't answer my question, she said.

Ibrahim doesn't know about Abdullah, does he? Eve asked.

Of course, he doesn't know, just like I don't know if Ibrahim had other lovers. The same as everybody, I have secrets. Now, people are finding out. Someone will think they have leverage. Will you let my secrets slip and suddenly somebody wants leverage? If someone knows I'm helping you, they want to use me and then you're a huge problem, she said. Norah was calculating, she was mapping and projecting possibilities, something she rarely did in front of people. Have you been spying on me? she asked. Do I have to be careful what I say at home?

No, said Eve, who was solemn. I promised we wouldn't and we have not.

Norah choked out a few incomprehensible bits of Arabic profanity. I want to be left alone, she said. Fix it without me. I'm sure you'll figure something out.

Eve went on offense, but gently. You should tell Ibrahim every-thing. Tell him you love Abdullah and tell him why. Confess completely.

There's no end to all this trusting, said Norah. Do I have to believe from now on that people won't hurt me? I can't keep believing what I know isn't true.

You can only trust people worth trusting, said Eve. If you can do that, you can send as much harm as you want to the Russian President. He's the one who ordered the Saudi King to send your suicide bombers to America. Did you know? It was the Russian President who killed Omar and almost killed Ibrahim. If you had been killed, he would have been fine with it. The man is a public enemy—yours, mine and everybody's. We have to contain him.

Maybe I refuse the Russian President. What then? And if I agree? What then? At some point, he thinks I'm a threat and then I'm dead. I want to live. It seems like I've been waiting forever, hoping I could live. The man has always been outside my door, ready to use me.

The best thing for you is to work with me, said Eve. The FBI is your protection. Call me any time and I can get you removed from any location.

You sound like them. If I hadn't gotten lucky and found DeAndre, if I hadn't had his knowledge to protect me, I'd be dead or in jail, said Norah. The FBI is lousy at protection.

You can't get rid of Victor, said Eve. He needs you. He won't let go. You're stuck with that. I'm the best help you'll ever get, and all you have to do is help me a little. I'll keep it to myself where my infor-mation came from. All on paper.

They'll never go away, these bullies, Norah said. They keep coming. Norah slid forward, ready to walk. If you need to see me, slip me another note, she said. Same as before—you can't put information about me in any computer and you can't tell anybody that your intel came from me. Nobody can know we've been in touch. She looked DeAndre in the eye. You too, she said.

I'm easy, said DeAndre. I'm your lawyer. I was already planning on dying with your secrets.

She stood up. Thank you for coming to warn me about Victor. I am grateful, but I have to leave. We can't be seen.

Eve handed her a tiny item, hardly bigger than a Kennedy half-dollar. Keep this, she said. If Victor comes to see you, touch this button and it will capture everything you say. Touch it again to stop. If you record what he says, it means you spend less time with me. I won't have to ask you so many questions.

Norah slid the item into her pocket and clutched at her face, as if a tooth hurt. I need you gone from my life, she said. I love you like a sister, but I need you gone.

On the gravel path, alone, Norah crunched the two miles back to town. Along the way, she didn't see a single soul.

At home, she undressed, climbed under the sheets and woke Ibrahim by spooning and running the front of her smooth legs against the back of his fuzzy ones. We need to talk, she said. It's important. She told him everything about her meeting with Eve, about Abdullah, about having sex with Abdullah when she was a teenager. She told him about Victor and the Russian President. I might never have said anything, said Norah, but Eve recommended it. I'm confessing to you. I wanted to keep secrets and I only decided to tell you because I had no other choice. I'm also apologizing. I should have known better than to keep these secrets.

She waited and watched for Ibrahim's reaction. He was too balanced to be angered, but he might feel hurt because the thing she'd planned to keep from him felt important. Maybe he'd be bruised because the reason for her honesty came from a selfish need to minimize her risks. He might think her too mercenary to trust completely. A good man might lose trust or affection. He might feel he could've avoided getting wounded if Norah had been more invested in him. He might find reason to untangle their lives.

One of the things I love about you is that your judgment is never absent, said Ibrahim. It was better for us both you didn't tell me until now. Thank you for that. He faced her and kissed her. She caressed the back of his neck, pulled at him and kept kissing, wanted him as close as possible. He was such a practical man, seemingly unwilling to lose faith in someone good. He was the person she wanted to be—one who knew how to get curious instead of afraid, one who saw problems as nothing bigger than a reason to search for a fix, and slow to find fault. He was a man whose judgment could be trusted, who seemed without guile. She could open herself to him in complete comfort. Never once had he judged or reached for advantage.

There are so many things I love about you, she said. I love that you always have a reason for why we should be calm, for why we should be curious. I love that I can trust you. Every day is better because of how lucky I am to have this whole man and he has me.

* * *

The second time Norah noticed the gentleman, she knew it was Victor, that he was following. He'd been easy to spot; if a man wears dress shoes in Maine, he's from away. The sight of him was the airy *whish* of a long blade before it landed and cut. Her neck seized.

She'd been standing in Hannaford's, her hand on a box of Kellogg's. Her first instinct was to retreat, to run—to be a rabbit and escape the jackal.

She'd push past the pounding of her heart. She'd breathe. She'd find a reason to admire the present and live in it. She'd manage her emotions, her fear. She paid for her groceries, left, loaded the Subaru and started it, ready to fly, to hide in her safe space, the home she shared with Jack and Annie and Ibrahim and their arsenal, where security came from blue steel. She could keep Victor at bay with lethal force. Nobody would come against that. Would they?

Of course, she'd have to tell the whole house. She'd make her loved ones worry. Jack and Annie would become frightened, vigilant victims like her. The four of them would stand watch on a rotating schedule for as long as it took. How long was that? They'd be on edge, on a never-ending alert, not daring to lower their guard.

She got curious. Wouldn't her adopted family be better off not knowing about Victor? They could live with the kind of peace that comes from knowing only what's necessary. She pulsed with a want to protect her loved ones. Did they need to hear this news? She remembered the long-ago *whummock* of Zarkawi's incoming shells, could hear them plugging into door jambs and shattering televisions. He'd approached in secret, had come so close to killing all four. If they'd been armed and on alert, he might not have gotten off a shot. Of course, she had to tell.

Pressure accumulated. She forgot to breathe. She slapped the Subaru's steering wheel. Hadn't she outlived this? Hadn't she escaped the strongmen? Fervently, she prayed for wisdom, for whatever she lacked that would leave her feeling strong.

Abdullah had told Norah, long ago, that Father offered prayers for her safety. Now dead, Father was no threat and with Abdullah as Crown Prince, neither was the Saudi King. Since then, it had been quiet. Norah had grown accustomed to believing life would go in the direction of her choosing. She'd dared to expect there would never be another leash around her neck.

Confronting Victor seemed the only way. She was quick out of her driver's seat, determined, turned on the FBI's pocket recorder. She sprint-walked across Hannaford's parking lot, where she confronted the man who'd been following. She had a strategy that would box Victor in. She was ready.

Victor saw her approach and held out a business card. It showed a shield over an embossed golden eagle. The eagle was holding a scepter and a cross as weapons and it was guarding the Russian flag. It was a symbol of Vladimir, the one who sought to control everything. Eve adjusted so she could read the card, but she didn't dare touch it. The Russians were dastardly clever about poisoning people.

He started to speak, began his attempt to gain her confidence. Norah shoved his words down his throat. Victor, I'm so glad we get to meet, she said, but it's dangerous for you. We can't be seen talking. She pointed at the pen in his shirt pocket, told him to write down her address. Meet me, she said. Eight thirty. We can talk. You're in danger. The FBI is watching you.

What he certainly wanted was to talk with her in private—and she'd dictated her terms. She had a grip on things. She'd redirected events that otherwise might have inspired dread. She'd been her own master, something more gratifying than the control she'd developed over her expansive capacity for fear. Directing events seemed to silence the cloying voice inside that was so bad at delivering self-assurance.

She turned to leave. He grabbed her wrist. You don't even know who I am, he said. Why give me your address?

His question might have given her legitimate reason to be wary and to question his motives. Norah saw it as a fraud intended to inspire false trust. He was trying to be disarming, except that he wasn't. She pointed at the business card. Victor Ivanov, said Norah. You and Father were lovers for decades. Until a year ago, you were one of the Russian President's top advisors. You were also his spy and his fixer. Father was your asset and you were his. When Father died, you had to leave Russia because you feared being killed and you came here to start over. Victor, I know exactly who you are. I knew you were coming and I know why. I want to help you.

Suddenly, there was reason for Victor to imagine a juicy reality. He could be wild with optimism. But Norah knew he'd have wondered: How could someone several degrees removed from him know so much? He'd operated in secret and kept up a façade that suggested a talent for things that were magically evil. The question might plague him.

He grimaced. As fast as a man could, he dropped his card back in his pocket. Fine, he said. Eight thirty.

In the Subaru, she checked her watch. For eight hours, Victor could whipsaw between hope and fury. He'd be energized by the prospect of a cooperative new asset. He'd feel endangered by what she'd injected under his skin. *You're in danger*, she'd told him. *The FBI is watching*. Arrest might be imminent—a risk serious enough to make him question the benefits of a connection with Norah.

Panting, she drove for home and the forest that surrounded it and gave the full story to her lover and their guardian housemates. Victor Ivanov was coming, she said. Here. Tonight.

Ibrahim was characteristically circumspect. What's your plan? he asked.

She shook her head and asked for his help bringing in groceries. We need to get them in right away, some things are frozen, she said. She tried to glide past the moment and tipped toward the Subaru with her eyes, an unrehearsed signal. She knew if Ibrahim was modestly concerned, Jack and Annie would be excessively so.

Norah's hint flew past Ibrahim without touching him. The Russian President's man coming here? he asked, his voice rising. He must have realized how he sounded. His tone softened. I'm sure it will work out fine, he said.

He's more afraid of us than we need to be of him, Norah whispered. Can you help me? She pointed at the car.

Annie and Jack were ready to take up arms. You gave him our address? demanded Annie.

Norah told them to relax but they wouldn't. Jack put on a gun belt. Annie kept caressing Margie and drew the curtains. The dang Russians could send a drone and attack us, said Annie. RPGs might be incoming any second.

I'll get my automatic out of the gun safe, said Jack. It'll take down anything airborne.

Norah walked them back from panic. She had a plan, she said. Jack and Annie needed to trust her. Please, could they?

Annie hugged Norah excessively and she waved in Jack because she wanted him to hug Norah too and, for a moment, the three became one. I'm not afraid to trust you, not in the least, Annie said. Also, I'm armed and I'm not afraid to shoot your bogeyman in his freakin' gonads.

Victor knocked on Jack and Annie's door—on time, as he'd been told. Norah touched the button on the FBI pocket recorder and rushed him inside, as if to conceal him from spies in the dark woods. She was quick to shut the front door and, with the help of Victor's need to appease, maneuvered him into a corner. Please don't stay long, she said. It's not safe. With the bend of one finger, she brought him into the kitchen.

Norah sat Victor at the heavy table, once a shield against Zarkawi's bullets. For two days, I have been following, Victor said. I waited to see if it was safe to talk. Some things you need to know. Nassir was no suicide. There was no shame in his death.

The Saudi King's men killed Father, said Norah. The palace announced it was suicide only to disgrace him.

Victor looked startled.

Don't pretend, said Norah. You know I know. Just like you knew this address and you wrote it anyway. She wasn't sure what he knew, but Father had told her that flattering statements about someone's apparent knowledge will often improve one's position.

He told her to be afraid. You need protection, Victor said. The Saudi King wants you dead, the same way he wanted Nassir dead. You're in serious danger.

Victor's story was fatally flawed and it stunned Norah that he'd not realized. Abdullah would disclose any threat from the House of Saud. Why now? demanded Norah. Father's been gone a year.

The Saudi King thinks you know things, said Victor. Whatever Nassir knew, King Saud says you know and what you know could ruin him. He's terrified.

Yes, but why *now*? she repeated. Then she pushed forward. And why didn't you answer my question the first time?

He sat straighter, elevated himself, looked her up and down. Are you one who refuses to see dangers? he asked. Are you that naïve? You'll be an easy target. Your friends, too. He gestured at Annie, Jack and Ibrahim.

Norah looked to Ibrahim and he smirked. The circumstances said it was time to go hard on offense. You're still not answering me? she asked. She pushed up her long sleeves, revealing forearms like copper cables. Stiff-wristed, she thumped the table. Father trained me better than you might like, she said. You're here because you want me to be your asset and you're planning to scare me and to promise protection until I feel I have no choice but to trust you. You think I can influence a certain man in Saudi Arabia and your president wants to take advantage. You raised Vladimir's hopes and told him I might lead you to other useful people. You'll play my fears and hope I won't trust my instincts. You want my anxiety to become your control knob.

Victor licked thin Russian lips.

Your threats are lies, said Norah. I've studied Father and I spied on him, she said. I know your methods and I know you, Victor. Did you know the FBI came here a week ago? When the FBI knew your plans, I had value. They want me as an asset—and all because *you* want me as an asset. Right now, their question is when to arrest you. Already, they see everything you send to your president.

Norah imagined that Eve, when she listened to the recording of the conversation, would be livid. In a few sentences, Norah had destroyed the FBI's chance to spy on Victor.

They're the ones lying, said Victor. The FBI is dangerous for you.

Victor, I'm sure you know what matters, she said. The FBI knows what you're doing. How else could they know in advance that you'd come here? Maybe because they're really good spies and you aren't. If the FBI thinks you have damaging intel, they'll want to arrest you before you can share it. Maybe after, they drop you in Moscow where someone stabs you because Russians think it's disgusting you are homosexual. Maybe the FBI spreads rumors with the Russian gangs in Brighton Beach and you have to go into hiding. She pulled the coin-sized recorder out of her shirt pocket and held it in plain sight. This is from the FBI and it's capturing our conversation, she said.

Victor pressed a fingertip against his lips. I need water, he said. Water. Please. Ibrahim fetched a glassful and placed it on the table. Victor's pause was obvious.

I didn't poison your water, Ibrahim said. Get a clean glass from the cabinet, pour your own. It's fine.

Victor demurred.

I'll drink from your glass if you want, Ibrahim offered.

Victor took his chances. He sipped, slowly.

You never know which drink is your last, said Ibrahim. You poor man, you have to worry all the time.

Coming from the balanced Ibrahim, Norah thought the cynicism nearly hostile. Had she emboldened him? Had she come that far? If you stay in America, your life has a bad end, Norah told Victor. This is the same FBI team that put Dirk in prison.

Victor tried to deny her. Norah, he said, the FBI only pretends to know things. They'll sacrifice you and you'll never see it coming. They take what's fake and make it look real. Think of who gives them orders and how terrible those people are.

Norah stood her ground. The FBI knows you asked Dirk to make a connection with Aceillo in prison, she said. They know Dirk's your asset. You showed him a ring with a hidden needle that could poison someone. They predicted you'd want me as your asset. If the FBI thinks I gave you anything, I'm guilty of treason and so are you. You should go maybe to Tanzania where it's peaceful and prosperous and they don't have nukes and then the President of Russia will ignore you. You never hear from a strongman if the strongman thinks you don't matter.

You've got it wrong, said Victor. You need my protection. You need the Russian President's protection.

I've decided to not believe you, said Norah. I think Victor should protect Victor.

You think I'd lie? asked Victor. The man who loved Nassir Saud his whole life would lie to Nassir's daughter? I promised Nassir I'd do this, that I'd protect you if I could.

When I told the President I was coming here, he wanted to use this meeting for his advantage, said Victor. After I leave here, he'll ask what happened. He'll want to know if you are someone he should worry about. So, what should I tell the Russian President?

She surveyed the room—Jack and Annie were speechless, still, seemingly torn between flight and fright. Victor, you should leave, said Norah. If you're with me, the FBI knows exactly where to find you. Whatever you tell me and whatever questions you ask, I'll tell the FBI everything.

You could be dead in a day, Victor said. No one but me will know how or when.

The FBI could walk in now, said Norah. She pulled out the recorder again and held it up. They'll arrest you because they heard me say you're a threat to my safety.

There was a click, metallic and unmistakable. Annie had taken her Marlin Golden from the wall rack and cocked it and she'd pressed the business end against the back of Victor's crown and kept pressing until Victor's chin had been shoved into his chest. Ever since that hammerhead Khrushchev banged his shoe at the U.N., I've wanted to shoot me a Russkie, said Annie. Put that in your pipe and smoke it, comrade.

Norah pulled the alarm: Her eyes went big, her shoulders reared back and she got breathless. *Annie!* she shrieked. Norah lifted the end of the barrel with a fingertip, made sure it was pointed away from Victor's head. Then, to Victor: This woman is your worst nightmare, she said. If it's not her, it's the FBI—or your president. What happens if he knows you couldn't close the deal with the asset you promised would replace Nassir Saud? You'll look incompetent. What if he learns you sent him intel even though the FBI was monitoring? You'll look incompetent *and* disloyal. But what happens if Victor stops spying for murderers and thieves and he disappears without a word? Think of how simple your life gets.

Victor took steps toward the door, his feet pointed that way; he would leave, yes, but not before having a last word. Nassir was one of the best, said Victor. He was much better than me and you're better than him. You could win always, if you wanted. You're smart enough to know that helping me might be the right thing. From now on, you'll remember that at this moment, this crossroads, you could have been seeing things the wrong way. You might be making a fatal decision because you refused to believe the truth. Maybe someone else from Russia comes here. Maybe they firebomb your house or poison your well. Don't forget the reason I'm here is to help you, he said.

You can't help me, said Norah. The FBI will know everything you say and whatever you ask because I'll tell them. From now on, you'll remember that at this minute you failed to enlist me and you disappointed your president. You gave him reason to question your value.

Victor looked pained, possibly angry.

I wish you no harm, said Norah, pushing him out the door. I only want you gone.

Victor's Cadillac Escalade, a luxury hulk, crunched uphill and away, along the gravel drive. His tires squealed when he hit pavement at the top. She'd guessed right—that he'd barrel west on Route 3, a fast two-lane, the fastest path to Augusta and the interstate highway, to places far more populated and far less beautiful than Maine.

Victor gone, she thought about the night air. Outside Jack and Annie's front door there were gnats and the *whoosh* of bats' wings close overhead. A sliver of moon was a badge of elegant white, offsetting infinite darkness. Coming from somewhere far away—a whiff of skunk. Norah stared up the driveway, was pleased. The only strongman who cared about her was afraid of her and had an incentive to stay away. It was everything she could have hoped for.

* * *

Eve, you can call him playground bully, mob boss or pedophile, or you can say that he's a war lord, a fascist, a rapist, a dictator, a sociopath or murderer. You can say he craves superiority the way an addict needs drugs. The core of the strongman's life is the hunger for supremacy. He's not hard to spot. If he wins by intimidation, by threat of force, it means he's a strongman. If he only reasons with you when he needs to scare you, he's a strongman. If he's always the most important one and it doesn't matter who he hurts, he's a strongman.

He offers no empathy, not if you're innocent and not even if you love him. He's a breed of predator and everybody else is a possible meal. No philosophy, only an attitude; he's entitled to dominate. If you threaten that, he's thinking of how to cut you and he'll want to watch you bleed.

The strongmen are mostly men, Eve. Have you noticed? I can't think of any woman who runs a country or a company like King Saud or Vladimir. The men are the ones most likely to think muscles and guns give them a right to rule. Look around. Organized crime—it's all men. If there's a coup, it's men, or if it's an armed robbery, men.

Strongmen come in all different sizes. A big one has terrorists kill people because a republic proclaims independence. The little one gives their spouse a black eye because they won't obey.

With Father, every person he met, he was wondering what they could do for him and how to gain control. Once, I saw him pretending not to understand a man who said something obvious and Father told me later he wanted to see if the man was naïve enough to offer help—if the man was easy to control. He wanted to use the man's generosity and patience against him, like borrowing a knife from somebody so you could stab him with it.

The people who don't dominate, Father needed them and he despised them, both at the same time. They were lambs—easy to manipulate, Father said. They were slow to become suspicious and ignorant in the ways that mattered most, he said. They were losers and deserved to be used. If you couldn't see that you were stupid and it didn't matter if you graduated Harvard.

What makes a person feel entitled to win and to get violent if he might lose? And why mostly men? I've always wanted to know. If we can ever find answers, God will have done us a great favor.

THE END

PARTIAL BIBLIOGRAPHY

This book's depictions of Saudi Arabia and Russia and its descriptions of the tactics of spies, terrorists and counter-terrorists are as accurate as I could make them, with a few liberties taken for the sake of a good story. Below is a list of some of the sources I relied upon.

Excellent Daughters: The Secret Lives of Young Women Who Are Transforming the Arab World by Katherine Zoepf. First published in 2016 by Penguin Press.

Nine Parts of Desire: The Hidden World of Islamic Women by Geraldine Brooks. First published in 1995 by First Anchor Books.

Be Careful with Muhammad! The Salman Rushdie Affair by Shabbir Akhtar. First published in 1989 by Bellew Publishing.

Nothing Is True and Everything Is Possible: Adventures in Modern Russia by Peter Pomerantsev. First published in 2015 by Faber & Faber Limited.

Putin Country: A Journey into the Real Russia by Anne Garrels. First published in 2016 by Farrar, Strauss & Giroux.

Left of Bang: How the Marine Corps' Combat Hunter Program Can Save Your Life by Patrick Van Horne and Jason A. Riley. First published in 2014 by Black Irish Entertainment LLC.

100 Deadly Skills: The SEAL Operative's Guide to Eluding Pursuers, Evading Capture, and Surviving Any Dangerous Situation by Clint Emerson. First published in 2015 by Simon & Schuster, Inc.

New York Times reporting on Saudi Arabia and Russia by Megan Specia, Katherine Q. Seelye, Andrew Roth, Neil MacFarquhar, Hassan M. Fattaj, Ben Hubbard and Robert Mackey.

The Authoritarian Dynamic by Karen Stenner. First published by Cambridge University Press in 2005.

APPRECIATION

Every book ever written required the help and encouragement of many people. Below is a list of the folks who helped and/or encouraged me in the writing and editing of this book—each of whom has my gratitude and respect.

My wife, Catherine. You gave me freedom to write a thousand times when I should have been helping you around the house or in the yard. You encouraged me and you proofread pages and you listened a thousand times to permutations of the story that became this book. Thank you and I love you.

The members of my writers' group: Rupa Basu, Michael Bowen, Russell Carr, Joe Demasco, Stella Donovan, Judy Kelly, Katherine Melvin and Joe Radko.

Editor Marlene Adelstein.

Beta reader extraordinaire and plot consultant Susan Farneth.

Beta readers Corinne Fasinski, Jennifer Grove, Rosemary Hess, Jack Hume, Jack Kornfeind, Kathleen Marsh, Julia Meyers, Michelle Niblock, Kristen Samonsky, Patricia Tilbury.

A shout out to Cliff Bellamy whose love of literature rubbed off on me and convinced me to become an English major.

Another shout out to author and journalist Katherine Zoepf, whose book *Excellent Daughters: The Secret Lives of Young Women Who Are Transforming the Arab World* was a terrific source of inspiration for the book you just read.

YOUR AUTHOR'S PLEA

If you enjoyed this book, please consider one or more of the following:

▶ Posting a review of *Blood Lily* at Amazon.com, at Goodreads.com, and at any other website where you buy or learn about books.

▶ Telling your friends and neighbors how much you enjoyed *Blood Lily*.

▶ Taking a selfie showing the cover of this book and posting it on social media.

▶ Suggesting *Blood Lily* to your book club.

▶ Recommending to people that if they buy this book, they do so directly through the website of Maine Authors Publishing, an authors' cooperative that was instrumental in the publishing of this book. www.maineauthorspublishing.com.